Thomas Reader

Remarks on the Prophetic Part of the Revelation of St. John

Especially the Last Three Trumpets

Thomas Reader

Remarks on the Prophetic Part of the Revelation of St. John
Especially the Last Three Trumpets

ISBN/EAN: 9783337065300

Printed in Europe, USA, Canada, Australia, Japan

Cover: Foto ©Andreas Hilbeck / pixelio.de

More available books at **www.hansebooks.com**

REMARKS

ON THE

PROPHETIC PART

OF THE

REVELATION

OF

St. JOHN:

ESPECIALLY THE

THREE LAST TRUMPETS.

By THOMAS READER.

Blessed is he that readeth, and they that hear the Words of this Prophecy, and keep those Things which are written therein; for the Time is at hand. Rev. i. 3.

Comparing spiritual Things with spiritual. 1 Cor. ii. 13.

LONDON:

Printed by J. W. PASHAM, Black-Friars;

And Sold by J. BUCKLAND, Pater-noster Row, G. KEITH, Gracechurch Street, and E. and C. DILLY, in the Poultry.

MDCCLXXVIII.

INTRODUCTION.

'HARDLY any one book of the New
' Teftament has more early, full, or
' authentick atteftations given to it,' than
this of *Revelation*; and, befides that fo
many of its prophecies have been already
accomplifhed, there are in the book itfelf
fuch internal marks of Divine infpiration,
that it would be needlefs to fay any more
on that head.

But obferving the very fingular and repeated demands of attention, which the
Lord Jefus has made, in the beginning,
middle and clofe of this prophecy, to the
things contained therein, (fee *Rev.* i. 3.
ii. 7, 11, 17, 29. iii. 6, 13, 22. xiii. 9, 18.
and xxii. 6, 7, 10.) I durft not imitate the
too common neglect by which many, even
worthy perfons, inadvertently difhonour
this myfterious part of the facred canon :
Yet when I had drank, with fome refrefh-
ment, of thefe holy ftreams, the miftakes
which many great and good men had, in
a long fucceffion, made in inveftigating

their

their courſe, for a conſiderable time deterred me from ſubmitting my apprehenſions about them to the public view: And afterwards, a firm perſuaſion that providence will ſoon throw ſuch a farther light upon this, and other obſcure prophecies, by their accompliſhment, as will in a great meaſure make many ancient and modern commentaries upon them uſeleſs, occaſioned a farther heſitation whether I ſhould go on with this deſign or not: But at length apprehending that, notwithſtanding involuntary miſtakes, from which I can ſcarcely hope theſe remarks are wholly free, they may be uſeful, to aſſiſt the views of others; or at leaſt to warn my contemporaries of ſome things which are intereſting to themſelves and their poſterity, I have ventured to lay them before the world; and ſhall greatly rejoice, if this piece ſhould be the happy means of aſſiſting others to ſtudy this precious part of God's word, with leſs labour and fatigue than it has coſt me.

That this revelation was given after our Lord was aſcended to Heaven, to prove the glorious ſufficiency of his atonement, and the prevalence of his continued interceſſion; as well as to diſplay the glories of his godhead, and the extent, duration, and

and uncontrouled fovereignty of his mediatorial government—That it was given to *the difciple whom Jefus loved*, in the decline of his days, and when himfelf and the caufe of his great mafter were oppreffed with the iron hand of tyranny—That it is the laft infpired meffage which the world will ever receive from heaven, till the confummation of all things; and contains an orderly feries of the grand events which are to befal the world and the church, from about A. D. 96 to the end of time, and to eternity—That it exhibits to every age fome new view of the wifdom and glory of the Lord Jefus, whilft it points out the defigns of men and devils againft his church, and the different fucceffive methods by which they will endeavour to accomplifh them; and at the fame time directs the faith and duty of every believer in his own time—And finally, That this book cafts fo ftrong a light on many other parts of the Old and New Teftament, and efpecially on fome ancient fcripture-prophecies, which it is impoffible for us fully to underftand, without a particular acquaintance with this book—All thefe confiderations may well endear this precious part of the word of God to us, by which the whole

world

world is now governed, as all shall be judged hereafter *according to the things which are written in this,* as well as in other of the inspired *books.*

Revealed things, says Moses, *belong to us and to our children for ever,* Deut. xxix. 29; and if the Jews, in their respective generations, had properly considered the threatenings in that, and the preceding chapter, they might have escaped the tremendous doom which has overwhelmed them ever since A. D. 70; so they who are effectually warned of the sins of the beast, will have nothing to fear from his plagues. And as the revelation may thus be perpetually useful to the men of this and other generations, whatever some great men have said, it seems to be no more *vain* and *presumptuous* in us, to enquire into prophecies which are not yet accomplished, than it was in the Old Testament prophets to *search what, or what manner of time the Spirit of Christ which was in them did signify, when it testified beforehand the sufferings of Christ, and the glory that should follow,* 1 Pet. i. 10, 11; nor can the present end of their publication be answered upon us without it. Who then shall set limits to that command

mand *search the scriptures?* *John* v. 39.——
But if *mirth*, or *malevolence* should call
my apprehensions about future things, *my
prophecies*; suffice it to assure the intelligent reader, that he will meet with nothing
here but my reasonings, and conjectures,
(I hope not immodestly offered) on *God's
prophecies*; and how far I have understood
them, the event will shew: At the same
time he will carefully distinguish, between
that degree of evidence which may be
expected now, and that which their future accomplishment will yield to every eye.

It is with great pleasure that I confess my obligations to Mr. Fleming, Mr.
Mede, Mr. Lowman, Bp. Newton and
others, for much of the knowledge which
I have of this book: And where I have
left my guides, I have submitted my reasons for it to the understanding and can-
dor of every reader, who must judge of
them as he can.

If it had not appeared of some importance, to give my reader a connected view
of the whole series of this prophecy, I
should have confined my remarks to the
three last trumpets, which would have cut
off about the first fifth part of this book:
But having, I imagine, something new to
offer, even on some of those parts of this
prophecy

prophecy where I have received moſt aſſiſt-
ance from others, I have thought it might
be agreeable, even to my learned reader,
and therefore have ſpent a few pages in
giving, I hope, a clear and conciſe view of
the events and times of the ſeven ſeals, and
the four firſt trumpets.

If I had dared to indulge any other object of attention, than that of declaring
the whole counſel of God, ſome unpopu-
lar ſentiments would certainly have been
concealed, which appear in the following
pages; but if *pleaſing men* was my great
aim, *I ſhould not be the ſervant of Chriſt.*
At the ſame time, as a judicious ſelf-love
cannot be offended with any word which is
really θεοπνευςος *divinely inſpired,* 2 *Tim.* iii.
16; ſo, if I have overlooked, or miſtaken
the will or work of God in any reſpect, it
is no more than many much greater men
have, eſpecially in their labours on this
book; and I aſk the indulgence which my
reader believes to be due to erring integrity.

The very imperfect knowledge which the
church of God had of this myſterious book,
A. D. 1611, when the preſent tranſlation
of the Bible was made, has occaſioned
many annotators ſince to give a new tranſlation of it; and I have attempted the ſame
on this prophetic part of it, with the aſſiſt-
ance

ance of Dr. Doddridge and others; yet without confining myfelf to any of them.

A few chronological obfervations are inferted in the following work; which, whilft they affift the unlearned reader, may in fome inftances, refrefh the memories of the more informed. And befides an index of the principal matters confidered in thefe remarks, which is fubjoined to them; I have alfo added one, of thofe Old Teftament prophecies and other fcriptures, which are more or lefs illuftrated in this work. Alfo; an index of the *Greek words* which are referred to in this piece.

I am in queft of further knowledge, and fhall rejoice to receive it from any quarter. At the fame time, I heartily thank every chriftian and minifter, who helped me in this work, either by his prayers to God for me, or by offering me any ufeful hints on any part of this book. But my thanks are particularly due to the Rev. Dr. Gibbons; and efpecially to my brother the Rev. Simon Reader, of Wareham, Dorfet; whofe unwearied pains beftowed upon my MS, preferved me from fome miftakes; and occafioned a more critical examination and difcuffion of feveral points.

If

If He who gave this Revelation to his church, will pleafe at all to glorify his own name by this feeble attempt, my higheft ambition is gratified; and with this hope I would devoutly lay it at His feet.

Taunton,
June 24, 1778.   T. R.

TWO

TWO ADVERTISEMENTS.

1. WHEN I delivered this piece to the Printer, I had not the most distant apprehension, that the year 1778 would have produced any thing so favourable to the Papists, as that act of the British legislature, which relieves them from certain (civil and religious) *penalties* and *disabilities*; which were imposed on them in the (eleventh and twelfth years of the) reign of king William the III. At the same time, my readers will observe, that what I have said of the future spread of popery, is not so much founded on the probabilities of things; as on the plain sense of those words, by which the blessed God has expressed his *judicial sentence* against the world; which he resolves to punish for their iniquities, by leaving them to the *infernal abominations* of popery.

2. The following words are sometimes printed by mistake for each other in this work; viz. *man* and *men*; *son* and *sun*; *who* and *whom*; *those* and *these*; *prophesy* and *prophecy*, which, it is hoped, will occasion the intelligent reader no great trouble; besides which he is requested to correct the following

ERRATA.

P. 75. l. 34. *f.* and, *r.* chap.
p. 83. l. 24. *f.* 315, *r.* 312.
p. 100. l. 16. *f.* p. 69, *r.* p. 96.
p. 101. l. 32. *f.* lion, *r. a lion.*
p. 111. l. 3. *f.* lam, *r.* lamb.
p. 126. l. 34. *f.* hast, *r.* has.
p. 130. l. 21. *f.* wrath, *r.* wroth.
p. 131. l. 27. *f.* event! *r.* events.
p. 136. l. 33. *f.* iii. *r.* 3.
p. 157. l. 16. *f. Lawds, r. Louds.*
p. 158. l. 22. *f.* tense, *r.* sense.
p. 288. l. 32. *f.* arranged, *r.* arrayed.

Any other trifling Errata that may have escaped notice, will, it is hoped, on account of the Author's distance from the Press, be readily excused by the candid Reader.

A
SCHEME
OF THE
REVELATION given to St. JOHN.

VII *Seals from* A. D. 96 *to* 395.

Chap. Verse.	Seal.	Times.	Persons and Things.
VI. 1, 2,	- - I.	- - A. D. 96 to the End of the World.	Christ conquers by his gospel.
3, 4,	- - II.	- - 98—134 - -	Jews and Heathens, destroy each other, in Trajan's and Hadrian's reign.
5, 6,	- - III.	- - 133—211 - -	Famine, &c. in the reign of the Antonine and Septimian families.
7, 8,	- - IV.	- - 235—284 - -	The sword, famine, pestilence, and wild beasts; from Maximin to Dioclesian.
9, 10, 11,	- - V.	- - 64—303 - -	The souls of the martyrs under the altar.
VII. 12 to 17,	- - VI.	- - 306—361 - -	The Pagan religion subverted; and peace established by Constantine, &c
VIII. 1—6.	- - VII.	- - 364—395 - -	A half hour's silence in heaven; the trumpets given to the angels.

VII *Trumpets from* A. D. 395 *to* 3125, &c.

7,	- - I.	- - 395—412 - -	The Goths, &c. break in upon the empire.
8, 9,	- - II.	- - 440—454 - -	Attila and his Huns fall upon the empire.
10, 11,	- - III.	- - 317—606 - -	Genseric and his Vandals; and Arius, Pelagius, and the Pope.
11,	- - IV.	- - 456—566 - -	The lights of the western empire put out.
13, A Warning		- - 566—606 - -	Of the three woe trumpets.
IX. 1—12,	- - V.	- - 606—756 - -	The Pope and Mahomet.
XI. 13 to 14,	- - VI.	- - 606-1866 - -	The Turks destroy the eastern empire; the two witnesses; and an earthquake at Rome.
7—10,	-	- 1862 - -	The two witnesses slain.
XXII. 15 to 21,	- - VII.	- -1866—3125, &c.	The end of the world, Judgment, and Eternity.

A
SCHEME
OF THE
SEVENTH TRUMPET.

Chap. Verſe.

XI. 15,	- - A. D. 1866.	- -	The ſeventh trumpet ſounds.
XIV. 1—5,	- - - - -	- -	The Jews return to their own land ; and multitudes of
6—10,	- - - - -	- -	Gentiles are converted : But
XIII. 11—17,	- - - - -	- -	the Mahometans become Papiſts.
	1872.	- -	The Mahometan chief calls himſelf the apoſtle of Chriſt.
	1882.	- -	He becomes the ſecond beaſt ;
	1886.	- -	and works miracles, as a falſe prophet, before the firſt beaſt.
XIV. 19, 20.	- - 1926.	- -	Many of the wicked are cut off.

VII *Vials from* A. D. 1936 *to* 1942.

XVI. 2,	- - I.	- A.D. 1936.	-	Is poured out on the earth.
3,	- - II.	- - 1937.	-	Is poured on the ſea.
4—7,	- - III.	- - 1938.	-	Is poured on the rivers and fountains.
8, 9,	- - IV.	- - 1939.	-	Is poured on the ſun.
10, 11,	- - V.	- - 1940.	-	Is poured on the throne of the beaſt.
12—16,	- - VI.	- - 1941.	-	Is poured on the river Euphrates.
17—21.	- - VII.	- - 1942.	-	Is poured on the air.

XVII. 16. From A. D. 1942 to 2016, the ten horns of the beaſt hate the whore, and burn her with fire.

XIX. 20, A. D. 2016, the beaſt is caſt into the lake of fire ; and Popery deſtroyed.

XX. 1—6, A. D. 2016 to 3016. The glorious millennium.

7—10, After 3016. Satan is looſed for a time.

11—15, A. D. 3125. The world ends, and judgment begins ; which may probably continue 225 years.

{ XXI. 1,
  to   The new Jeruſalem comes down to the new heaven and
XXII. 5, earth, where the ſaints dwell with God.

6—21, A moſt gracious call ; a ſolemn warning ; and a parting benediction.

REMARKS

ON THE

REVELATION of St. JOHN.

REVELATIONS,

CHAP. IV.

THE beloved difciple, having feen in the two preceeding chapters, *the things that are*, to raife his attention to *the thing which fhall be hereafter*, (Rev. i. 19.) and to give him clear ideas of the wifdom, power and faithfulnefs, which will be difplayed in the grand events which are to take place in the world; is, in this chapter, honoured with a vifion of God himfelf, feated on his throne in heaven, incircled with a glorious hoft of angels and faints, (who here appear as *fitting together with* Chrift *in heavenly places*), the adoring fpectators of thofe things which will certainly be accomplifhed, in their refpective times, exactly as heaven and earth here behold them.

1. After

1. After this I looked, and behold a door was opened in heaven: and the firſt voice which I heard was, as it were, of a trumpet talking with me; which ſaid, Come up hither, and I will ſhew thee things which muſt be hereafter.

The firſt Adam's apoſtacy ſhut up heaven againſt himſelf and his poſterity; but the ſecond Adam opens it: ſo the heavens were opened to *Ezekiel*, chap. i. 1; at Chriſt's baptiſm, *Matt.* iii. 16; to dying Stephen, *Acts* vii. 56; to Peter, when the goſpel was to be preached to the Gentiles, *Acts* x. 10; and here to our apoſtle. And being opened, to rouſe him and us to the moſt devout and fixed attention, *the firſt voice which he heard was, as it were, of a trumpet, talking with him.* Under the law it was commanded, *Numb.* x. 4. *If they blow but with one trumpet, then the princes which are heads of the thouſands of Iſrael, ſhall gather themſelves unto thee;* hearken particularly then, ye heads of our goſpel-Iſrael.

2. And immediately I was in the ſpirit: and behold a throne was ſet in heaven; and one ſat upon the throne.

Endeavoring to obey the divine order, the Spirit came upon him in an extraordinary and miraculous manner, *Ezek.* viii. 1. *Acts* x. 10. 2 *Cor.* xii. 2. for what God commands, he gives to his ſervants: and being in the Spirit, he could obey this order, *Come up hither.* Thus raiſed in Spirit, he ſaw God the Father, chap. v. 1; who never appeared, as Chriſt had done, in bodily parts and proportions, chap. i. 13—16.

3. And

3. And he that fat was to look upon like a jafper, and a fardine ftone: and there was a rainbow round about the throne, in fight like unto an emerald.

The brilliant jafper, and red fardine ftone, might intimate that he is *a juft God and a Saviour*: And probably the Lord appeared in the fplendor of thefe two ftones, which were the firft and laft upon Aaron's breaft-plate of judgement, Exod. xxviii. 17—21, that he might vifibly feal the whole of his covenant with the twelve tribes of Ifrael, through the great High Prieft of our profeffion, as well as to affure his people that he would bring them to that city, of which thefe were two of the foundations, *Rev.* xxi. 19, 20. A rainbow too furrounded the throne, both to fatisfy us of his care of every thing living, *Gen.* ix. 12—17; and that he is not afhamed, or unmindful of the peculiar covenant which he has made with his own people, *Ifa.* liv. 9. *Ezek.* i. 28; which fhall be confirmed and guarded, by every order which fhall ever proceed from that throne.   And the prevailing green, or emerald colour of this rain-bow, was defigned to fhew, that God's covenant will never grow old or decay, but produce the moft precious fruit; and afford ever frefh delight to the believing eye that gazes upon it.   Chrift alfo appears with the fame enfign of divine glory upon his head, chap. x. 1; for *he thought it not* an act of *robbery to be equal with God*, Phil. ii. 6. So αρπαγμος fignifies in Plutarch: and this is agreeable to the ufual fenfe of Greek verbal nouns, which end in μος.

4. And round about the throne were four, and twenty thrones: and upon the

thrones

thrones I faw four and twenty elders fitting, clothed in white raiment; and they had on their heads crowns of gold.

These thrones were prepared, not for the four animals or minifters, but for the twelve patriarchs and apoftles, who were the reprefentatives of the Jewifh and Chriftian church : and if archbifhops confider themfelves as the fuccefiors of the apoftles without either their credentials or accomplifhments, it might, at leaft, have been better if they had waved being *enthroned* till they came to heaven, where the apoftles were fo : But if our author, who was now the only furviving apoftle, not only knew the twelve Jewifh patriarchs, as he knew Mofes and Elijah on the Mount of Tranfiguration, *Matt.* xvii. 1—3 ; but beheld his well-known eleven brethren thus arrayed in white, with crowns of gold upon their heads; and faw his own future countenance in the appearance of one of the twelve, what unimagined tranfport muft fill his heart, when in vifion he faw thofe words accomplifhed, whilft yet in the body, *Ye are they which have continued with me in my temptation; and I appoint unto you a kingdom, as my Father hath appointed unto me; that ye may eat and drink at my table in my kingdom, and fit on thrones judging the twelve tribes of Ifrael.* Luke xxii. 28—30. And, *To him that overcometh, will I grant to fit with me in my throne; even as I alfo overcame, and am fet down with my Father in his throne,* Rev. iii. 21. See chap. xx. 4. and *Eph.* ii. 6.

5. And out of the throne proceeded lightnings, and thundrings, and voices : and there were feven lamps of fire burning before

fore the throne, which are the seven spirits of God.

These seven Spirits of God, which *are sent out into all the earth*, are declared to be *the seven horns, and seven eyes of the* Lamb, chap. v. 6; see also i. 4. and iii. 1. And, to testify the divine power and wisdom, with which our Lord effects his designs in the church and world by these seven spirits, they are described as *lamps of fire*; which, as well as a *horn*, a *reed* and *rod*, are scripture emblems of authority and government, *Psal.* cxxxii. 17. *I have ordained a lamp for mine anointed*; see 1 *Kings* xv. 4. *Isa.* lxii. 1. *Rev.* viii. 10. So it is said of Christ, *Isa.* xlii. 3. *The smoking flax*, that weakest ensign of his government in the soul, *shall he not quench.* The Lord made a covenant with Abraham, by one *lamp of fire*, passing between the divided parts of his sacrifice, *Gen.* xv. 17; but now, as *the light of the moon* of Jewish ceremonies, is become *as the light of the sun* of righteousness; so that *light of the sun* will become *seven-fold, as the light of seven days, in the day when* the Lord comes down to *bind up the breach of his* Jewish *people, and heal the stroke of their wound, Isa.* xxx. 26. These seven spirits of God, which are still before the throne, whilst shedding their most potent influences upon the earth, were typified by the seven lamps which were continually kept burning in the tabernacle, *Exod.* xxv. 37; see *Ainsworth in loc*: and they are said to be *seven*, for the supply of the seven candlesticks, or churches; and to comfort God's people in the times of the seven seals, seven thunders, seven trumpets, and seven vials; and also to illuminate, chear and purify his ministers through all the seven days of the week; of each

of

of which he has ſaid, *Lo, I am with you* πασας τας ημερας *all days, even to the end of the world,* Matt. xxviii. 20; and that through the ſeven thouſand years which the world will certainly continue, before the eternal ſabbath begins; ſee chap. xx. 1—6.

6. And before the throne there was a ſea of glaſs, like unto cryſtal: and in the midſt of the throne, and round about the throne were four animals *or living creatures,* full of eyes before and behind.

It was the more improper to render the word ζωα *beaſts* in this place, as two θηρια *beaſts,* properly ſo called, appear in this book, in characters ſo diametrically oppoſite to that of theſe four *animals,* chap. xiii. 1, 11.

The four living creatures in *Ezek.* i. 5. whom the LXX call ζωα, are generally apprehended to be angels; and as *their* miniſtry was employed in ordering and diſpoſing many of the great affairs of the Jewiſh church, (*Pſal.* lxviii. 17. *Acts* vii. 53. *Gal.* iii. 19.) that church was *put into* a kind of *ſubjection* to the angels, as officers acting under the captain of our ſalvation, *Heb.* ii. 2, 5: but though there is ſome affinity between that viſion and this; I cannot underſtand theſe four animals as hieroglyphical repreſentations of the angelic nature, but rather of earthly miniſters (on whom God has now, in Chriſt's time, beſtowed the name of angels, and the viſible part of their ancient miniſtry,) 1. Becauſe they ſing, chap. v. 9, 10. Thou *waſt ſlain, and haſt redeemed us to God by thy blood, out of every kindred, and tongue, and people, and nation; and haſt made us unto our God kings and prieſts: and we ſhall reign on the earth;* none of which things can be

be ſaid of angels. 2. They are expreſsly diſtinguiſhed from the angels, and placed nearer the
throne than they; on account of their nearer relation to the God-man mediator, chap. v. 11.
I beheld, and I heard the voice of many angels round
about the throne, and the animals, and the elders:
and, though their brightneſs was very far from
eclipſing the glory of the four animals, *the num-*
ber of them was almoſt inconceivably greater than
theirs; for it was *ten thouſand times ten thouſand,*
and thouſands of thouſands. 3. Though ζαω and
ζωη expreſs *life* in general, yet as ζη is the ſound
which we make in breathing; and ζωα is never
applied in the New Teſtament, to any other beings but ſuch as have animal life; (ſee *Heb.* xiii. 11.
2 *Pet.* ii. 12. *Jude* 10.) it is moſt reaſonable to underſtand it of the miniſters who were upon earth
A. D. 96 and following, though the ſcene is
here laid in heaven. 4. If the four and twenty
elders are the repreſentatives of the Jewiſh and
Chriſtian churches, it ſeems natural to underſtand
the four animals, who are joined with them, of
the miniſters ſent out into the four parts of the
earth; who are therefore repreſented as *full of*
eyes before, behind and *within,* ver. 6, 8; though
they are by no means equal to the angels in
knowledge; of whom it is ſaid, *Ezek.* x. 12.
Their whole body, and their backs, and their hands,
and their wings, as well as the *wheels* which went
by them, *were full of eyes round about.* 5. The
large glaſs veſſel, called a *ſea of glaſs, like unto*
cryſtal, which John ſaw near theſe four animals,
is not wanted for the purification of angels, but
of goſpel miniſters yet upon earth: And this
ſea, which ſtood before the throne to teſtify
God's particular and gracious care for the ſanc-
tification of his miniſters, was typified by the
lavers of braſs in the tabernacle, and the molten

fea in Solomon's temple; in which the priefts
wafhed, not the people or the facrifices, but
their own hands and feet, when they approached unto God, *Exod.* xxx. 18. 2. *Chron.* iv. 2.—6.
Note, Jewifh priefts were cleanfed with water
and blood; but gofpel minifters with water, the
fire of the Spirit, ver. 5, 6. *Mal.* iii. 3, and of
awful trials, *Rev.* xv. 2. *Ifa.* xxxi. 9; as well
as with blood, *Lev.* viii. 23, 24. *Heb.* ix. 22;
the latter of which, however, it was not neceffary
to reprefent in this vifionary fcene, as the Lord
Jefus himfelf, by whofe blood only they can be
cleanfed, *ftood before the throne, as a lamb that
had been flain,* chap. v. 6.

I only add here, when the word ζωα fignifies
angels, as in, *Ezek.* i. 5, according to the LXX,
it would be very proper to render it *vital beings,*
as thofe pure intelligences have no principle of
decay in their nature; but *animals,* or *living
creatures* feems a more proper appellation for
earthly *minifters,* whofe ftrength goes away with
their time, and who are dying whilft they are at
their work.

7. And the firft animal was like a lion;
and the fecond animal like a calf; and the
third animal had a face as a man; and the
fourth animal was like a flying eagle.

Every one of the cherubim had all thefe four
faces, *Ezek.* i. 10; but in earthly minifters, we
can only expect to find the ftrength and courage
of a lion in one; the patience of an ox in another;
the ftrong reafon of a man in a third; and the
quick fight and admirable velocity of the eagle
in a fourth. And probably the order in which
they here appear, may be defigned to teach us,
that the primitive minifters, who were to begin
the attack upon fatan's kingdom, were courage-
ous and undaunted as a lion, who is made without

out fear; see *Gen.* xlix. 9. *Dan.* vii. 4: That
these should be succeeded by others, who would
abide firm and persevering in labour and sufferings as an ox, till the world should feed upon
them: And after them should arise a third sort
of ministers, able and determined to defend the
cause of their Lord, with the perspicuity and for-
titude of a man; whilst the high soaring eagle
may describe the rapid motion, and great heavenly mindedness which will probably characterize
the ministers of God in the latter days, *Isa.* xl. 31.
Yet this is no reason why we should not look for
all these characters in different ministers in every
age: accordingly we hear a voice uttered in the
midst of the four animals, at the opening of the
third seal, chap. vi. 6; as they all advance in succession to our view in the three first centuries,
within which the four first seals are generally
thought to have been opened; at the opening of
which respectively one of them cried, *Come and
see*, ver. 1—7.

But 'about the middle of the third cen-
' tury, says *Bengelius*, there arose gradually
' an indiscreet aversion to the' millennium 'it-
' self'; nay, even to the whole prophecy' of
this book, (*Introduction to his exposition of the
Apocalypse by Dr.* Robertson, p. 288.) which
may be one reason why they cry no more, at the
opening of the following seals, Come and see.
And though we find them still before the throne
in the fourth century, under the sixth seal, chap.
vii. 11; they are there silent inactive spectators of
what passes; and after that time we hear no more
of them, under the name of animals, till,
under the seventh trumpet, or A. D. 1866,
chap. xi. 15; when they resume their activity,
and renew their worship, chap. xiv. 3. xv. 7. and
xix. 4.

8. And

8. And the four animals had each of them fix wings about him; and they were full of eyes within: and they reſt not day and night, ſaying, Holy, holy, holy, Lord God Almighty, which was, and is, and is to come.

See ver. 6. They give glory to the Father, Son, and Spirit, as the ſeraphim, *Iſa.* vi. 2, 3; and had the ſame number of wings as they. Our Lord aſſerts the ſame, and like glorious things of himſelf, chap. i. 8; for if thoſe had been the words of the Father, to have anſwered their end, they muſt have contained his own diſtinguiſhing and appropriate characters, which no holy creature whatever would therefore have dared to apply to himſelf: But our Lord aſſumes ſome of the ſame appellations immediately, ver. 11; ſee alſo chap. xxii. 13. But if Chriſt was Alpha and Omega, conſidered only as mediator, then thoſe words could not belong to the Father. I conclude therefore that ver. 8, can be the words of no other perſon but the Lord Jeſus, who gave this revelation to John; for the Father never ſpoke to him in this viſion: *Ye have neither heard his voice at any time, nor ſeen his ſhape, John* v. 37; ſee *Rev.* xix. 6, 13.

9. And when thoſe animals give glory, and honour, and thanks to him that ſat on the throne, who liveth for ever and ever,

10. The four and twenty elders fall down before him that ſat on the throne, and worſhip him that liveth for ever and ever; and caſt their crowns before the throne, ſaying,

11. Thou

11. Thou art worthy, O Lord, to receive glory, and honour, and power: for thou haſt created all things, and for thy pleaſure they are, and were created.

If this worſhip was all heavenly, theſe words inform us of its order: but as this viſion chiefly reſpects the affairs of the church militant, we may obſerve, that when miniſters are burning and ſhining lights, that light will inſtrumentally inſtruct and invigorate others; and their zeal will provoke every one whoſe heart is, like their own, attuned to the high praiſes of God.

C H A P. V.

The viſion of the ſcaled book, which the Lamb only was found worthy to open; who, on that account, received the united acclamations of heaven and earth.

1. AND I ſaw in the right hand of him that ſat on the throne, a book written within, and on the backſide; ſealed with ſeven ſeals.

By appearing with this book in his hand, he that ſat on the throne teſtified to this grand convention of men and angels, that all his works were wrought *after the* immutable *counſel of his own will, Eph.* i. 11. *Heb.* vi. 17; and expreſſed his gracious deſire that they might be made acquainted with his ſecrets: Yet looking to this ſcroll, or volume, rolled up, the beloved diſciple could only at preſent diſcover, that its ſeven

leaves

leaves had each a diſtinct ſeal upon it; and that it was written on both ſides, or within and without; though its ſurrounding brightneſs and glory prevented his gazing ſo attentively upon it, as even to read any of the outſide writing; ſee ver. 3.

2. And I ſaw a ſtrong angel proclaiming with a loud voice, who is worthy to open the book, and to looſe the ſeals thereof?

3. And no one in heaven, nor in earth, neither under the earth, was able to open the book, neither to look ſtedfaſtly thereon.

4. And I wept much, becauſe no one was found worthy to open and to read the book, neither to look thereon.

If he who ſits upon the throne appears with this book in his hand, it cannot be to raiſe deluſive hopes in the hearts of his ſervants; therefore, when heaven and earth have confeſſed their inſufficiency for it, himſelf will find a perſon to open it. Obſerve 1. The apoſtle *loved much*, and therefore *wept much* at the thought of having God's ſecrets concealed from him; but 2. The faith which produced that love cannot act in any inſtance, without the immediate exertions of divine power. And, 3. Nothing is more common than for good men to diſcover their unbelief, even whilſt ſhewing their love to God. 4. To look only to creatures for the opening of God's book to us, though himſelf ſtands cloſe by us, is a work of unbelief; and the way to have ſorrow enough. 5. They differ *much* from the ſpirit of our apoſtle, and from the views of angels, who are contented to be ignorant of the things contained in this book, now they are revealed.

5. And

5. And one of the elders faith unto me,
weep not: Behold the lion of the tribe of
Judah, the root of David, hath prevailed to
open the book, and to loose the seven seals
thereof.

This elder, filled with the love of God, was
glad to comfort our apoftle, by pointing out an
unobferved Jefus, and fome unnoticed glories
of his name to him: And as this vifion refpects
the affairs of earth, thefe words inform us, that
even an aged apoftle may receive direction and
affiftance from others; for no member of Chrift's
myftical body can fay to any other, *I have no
need of you.* But as the fcene is here laid in
heaven; we may obferve, that an elder enthroned above could fee and draw confequences, with
more clearnefs and certainty than our yet embo-
died apoftle; and they moft refemble the faints
in heaven, who can moft clearly deduce, from
eftablifhed principles, fuch conclufions as may
fupport them under temptations, and animate
to duty. 'Confider then,' as though he had
faid, '*the lion* which fprang out *of the tribe of*
' *Judah, Gen.* xlix. 9. *Heb.* vii. 14. who had not
' his might and terriblenefs in vain; he has con-
' quered ενικησεν; (for I muft ufe a word which
' will lead thy thoughts to a view of his victory
' over) thofe fpiritual enemies, who, whilft they
' held us captive, locked up God's fecrets from
' us, and rendered us indifpofed, and even
' dead to an acquaintance with them: but ha-
' ving overcome them, both himfelf and we
' muft reap the fruits of his victory; one of
' which will certainly be his *prevailing* with the
' Father for the opening of this fealed book,
' which he now holds forth in our fight. He is
' alfo the immortal *Root* from whom the victori-
' ous

' ous *David*, and all his renowned fucceffors
' fprang, *Ifa.* xi. 1. *Matt.* xxii. 42. *Rom.* xv. 12;
' and as that great patriarch, who was fo emi-
' nent a type of him, enjoyed the bleffings of
' prophecy as well as of the fword, fo furely will
' this his root, now planted in heaven, yield us
' all *the fure mercies of David,*' Ifa. lv. 3.

6. And I beheld, and lo, in the midft
of the throne, and of the four living creatures, and in the midft of the elders, ftood
a lamb as it had been flain; having feven
horns and feven eyes, which are the feven
fpirits of God fent forth into all the
earth.

While this elder is fpeaking of Chrift, himfelf
appears; or, if he was vifible before, the *eyes* of
our apoftle had been *holden* that he fhould not
know him, *Luke* xxiv. 16, 36.   But obferve
where and *how* he appeared.   1. *Where*; viz. *in
the midft of the throne*; for Chrift is a middle
perfon between the Father and the Spirit, the
centre of their gracious thoughts and works;
and he in whom *mercy and truth are met together,
righteoufnefs and peace have kiffed each other,*
Pfal. lxxxv. 10.   Who is fit to be in the midft
of the throne, but the God-man mediator? And
what becomes of reafon and religion, if we would
place a mere man, or any mere creature there?
He is alfo in the midft of the *four living creatures*
or minifters, to maintain their life; and to pre-
ferve peace and order amongft them, by com-
municating of his own light and grace to each.
And for the fame purpofe he is in *the midft of
the* four and twenty *elders*, on earth and in heaven; to *feed them*, and to *lead them to living fountains of water*: His influence upon them makes
them

them fweet and favoury to one another; and
when thofe of them who are here, derive virtue
from him mutually to refer their different apprehenfions and interefts to this great mediator between them, there can be no contentions among
them. 2. *How* he appeared; among his enemies
he had roared as a lion tearing the prey; but, as
divine juftice could be no other way difarmed,
but by his dying as a facrifice, therefore in the
midft of the throne, he ftood as *a Lamb that had
been flain*, with confpicuous marks of flaughter
upon him, *Gen.* xxii. 8. *John* i. 29. As flain for
us, he is our way to God, and our peace: and there
is reafon to fear, that profeffors who deny his
atonement, have never yet favingly tranfacted
any bufinefs with God before this throne. This
Lamb had alfo *feven horns, and feven eyes, which
are the feven fpirits of God fent forth into all the
earth: thefe could not be the feven angels which
ftood before God*, chap. viii. 2; for, befides that
no creature can be the horn or the eye of the
Lamb, or as it were an effential conftituent part
of the mediator, thefe feven fpirits are actually
invoked, chap. i. 3, 4, which is an honour peculiar to God himfelf; *Grace be unto you, and
peace from the feven fpirits which are before the
throne*: Therefore by thefe *feven fpirits, or feven
lamps of fire*, chap. iv. 5, is meant the eternal
Spirit, fo called with reference to his different operations and influences, which are directed by
thofe feven eyes of Jehovah the Lamb, *which run
to and fro through the whole earth*, to light *the
feven lamps* of the church; and to fee *the feven
pipes* which fupply thofe *feven lamps*, furnifhed
with holy oil; fee *Ifa.* xi. 2. *Zech.* iv. 2, 10, and
John i. 4. And who but the true God can direct, or fend out thefe feven fpirits into all the
earth, as the Lord Jefus does? and though the
above

above prayer to the Spirit, proves that he has a distinct subsistence from the Father and Son ; yet these seven spirits, being called the seven horns and eyes of the Lamb, testifies the intimate and indissoluble union between Christ and the Spirit ; that these seven spirits are essential to the mediator as his horns and eyes ; that where ever they are sent he is personally present ; and that the wisdom and power of these horns and eyes are his wisdom and power : and finally, as no one can receive any of these seven spirits but from Christ, so they who are nearest to him shall communicate most with him of his wisdom and power : and all who see with the eyes, or push their enemies with the horns of this Lamb, will certainly give him the praise of all they enjoy or perform.

7. And he came and received the book, out of the right hand of him that sat on the throne.

For the father willingly reached out this book to him, that he might go on with his prophetic office ; to open God's designs, and consequently shew his people what will be their Lord's employments, cares, and intercessions for them in every age.

8. And when he received the book, the four living creatures, and the four and twenty elders fall down before the Lamb ; having every one of them harps, and golden vials, full of odours, which are the prayers of saints.

Harps and censers, which seem to be here intended by the vials, were well-known instruments of Jewish worship ; and are proper emblems of
                                                        prayer

prayer and praife. And if our Lord will tranflate the defigns of Deity into the language of earth, fhall we not entertain him with the harps of our praife, and prefent the pleafing incenfe of prayer, *Pfal.* cxli. 1, that we may underftand and improve thefe myfteries of God? But thefe words no more favour inftrumental mufic in our public worfhip, than the ufe of cenfers and incenfe, both of which came in, and went out with Mofes, *Pfal.* lxxxi. 2—5. *John* i. 17.

9. And they fang a new fong, faying, Worthy art thou to take the book, and to open the feals thereof: for thou waft flain; and haft redeemed us to God by thy blood out of every tribe, and tongue, and people, and nation;

10. And haft made us unto our God, kings and priefts; and we fhall reign on the earth.

Thefe minifters and elders, who were of every kindred, language, people, and nation, animated with the fame fpirit, united their different tongues, in ftrains grateful to the Redeemer, though not underftood by each other; whilft they praifed him, (1.) For what he had done, *thou haft redeemed us to God*; and as redeeming love is the burden of all their fongs, if faints lived nearer the throne, they would fee more clearly their intereft in the great redemption. (2.) For what they were therefore fure he would do; *we fhall reign on the earth*, firft in our own perfons, and afterwards in others, to whom God will make us inftruments of tranfmitting the fame fpirit and hopes, chap. xx. 6. We fhall reign over ourfelves by the power of that life of God,

C which

which is given to every believer to controul the
interefts, and propenfions of every other life in
him.   And over the lufts of others too we fhall
reign.   1. By the interefts we always have in
heaven, chap. xi. 6: So Shadrach, Mefhech, and
Abednego, by yielding their bodies to be burned,
changed even Nebuchadnezzar's *word, Dan.* iii.
28.   See *Job* xxxvi. 7. *Prov.* xxi. 1.   2. By the
great advantages which the revelation, our Lord
is going to give, will afford us, under the influence
of his Spirit, for the direction of our conduct before men ; which cannot but have fome effect
upon the ftates and kingdoms with which we are
connected.   The words alfo will have a further
accomplifhment in the Millennium, chap. xx. 4.
Pfal. lxvi. 6:   And the faints fhall reign with
Chrift for ever, in the new heaven and the new
earth, chap. xxi. 1.

11. And I beheld, and I heard the voice
of many angels round about the throne, and
the living creatures, and the elders : and
the number of them was ten thoufand times
ten thoufand, and thoufands of thoufands ;

12. Saying with a loud voice, Worthy
is the Lamb that was flain to receive power,
and riches, and wifdom, and ftrength, and
honour, and glory, and bleffing.

13. And every creature which is in heaven, and on the earth, and under the earth,
and fuch as are in the fea, and all that are
in them, heard I, faying ; Bleffing and honour, and glory, and power be unto him
that fitteth upon the throne, and unto the
Lamb for ever and ever.

14. And

14. And the four living creatures said,
Amen. And the four and twenty elders
fell down and worshipped him that liveth
for ever and ever.

In this grand chorus of heaven and earth,
observe the *singers* and their *songs*. The *singers*,
are first the angels, who are innumerable; and who
magnify the once slaughtered Lamb for opening
to them, as well as us, the things which concern the church and world: And though meaner
beings could not reach to join their notes, yet
every creature in heaven, and earth, in his different way, prolongs their praises; to which the
animals and elders, in a devout transport, add
their joyful *Amen.* Their *song* is, (1.) The highest
possible ascription of praise to the Lord Jesus,
by the bright intelligences of heaven, ver. 12;
in seven words, which might perhaps have some
reference to the seven seals which he was going
to open: And, (2.) when their acclamation was
finished, all the creatures in heaven and earth
with all their might, join in four words (which
might have a respect to the four parts of the
earth or the creation, which these seals concern,)
in ascribing exactly the same glory to the Father
and the Son, ver. 13. And as this scripture certainly contains a just representation of things, I
beseech my anti-trinitarian reader to consider,
whether it is possible for *that* scripture to have
been rightly understood, which seems to contra-
dict the plain sense of *this.* Surely all men must
give the same honour to Christ at the day of
judgment as to the Father, whatever they do now,
Rom. xiv. 10—12. *Phil.* ii. 10. *Isa.* xlv. 23.

CHAP. VI.

An account of the opening of the six first seals; and the great events which they disclose.

1. AND I saw when the Lamb had opened one of the seals; and I heard one of the four living creatures which said, as with a voice of thunder, Come and look attentively.

2. And I saw, and behold, a white horse; and he who sat thereon had a bow; and there was given to him a crown, and he went forth conquering and to conquer.

As nothing could be more desirable to this aged Apostle, now banished to *Patmos*, than to see his divine master taking the field as a warrior, with that ease, dignity, speed, and certainty of success which are peculiar to himself, to rescue sinners from their infernal slavery; so it will scarcely admit of a doubt, but that this, and the following scriptures speak of the same person; *Psal.* xlv. 3, &c. *Gird thy sword upon thy thigh, O most mighty, with thy glory and thy majesty; and in thy majesty ride prosperously, &c. thine arrows are sharp in the heart of the king's enemies, whereby the people fall under thee,* Rev. xix. 11, &c. *I saw heaven opened, and behold, a white horse; and he that sat upon him was called faithful and true; and in righteousness he doth judge and make war—and on his head were many crowns—and he was clothed with a vesture*
dipt

dipt in blood; *and his name is called the word of God. And the armies which were in heaven followed him upon white horses.* See also, chap. xvii. 14. The purity, beauty, joy, and triumphs of our Lord which are displayed in the gospel's wondrous frame, are well expressed by the colour of his horse. We call that object *white* which reflects all the colours of the rainbow; so the *gospel* reflects every glory of God to our view, which we can behold in the present state; for which reason our Lord, in his spiritual kingdom, constantly rides this horse, and inforces moral duties from evangelical motives. Yet many are ashamed of the gospel and paint it according to their own distempered fancy; whilst thousands more quarrel with its purity, because they are blind to its beauty. But whatever others do, *the armies which* are in *heaven,* will *follow* Christ *upon white horses,* chap. xix. 14, and they that leave the gospel, desert to the dragon and his army, chap. xii. 9; for we know who hath said, *He that is not with me, is against me; and he that gathereth not with me, scattereth abroad, Matt.* xii. 30.

A.D. 96, John saw his Lord taking the field upon this horse; and as we have no account of his return, so we are sure he never will return till all the elect are gathered in : Therefore the first seal extends to the end of the world; and furnishes the saints with a *joy unspeakable and full of glory,* through all the darkest scenes of the succeeding seals and trumpets: And attention to this, is properly demanded by a *son of thunder,* or by a *lion*-like minister, *Mark* iii. 17.

3. And when he had opened the second seal, I heard the second animal saying, Come and see.

4. And

4. And there came out another horse that was red; and it was given to him who fat on it, to take peace from the earth, and that they fhould kill each other. And there was given to him a great fword.

In the kingdom of nature our Lord rides horfes of different colours, which immediately reflect the glory of only fome of the divine perfections: So after the deftruction of the firft temple, Zechariah faw him upon a *red* horfe; his angels following him upon the *red*, *fpeckled*, and *white* horfes of different and mixed difpenfations, chap. i. 8—11. In A. D. 66, he brought the Romans upon the Jews; who deftroyed one million and a half fay fome, or, as others, two millions of them, agreeable to the predictions of Mofes and our Lord, *Deut.* xxviii, and *Matt.* xxiv. This dreadful war continued feven years; ended A. D. 73; and Jerufalem was taken in the beginning of September, A. D. 70, fays Mr. Blayney in *his Differtation on* Dan. ix. 20—27, p. 58. Thus literally *in the midft of the week* of their feven years war, *he caufed the facrifice, and the oblation to ceafe* for ever, ver. 27. But this flaughter being now paft, the deftruction intended under this feal, is generally thought to be that which the Jews and Romans, thofe mutual enemies of Chriftianity, made of each other in the reigns of Trajan and Adrian; in which the former, provoked by the idolatrous worfhip of Jupiter Capitolinus, killed fome hundred thoufands of the Romans; but they on the other hand had a thoufand cities and fortreffes deftroyed with the flaughter of above 580,000 men. This they gained by following that falfe meffiah *Barchochab*, the fon of a ftar; and thus the potfherds of the earth ftrove with each other, from A. D. 98, and

especially

especially from A. D. 107, to A. D. 134; see
Mr. Mede, and Mr. Fleming: But bishop Newton
extends this seal through the reigns of Trajan,
and his successors, by blood or adoption, for the
space of 95 years. Observe, if men appoint the
sheep of Christ for slaughter, they will soon
bring their royal Shepherd into the field, in a
garment dipt in blood; see *Isa.* lxiii. 1. And
it was doubtless a great support to the primitive
Christians to read this prediction; to which attention is very properly demanded by a living
creature like an ox, who expected himself to be
brought to the slaughter for the name of Jesus;
for though this scene is laid in heaven, it manifestly respects the affairs of earth.

5. And when he had opened the third
seal, I heard the third animal, saying, Come
and see. And I saw, and behold a black
horse; and he that sat upon him had a pair
of balances in his hand.

6. And I heard a voice in the midst of
the four animals, saying, A measure of wheat
for a penny, and three measures of barley
for a penny! yet see that thou injure not
the oil or the wine.

The rider here is either the same as on the
former horse, or some angelic instrument, by whom
our Lord saw proper to effect his wise and awful
designs in the kingdom of providence, for his
own and his Father's glory.

The seals, like other parts of scripture, are
of no *private interpretation*; therefore we must
not confine them to any one connection of circumstances, to the exclusion of all others which
are similar. But as the church of God had much
concern with the Roman empire at this time, we

are

are naturally led to look there especially for the
events here described. And, understanding this
seal of the affairs of that empire, during the reigns
of the *Antonine* and *Septimian* families, we find
the events here specified between A. D. 138, and
A. D. 211, viz, (1.) A grievous famine, intimated by the black horse; *Lam.* v. 10. *Our skin
was black, like an oven, because of the terrible famine.* And the divine order respecting the oil
and the wine; or rather this humble request of
the four ministers, that our Lord would not withhold his usual blessing from these two articles,
(that his power and goodness might the more visibly appear, in the midst of deserved wrath) implies that the other fruits of the earth were to be
hurt: And the distress must be great, when
wheat was, as we should express it, at more than
twenty shillings a bushel, or when a chœnix or
measure of it, which says Grotius, was no more
than an allowance for a man for one day, cost a
Roman penny, or 7d. ¼, which was a labourer's
daily wages, *Matt.* xx. 2; and the barley in proportion; viz, three times that quantity, for the
same money.

According to this prediction, Mr. Lowman
quotes, from the Roman historians, accounts of
famine in the reigns of *Antoninus Pius*, *Antoninus
Philosophus*, and *Commodus*; which *Tertullian* pointed out as a judgment from God, for their persecuting the Christians: And when in some of these
famines, the Christians saw wheat and barley sold
exactly at the price here specified, they could not
but devoutly adore him who foretold the exact
price of bread in this famine; to make his own
hand the more visible in it, to fill them with an
awe of his word, and at the same time to reconcile
them the more to their own share in this calamity. (2.) Under this seal we have an account of

the

the plentiful provifion of wine and oil, which was
ordered not to be hurt : So *Severus* fet himfelf to
guard, as much as poffible, againft that fcarcity
of provifion which the empire had experienced
in the reign of the *Antonines*; and kept particularly
a five years ftock of wine and oil in hand.
Within this period too, (3.) we find juftice
ftrictly adminiftered, of which a pair of balances
is the ufual emblem, both by the *Antonines*, and
by *Septimius* and *Alexander Severus* ; the latter of
whom was fo ftruck with the Chriftian maxim,
*whatfoever you would not have done to you, do not
you to another*, that he commanded it to be en-
graven on his palace, and on his public buildings.
Bifhop *Newton*. Yet fome refer the pair of balances to the famine mentioned above, and underftand it of their eating their bread *by weight
and with care*, Ezek. iv. 16. But if we take the
word ζυγον *a pair of balances*, in its ufual fenfe
for a *yoke*, this yoke was defigned to fhew, that,
as peftilence is a judgment which can fcarcely
come alone, fo if this did not humble his enemies,
they muft expect to encounter that quaternion of
deftroyers the fword, famine, peftilence, and wild
beafts, which will come *yoked* together under
the next feal, death's hollow fquare, with hell
in its train. But they would not believe, therefore the four-fold vengeance advances, as the
next verfes inform us.

7. And when he had opened the fourth
feal, I heard the voice of the fourth animal
faying, Come and fee.

8. And I faw, and behold, a pale horfe ;
and he that fat upon him, his name was
death, and hell followed with him : and
there was given to them, power to kill,
over

over the fourth part of the earth, with sword, and with famine, and with death, and with the wild beasts of the earth.

It was the sin and shame of the Roman emperors and people, that, when they saw the blessed fruits of the gospel in the holy lives of many around them, *Matt.* xxi. 32, they not only refused subjection to the LORD JESUS, who was gone forth into their provinces on his white horse; but when his red and black horse advanced to punish their insolence, they were so far from taking warning, that they even charged the Christians with being the occasions of those judgments, by which the Lord was avenging their blood—But when he judges, he will overcome; therefore under this seal we see him going forth on a pale horse; *Death* and *Hell*, (ἁδης an invisible, yet conscious and most sensible state,) in his train, which opens upon the execution of these his four sore judgments; *viz.* the sword, famine, wild beasts, and pestilence, *Ezek.* v. 17. xiv. 21. and xxxiii. 27. The last of these seems to be called by the name of the rider of this horse, *viz. Death*, as in *Jer.* ix. 21; and the pestilence in *Exod.* ix. 15, is in the Greek and Chaldee, *Death. Ainsworth.* It is the same word too in the LXX, 1 *Chron.* xxi. 12, where David is allowed his choice, whether the Lord should send his black, red, or pale horse, when he designed to punish him for numbering the people; but God's enemies have nothing to do with the *sure mercies of David*; much less with those, which were more than God had ever promised even that patriarch himself. Yet though this four-fold vengeance is not confined to the Roman empire, it is mercifully restricted to the fourth part of the earth; and executed, not all at once, but gradually; *viz,* from the reign of the emperor Maximin to Dioclesian,

clefian, or from A. D. 235, to A. D. 284: Within which period, (1.) the fword went forth awfully,
for there were more than twenty emperors in the
fpace of fifty years; moft of whom died in wars,
or were murdered by their own foldiers, or fub-
jects: And, befides lawful emperors, there were,
in the reign of *Gallienus,* thirty tyrants or ufurpers;
who fet up in different parts of the empire, and
came all to violent and miferable ends: Thus of the
Roman empire it might be faid, as of Nineveh,
Thy crowned are numerous *as the* devouring *locufts*
who come as a plague from God; *and thy captains
as the grafshoppers, which camp in the hedges in the
cold day;* but *when the fun arifeth, they flee away;
and their place is not known where they* are, *Nah.*
iii. 17. (2.) Thefe wars produced famine; which
was alfo brought on by other providential means,
caufing the earth to withhold its increafe: Befides
which, (3.) a moft dreadful peftilence went through
many provinces of the empire, A. D. 251, and for
fifteen years made unexampled havock of human
nature. (4.) By this means wild beafts were greatly
multiplied, fo that ' 500 wolves together entered
' into a city which was deferted by its inhabi-
' tants.' See Mr. *Lowman;* Bifhop *Newton; Univerfal Hiftory;* Dr. *Cave's Lives of the Primitive
Fathers;* and *Eufebius's Ecclefiaftical Hiftory.*

But I muft not conclude this fhort account of thefe
fore judgments without obferving, that the word
which expreffes the colour of this laft horfe $\chi\lambda\omega\rho\sigma\varsigma$
pale, every where elfe in fcripture fignifies *green
as grafs,* fee *Mark* vi. 39. *Rev.* viii. 7. and ix. 4;
which may teach us, that, as the graces of the
faints commonly *flourifh* moft when their temporal comforts *fade,* fo defolating judgments are
adapted to produce, and commonly fucceeded
by, a moral verdure over the world; as was the
cafe in the Roman empire foon after thefe four
judgments,

judgments, *Isa.* xxvi. 9; though the account of it is delayed till under the sixth seal, by the inter-jected history of what passed in the invisible world under the fifth. See *Brightman in loc.*

9. And when he had opened the fifth seal, I saw under the altar, the souls of those who were slaughtered, on account of the word of God, and for the testimony which they held;

10. And they cried with a loud voice, saying, How long, O Lord, holy and true, e'er thou dost judge, and avenge our blood upon those who dwell upon the earth?

11. And there were given to each of them white robes; and it was said to them that they should rest yet for a little time, till their fellow-servants and their brethren, who should be killed as they, should be fulfilled.

The ten primitive persecutions, (though there were not so many, says *Mosheim,* if we under-stand them of those which were universal through-out the Roman empire; but many more, if we take in those which were only provincial, and less remarkable,) are thus reckoned by Dr. Cave; *viz.*

Persecution	Time	Emperors
1. began A. D.	64 under	Nero.
2.	90	Domitian.
3.	107	Trajan.
4.	118	Adrian.
5.	162	Verus.
6.	202	Severus.
7.	235	Maximinus.
8.	250	Decius.
9.	257	Valerian.
10.	303	Dioclesian.

But

But the contents of this seal forbid us to restrict it to any one of these persecutions; yet it is commonly thought to refer immediately to the last of them, which was more extensive and bloody than any preceeding, and raged incessantly for ten years, (or *ten days*, as the blessed God, and the faith of his people are ready to call them, chap. ii. 10;) for it is often darkest just before the day breaks, and so it was before Constantine the Great arose to relieve the groaning empire.

It is probable the four living creatures, did not see these souls of the martyrs; but whether their attention was drawn off to something else; or whether it was not given them, as to John, to see them, at least they do not cry, as at the opening of the four first seals, *Come and see*. See the note on chap. iv. 7. But John saw them, either by means of some aerial vehicle with which they were clothed, to be visible to him; or his being in the Spirit enabled him to see and hear them, to certify us, that unbodied spirits, do not sink into insensibility till the resurrection. He saw them under the altar; but whether under the brazen altar of atonement, or the golden altar which was before the throne; (both of which he saw in this vision, chap. viii. 3, 5;) we are not informed: As glorified spirits, they had no further need of atonement to be made for them; therefore, if they are under the brazen altar, it must be either to contemplate the wonderful price which was paid for their ransom, or the awful fire which will be taken from thence, and cast down among their enemies upon earth, chap. viii. 5: But, as their Lord might perhaps yet have work to do, on behalf of their bodies, at the altar of incense, which stands before the throne, to this I rather consider them as repairing; and here, the glory of God bursting upon their sight, they feel such an

indignation

indignation at the contempt caft upon him in our world, as breaks out in this devout exclamation; *How long, O Lord, holy and true, e'er thou doft judge and avenge our blood, on them who dwell on the earth!* In anfwer to which; (1.) Their purity, beauty, and triumph, are compleated: By a lively faith in the atonement, they had in this world, *wafhed their robes, and made them white in the blood of the Lamb,* chap. vii. 14.; and now, not only is every thing tempting, deforming and degrading removed, but *white robes were given to every one of them,* as they fucceffively arrived at that blifsful world; for it was promifed them, that they fhould *walk with* Chrift *in white,* chap. iii. 4. and vii. 13. (2.) They are commanded to *refrefh* αναπαυσωνται, and folace themfelves in God. And, as glorified faints cannot poffibly take in every part of divine knowledge, immediately upon their arrival in heaven, (3.) they are inftructed in what they yet knew not ; *viz.* the wide reach of divine wifdom and patience, which would ftill permit the fame caufes to operate upon earth, which had haftened them to glory: Therefore it was faid to them, that they fhould *refrefh* themfelves ετι χρονον μικρον *for a little time*; yet I cannot apprehend that the word *chronos* informed them how long they were to wait for the avenging of their blood.

A *time* or *chronos,* fays the learned *Bengelius,* and his admirer Mr. John Wefley, is 1111 years ; but at whatever probable time this feal was begun or ended, I cannot find that 1111 years (with the fraction annexed to it,) could either inform them when their brethren, the martyrs under the man of fin, fhould either begin to come to them, or be all gathered in ; or confequently when their blood would be avenged, which was avenged upon the Roman empire from A. D. 395, to 560; chap. viii. 7—12; but will not be fo upon the beaft, till under the

the feventh trumpet, chap. xviii. 20, and xix. 2. Suffice it to add, that having read no more of this great man's ERKLARTE OFFENBARUNG, (written from the *Convent* of Denkendorf, A. D. 1740,) than Dr. Robertfon's tranflation of his introduction to it, I do not apprehend there are any fuch fractions in the divine arithmetick of time as he would introduce: Mr. Wefley has therefore wifely rejected them; and without the arithmetical and fractional fkill which *Bengelius* has difcovered, we hope fuch a rational and confiftent account may be given of many things in this book, as lies level with the capacity of plain Chriftians, for whofe ufe divine revelation was indifputably defigned.

12. And I faw when he had opened the fixth feal, and behold there was a great earthquake; and the fun became black as fackcloth of hair; and the moon became as blood.

13. And the ftars of heaven fell upon the earth; even as a fig-tree cafteth her untimely figs, being fhaken by a mighty wind.

14. And the heaven departed as a book that is rolled together; and every mountain, and ifland were moved out of their places.

15. And the kings of the earth, and the grandees, and the rich men, and the chief rulers, and the mighty men; and every flave, and every free man, hid themfelves in the caverns, and in the rocks of the mountains.

16. And they faid to the mountains, and to the rocks, fall upon us, and hide us from

the

the face of him that fitteth upon the throne, and from the wrath of the Lamb :

17. For the great day of his wrath is come, and who can be able to ftand.

C H A P. VII.

1. AND after thefe things, I faw four angels ftanding at the four corners of the earth; holding the four winds of the earth; that the wind fhould not blow on the earth, nor upon the fea, nor upon any tree.

2. And I faw another angel afcending from the rifing of the fun, having the feal of the living God; and he cried with a loud voice to the four angels, to whom it was given, *even* to them, to injure the earth and the fea :

3. Saying, hurt not the earth, nor the fea, nor the trees, till we have fealed the fervants of our God in their foreheads.

4. And I heard the number of thofe that were fealed; an hundred forty-four thoufand were fealed, out of all the tribes of the children of Ifrael.

5. Of the tribe of Judah, *were* fealed twelve thoufand. Of the tribe of Reuben, *were* fealed twelve thoufand. Of the tribe of Gad, *were* fealed twelve thoufand.

6. Of

6 Of the tribe of Aſher *were* ſealed twelve thouſand. Of the tribe of Naphthali *were* ſealed twelve thouſand. Of the tribe of Manaſſeh *were* ſealed twelve thouſand.

7. Of the tribe of Simeon *were* ſealed twelve thouſand. Of the tribe of Levi *were* ſealed twelve thouſand. Of the tribe of Iſſachar *were* ſealed twelve thouſand.

8. Of the tribe of Zebulun *were* ſealed twelve thouſand. Of the tribe of Joſeph *were* ſealed twelve thouſand. Of the tribe of Benjamin *were* ſealed twelve thouſand.

9. After this I ſaw, and behold, a great multitude which no one could number, out of every nation, and tribe, and people, and language, ſtanding before the throne, and before the Lamb, clothed in white robes, and palms in their hands;

10. And crying with a loud voice, ſaying, ſalvation to our God, who ſits upon the throne, and the Lamb.

11. And all the angels ſtood round about the throne, and *about* the elders, and the four living creatures; and they fell down on their faces before the throne, and worſhipped God,

12. Saying, Amen: The bleſſing, and the glory, and the wiſdom, and the thankſgiving, and the honor, and the power, and the ſtrength *be* to our God for ever and ever. Amen.

13. And one of the elders anſwered, ſaying to me, Theſe who are clothed in white

D   raiment,

raiment, who are they, and whence did they come?

14. And I said unto him, Lord, thou knoweft. And he faid to me, thefe are they who are come out of much tribulation; and have wafhed their robes and made them white in the blood of the Lamb;

15. Therefore they are before the throne of God, and worfhip him day and night in his temple; and he who fitteth upon the throne tabernacles upon them.

16. They fhall hunger no more, neither fhall they thirft any more; nor fhall the fun fall upon them, nor any fcorching heat;

17. For the Lamb, who is in the midft of the throne fhall feed them, and fhall lead them to living fountains of waters; and God fhall wipe away every tear from their eyes.

We may reckon the time of this fixth feal from A. D. 306, to 361; under which fix things open upon our view; viz, (1.) The fubverfion of the Pagan religion in the world, and particularly in the Roman empire. (2.) The perfecutors of God's people, are feized with inexpreffible horror. (3.) Their deftruction is followed by an univerfal peace in the empire, for a little time: In which time, (4.) many of the Jews are converted: And, (5.) yet more of the Gentiles: (6.) Whofe glory in heaven produces the moft triumphant fhout from faints and angels, to him who fits on the throne, and to the Lamb. This feal begins,

1. With an account of the fubverfion of the Pagan religion in the world, chap. vi. ver. 12,
13, 14.

13, 14. The Holy Ghost has taught us, in *Isa.*
li. 15, 16, to consider every kingdom, as a kind
of world in miniature, dependent on him, covered
with a heaven; whose luminaries or magistrates
are to minister to its comfort day and night for
his praise: But if the Heathen emperors, consuls,
priests and augurs, those persecutors of God's
people, have been considered as the sun, moon,
and stars of the world in general, and their power
and influence regarded as immoveable as mountains, and the frame of nature; it becomes him,
who has all power in heaven and earth, to speak
to them in his wrath, and vex them in his hot dis-
pleasure; especially as they refused to take warning by any of the judgments which he had executed upon them, under the four first seals. It became him therefore to make this sun *black as sackcloth of hair*; to turn the moon, the regent of the
night, into a bloody hue; with a solemn nod, to
frown these *stars* down to the *earth*; even *as a fig-
tree casteth her untimely figs, when she is shaken of a
mighty wind*; *to bid the heavens,* which had shed
such a pestilential influence upon the church and
the world, *depart as a volume when it is rolled
together*; and remove *these* huge *mountains* or
men, and *the islands* in general (which proudly
reared their heads in the midst of the seas; and
especially those which they had built in the sea,)
out of their places.

In the same lofty strains the destruction of
Babylon is predicted, *Isa.* xiii. 10. *The stars
of heaven, and the constellations thereof, shall not
give their light; the sun shall be darkened in his
going forth, and the moon shall not cause her light
to shine.* And that of Idumea, chap. xxxiv.
4. *All the host of heaven shall be dissolved: And
the heavens shall be rolled together as a scroll; and
all their host shall fall down, as the leaf falleth from
the vine, and as a falling fig from the fig-tree, and*

D 2　　　　　　　　that

that of Egypt, *Ezek.* xxxii. 7 ; yea of Judah, and Jerufalem, *Jer.* iv. 23, 24. *Joel* ii. 10, 11, and *Matt.* xxiv. 29, fee alfo the fame mataphors again in this book, chap. viii. 12. ix. 2. and xii. 4.

Thefe ftriking images are fo often repeated to teach us, in every cataftrophe, and even in every revolution of the nations, to contemplate the folemnities of the great judgment day, (to which our Lord immediately leads our thoughts from Jerufalem's deftruction in *Matt.* xxivth ;) when *all thefe things fhall be diffolved,* and *the heavens fhall pafs away with a great noife, and the elements fhall melt with fervent heat ; the earth alfo, and the works that are therein, fhall be burnt up.* 2 Pet. iii. 10, 11. In this view we alfo, as well as the men of that generation, fhall hereafter be called to an account for this *great concuffion,* σεισμος μεγας ver. 12, here called an earthquake ; but which manifeftly affected both heaven and earth, ver. 12, 13, 14 ; and produced an effential change of men and meafures, efpecially in the Roman empire, to eftablifh Chriftianity on the ruins of Pagan idolatry. So the Lord thus expreffes the removal of Judaifm ; *I will fhake the heavens, and the earth,* fignifying, fays the Holy Ghoft, *the removing of thofe things that are fhaken, as of things that are made ; that thofe things which cannot be fhaken may remain.* Heb. xii. 27 ; fee Hag. ii. 6 : He adds, ver. 21, 22, *I will fhake the heavens, and the earth ; and I will overthrow the throne of kingdoms : And I will deftroy the ftrength of the kingdoms of the heathen : And I will overthrow the chariots, and thofe that ride in them, and the horfes and their riders fhall come down, every one by the fword of his brother.*

Not to mention the inftances in which this prophecy had been fulfilled, before the opening of this feal, as it will alfo be hereafter ; it received a manifeft accomplifhment in the

civil

civil and religious victories of *Constantine the Great*, the son of *Constantius*, who began to reign A. D. 306 ; and who, after the defeat of Maximian, Galerius, Maximin, Maxentius, Licinius, and their adherents, openly defended the Christian religion.

This was the person by whom the church was to be *holpen with a little help* ; after they had *done exploits* in the ten heathen persecutions, and *instructed many* by their invincible patience ; whilst they fell *by the sword, by flame, by captivity and by spoil many days* : But when the sun of prosperity shone upon the church, many *cleaved to them with flatteries* ; and afterwards, when Arianism had poisoned the empire, *some of them of understanding fell*, as they had under the heathen Emperors ; *to try* the church, *and to purge, and make them white even to the time of the end*. Dan. xi. 32, 35; see further of this prophecy at *Rev.* xiv. 1—5.

In the beginning, and at the close of his reign, Constantine seems to have fluctuated between the heresy of Arius and the Athanasian doctrine : Afterwards his son Constantius became an Arian ; whose successor was the infamous Julian the apostate, the nephew of Constantine.—But though Christ had said, *my kingdom is not of this world*, and expressly forbidden his servants, to *exercise* that *lordship* and *dominion* over one another, in spiritual matters, which *the Gentiles* exercise over their subjects, *Matt.* xx. 25—28. *Mark* x. 35—45. *Luke* xxii. 24—30, this great man Constantine took upon him to secularize the ecclesiastical hierarchy, and adapt the government of the church to that new form of government which he had established in the state; see *Bower's hist. of the Popes*, vol. 1. p. 99—110. 'In his reign', says he, ' it was that the titles of patriarchs, ex-
                  ' archs

' archs and metropolitans were first heard of, or
' at least had any power, authority or privileges
' annexed to them.' And he particularly shews
us the exact agreement between the civil and ecclesiastical polity of Rome and Italy: ' Under
' the præfect of Italy, says he, were three
' dioceses, namely, Italy, West Illyricum and
' West Africa. The diocese of Italy was divided
' into two vicarages, and governed by two
' vicars; the one called the vicar of *Rome*, and
' residing in that city; the others styled the vicar
' of *Italy*, and residing at *Milan*; under the for-
' mer were ten provinces, and seven under the
' latter. Such was the civil government of Italy;
' and entirely agreeable to the civil, was the ec-
' clesiastical;' for the bishops of Rome and Milan enjoyed all the privileges of metropolitans,
over the bishops of the provinces which were respectively subject to the vicarages of *Rome* and
of *Italy*.

But these bishops were only metropolitans,
' whose power was confined within the li-
' mits of their respective vicarages:' And 'as
' neither of them had the charge of an whole dio-
' cese, they were not like several bishops in
' the east, distinguished with the title of ex-
' archs;' who, says the same author, ' were em-
' powered to ordain the metropolitans, to con-
' vene diocesan synods, and to have a general
' superintendency over their respective dioceses,
' such as the metropolitans had over their respec-
' tive provinces.' Sir Peter King in his *enquiry*
about the *Primitive Church*, has proved that in
the three first centuries, bishops or ministers had
the care only of one parish or congregation; but
Constantine secularized the ecclesiastical government; and so laid the foundation of that Anti-
christian hierarchy, which the Pope has since established at Rome; and of those other corrupt
                                              establish-

establishments, which have debased Christendom
ever since the fourth century.—Thus soon after
its glory, began the *spiritual* disgrace of that
bloody city Rome, which is at this hour the most
execrable spot upon earth: Constantine also began its *temporal* disgrace; for, about five years
after he became sole lord of the Roman empire,
A. D. 330, he removed the seat of the empire
from Rome to Constantinople, so called after his
name. He died A. D. 337; and the empire was
divided into the eastern and western, A. D. 395.

But to return—While the heathens were dis-
tressed to see their baneful *Sun, Moon,* and *Stars*
extinguished; the blood of God's servants, which
they had so wantonly spilt, cried aloud in their
consciences; and, to testify the Redeemer's power
over the spirits of his enemies,

2. These persecutors are seized with inexpressible horror; which is described in such language, as points our thoughts **again** to the mighty terrors which will fall upon the wicked, and
especially upon persecutors, at the day of the
Lord. The Spirit of God told us, *Isa.* ii. 10,
19, 21, *They shall go into the clefts and holes of
the rocks, into the tops of the ragged rocks, and
into the caves of the earth; for fear of the Lord,
and for the glory of his majesty, when he ariseth to
shake terribly the earth.* And to verify this prediction, ver. 15, 16, 17. *The kings of the earth,
and the grandees, and the rich men, and the chief
rulers; and the mighty men, and every slave, and
every free-man hid themselves in the caverns and in
the rocks of the mountains: And they said to the
mountains and to the rocks, fall upon us, and hide
us from the face of him who sitteth upon the throne,
and from the wrath of the Lamb; for the great
day of his wrath is come, and who shall be able to*
stand?

stand? To say nothing of the common slaves or freemen, who had been the active tools of Heathen vengeance, to drag the sheep of Christ to the slaughter, whose dying horrors are forgotten with their names; Galerius, Maximin and Licinius made a public confession of their guilt in this respect; revoked their edicts and decrees against the Christians; and acknowledged the just judgment of God in their destruction: The former died by a loathsome disease, ' whose compli-' cated horrors no language can express;' the second ended his life by poison in despair; and the last of these was strangled. Their destruction was succeeded,

3. By a general peace in the empire for a time, chap. vii. 1, 2, 3. *Four angels* stood *at the four corners of the earth, holding the four winds of the earth,* that none of them should *blow on the earth, sea, or trees; till the servants of God* were *sealed in their foreheads.* Observe, the affairs of this world are ever fluctuating, uncertain and empty, yet noisy, strong and terrible as the four winds of the earth; but God who holds the winds in his fist, here prevents those confusions, which the jarring passions and interests of men would have produced, by the ministry of four of those angels, who stand before him for orders from his throne, chap. viii. 2; the same probably who founded the four first trumpets, which shook down the western Roman empire; to whom however the Lord Jesus commanded, *saying,* though you know a dreadful work is assigned you, yet at present *injure not the earth,* neither *the sea, nor the trees; till* I and my servants have *sealed the servants of God in their foreheads,* or till I have accomplished that great work the conversion of Jews and Gentiles, which shall be affected
ted

ted by the inſtrumentality of Conſtantine; who, though born in Britain, may be ſaid to have *aſcended,* as *an angel from the eaſt, having the ſeal of the living God*; as, under the direction of ſome celeſtial angel, he ſhed from Conſtantinople in the eaſt a ſalutary influence upon the empire; and perhaps advanced the intereſts of Chriſtianity more from thence, than if his royal reſidence had been amidſt the augurs and temples of Rome, ver. 2. Accordingly we immediately hear,

4. Of the converſion of a great number of the Jews, who muſt certainly be the people intended by the twelve tribes of Iſrael, ver. 4—8, as diſtinguiſhed from the Gentiles, ver. 9; for converted Gentiles cannot be diſtinguiſhed *from,* though they are here diſtinguiſhed *among,* themſelves, by the reſpective countries, to which, they belonged. Beſides the Jews converted in Chriſt's time; at the day of Pentecoſt; by the apoſtles; and after the deſtruction of Jeruſalem, here is a bleſſed ingathering of a hundred and forty-four thouſand, that is, twelve thouſand out of every one of the tribes of Iſrael; as a pledge of their general return to God, and to their own land in the latter days; of which we ſhall hear under the ſeventh trumpet, chap. xiv. 1—5. And ſays Dr. Sharpe, ' The infliction of penalties, tortures and death, ' in the ten grievous perſecutions under the Hea-' then emperors, ſo remarkably increaſed the ' number of believers, that in the time of Con-' ſtantine the Great, it was doubtful, whether in ' the Roman world, the Heathens or the Chriſ-' tians were the more numerous.' *Introduction to Univerſal Hiſt. p.* 141. And if above twelve thouſand Jews and Idolators were baptiſed at Rome, A. D. 312, beſides women and children; (ſee bp. Newton,) it is eaſy to ſuppoſe that, in the

whole

whole empire, during the thirty one years of
Conftantine's reign, the number here mentioned
fhould be brought home to God; though it is
from this prophecy alone, that we can expect to
learn the number converted in each tribe.

A mark on the forehead may ferve for diftinction and fafety, *Ezek.* ix. 4; but *fealing* expreffes covenant tranfactions between God and them:
And this being externally miniftered by men, our
Lord fays, ver. 3, *till we have fealed the fervants
of God in their foreheads.* The *holy fpirit of promife* feals the foul, 2 *Cor.* i. 22; but on their bodies too, the Lord will notify his *authority* over,
and *propriety* in them, and their *feparation* for his
ufe, by the common feal of his kindom; which
alfo witneffed before men their *relation* to him,
and confequent *fecurity* and *prefervation:* Though,
at the fame time, as things are fealed for *fecrefy,*
fo the life of a Chriftian is much hidden in its
origin, nature, actings, fupports and glorious
iffue, *Col.* iii. 3. Circumcifion had been a feal
of God concealed in their flefh, *Rom.* iv. 11;
and under the Heathen perfecutions Chriftians
had been much compelled to worfhip God in
fecret: But now Jews and Gentiles made a free,
open, and public confeffion of their faith by *bap-
tifm*; which was then commonly called the feal
of falvation, *Gal.* iii. 27, 28: And this feems to
be, intended by their being *fealed,* and having
the Father's name written in their foreheads, ver.
3, 4, and chap. xiv. 1; which phrafes greatly
favour the method of baptizing by fprinkling:
Yet in no fenfe whatever can thefe expreffions be
taken exactly literally.

But whatever apprehenfions we form about
that crofs in heaven, which Conftantine is faid
to have feen, A. D. 312, as he was going to
Rome

Rome to fight Maxentius : And though himself, says Eusebius, was signed with the cross in baptism, as thousands still are; neither this Expression of *sealing,* nor any other in scripture, ever laid any foundation for this airy sign in that ordinance ; which therefore is as really will-worship, as if we should imprint any self-invented marks of Christ in our flesh, such as some of the Heathens bore of their masters and gods, to which custom these words seem to allude; see chap. xiii. 16. xiv. 1. xx. 4. and xxii. 4. Scripture silence is as directive and decisive as scripture-words; for what God has not appointed in his worship, no man or body of men have any right to appoint; see *Jer.* xix. 5. *Heb.* vii. 3, 14. If this had been believed in queen Elizabeth's days, when the delaying shades of papal night were yet struggling with the advancing morning; at which time the Popish habits were so shamefully imposed, England had been probably excused, from most of the miseries which it endured under the four following reigns. When the brazen serpent was idolized, Hezekiah broke it in pieces, and called it Nehushtan, *Brass-work,* 2 *Kings* xviii. 4. But this sign never was injoined from heaven; therefore the faith employed about it, stands only in the wisdom of men, and not at all in the power of God. We cannot enough *glory in the cross of Christ, Gal.* vi. 14; but the sign of the cross is the vain amusement of multitudes in Christendom : May God remove this stumbling-block of their iniquity out of the way of the Papists ; and form professing Christians of every name, to the unadulterated simplicity of gospel obedience.

The number here converted, is the same as will hereafter return to their own land, chap. xiv. 1: And the number must be so far definite in both places, that there must be at least 144,000

in

in all; and here of each tribe 12,000—And in
this account obferve, that there are children of
the bond-woman, as well as children of the free,
Gal. iii. 28. That Judah is named firſt, becauſe
the Meſſiah, the fountain of honour, deſcended
from him; that Levi, who had no temporal inheritance with his brethren, had neither more nor
leſs inheritance in God than they; that Ephraim,
infamous for idolatry, is here called by the better name of his father Joſeph: But idolatrous
Dan is not named at all in this account of the
tribes; which intimates, that, if he had any ſhare
in the grace of this ſeal, it was much leſs than
the others: Yet this no more proved the tribe ex-
tinct, than omitting the name of Levi, *Numb.*
xiii, or, of Simeon, *Deut.* xxxiii, proved them
ſo at thoſe times. But if Dan had been a *ſon of
perdition*, we ſee here, that the tribes would be as
compleat without him, as the twelve apoſtles
were after Judas was gone to his own place, *Acts*
i. 26: Yet I apprehend that tribe will not appear
to have been loſt hereafter; ſee chap. xxi. 12.

The ſignification of the names of theſe twelve
tribes of Iſrael, in the order in which they are
here placed, which is not the order of their birth,
is thought by Mr. Mede to have ſomething in-
ſtructive in it to us; for when we *confeſs to God*
by *looking* to his *Son*, as the words *Judah* and *Reuben* remind us to do; a *troop* of *happy* perſons or
things cometh, as *Gad* and *Aſher* ſignify. But even
theſe happy perſons are to *wreſtle* with thoſe who
forget their *obedience* to God; as the words *Naphthali*, *Manaſſeh* and *Simeon* import: But who ever
cleaves to the Lord Jeſus, ſhall have a great *reward*;
for God himſelf ſhall be their *dwelling*, and *add*
them to the *Son* of his *right hand* in heaven, as
the remaining names of theſe tribes teach us, *viz.*
Levi, *Iſſachar*, *Zebulun*, *Joſeph* and *Benjamin*.

5. The

5. The converfion of the Gentiles, ver. 9. *After this I faw, and behold, a great multitude which no one could number, out of every nation and tribe, and people, and language, ftanding before the throne and before the Lamb*; for fatan can detain none of the prey, whom Jefus refolves to refcue; and this is the infcription on every new-creature, *I that fpeak in righteoufnefs, mighty to fave*, Ifa. lxiii. 1. And though their being fealed is not mentioned; yet their ftanding before the throne, and before the Lamb implies it, as harveft fuppofes fpring and fummer, or as the end of a journey includes the way: Yet it is exprefsly hinted too, chap. ix. 4, that all, whether Jews or Gentiles, who are preferved from the Mahometan and Papal locufts, have been fealed in their foreheads. And if there were *Jews* in this glorified company, who were *of every tribe* φυλων, as well as of every nation, people, and language, *their* being fealed implied that *all* the company were fo; for there can be no invidious diftinctions made in God's family, *Eph.* iii. 15: Yet it was the more neceffary to fpeak of God's fealing the Jews particularly, to teftify the immutability of his covenant engagements to that people; as their defcendents were to fhare but little of the bleffings fettled upon their progenitors after this time, for about fifteen hundred years.

6. Their glory in heaven produces a triumphant fhout from faints and angels, ver. 9—17. *God is a rock, his work is perfect:* And if Chrift perfeveres in his love to his people, they will perfevere to eternal life. Accordingly our apoftle faw this, once fealed, and now glorified, company before the throne, and before the Lamb; from whofe blifsful vifion and enjoyment they fhall no more depart. He faw them *cloathed in white robes of* perfect purity, beauty and triumph, with

with *palms* of victory *in their hands ; and they cried with a loud voice, saying, Salvation to our God who sitteth upon the throne, and unto the Lamb. And all the angels stood round about the throne, and about the elders, and the four living creatures ;* the living creatures being nearest the throne, the elders next, and the angels outermost ; *and fell before the throne on their faces, and worshipped God ; saying, Amen* to the preceding praises of this ransomed multitude. And, though they needed no share in their salvation, and could not therefore join in the words of their song, they subjoin another sevenfold ascription of glory to God, as they had done, chap, v. 12, *saying, Amen ; blessing, and glory, and wisdom, and thanksgiving, and honour, and power, and might be unto our God for ever and ever. Amen.*

And as this song of praise touched the beloved disciple's heart on its tenderest strings, *one of the elders* seeing, as though he had said, a visible joy upon my countenance, *answered* to that joy ; though thou canst know but little at present about the angels, yet as for *those who are arrayed in white robes,* on which I see thy eyes are fixed, *who are they ? and whence did they come ? and I said unto him,* Κυριε *Lord* or Sir, (the word commonly signifies a master or governor ; and whoever teaches another, is so far his governor) *thou knowest ;* and canst inform me more particularly of that salvation, which I heard them just now ascribe to him that sitteth on the throne, and to the Lamb. *And he said unto me, these are they who came out of great tribulation ; and have washed their robes, and made them white,* not in their own, but *in the blood of the Lamb.* Observe, blood would defile in every other view but that of making an atonement, for which it was shed : But Christ's blood does not wash the robes of our own natural righteousness,

Matt.

Matt. **v.** 20. *Rom.* **x.** **3**, which muft be put off, *Rom.* vii. 6 ; but thofe *garments of falvation* which we received from God himfelf, *Ifa.* lxi. 10, and which we have defiled, *Ifa.* lxiv. 6 : Yet wafhing thefe robes, it does not make them of its own colour *red*, leaft the righteoufnefs of believers fhould feem to have any concern in their juftification, *Phil.* iii. 9 ; but it makes them *white*, which is the emblem of purity, beauty, victory, joy and glory. *Therefore* being juftified by that blood, and fanctified by the fpirit which flows in and with it, *they are before the throne of God, and ferve him day and night* in unwearying miniftrations *in his temple ; and he that fitteth on the throne*, fhall pitch his *royal tabernacle over them :* And, agreeable to the promife made to them in *Ifa.* xlix. 10, *they fhall hunger no more*, either in foul or body (when the latter is raifed from its dufty bed,) *neither thirft any more ; neither* fhall the natural, or any metaphorical diftreffing *fun light upon them, nor any fcorching heat : For the Lamb which is in the midft of the throne, fhall feed them, and fhall lead them to living fountains of water*, till he gives up the mediatorial kingdom to the Father ; *and* as they are paffing over into the loving hands of an abfolute *God*, he fhall *wipe away all tears from their eyes*, and ftop up for ever the fountain which fo long fupplied thofe briny ftreams.

But though the fcene is here laid in heaven, to affure us of the faints admiffion to glory immediately upon their leaving the body ; and in that world only can the expreffions here ufed receive their full accomplifhment, yet many of them may be accommodated to a ftate of grace here, which is glory begun, 2 *Cor.* iii. 18.

C H A P.

‡—•━━━━━━━━━━━▶•◀◀━━━━━━━◀•‡

C H A P. VIII.

The opening of the seventh seal; the sounding of
four of the trumpets; and a very solemn alarm given
with respect to the three remaining.

1. **A**ND when he had opened the seventh seal, there was silence in
heaven about half an hour.

2. And I saw the seven angels who stood
before God; and there were given to them
seven trumpets.

3. And another angel came, and stood
at the alter, having a golden censer; and
there was given to him much incense, that
he might give it to the prayers of all the
saints, upon the golden altar which was
before the throne:

4. And there went up the smoke of the
perfumes, with the prayers of the saints,
from the hand of the angel before God.

5. And the angel took the censer, and
filled it with fire of the altar, and threw it
upon the earth; and there were voices, and
thunders, and lightnings, and an earthquake.

6. And the seven angels, which had the
seven trumpets, prepared themselves that
they might sound.

The

The seventh seal introduces the seven trumpets: But before they sound, we have here an account of six things; viz, 1. A half hour's silence in heaven. 2. The trumpets are given to the seven angels. 3. The saints are very earnest in prayer. 4. Christ presents their prayers with his much incense. 5. Fire taken off from the altar, produces great commotions in states and kingdoms. 6. This gives a signal to the angels to prepare themselves to sound, each in his place and order.

The time of these events seems to have been from about A. D. 364 to 395; in which time,

1. We have an account of a *silence in heaven about half an hour*, ver. 1. As there can be no cessation of worship or pause of blessedness in heaven above, it seems necessary to understand this silence of the affairs of the church below. Commotions of any kind in a society produce noise and *voices*, ver. 5. chap. iv. 5. xvi. 17, 18. xviii. 2. and xix. 6; and when the kingdom of Christ shall be set up more universally in the world, there will be great voices in heaven, chap. xi. 15. and xiv. 2: In opposition to which, we may well understand this silence in heaven, of a season in which little was done for the advancement of Christianity in the world: And such a time we find between the reign of Jovian and Theodosius the Great, from A. D. 364 to 379; in which time the Alemans, Picts, Goths, Saxons, Sarmatians, Quades and Persians, so harrassed the different provinces of the Roman empire, as left God's servants but little time to oppose the Gentile superstitions, in the reigns of Valentinian I, Gratian and Valentinian II: and by a method of computation which will be explained, chap. xx. 1—6, this time might be called *about half an hour*; for the holy Ghost did not design, by this phrase, to mark the pre-

cise

cise time, in which his people had been providentially hindered from spreading the honours of his name: And though this obstruction did not continue a full *half hour*, yet the mentioning *about* that time, was very proper to express how displeasing the hindrance of it was to God, and to his servants. Or this *silence in heaven* might refer to what was done in the temple, which resounded with songs, trumpets, and other instruments of musick, whilst the burnt offering was consuming upon the altar, 2 *Chron.* xxix. 25—28; but afterwards the people prayed in silence *without*, in the courts of the temple, whilst the priest was gone in to offer incense before God, *Psal.* lxv. 1. *Heb. Luke* i. 10; and accordingly we hear of many prayers ascending from all the saints at this time, ver. 3; for however God's servants may be obstructed in his other work, they cannot be taken off from praying to him. But before we come to consider this, the text calls us to observe,

2. That seven trumpets are given to the seven angels, ver. 2. *I saw the seven angels who stood before God; and there were given to them seven trumpets.* See the notes on chap. v. 6. Observe, so important is the number *seven* to us, with respect to the Lord's day, which is a seventh part of our time, that the Lord not only makes the age of the world seven thousand years, and manages the affairs of the last three thousand of it, in this book, by sevens; viz, seven seals, seven trumpets and seven vials; but he has also represented his own court in heaven, as having seven angels especially standing before him, distinguished amidst *the thousand thousands who minister to him, and the ten thousand times ten thousand who stand before him, Dan.* vii. 10. (so the Persian chief had *seven princes which saw the king's face, and sat the first in the*
kingdom

kingdom as his *counsellors, Esth.* i. 10—14. *Ezra*
vii. 14; who were called, says Xenophon, the
eyes and *ears* by which the king saw and heard.)
And though Jehovah needs none of the services
of his creatures, yet, to these grand ministers of
our God, the seven trumpets are given; which
reach to the end of the world, and disclose the
grand events which await nations and the church
of God: But these trumpets being all given to
them at the same time, proves that they are angels properly so called, not living men. Yet it
does not appear, that John saw or observed these
angels, till the instruments of their service were
delivered to them; for holy beings must be, and
desire only to be, noticed in the display of their
abilities, and the improvement of their talents
for God's glory. But though we hear of *voices,*
thunders, lightnings, and an earthquake under this
period, ver. 5; yet the incursions of the nations
upon the empire, spoken of above, which were
represented by them, were not crowned with such
success as afterwards; because the first of these
angels had not yet sounded: They began before
God's time, and therefore could not effect their
designs.

3. The saints are very earnest in prayer at this
period, ver. 3, 4. when the Spirit, Christ's glo-
rifier, has made known that substantial *word* in
the heart, an everlasting intercourse is opened between God and that soul; and the persons who
enjoyed this intercourse, were now very numerous in the different parts of the empire, especially in the reign of Theodosius: And the invasions of their enemies, but drove good men the
more to their knees, and their God; for storms
are God's messengers sent to hasten his doves to
their windows; and *I—prayer* is the language of
every new-born soul, when his *enemies* are *strong*

and

and lively, Pfal. xxxviii. 19—22 and cix. 4. *Heb.*
and he that will do no other good in the world,
may ferve as a fcourge to drive good men to God
and heaven.

4. Chrift, being omnifcient and omniprefent,
hears and prefents the prayers of each of them,
with his own much incenfe before the Father,
ver. 3, 4. *Another angel came and flood at the
altar,* &c. This could not be a created angel,
for they were never called to be priefts unto or
before God, *Heb.* v. 4. *Gr.* and therefore have
nothing to do at the *golden altar before the throne,*
ver. 3. But our Lord is called an angel in many
places befides this, *Gen.* xlviii. 15, 16. *Hof.* xii. 4.
Mal. iii. 1. *Rev.* x. 1. xviii. 1. and xx. 1. And
as many prayers were now afcending in their na-
tional troubles, it feemed needful that the beloved difciple fhould be able to inform the churches
of the certain fuccefs of them, through their Redeemer's interceffion; agreeable to the hopes
which other parts of fcripture had given them,
Rom. viii. 34. *Heb.* vii. 25. 1 *John* ii. 1.

But that the favourites of heaven may not fuppofe that their prayers are accepted on their own
account, they are here taught, that in order for
their acceptance, 1. There muft be under them,
the fire of that juftice and jealoufy of God againft
fin, and love to men, which preyed upon the
great facrifice Chrift, otherwife they cannot afcend to God; fo the Jewifh prieft took fire from
off the brazen altar with his cenfer, to offer incenfe on the golden altar which was before the
mercy-feat, *Lev.* ix. 24. x. i. and xvi. 12, 13.
The Spirit both affifts believers to wafh their facrifices by previous preparation, *Lev.* i. 9, 13.
and alfo to feel fomething of this fire in their ap-
proaches to God, to quicken and purify their
prayers: Yet our great high prieft too muft take
of

of this fire himself, (or be impressed with a present sense of that justice which preyed upon him for our sins,) in order to enable our prayers to ascend as a delightful perfume, in his gracious intercessions. 2. They must be presented on the golden altar of Christ's divine nature before the throne. 3. Our Lord must mingle his own fervent desires with ours; and as he offered himself a sacrifice of a sweet smelling favor to God, *Eph.* v. 2, so, to overcome the offensiveness of our corruptions, which mingles itself with our prayers, he will perfume them with the much incense of his most pure and perfect desires or intercessions. And this incense is said to be given him, as the incense-keeper gave out what was to be offered, every morning and evening, on the golden altar, *Exod.* xxx. 7. *Numb.* iv. 16. 1 *Chron.* ix. 29, 30. 2 *Chron.* xiii. 11. Accordingly, to testify the Father's concurrence and delight in this part of our Lord's priestly office, to which he had called him, *Isa.* liii. 12; he is represented as giving him every desire which rises in his heart, that he may offer it with the virtue of his atonement for his redeemed people: Therefore says he, *I know that thou hearest me always*, John xi. 42; for *he whom God sent, speaketh the words of God*, on earth and in heaven. The Lord has respect to these three things in the prayers of his people; therefore they may be satisfied, that he will be with and preserve them, amidst the confusions which the seven trumpets announce to the world.

3. In the censer in which our Lord had offered the prayers of his people, he took fire from off the brasen altar, which had preyed upon himself (and which still continues burning as hot as ever against impenitent sinners, and against the corruptions of good men, *Heb.* xii. 29;) and threw

it

it into the earth; yet wifely directing it to every
defigned fpot, ver. 5, fee *Ezek.* x. 2; to con-
fume the wicked, *Pfal.* lxxxiii. 14, 15. *Ifa.* lxvi.
15. *Ezek.* xxii. 20—22. *Nah.* i. 6; and at the
fame time to purify the righteous and prepare thefe
offerings of God to be fet before him, *Ifa.* vi.
6, 7. And as foon as it was kindled; a general
cry was heard from numerous terrified *voices*,
when the nations broke in upon the empire from
A. D. 364 to 395; and as general a horror was
fpread, as when *thunder, lightning, and earthquakes* convulfe the frame of nature, and predict
its diffolution: For to Heathen Rome, that
flaughter-houfe of the Redeemer's fheep, it was
now cried, as once to Jerufalem, *Thou fhalt be vifited of the Lord of hofts, with thunder, and with
earthquake, and great noife; with ftorm, and tempeft, and the flame of devouring fire, Ifa.* xxix. 6.
Thefe dreadful guards attended when the Lord
gave forth his fiery law at Sinai, *Exod.* xix. 16—
18; and the fame awful artillery will be difcharg-
ed when the feventh trumpet founds, chap. xi.
19; and efpecially when great Babylon, worfe
than the ancient, comes to be vifited of God,
chap. xvi. 18.

6. Upon this fignal given, the angels prepare
to found their trumpets, each in his own place
and order, ver. 6: And though one of them has
not yet founded, after fo many hundred years,
the apoftle faw them all preparing; to affure us
that, when the time is come, there will be no delays; and that angels are waiting, as well as we,
for the accomplifhment of the things here predicted.

Obferve, *feals* may be broken and *vials* poured
out without noife, whatever commotions may be
confequent upon them, chap. vi. 4, 12, &c. vii. 1.
viii. 1. and xvi. 12—21; but a *trumpet* intimates
a loud

a loud noise, addressed to our senses, to awake and rouse us, especially when this trumpet is in the hand of an angel; for *the sound of the trumpet is the alarm of war, Jer.* iv. 19; and such is every one of these seven trumpets. And it seems reasonable to suppose, that an intelligent ear should be able to distinguish, both when each sound begins and when it ceases; and consequently to discover how long the ministry of each of these seven angels, and of those celestial attendants who are ranged under his order, continues; which no doubt continues during the whole time allotted to his trumpet; see chap. xvi. 4—7.

We may further observe, that, as the voice of the arch-angel and the trump of God, will hereafter summons the hosts of heaven, and dissolve all nature's frame; so the first four trumpets of these angels, are generally thought to have shaken down the Roman empire: which never was more than about the third part of the known world, though they vainly boasted of universal empire: For America was not discovered by Christopher Columbus, till eleven hundred years after this time; viz. A. D. 1492: But Rome possessed about as much in Asia and Africa, as it wanted of the whole sovereignty of Europe. And though Rome could now boast its Christian emperors; yet this can no more prevent the avenging of the blood of God's servants, upon them, than Josiah's reformation prevented God's avenging upon the kingdom of Judah, the innocent blood with which Manasseh had stained that long-favoured country.

7. And the first angel sounded, and there was hail and fire mingled with blood, and it was cast down upon the earth; and the

E 4   third

third part of the trees were burnt up, and the green grafs was burnt up.

It was an entertainment to the great Mr. Mede, to obferve from *Achmetes*, and the documents and monuments of the *Indians*, *Perfians* and *Egyptians*, that fome of the fame bold figures, which adorn the pages of infpiration, were in ufe amongft them; and applied to the fame things as they are in fcripture, but the fcriptures are wonderfully fufficient to explain themfelves, as thefe trumpets fhew; with refpect to the firft of which Sir Ifaac Newton obferves ' That ftorms ' of thunder, lightning, hail and overflowing ' rain, are, in the prophetic language, put for ' a tempeft of war defcending from the heavens ' and clouds politic:' And as blood is here mingled with the hail and fire, this naturally leads our thoughts to the defolations of war; fo that the words muft have a metaphorical, whatever literal, accomplifhment they have; fee *Exod.* ix. 23.

Mr. Mede begins this trumpet at the death of Theodofius the Great, A. D. 395; at which time, ' The Huns, Goths, and other barbarians,' (excited by the perfidy of Rufinus, prime minifter to Arcadius the Eaftern emperor) ' like hail for mul- ' titude, and breathing fire and flaughter, broke ' in upon the beft provinces of the empire, both ' in the Eaft and Weft, with greater fuccefs than ' they had ever done before.' The fame year the famous Alaric, with his Goths ' began his ' incurfions: Firft he ravaged Greece, then waft- ' ed Italy; befieged Rome, and was bought off ' at an exorbitant price: Befieged it again in the ' year 410; took, and plundered the city, and ' fet fire to it in feveral places.'

So the Lord *fent a mighty and ftrong one,* the king of Affyria; *who, as a tempeft of hail, and*
deftroying

*destroying storm, as a flood of mighty waters over-
flowing, cast down* the house of Israel *to the earth
with his hand*, Isa. xxviii. 2: And this Gothic
storm spared neither high nor low, young nor old;
but came resistless as *hail mingled with fire*, upon
the *trees* of the field, and upon the *green grass*, to
which respectively men of high and low degree
are compared in scripture; see *Ecclef.* xi. 3. *Isa.* ii.
12, 13. and xl. 6. *Ezek.* xvii. 24. and xxxi. 8, 9.
Dan. iv. 10, 15, 26. *Zech.* xi. 2. *Matt.* iii. 10.

And besides the sword of the barbarians,
which destroyed the greatest multitude of men,
Philostorgius who lived in, and wrote of these
times, saith; " That among other calamities, dry
" heats with flashes of flame, and whirlwinds of
" fire, occasioned various and intolerable ter-
" rors: Yea, and hail fell down in several places,
" weighing as much as eight pounds." See
bishop *Newton*, and *Universal History*.

Thus these words were both literally and metaphorically accomplished, from about A. D.
395 to 412; which we therefore reckon the proper time of this trumpet.

8. And the second angel sounded, and as
it were a great mountain, burning with fire,
was cast into the sea; and the third part of
the sea became blood.

9. And *there* died the third part of the
creatures in the sea, which had life; and a
third part of the ships were destroyed.

The blood under this trumpet, intimates that
the desolations of war are intended here, as well
as under the former; the instrument of which is
represented by a grand metaphor, *as if a great
mountain, burning with fire, was cast into the sea;*

us

us *as if*, for no such mountain really fell into the
sea; and if it had, it could not have turned it to
blood, much less could the fall of any one mountain, so generally affect the third part of the sea,
and the living creatures in it. Besides, to produce blood, the sea into which it falls must be
peoples, multitudes, nations and tongues, chap. xvii.
15. And if such a mountain as Attila and his
Huns, fall upon the Eastern and Western empire, he will crush them to death; and at the
same time *burn them with fire.* This man called
himself *the scourge of God*, and *the terror of men*;
and so he was literally, especially to the Western
emperor Valentinian the third, with his 700,000
attending barbarians. See the Roman histories
from A. D. 440 to 454, within which time this
royal murtherer and others not only crushed the
third part of men, as if a mountain had been
thrown down out of the clouds upon the fishes
of the sea; but also destroyed the third part of
the ships trading, or taking their pleasure thereon.

Observe proud men esteem themselves as mountains, *Isa.* ii. 12—14. and xl. 4. *Zech.* iv. 7. *Rev.*
vi. 14; and haughty oppressors are burning mountains: Such *a destroying mountain* was Babylon,
till the Lord *rolled it down from the rocks*, Jer. li.
25; see also *Psal.* xxx. 7. and lxv. 6. *Dan.* ii.
35, 44, 45. But Sion need not fear, whatever
mountains are *carried into the midst of* whatever
seas; for *God is in the midst of her, she shall not
be moved:* And whatever fires kindle upon the
first Adam's world, under the preceding and following trumpets, previous to the general conflagration, *God shall help her right early.* Psal.
xlvi. 2, 5. Rev. xvi. 18, 19.

10. And

10. And the third angel founded, and there fell from heaven a great ftar, burning like a torch; and it fell upon the third part of the rivers, and upon the fountains of waters.

11. And the name of the ftar is called wormwood; and a third part of the waters became wormwood : and many men died of the waters, becaufe they were made bitter.

A *ftar* in prophetic language, is a ruler in the church or ftate, a *prince* or a *prophet*. It is applied to Chrift, that *morning ftar of Jacob*, Numb. xxiv. 17. Rev. xxii. 16, and to the fons of Jacob, who were the heads of the tribes of Ifrael, *Gen.* xxxvii. 9, 10. When the word *ftars* is joined with the *fun* and *moon*, it fignifies inferior officers in the ftate, *Ifa.* xiii. 10. *Ezek.* xxxii. 7, 8. But a *ftar* is a very common, and moft fignificant hieroglyphic of a prophet or minifter in the church, *Dan.* viii. 10. *Jude* 13. *Rev.* i. 20. ix. 1. and xii. 1, 4. And, whether this was a religious or political ftar, it fell fudden and unexpected from the lower heaven, down ro the earth, *burning like a torch*; and though it could neither burn up the *rivers* nor *fountains*, nor even make them change colour, chap. xvi. 4; yet it impregnated them with fuch a bitternefs, as ended in death to wretched multitudes.

Such a ftar was Genferic; who, having founded a kingdom in Africa, A. D. 427, ' embark-' ed with 300,000 Vandals and Moors, and ar-' rived upon the Roman coaft in June 455; the ' emperor and people not thinking of any fuch ' enemy: he landed his men and marched directly ' to Rome; whereupon, the inhabitants flying ' into the woods and mountains, the city fell an

easy

' eafy prey into his hands: He abandoned it to the
' cruelty and avarice of his foldiers, who plun-
' dered it for fourteen days together. He then
' fet fail again for Africa, carrying away with him
' immenfe wealth, and an innumerable multitude
' of captives; and left the ftate fo weakened, that
' in a little time it was utterly fubverted.' Bifhop
Newton.

Underftanding this ftar politically, we may
begin the time of this trumpet from the above
year; viz. 455, and confider its effects as continued till the time of the founding of the following trumpet; which period was a time of as great
bitternefs to the Roman empire, as if the rivers
and fountains, which fupply cities and countries,
were impregnated with wormwood. And perhaps Rome, which had been confidered as a *fea,*
or collection of people under the former trumpet, now greatly diminifhed, might be as fitly
reprefented by *rivers* and *fountains,* which were
running faft towards another *fea* or collection of
people, that is, to a different government. Drying up rivers and fountains would produce a fcarcity of the neceffaries of life, *Hof.* xiii. 15. *Ifa.*
xix. 5, 6; and, though this trumpet does not
dry them up, they are *imbittered*; fo that *many*
died by drinking of them.

Some years before this, the Romans had given
up the defence of Britain; which called in the
Saxons to its aid about the year 450: And in
A. D. 456, fays Mr. Mede, the Roman empire
was crumbled into ten kingdoms, which are afterwards called the *ten horns* of the *beaft*; fee chap.
xiii. 1. and xvii. 7, 12, 16.

But underftanding this *great ftar* of a religious
governor, we may obferve, that, as Genferic was
a perfecuting Arian, fo Pelagianifm rofe up in
this century, about the year 410; and, joining

ing its forces with the Arianism of the former century, dreadfully poisoned the *rivers* and fountains of the church; so that many died, both temporally and spiritually, of one part or other of this double root of bitterness, which bore *gall and wormwood*; see *Deut*. xxix. 18. *Jer*. xxiii. 15. *Amos* vi. 12: Or confining ourselves yet more closely to that sense of the word star which the holy Ghost has given us in this book, *Rev*. i. 20, by this *great star* may be meant *the Bishop of Rome*; whose proud affectation of superiority over all other bishops, produced such awful political and religious contentions, in the East and West, from A. D. 312 to 606; or from the time that the empire became Christian, till he had gained his airy point. After this *star* had compleated its fall *from heaven*, our author at A. D. 606, saw *the key of the well of the* abyss *given* to him, as we shall see, chap. ix. 1; but here he saw his fall, and marked its bitter effects upon the *rivers and fountains of water*; which poisoned *many*, though not all the *men* who drank of them.

But as his fall has been so fatal to the world, for our own warning for the future, suffer me to point out the circumstances which facilitated his descent.

And here not to say that the *mystery of iniquity* had been working in the church, ever since the apostle Paul's time; or that unguarded hyperbolical expressions, which some of the primitive fathers of the three first centuries had used, about the Virgin Mary; ministers and saints (if their writings have not been interpolated or altered) ministered an occasion of promoting the papal cause; 1. When the bishop of Rome became preacher to the head of the Roman empire, through the corruption of nature, this both excited an improper elatement in his own breast, and gave him an undue consequence among his brethren.

brethren. 2. When Conſtantine had ſecularized the eccleſiaſtical government, in the manner explained at chap. vi. 12, &c. this gave a fair opportunity for the further exertion of his lordly pride; eſpecially as from the beginning, ' the ' power of the biſhop of *Rome* far exceeded, ' within his juriſdiction, that of other metropoli- ' tans.' Mr. *Bower*, vol. 1. page 105. And, 3. When the biſhop, or patriarch of Conſtantinople, after the ſeat of the empire was removed thither, became his rival; this only put an edge upon his thirſt after unlimited power, and excited dreadful conteſts, before he could attain the arrogant title of *Univerſal Biſhop.*

But the moſt eſſential thing in popery is its leading doctrines, which may be all reduced to theſe two; viz, *degrading Chriſt*, and *ſetting up the creature:* The firſt of theſe was effected by Arius, A. D. 317; and when they had taken off the crown from Chriſt's head, it was eaſy to ſee for whom they deſigned it; though Pelagius did not ſet it upon the head of free-will, till almoſt a hundred years after that time. Theſe two abominations, nouriſhed by a worldly ſpirit, produced popery A. D. 606: And as the ſpirit of the world has ſtill dominion in the church, and its rivers and fountains are not yet healed of their Arian and Pelagian bitterneſs; therefore, as every ſeed will have its own body, there is reaſon to apprehend that the modern contempt caſt on the perſon and offices of Chriſt, and that Arminianiſm which has deluged Chriſtendom ever ſince A. D. 1602, will again produce popery, and give it another infernal triumph in our world; ſee chap. xiii. 11—18. And how far it is already begun, in the ſilence of the friends of the goſpel, and in the impudence of its enemies, I

leave

leave to their confideration who have the moral ufe of their intellectual fight.

Underftanding this trumpet, in this laft fenfe, I reckon the time of it from A. D. 317 to 606; all that time the pope lay upon earth, ftruggling with the church and ftate for pre-eminence; and when he had gained it, Pelagian and other errors were abforbed in popery, that grand collection of almoft every error with which the devil was ever permitted to torment the Chriftian world.

12. And the fourth angel founded, and the third part of the fun was fmitten, and the third part of the moon, and the third part of the ftars; fo that the third part of them was darkened: And the day did not appear for the third part of it; and the night likewife.

This trumpet predicts the darkening of the great lights of the empire; as we have feen the fame metaphors explained under the fixth feal, chap. vi. 12, 13; but, though the images are in both places nearly the fame, there is an obfervable difference, between the defcription which the holy Ghoft there gives of that *religious reformation* in Conftantine's time, and the *political diffolution* of the empire which thefe words announce. In the former cafe, the *fun* became *black as fackcloth of hair*, but foon put off its mourning to congratulate the victories of Conftantine; *the moon became as blood*, but at the next lunation fhe fhewed a fairer face; yet the inferior officers in general were removed at that time, to make way for better men; which is thus expreffed in prophetic language, *the ftars of heaven fell unto the earth, even as a fig-tree cafteth*

eth her untimely, and therefore unfavoury, *figs when she is shaken of a mighty wind:* But in this diffolution of the empire the fun, moon and ftars are *fmitten*, *darkened* and *shine not*; for they could not fhine as lights of the empire, when there was no empire to be illuminated. There is alfo this further difference, that *religious reformation*, under the fixth feal, extended further than the Roman empire; this *revolution* concerned that empire only, for it darkened but *the third part* of the heavenly luminaries. In the former cafe too, an extreme horror, down from the throne to the cottage, for the great fin of having perfecuted God's fervants, made way for the removal of the Pagan religion and government, ver. 15, 16; but we read of no fuch horror *here*; nor was there fuch a caufe for it in the prefent, as in that cafe: This was a forrow not unufual in the world; though fpreading wider than in former inftances; a forrow at the funeral of an empire, at which were interred the hopes and joys of weeping multitudes: For Rome, having ftruggled with its fate, through eight turbulent reigns, was at length ruined in the year 476, under Momyllus or Auguftulus, as he was called in derifion, by Odoacer king of the Heruli; who being flain A. D. 493, Theodoric founded the kingdom of the Oftrogoths in Italy, which continued about fixty years. Yet the *moon* and *ftars* ftill fubfifted; for the fenate, confuls and patricians were not wholly extinguifhed till A. D. 566, when Italy was conquered by the eaftern emperor Juftin II; who governed it by the exarchs of Ravenna, under whom Rome was made only a dukedom: and this was the feventh form of government there, after kings, confuls, dictators, decemvirs, military tribunes with confular authority, and emperors; fee chap. xvii. 10. Therefore we may

3

reckon

reckon the time of this trumpet from A. D. 456 to 566.

Rome, often warned, would not obey that solemn mandate, *Jer.* xiii. 16. *Give glory to the Lord your God before he cause darkness, and before your feet stumble upon the dark mountains, and while ye look for light, he turn it into the shadow of death, and make it gross darkness*; therefore Egypt's doom became theirs, *Ezek.* xxxii. 7, 8. *When I shall put thee out, I will cover the heavens, and make the stars thereof dark: I will cover the sun with a cloud, and the moon shall not give her light. All the bright lights of heaven will I make dark over thee; and set darkness upon thy land, saith the Lord God.* See also *Isa.* xiii. 10, 11.

13. And I beheld, and heard one angel flying in the midst of heaven, saying with a loud voice, Woe, woe, woe to those that dwell upon the earth; because of the remaining voices of the trumpet of the three angels, who are yet to sound.

This angel, flying *alone*, *brings* the most interesting and alarming *tidings*, 2 *Sam.* xviii. 25. And each trumpet here spoken of, has a distinct woe of its own; which concerns those who dwell upon the earth in general, from the rising of the sun to the going down thereof. For if the holy Ghost had only designed to denounce a woe against the world in general, from some or other of these trumpets, the words must have run thus, *Woe to the inhabitants of the earth, because of the voices of the trumpets*; but the *trumpet* being in the singular number, extends the woe of each to the east and west. True, the singular number is often put for the plural, where no possible mistake can be made by it, as in *Psal.* xii. 2.

F   xxii. 26.

xxii. 26. xxxi. 24. xxxiii. 19, 20, 21. xliv. 18, 21.
and xlv. 5. and many other places; but though
the woe-trumpets are certainly three, if the word
trumpet had been in the plural number, it would
have produced this miſtake, that each trumpet
had not a woe for every part of the profeſſing
world. And for the ſame reaſon as the *trumpet*
is ſingular, the *voices* are plural, to intimate that
each trumpet ſounds an alarm both againſt the
eaſt and weſt. Accordingly under the fifth trumpet, the locuſts are a woe to the eaſt and weſt,
chap. ix. 7—10: Under the ſixth the Turks are
a woe to the eaſt, chap. ix. 13—19; and (to
ſay nothing of the ſpiritual judgment mentioned
in the two laſt verſes of that chapter) the earthquake at Rome is a woe to the weſt, chap. xi.
13: And under the ſeventh, the two beaſts are
a woe to both, chap. xiii. 1, 11.

Perhaps the *trumpet* may alſo be made ſingular, to inform us that but *one* ſubjeᢏt is purſued
through all the woe-trumpets, though that ſubjeᢏt is twofold: Accordingly we find that the firſt
of them deſcribes the riſe of popery and mahometaniſm; the ſecond amplifies the account of both,
and puts an end to the latter; and the third ſhews
us, that after mahometaniſm is ſwallowed up in
popery, the two popiſh beaſts ſhall be deſtroyed:
After which we have an account of what ſaints
and ſinners have to expeᢏt from God, from that
time to all eternity. If we hope to *decipher* the
charaᢏters of this book, we muſt carefully attend
to every word.

According to the order of this prophecy
this warning falls between A. D. 566 and 606:
And indeed the ſixth century concluded, as the
ſeventh began, with very clear moral prognoſti-
cations of thoſe two infernal evils, which at
A. D. 606 poiſoned the eaſt and weſt; the approach

proach of both of which is here announced to the church, by this celestial messenger.

Kind Spirit! it was God himself who sent thee to give men this needful warning. Thy voice too was loud enough to have roused the east and west; and thy flight low enough, even in the midst of the heavens, where the birds fly, chap. xiv. 6. and xix. 17. And oh! that the world had attended thy faithful admonitions from God! or would even now, in its old age, hearken and receive thy long-neglected instructions, which are still addressed to sinners of Adam's family.

C H A P. IX.

1. AND the fifth angel sounded, and I saw a star fallen from heaven to the earth : And there was given to him the key of the well of the abyss.

2. And he opened the well of the abyss ; and a smoke ascended from the well, as the smoke of a great furnace : And the sun and the air were darkened by the smoke of the well.

3. And out of the smoke, there came locusts upon the earth ; and power was given to them as the scorpions of the earth have power.

4. And it was commanded them, that they should not injure the grass of the earth, nor any green thing, nor any tree ; but the men only who have not the seal of God in their foreheads.

5. And

5. And it was given them, not that they should kill them, but that they should be tormented five months : And their torment *was* like the torment of a scorpion, when it strikes a man.

6. And in those days shall men seek death, and shall not find it ; and they shall desire to die, and **death** shall flee from them.

7. And the resemblance of the locusts, *was* like horses prepared for war ; and on their heads as it were crowns, like gold ; and their faces as the faces of men.

8. And they had hair like the tresses of women ; and their teeth were as those of lions.

9. And they had breast-plates like breast-plates of iron : And the sound of their wings was like the noise of chariots, *with* many horses running to battle.

10. And they had tails like scorpions, and stings were in their tails : And their power was to hurt men five months.

11. And they had a king over them, the angel of the bottomless pit ; whose name in Hebrew *is* Abaddon, and in the Greek tongue he has the name of Apollyon.

12. One woe is past ; behold two woes more are coming after.

A falling star is a globule of fire composed of oily, sulphurous and nitrous exhalations from the earth ; which, upon the clash of two clouds, breaks, shoots out in a fiery stream, and immediately disappears : And many esteem this a proper

per hieroglyphic to reprefent the Pope and Mo-
hammed, or Mahomet; in both of whom the
characters of a *prince* and *prophet* are united, as
we have feen the word *ftar* explained, chap. viii.
10, 11. But though a *ftar* may defcribe a
falfe, as well as a true, minifter, chap. viii. 10,
11; yet the further account given of this *ftar*, as
fallen from that *heaven* the church *to the earth*,
by no means agrees to Mahomet, who never was
in heaven, either before or after the year 606;
and therefore could not fall from thence; nor
had he even the honour of his famed predeceffor
Balaam in the eaft, who uttered true prophecies
from God. But this character exactly agrees to
that minifter who had long been in the church,
before the bloody emperor Phocas declared him
univerfal bifhop, A. D. 606; and who had de-
fired to fet *his throne above the ftars of God :* But
finding that he could not be the only oftenfible
figure in the fkies, his earthly nature (which was
not at all changed by his heavenly fituation) ope-
rating ftrongly upon him, brought him down
with the rapidity of a fiery meteor, blazing all
the way, in hafte to gain the parent earth.

A ftar, fays bifhop Warburton, in the Egyptian
hieroglyphics, alfo denoted God, *Amos* v. 26.
*Ye have born the tabernacle of your Moloch, and
Chiun your images, the ftar of your God which ye
made to yourfelves;* and how applicable this is to
him who *fitteth in the temple of God, fhewing himfelf that he is God,* is plain to every intelligent
proteftant, 2 *Theff.* ii. 4.

If this man had refembled a watery exhalation
from the earth, he might have returned to it as a
generous refrefhing fhower; but as the holy Ghoft
has reprefented him by a body of an oily, ful-
phurous and nitrous nature, it was not likely he

fhould

should *descend* to it as good angels do, chap. x. 1.
xviii. 1. and xx. 1; but in a fiery stream, predictive
of the burning which he will kindle here. So
fell the pope, from that *heaven* to which he was
not adapted: He fell almost from the first hour
that the empire became Christian; and especially
from the time when he so far cast off subjection to
Christ, as to become a metropolitan. Then it
was that our author saw him fall, chap. viii. 10,
11; though this promotion was but the begin-
ing of his perdition, yet his fall was not generally taken notice of till A. D. 606, when he
shamefully accepted the title of universal bishop,
which he had so scandalously solicited: From
that time it became visible that he *had been
fallen* before; and that the church of Rome was
no more a church of Christ, but a part of the
common earth to which this star was fallen.
But our author has awful things to see after he
was fallen; for to blaze for a moment and then
die (which is all the glory of a falling star) could
give us no adequate idea of the designs and works
of this earth-born vapor; therefore, observing
him when he was *fallen* πεπτωκοτα, he saw *the
key of the well of the abyss given to him.*

It was not consistent with the scheme of divine
grace in Christ Jesus, to give him the key of the
abyss itself; but, in righteous indignation against
the hypocrisy of the east and west, the Lord
gave him *the key of* its *well.* Observe, (1.) God
alone can open heaven; but men could in some
measure have opened hell, if he had permitted
them; and he has given the key of its *well* to
this man of sin. Well therefore might 'the
' whole system of nature put on mourning at his
' birth, to sympathize with the church's afflic-
' tion:' And so historians tell us, that about this
time, ' the air grew pestilent; the earth became
                                        ' barren;

' barren; the sea overflowed its banks; and a
' mighty mortality of men, beasts and fishes
' ensued.' *Hist. of Popery*, vol. 1. p. 59. (2.)
Schemes to do mischief, like a well, furnish
hell with all the entertainment which it has:
With these satan attempts to mitigate the torment
of his burning rage against God; yet every
draught he takes increases his scorching thirst
after more wickedness, whilst the moments of
even this cruel pleasure shorten apace.

(3.) As all believers are daily employed in drawing *water out of the wells of salvation*, which God has
opened on mount Sion, *Isa.* xii. 3; so eminent sinners
take the same methods to quench their infernal
thirst as satan does; and for this purpose the
pope *opened the well of the abyss:* Therefore, (4.)
Popery and its appendages, proceed from infernal depths. And, (5.) That enmity to God,
which supplies hell with its successive schemes of
pride, deceit and cruelty, supplies also the Papists with theirs: This is the well to which this
shepherd leads his flock of goats, to quench their
thirst; and no other key but this was ever
given him. Yet, (6.) As wells are deep, and their
bottoms generally unseen, we can form no compleat idea of the wickedness or misery of hell, by
any infernal religions; or other things, which
proceed from thence. But; (7.) If men may
be so wicked on earth, as to open the well of the
abyss, to torment and damn their fellow-crea-
tures; what will the inhabitants of hell do against
one another to all eternity, who are for ever lost to
every virtue and hope!—Observe also the difference between Christ and Anti-christ; the latter
has only the *key of the well of the abyss*, and that
given him; the former has the *key of the abyss*,
itself, which is his own property as God, chap.
xx. 1: And Anti-christ brought up *Abaddon* and

F 4 *Apollyon*

Apollyon from hell; but Christ *shuts* him up there, and *sets a seal* upon him, ver. 2, 3.

But to proceed—Anti-christ, being fallen from all that common grace of God, which preserves even the wicked within some bounds of moderation and decency; and not knowing the horrors of that *bottomless pit*, to which the devils besought our Lord not to command them to return, *Luke* viii. 31, having received *the key of this well*, he resolves (upon an infernal journey)

Flectere si nequeam superos, acheronta movebo :
and, following the propensions of his own heart, which still led him downward, *he opened the well of the abyss*, and took an oath of allegiance to satan : The common wickedness of earth would not suffice him, therefore he digs down to open the infernal store-house, to fetch from thence the thickest shades to vail the day ; for he *loved darkness rather than light, because* his *deeds were evil.*

We cannot doubt the propriety of applying this to that grand enemy of the church of God, who is so much spoken of, and so fully described from this place to the end of the xixth chapter ; not only because every character here given exactly suits the Pope, but because it is expressly said of the same person, when he became a *beast*, A. D. 756, that he *ascendeth out of the bottomless pit*, chap. xi. 7. and xvii. 8. The holy Ghost says of Christ, *Eph.* iv. 10. *He that descended, is the same also that ascended up far above all heavens :* Reverse the words, and they are true of Anti-christ, *He that ascended is the same also that descended* ; for he could not *ascend*, if he had not first *descended :* Yet as no key but that of the *well of the abyss* had been given him, we are naturally led to understand, that he both descended to, and ascended from the bottomless pit, through the well of it,

I   which

which communicates with the abyfs; for we have no account of his opening the abyfs itfelf immediately, though he opened its *well*, A. D. 606; which will not be fhut till A. D. 2016, chap. xx. 1, 2. It was the beaft then, and not Chrift! who *defcended into hell:* But as we cannot underftand this of a local hell, to which he could not defcend clothed with an animal body, I am ready to afk, how did he defcend to open this well of the abyfs? certainly he could go down no other way than through his own vicious heart; nor could he defcend further than his own inclinations, inftigated by fatan, fhould lead him; and they led him downwards till he came to the bottomlefs pit: And as all human hearts are naturally alike, *Matt.* xv. 19, it is only the reftraint of providence which keeps every man from opening the well of the abyfs as the pope did; for if God fhould leave every man to himfelf, he would prove, as he did, that the bottom of hell is the bottom of his heart.

Satan gladly affifting the defigns of this *man of fin,* he found it eafy to turn the key of this well of the abyfs; and immediately *a fmoke,* like that *of a great furnace, afcended from the well; and the fun and air* in general *were darkened by the fmoke of the well,* efpecially in thofe parts which were neareft to Rome, where this well was opened, ver. 2. *And,* every part of this *fmoke* being prolific, *out of it there came locufts upon the* earth, ver. 3, which filled every place which this fmoke had darkened. Thefe locufts were the Saracens and Mahometans in the eaft; who, like other people (though unlike the natural locufts, *Prov.* xxx. 27.) *had a king over them, the angel of the bottomlefs pit;* who came forth in this fmoke unobferved, to fpread death all around him: But in the weftern part, nearer the mouth

of

of this well, this smoke produced the monks and friars and other religious orders amongst the Papists, who had the same *king over them* as the eastern locusts ; who, under the Hebrew *name of Abaddon*, employed some of these armies against the Jews ; and others against the Gentiles, under the *name of Apollyon*, ver. 11.

If it should be asked, how could the pope's opening the well of the abyss affect the east, as well as the west ? I answer ; (1.) the pope was at that time considered as the *eye of the world* ; and when *the light* which was in the world *was become darkness*, the whole *body* must be *full of darkness*, *Luke* xi. 34, 35 : Nor could that *false prophet* Mahomet have established his arrogant pretensions, if an extreme darkness had not sat upon the face of the churches of God in general, at A. D. 606. (2.) This smoke ascending out of the bottomless pit, would naturally move which way ever the wind drove it ; and, as it continued to rise all the time of this trumpet, the changing winds would in such a length of time, necessarily drive it to every quarter of the heavens—Besides, though the pope alone opened the well of the abyss, yet, (1.) It has been already proved that every trumpet has at least two *voices*, or a woe *to those who dwell on the earth* in general, chap. viii. 13 ; therefore this trumpet has a woe for the places where the Saracens did, and where they did not come. (2.) As we shall find the two witnesses prophesying both against Popery and Mohometanism, during the whole time of this trumpet, as well as long after ; see chap. xi. 1—13, no doubt this angel from the beginning announced both these evils, against which they are subpœnaed to witness. (3.) *The sun and the air* in general *were* said to be *darkened*, by this *smoke of the well* ; agreeable to which, both the Papists and
Mahometans

Mahometans are reprefented as in a ftate of comparative darknefs, chap. xi. 2, 3: And Rome efpecially is known to have been as full of chofen darknefs in the feventh century, as it will be of judicial darknefs when the fifth vial is poured out, under the feventh trumpet, chap. xvi. 10. In confequence of this darknefs it was, that even profeffing Chriftians took up with *maffes* and *altars*; with *images* and *pictures*; with *cups, croffes* and *candle-fticks*; with *relicks, garments, holy water, number-ed prayers, pilgrimages*, &c. &c. inftead of Chrift: For the fmoke, not of a common fire, but *of a great furnace* arofe in thick and awful pillars around them, *and darkened the fun and air* in general: Accordingly the Papifts ufe candles in their worfhip at noon-day, chap. xviii. 23, as if to light Proteftants to fee their darknefs. And though thefe pillars of fmoke might be fomething leffened, in the time they would take in moving from Rome to Arabia, yet the darknefs was alfo great there; which feems to have been notified to the eaftern nations, in a language which they were likely to underftand; viz, by the literal darkening of the fun and air, which was probably effected by the miniftry of the angel who founded this trumpet. So bifhop *Newton* quotes an Arabian hiftorian, who fays that half the body of the fun was eclipfed, fo that little of its light appeared from October, A. D. 626, to June 627; at which time Mahomet was exercifing his followers in depredations at home, for greater conquefts abroad.

The prophet Daniel feems to have predicted both thefe evils together, chap. xi. and xii. and xi. 4, the angel foretells the deftruction of Alexander's empire, and ver. 5—29 defcribe the conteft which was between two of the four horns, or kingdoms into which Alexander's dominions
were

were broken; viz, Egypt and Syria, called the
kings of the south and of the north, whose alternate
successes affected the land of Israel, which lay between them. And having spoken of the Roman
empire, ver. 30—35; the angel led him to a view
of both these abominations, ver. 36—43. Popery is described, ver. 36—39. *The king shall do
according to his will,* more than any other king
ever did ; *and he shall exalt and magnify himself
above every god* ; *and shall speak marvellous things
against the God of gods, and shall prosper, till the
indignation* designed against the world *is accomplished.* It is added, ver. 37, that he shall apos-
tatize from *the God of his Fathers*; and not *regard
the desire of wives*, or conjugal affection, ver, 38,
39. He *shall also honour* Mahuzzim; viz, the
Virgin Mary, saints and angels, whom he con-
siders as the *bulwarks, fortresses, protectors,* and
guardians of mankind : *He shall acknowlege and
increase them with glory : And he shall cause them to
rule over many* ; *and shall divide the land* among
them *for gain:* ' St. George shall have England ;
' St. Andrew, Scotland ; St. Denis, France ; St.
' James, Spain ; St. Mark Venice ;' &c. see Mr.
Mede, and bishop *Newton*. What follows, ver.
40—43, is probably an account of the *Saracens*,
who sorely wounded the Greek empire, and of
the *Turks* who totally ruined and destroyed it ; as
we shall see at chap. ix. 13—19 : And we shall
find the two last verses of that chapter, ver 44, 45,
and some things in chap. xii, accomplished under
the seventh trumpet ; see *Rev.* xvi. 12—16. But
to return,

1. The Mahometans are indisputably intended
by the *locusts* which this smoke produced in the
east, ver. 3—11. Mahomet was born at Mecca
A. D. 571, and when he began to vent his imposture, there was but one man in that city who
could

could read or write; which made it the more easy for him to feign an intimacy with heaven, in order to make himself great upon earth. He retired to his cave near Mecca, A. D. 606, where he pretended to converse with the angel Gabriel: And, by the affistance of a Chriftian Monk and a Perfian Jew, he manufactured and fabricated that false religion; **which**, like the moift, filthy and fuffocating *fmoke of a great furnace* has filled the eyes of many with tears, and of more with darknefs: And by this fmoke, and the Saracen locufts which proceeded out of it, *the fun* or governor of many a city and kingdom, *was* both morally and politically *darkened*; fo that *the air* itfelf forgot the light which ufed to fhine joyfully through it. And to fupport his pretenfions, this monfter of ambition and luft, afterwards feigned an afcent to heaven from Jerufalem, upon a ladder of light, attended by the angel Gabriel: **And**, having taught his followers that his religion was to be propagated by the fword; **and** flattered their hopes with every fenfual enjoyment, in that paradife to which he affured them, that they fhould go, if they **fell in his** wars; arrayed in armour and in blood he rode in triumph over the fpoils of thoufands and ten thoufands, till he had founded the Saracen empire, ‘ which, in eighty years ‘ time, extended its dominion, over more king- ‘ doms and countries, than ever the Roman could ‘ in eight hundred: But it continued in its ‘ ftrength not much above three hundred years;’ fee *Prideaux's Life of Mahomet*.

These Arabian, Hagarene, or (as they proudly called themfelves from Sarah the free woman) *Saracen* invaders of the eaftern empire, are properly called *locufts*, not only for their number and devouring nature; but becaufe locufts are the natural produce of Arabia, which feems to have

taken

taken its name from them, *Judg.* vii. 12. Heb.
They also made their chief inroads upon those
parts of Christendom, where locusts are wont to
be seen; and nearly in the same proportion too,
as to time and degree. Locusts are bred in pits,
and the schemes of these men proceeded from the
bottomless pit; the smoke of their religion urg-
ing them forward in quest of prey, ver. 2, 3.

The strength of these Arabians also consisted
much in their cavalry; therefore, like locusts,
their *resemblance* was that of *horses prepared unto
battle: And their teeth were as the teeth of lions*,
tenacious of every thing they seize. And as the
locusts have a hard shell upon their breasts, to
prevent them from being hurt on whatever they
light; so these had *breast-plates, as it were breast-
plates of iron:* And, flying with great rapidity
upon their prey, *the sound of their wings was as
the noise of chariots, with many horses, running to
battle*, ver. 7, 8, 9; see *Joel* i. 6, and ii. 3—8;
for they came as a judgement from God, and the
nations could no more resist them than they can
locusts. And, to intimate their relation to *the
serpent, the old one*, who (being so much older
than us) deceiveth them that dwell on the earth,
chap. xii. 9. and xx. 2. Gr. it is added, ver. 3. *Power
was given to them as the scorpions of the earth have
power;* for *they had tails like scorpions*, which,
says Mr. Brightman, carries its sting out of its
tail, awry and unobserved, ready to strike a blow
any moment; *for their stings were in their tails*, ver.
10; and the anguish they gave *was as the torment of a scorpion when he striketh a man*, ver. 5:
Such was the torment of their false religion, and
of the brutal cruelty and oppression which it coun-
tenanced; the sting of which they left in the
souls and bodies of men wherever they came: And
what better could be expected from the bottomless

less pit, and from *Abaddon* and *Apollyon* their king, ver. 11, if men would but have traced their infernal origin and direction!

It is added, ver. 7, 8, They had *on their heads as it were crowns like gold*, alluding to the turbants or mitres which these proud Arabians wore; as well as to intimate the prodigious number of kingdoms which they should conquer; Mr. Mede mentions about eighteen. They had also *faces as the faces of men*, with beards or mustachoes: And it was the more proper to take notice of their faces, if they were as large as they are pictured. And they *had hair as the tresses of women*, long, flowing or plaited, agreeable to the lascivious genius of that people; by their manner of dressing or plaiting which, one part of them was distinguished from another.

Yet to satisfy us that these are not natural, but symbolical, locusts, *it was commanded them*, ' by ' the secret power of God upon them,' ver. 4, *that they should not hurt the grass of the earth, neither any green thing, neither any tree*; and this order was literally obeyed, in the care which the first Saracen leaders took, to spare as much as possible the countries they invaded : Or, taking the words *grass*, *green things*, and *trees* figuratively, as in chap. viii. 7, they were commanded not to hurt those of *low*, *middling* or *high* degree in the world, *but the men only who had not the seal of God in their foreheads*; viz. the Jews, and those idolatrous Christians in the east and west, who, if they ever had the seal of God set upon them, had violated and profaned it by worshipping saints and images; who Mahomet and his followers pretended to chastise for their idolatry : And when their avarice carried them beyond their commission, falling upon those who had the seal of God in their foreheads, 'in Savoy, Piedmont, and the ' southern

' southern parts of France, (which were after-
' wards the nurseries and habitations of the Wal-
' denses and Albigenses) they were defeated with
' great slaughter, by the famous Charles Mar-
' tel, in several engagements;' see bishop *Newton*, and *Universal Hist.* vol. xix. p. 670. And
as to those who had not this seal, *it was given
them, not to kill*, but *to torment them*, ver. 5;
therefore when they besieged Constantinople, A.D.
672, and again in 718, ' they were forced to de-
' sist by famine, pestilence, and losses of various
' kinds;' for the putting an end to the Roman
empire was reserved for the Turks, as we shall see
under the next trumpet: Yet they *tormented them*
by their invasions, by their brutal lusts, and by
what they obliged them to pay for liberty to pro-
fess their own religion; till *in those days* men *sought
death and found it not, and* earnestly *desired to die,
but death fled from them*, ver. 6.

But though this trumpet speaks expresly of
nothing but woes, yet mercy is always mixed with
the sorest judgments in this world: Accordingly
we shall hereafter find, chap. xi. 3, &c. that the
two *witnesses* began to deliver their testimony, in
the east and west, at the same time that this trumpet was sounded: And with respect to these locusts too, here are three restrictive clauses in the
power given to them; viz, as to the *persons* whom
they may injure; the *degree* of injury to be done
them; and the *time* to which they are limited,
which is *five months*, ver. 5: So long the locusts
live; viz, from April to September; and scorpions too are said to be noxious for no longer
time; after that they become torpid and inactive.
So the Saracens made their incursions in the five
warmest months of the year; then retired, and
dispersed themselves to their own homes for the
winter.

winter. And as the words had thus an annual accomplishment, so taking a day for a year, as in chap. xi. 2, 3, the *five months* inform us, that they were to continue their tormenting invasions for a hundred and fifty years: And accordingly, we find the chief part of their religious and political conquests, **between A. D.** 606 and 756. The year before that; **viz, A. D.** 755, says the *Gospel Magazine* for *May* 1777, 'the Turks, bursting ' **forth in** great numbers out of Tartary, seemed ' to carry all before them: They fought for a ' considerable time, and with various success ' against the Persians and Saracens; at last they ' obtained a peace from the Saracens, and a ' quiet settlement in Asia, upon condition that ' they should adopt the Mahometan religion, and ' unite their armies with them against the Chris- ' tians'—some therefore reckon the above **the** proper time of this trumpet, as it respects **the** Mahometans: But if the repetition of the *five months* ver. 10, intimates that another hundred and fifty years is to be added **to the account,** the whole three hundred years will give us the whole time in which the Saracen empire had power to hurt men, before it was broken into several principalities or kingdoms; See Mr. *Mede,* Mr. *Lowman,* and bishop *Newton.*

Sir Isaac Newton reckons the times of the Saracen conquests from A. D. 637 to 936 inclusive: Others, looking only upon the Mahometan and Saracen conquests, begin this trumpet some at 612, when Mahomet began to call himself the *apostle of God*; others at 622, when he *fled from Mecca,* from which the Arabians date their Æra or Hegyra; or they might be dated from A. D. 626 when the *Sun was darkened* in the east, as we have seen before. But these different times, seem rather to look at the different incidents which

G   occur

occur under this trumpet, than at the time when
the pope became a universal bishop A. D. 606.

This was the beginning of this trumpet; and as
human affairs move on in succession, the opening of the well of the abyss, the ascent of the
smoke, the darkening of the sun, and air, and
the coming forth of the locusts, must be considered as events gradually opening after the above
time—But it is not necessary to determine how
long this trumpet is to continue ; for, as I hope
hereafter to prove that the sixth trumpet will
commence at the same time with this, and its sound
will be prolonged 1260 years, consequently it
must coincide with the whole time of this trumpet; whether that is reckoned 300, or only 150
years. Only we may observe, that the repetition
of the *five months*, ver. 10, which is certainly designed to secure a particular attention to the 150
years of this trumpet, no more necessarily implies
that another 150 years are to be added to those
mentioned ver. 5, than the doubling of Pharoah's
dream, *Gen.* xli. implied any addition to the mercy
and judgment of the first part of that dream. Yet
as this was not an age for reformation, we are not
to expect to see the stings of these scorpions ex-
tracted from the souls or bodies of men for many
hundred years: Nor did Popery or Mahometanism
conclude with this trumpet, whether it ended at
A. D. 756 or 906, at 936 or even at 1067, when
Tangrolipix the Turk put a final end to the Saracen empire, by conquering the caliph of Persia; for alas! both Mahometans and Papists
continue to our own times, though the sound
of the fifth trumpet has long ago ceased. But
this reminds me to return from the East, to take
a view,

2. Of those locusts the *monks* and *friars*,
and other religious orders among the Papists, which came out of the *smoke of the bottom-*
less

less pit, near where the mouth of its *well* was opened: Thefe, Mr. Brightman, Mr. Fleming, Mr. Durham and Dr. Gill, underftand by the locufts here fpoken of: And if they were a plague to the world; if they originated from the bottomlefs pit, in the time of this trumpet; if what is faid of thefe locufts is an exact defcription of them; and if it fhould hereafter appear, that Popery is one of the abominations which the witneffes teftified againft, in the time of this trumpet, I know of nothing that can be wanting to compleat the demonftration, that they are as really intended by thefe locufts, as the Saracens; efpecially as it is not probable that this fmoke, which was fo prolific at a diftance in the eaft, fhould be wholly barren near the mouth of that well at Rome from which it proceeded; and as the *Greek* and *Hebrew* name of *their king* ver. 11, affures us that thefe locufts will be employed againft Jews and Gentiles in general, both in the eaft and weft.

The ground about this infernal well at Rome had continued fmoking five or fix hundred years, 2 *Thef.* ii. 6, 7; and this fmoke eminently increafed after A. D. 315, chap. viii. 10, 11, and efpecially from A. D. 566 to 606, ver. 13 of that chapter; when the fire of this furnace could be no longer concealed: Then it was that the pope began to lord it over God's heritage, under the character of a univerfal bifhop; for the fupport of whofe throne, fuperftition had been long preparing well adapted materials, fuch efpecially were the monks and friars, and other religious orders among the Papifts; who had the fame king over them as the eaftern locufts; who, under the name of Abaddon, employed fome of thefe armies againft the Jews, and others againft the Gentiles, under the name of Apollyon.

And

And it is remarkable that, though the monastic life began to be held in undue veneration as early as the fourth century, yet these religious orders were not raised to a level with, or set above the priests till A. D. 605. *Hist. of Popery*, vol. ii. page 422.   Then was satan's hour, and the power of darkness; for after this, these holy fathers (who had long lived, like locusts, upon the labours of the industrious) leaped from place to place in infernal swarms, leagued under Abaddon and Apollyon, under the lying pretence of subjection to Christ; and tormented those who had not the seal of God in their foreheads, by tricking heirs out of their estates, and filling the dying with a mortal horror of the fires of purgatory (which were first feigned about five years before; viz, A. D. 600) till men *sought death*, but could not *find it*; and *desired to die, but death fled from them*: For their shewy religion increased the miseries of life, yet added new horrors to the grim visage of death.

These cattle were fierce as *horses prepared for battle*: For they were champions for the pope against Christ; and many thousands of them entered, into the wars against the Albigenses, and others of God's servants—*And on their heads* they had, not really, but *as it were crowns like gold*; which Mr. Fox and Mr. Brightman understand of their shaving the top of their heads, that it might resemble a crown standing above their temples: This shaven crown they gloried in as much as princes in their golden crowns: And the modern monks are distinguished by something upon the crown of their heads.   Yet the more artfully to compass their impious designs, *they had faces courteous* and humane; *as the faces of men*: And possibly between their faces and their shaven crowns, *they had hair as the tresses of women*, the

more

more to refemble the Virgin *Mary*, whom they
confidered as the patronefs of their orders ; as the
Saracens took their name from another woman ;
viz, *Sarah:* But as all the Popifh orders are thefe
locufts, their *hair* may defcribe their nuns.   *And
their teeth were as the teeth of lions,* which will let
nothing go, on which they faften.   And for their
defence, *they had around their hearts breaft-plates*
of pretended righteoufnefs, but of real impenitence, hard *as iron*: And Mr. Fox the martyrolo-
gift fays, That fome of the monks wore coats of
mail next their flefh.   And when they vifited any
place, it was with pomp, fpeed and terror ; and
the found of their wings, when they clapped them
together, *was as the found of chariots with many
horfes,* ver. 7, 8 : Yet many deluded perfons, received them with reverence and tranfport, as if
they had been *the chariots of Ifrael and the horfemen thereof*; though they had not deliverance,
but *ftings in their tails, like fcorpions,* ver. 5, 10 ;
efpecially fo in their *begging friars,* who were the
laft, and the *loweft* of their orders.

On fome accounts, there feems to be more uncertainty in fixing the time of this, than of any
other of the trumpets : We have heard before,
that it may be 150 years ; or, adding the *five
months,* ver. 10, to thofe at ver. 5, it will be 300
years ; or reckoning thofe times together, and
allowing one 300 years for the *Saracen,* and another for the *Roman* locufts, the whole time of this
trumpet will be, as Mr. Brightman reckons it,
600 years.   In this way of computing it will end
A. D. 1206 ; which will conclude this wœ 75
years before A. D. 1281, when the wœ of the
fixth trumpet begins ; but I have reckoned it only
150 years, for a reafon before affigned ; and this
time well agrees with what is here faid of thefe
Roman locufts ; who (though they may probably

continue

continue even more than 1260 years) had not *power to kill*, but only to *torment* men for the *five months* of this trumpet; viz, from A. D. 606 to 756, when the pope received his secular power as a *beast*; after that they became more abundantly mischievous: And the nests of these locusts were not destroyed in England till A. D. 1540, by king Henry the VIIIth.

But whatever is the real time of this trumpet, the mentioning of the *five months* twice, ver. 5, 10, tends to prepare the mind to contemplate a remarkable 150 years, which occur at the beginning of each of the following trumpets; one of which, as a part of the time of the two witnesses, coincides with the supposed time of this fifth trumpet, chap. xi. 3—7: And the other, under the seventh trumpet, is the time when the beast will become a dragon, supported by the approach and by the power of the second beast; viz, from A. D. 1866 to 2016; see chap. xii. 6. xiii. 11.

It is added, ver. 12. *One woe is past*; which being in effect called the first, chap. viii. 13, supposes another or others coming, and prepares the mind to contemplate them: So at the close of the sixth trumpet it is said, *The second woe is past*, chap. xi. 14; yet the two witnesses, of whom that trumpet speaks, were no woe to the world; therefore, if we should find that they prophesied in the times of the fifth trumpet, as well as under the sixth, this will be no contradiction to these words, *one woe is past*: For the woe denounced signifies some sin to which the world is left, or the punishment of sin; besides which the two last trumpets manifestly speak of the triumphs of God's grace. *Behold two woes more are coming hereafter*; of both which warning is here given, (1) because little or no time will intervene between the two last woes, chap. xi. 14; and (2) because there is this

circum-

circumftance common to them both, that under each trumpet, there is a period of 1260 years referred to; one to be employed in God's work, and the other in the devil's. **But this** phrafe *two woes come μετα ταυτα hereafter*, intimates that the fecond woe will not come, **till fome time after the time** of this trumpet is expired: Accordingly (that which the world would reckon a woe) the eaftern **woe did not come till A. D. 1281;** fee chap. ix. **13—19,** though the holy city was trodden down from A. D. 606, chap. xi. 2: And the weftern woe will not come till the very hour when the fixth trumpet concludes, chap. xi. **13;** *fer the Lord is flow to anger, and of great mercy.*

13. And the fixth angel founded, and I heard a voice from the four horns of the golden altar, which is before God;

14. Saying to the fixth angel who had the trumpet, Loofe the four angels, who are bound by the great river Euphrates.

15. And the four angels were loofed, who were prepared for an hour, and a day, and a month, and a year; that they might kill the third *part* of men.

16. And the number of the armies of horfemen *was* two hundred millions; and I heard their number.

17. And I faw the horfes thus in *their* appearance, and thofe who fat upon them, having breaft-plates of fire and hyacinth and brimftone: And the heads of the horfes were as the heads of lions; and out of their mouths proceeds fire and fmoke and brimftone.

18. From

18. From these were the third *part* of men killed; out of the fire, and out of the smoke, and out of the brimstone, which proceeded out of their mouths.

19. For their powers are in their mouths, *and in their tails*; for their tails are like to serpents having heads, and with them they do hurt.

20. And the rest of the men, who were not killed by these plagues, repented not of the works of their hand; that they should not worship demons, and idols of gold, and silver, and brass, and stone, and wood; which can neither see, nor hear, nor walk.

21. And they repented not of their murders, nor of their sorceries, nor of their fornication, nor of their thefts.

CHAP. X.

1. AND I saw another mighty angel coming down from heaven, clothed round with a cloud, and a rain-bow on his head; and his face as the sun, and his feet like pillars of fire.

2. And he had in his hand a little book open: And he placed his right foot upon the sea, but his left upon the earth.

3. And

3. And he cried with a loud voice, as a lion roars; and when he had cried, the seven thunders uttered their voices.

4. And when the seven thunders had uttered their voices, I was about to write; and I heard a voice from heaven, saying unto me, Seal up the things which the seven thunders have spoken, and write them not.

5. And the angel which I saw standing upon the sea and upon the earth, lifted up his hand to heaven,

6. And sware by him who liveth for ever and ever, who created the heaven, and the things in it, and the earth, and the things in it, and the sea, and the things in it; That the time shall not be yet:

7. But *it shall be* in the days of the voice of the seventh angel, when he shall be about to sound *his* trumpet, and the mystery of God shall be fulfilled; as he hath declared the glad tidings to his servants the-prophets.

8. And the voice which I heard from heaven spake with me again, and said, Go thy way, take the little book, which is open in the hand of the angel who is standing upon the sea, and upon the earth.

9. And I went away to the angel, saying to him, Give me the little book; and he said to me, Take and eat it up; and it shall make thy belly bitter, but in thy mouth it shall be sweet as honey.

10. And I took the little book out of the hand of the angel, and eat it up; and it was

was in my mouth sweet as honey ; but when I had eaten it, my belly was bitter.

11. And he saith to me, Thou must again prophecy to, *or concerning* many people, and nations, and tongues, and kings.

C H A P. XI.

1. AND there was given me a reed, like a rod; and the angel stood saying, Arise and measure the temple of God, and the altar, and those who worship in, *or at* it.

2. And the court which is without the temple cast out, and measure it not; for it is given unto the Gentiles; and the holy city shall they tread under foot forty-two months.

3. And I will give *power* unto my two witnesses ; and they shall prophecy a thousand two hundred and sixty days, clothed in sackcloth.

4. These are the two olive trees, and the two candlesticks, which stand before the God of the earth.

5. And if any one will hurt them, fire proceedeth out of their mouth, and devoureth their enemies ; and if any one would injure them he must thus be killed.

6. These have power to shut heaven, so that no rain may be showered down in the

days

days of their prophecy: And they have power over the waters, to turn them to blood; and to fmite the earth with every plague, as often as they will.

7. And when they fhall have finifhed their teftimony, the wild beaft which afcends out of the bottomlefs pit, fhall make war with them; and fhall overcome them, and kill them.

8. And their dead bodies *fhall lie* in the ftreet of the great city, which is fpiritually called Sodom and Egypt, where alfo our Lord was crucified.

9. And *they* of the people, and tribes, and tongues, and nations, fhall view their corpfes three days and a half, and fhall not fuffer their corpfes to be laid in graves.

10. And they who dwell upon the earth fhall rejoice over them, and make merry, and fhall fend gifts to one another; becaufe thefe two prophets tormented them who dwell upon the earth.

11. And after three days and half, the Spirit of life from God entered into them, and they ftood upon their feet; and great fear fell upon thofe who looked upon them.

12. And they heard a great voice from heaven faying to them, Come up hither. And they afcended up to heaven in a cloud; and their enemies looked on them.

13. And in the fame hour there was a great earthquake, and the tenth part of the city fell; and there were killed in the earthquake

quake feven thoufand names of men : And
the reft were terrified, and gave glory to the
God of heaven.

14. The fecond woe is paft; behold, the
third woe cometh quickly.

This trumpet demands our attention, (1.) To
the deftruction of the eaftern Roman empire by
the Turks; and, (2.) to the impenitence of the
weftern Chriftians, and of the world in general,
under the warning which that deftruction gave
them.   After which, (3.) the Lord Jefus appears to his fervant John *having falvation*; (4.)
orders him to meafure the temple; (5.) gives
him an account of his two witneffes, and what
fhould befal them; and (6.) of an earthquake
which fhould fall upon the court part of the city
of Rome.

1. The deftruction of the eaftern Roman empire by the Turks; which is reprefented by the
loofing of four evil angels, who had been *bound by
the river Euphrates*; whofe reftraint being taken
off, they go forth at the head of a moft formi-
dable cavalry, with thundering engines of war,
chap. ix. 13—19.

That thefe words are to be underftood of the
Turks, not the Saracens, many things perfwade
us; viz, (1.) their being *bound at the great river
Euphrates*, chap. ix. 14, agrees to the four fultanies, or principalities from which the Turkifh
nation originated; not to the Saracens or Arabians, who in a fenfe were never bound any where,
though they received a limited commiffion, ver. 4.
(2.) The Saracen locufts refembled *horfes prepa-
rd to battle*, ver. 7; but without fuch a term of
fimilitude, this army is exprefly called *horfemen*,
ver. 16; which well agrees to the Turkifh armies,

mies, which are still so remarkable for their numerous cavalry; and whose success against the Roman emperor seems to be predicted, *Dan.* xi. 40—43. *At the time of the end* of the Roman empire, *the king of the south;* viz, the Saracens, *shall push at him* and wound him; and afterwards *the king of the north,* that is, the Turks, who were originally of the Scythians, and came from the north, *shall come against him, like a whirlwind, with chariots, and with horsemen, and with many ships: And he shall enter into the countries, and shall overflow and pass over. He shall enter also into the glorious land* of Israel; *and many countries shall be overthrown: But these shall escape out of his hand, Edom, and Moab, and the chief of the children of Ammon;* whose countries are now possessed by the Arabians, who the Turks could never conquer. *He shall stretch forth his hand also upon the countries; and the land of Egypt shall not escape: But he shall have power over the treasures of gold, and of silver; and over all the precious things of Egypt: And the Lybians and the Ethiopians* in Africa *shall be at his steps.* The prophet Ezekiel also speaks of them under the same name of *horsemen, clothed with all sorts* of armour, chap. xxxviii. 4, 5, and xxxix. 20; for this is the same people who will come up against Judea, after the Jews are returned to their own land; as we shall see under the sixth vial, chap. xvi. 12—16. (3.) Their colours, which were a fiery red, blue, and yellow ver. 17, speaks this army Ottoman, not Saracen. (4.) The use of fire arms, cannon, and military ordnance, which are supposed to be referred to in these words, *out of their mouths proceeds fire, smoke and brimstone,* ver. 17, confines our thought here to the Turks; for gun-powder was but little used in war till about the year 1342, which was after

the

2

the Saracen empire was broken to pieces: But by means of this invention the Turks took Constantinople A. D. 1453; and it is well known that these horsemen trampled down, and put a final end to the Roman empire, here called *the third part of men,* ver. 18; which is the constant description of that empire under the four first trumpets, chap. viii. 7—12. Those four trumpets shook down the Latin or Western empire; and the fifth had greatly weakened the eastern or Constantinopolitan part of it, by the incursions of the Saracens: Yet they would not take warning; therefore their time comes totally to fall by another enemy.

To prepare the way for this destruction, when the sixth angel had sounded, John *heard a voice from the four horns of the altar,* that is, from each of them, or from among them. This voice came not from the brasen altar of atonement, but from *the golden altar* of incense *which is before God;* on which our Lord had offered the prayers and intercessions of his people, chap. viii. 3. Aaron offered incense in the tabernacle, not for Heathen nations, but for the Israel of God, *Exod.* xxx. 10; and Christ says of his own people, *I pray for them, I pray not for the world, but for them which thou hast given me; for they are thine, John* xvii. 9. But this altar, which was erected on behalf of God's people, in great indignation against an empire of hypocritical Christians, seems to cry to the angel who had sounded this trumpet; *saying,* As God has given the elect angels as well as to saints on earth, a dominion over beings of their own rank and nature, who live in enmity to himself; so, the time which infinite wisdom had fixed for this work being arrived, to thee it is commanded, *Loose the four evil angels,* who, like the princes

of

of the kingdoms of Perfia and Media, *Dan.* x. 13, 20, (under the *prince* and *God of this world*, *John* xii. 31. 2 *Cor.* iv. 4.) prefide over the four fultanies, or Turkifh principalities, which were founded at Bagdat, Damafcus, Aleppo and Iconium between A. D. 1055 and 1080; all of them bordering upon the great river Euphrates. Thefe angels had been bound, or reftrained from leading forth the Turks to extend their conquefts further than the neighbourhood of that river for many years; particularly by the Croifades, thofe murtherous expeditions of the Chriftians, into the holy land, in the eleventh, twelfth and thirteenth centuries. But when an end was put to thefe unholy wars of the Chriftians, the four angels were loofed A. D. 1281, and fuffered to follow their own propenfions in plundering and deftroying the Chriftians.

The Turks had long been prepared to execute this defign any *day, hour, month* and *year*, in which God fhould permit them to follow their ambitious aims, ver. 15: But, underftanding thefe times prophetically, fome begin them A. D. 1057, when Tangrolipix the Turk was invefted with the imperial robe upon his taking Bagdat, and end them, A. D. 1453, when Conftantinople was taken. Or, if inftead of ending, we begin them at the year 1453, they will end not far from the year 1849, about which time fome have expected the period of papal ufurpations. But, waving fpeculations, the text requires us to begin them from the time when the four angels were loofed from the river Euphrates, which was in 1281: Add to this a prophetic year, or 360 years; a month 30 years; and a day one year, and the whole 391 years contains the exact time in which the Turks were to flay the third part of men, that is of the Greek Roman empire: And this
added

added to 1281 brings us to A. D. 1672, at which time, says bishop Newton, the last of their conquests was gained over the Christians, by taking Cameniec from the Poles. And though no notice is here taken of the *hour*, or fifteen days; when Christianity shall more illuminate the east, probably as great exactness will be discovered with respect to the day, as has been already observed in the year which put an end to their victories; viz, 1672. Since that time the Ottoman affairs have been visibly declining, especially so in their late war with the Russians: Yet we shall hereafter find, that the Turkish empire will not be finally brought down, till the sixth vial is poured out under the seventh trumpet, after the Jews are brought back to their own land; though they will cease to be Mahometans before that time.

The means of their victory are further described ver. 16—19; *The number of all the armies*, which were successively led into the field against the Christians, during the 391 years of the Turkish conquests was *two hundred millions*. Xerxes, the fourth king of Persia, after Cyrus (who *by his strength, through riches, stirred up all against the realm of Grecia, Dan.* xi. 2.) brought the largest army together which the world ever saw at one time, by sea and land; viz, 5,283,220 men, as Herodotus reckons them: But the divine omniscience foretold that, at different times, 200,000,000 would be employed in these expeditions. *And I heard the number of them*; not indeed from the principal of those four evil angels, who was to lead them on to the war; who would have been ready enough to boast of such a number to imploy against the Christians, if he had known it; but he knew not their number, till he had read this prophecy. But John heard their number,
either

either from the angel who blew this trumpet, or rather from the Lord Jesus Christ himself.

Ver. 17. *And thus I saw the horses in the vision, and them that sat on them, having breast-plates* red as *fire*, light-blue as *jacinct*, and yellow as *brimstone*. The Turks much affect these colours; as the whore of Babylon does purple and scarlet, chap. xvii. 4: But observe, they have left for the followers of the Lamb, the livery of heaven and earth; viz, the sky blue, and the living green, as well as the pure white, chap. iv. 3. vii. 14. *Ex.* xxiv. 10: And when the saints have done with their mourning, the wicked shall put it on to all eternity.

It is added, *the heads of their horses were as the heads of lions*; and their riders firing their pieces over their horses heads, it appeared as if *out of their mouths issued fire, and smoke, and brimstone:* And—ὑπο *From these were the third part of men killed*, in their different engagements with the Christians; *out of the fire, and out of the smoke, and out of the brimstone, which issued out of the mouths* of their heavy cannon; *for their power is in their mouths*, which inforced, in word and deed, the same cursed religion as the Saracens had before them: Nor failed they of success; for to all the force of power, they added the craftiness of the serpent; nor could they conceal their relation to the old serpent, *for their tails were like unto serpents, and had heads* like the Amphisbæna (so called from its moving either end foremost; *and with them they do hurt* to the Greek church, and indeed to every one to whom they come.

But can such a rod of God be stretched out, for so many hundred years, almost in vain? alas! the next words inform us,

II. That *the rest of the men*, the other two thirds *who were not killed by these plagues*, whether

they

they were Heathens or Chriſtians; and particularly thoſe of the Latin, or weſtern church, who
have been ſpoken of ſo much under the four firſt
of theſe trumpets, theſe walked as *men*; and amidſt
the empty boaſt of being the only Chriſtians, having long indulged to ſuch infernal works as were a
daring inſult upon that honoured name, the holy
Ghoſt may well call them, with an emphaſis, MEN:

For, whilſt theſe judgments of God were abroad
in the earth, neither in the beginning, nor at
the end of them *repented they of their works;
that they ſhould not worſhip* δαιμονια *devils*, as
the Heathens; or ſuch mediatory gods and god-
deſſes, has have been the reproach of Chriſtendom; viz. thoſe Mahuzzim the Virgin Mary,
ſaints and angels, to whom the apoſtate church
of Rome applies as their *bulwarks, guardians and
protectors*, according to the prediction, *Dan.* xi. 38,
39; ſee p. 57. This was robbing God of the
brighteſt jewel of his crown, *Pſal.* xxvii. 1. xxviii.
8. xxxi. 3, 5, and xxxvii. 39. Yet heathens and
pretended Chriſtians ſtill perſiſted in their *worſhip
of idols of gold, and ſilver, and braſs, and ſtone, and
wood; which neither can ſee, nor bear, nor walk:*
And this they did all the time from A. D. 1281
to 1672; even while the Lord was puniſhing the
Greek empire, for theſe as well as other ſins:
Neither repented they of the Latin Church, any more
than the Heathens, *of their murders*, committed
upon thoſe whom they called hereticks, and upon
their own baſe-born infants (who fell, in awful
crouds, the victims of papal inhumanity; *nor of
their ſorceries*, by pretended miracles and revelati-
ons; nor of their temporal and ſpiritual *poiſonings*,
as the word φαρμακεια often ſignifies, for which
Rome has been ſo infamous; *nor of their fornications*, for which this mother of harlots acts
as procureſs. And as this is the firſt of the ſeven
times

times that the word πορνεια *fornication* occurs in this
book, as applied to Rome papal ; and this word
properly signifies the lewdness of an unmarried
person, suffer me to say, the bible is the wrong
place for this whore to look into, for a certificate
of her marriage with the Lord Jesus: On the
contrary he here disclaims her ; and all her progeny, as hers, are bastards and not sons. And
what has she to do in his house, who has been so
intimate with the dragon? Accordingly Rome is
represented in this prophecy by Sodom and Babylon, chap. xi. 8. and xvi. 19 ; neither of which were
ever married to God, or could therefore be guilty
of spiritual *adultery*. It is added, *nor* repented
they *of their thefts*, which they had committed by
means of their priests, their pardons and purgatory, ver. 20, 21 : For God, in righteous vengeance, sent them *strong delusions*, which hold
them fast to this fatal hour, *that they should believe a lie* ; that they *all might be damned, who believe not the truth, but have pleasure in unrighte-
ousness*, 2 *Thess*. ii. 11, 12.

Of what a hardening nature is sin ! and how
horrible the moral ruin which has deluged the
world ! Therefore nothing has hitherto appeared
under these two woe trumpets ; viz, from A. D.
606 to 1672, but desolation and destruction to
the souls and bodies of men, except the restrictive clauses under the former trumpet, in favor
of the men who have the seal of God in their
foreheads : Yet the Lord lives and loves ; and
the great head of the church is still in office saving
souls, in spite of satan's rage : And even whilst
storms of divine vengeance are falling upon people and nations, every eye of faith sees and adores
him, through all the darksome scene.

But before I enter upon the consideration of those
works of grace, which are published under this trum-

pet, I muft obferve; that, though the angel who
founded this trumpet, will be employed, with other
angels, in miniftering to God's earthly witneffes,
during the whole of their 1260 years, *Heb.* i. 14;
yet not a word more is faid of him under this
trumpet, after he has loofed the four angels, ver.
14: For though angels have a minifterial dominion over the devils; yet the works of grace are
too mighty for them, as well as for us; *falvation
belongeth* only *unto the Lord.*   At the fame time,
as *the found of the trumpet is an alarm of war, Jer.*
iv. 19, fo, as far as the external miniftry of this
angel is employed in founding this trumpet, re-
fpecting the Turks we muft reckon the time of it
as before mentioned, viz, from A. D. 1281 to
1672; fee p. 69: Yet ftrictly fpeaking, the time
of a trumpet, muft be the time which all thofe
events take up which fall under it; which under
this trumpet is 1260 years, as we fhall fee when
we come to the *time* of the witneffes.   Therefore
paffing away from this action of the angel, obferve,

III. Our **Lord** appears to his fervant John, for
his and our comfort; fee chap. x. throughout.
Ver. 1. *And I faw another mighty angel;* (for
Chrift, being ftill mediator between God and us,
will wear this name *angel* till the day of judgment)
come down from heaven; for Chrift muft come
down, or there can be no good work going on
upon earth, *John* xv. 5: We afcend as our Lord
defcends; and he muft come very low, if we rife
very high.   Thus he came down to begin to
the reformation from popery, A. D. 1517; which
had made confiderable progrefs by the year 1672
above named; at which time king Charles II.
gave a general indulgence to the Englifh noncon-
formifts.—He came *clothed with a cloud,* the ufual
emblem of the Divine Prefence; which yet concealed

cealed him both from saints and sinners—*and a rainbow*, which surrounded the throne of his father, was also *upon his head*; to assure us that he is ever mindfull of all the articles of his well ordered covenant; see chap. iv. 3.—*And his face was* bright and glorious *as the sun*; *and his feet as pillars of fire*, ready to consume what he trampled upon, chap. i. 15, 17. *Mal.* iv. 1, 2.

Ver. 2. *And he had in his hand*, not a book as large as the bible, nor yet βιβλιον, as large as the whole revelation of this prophecy, chap. **v.** 1; but βιβλαριδιον *a very little book open*; which, probably contained an illustration of the great design of the three woe-trumpets, which serve as a key to the whole revelation. And this book now lay open in Christ's hand, to intimate that this *revelation*, which was in fact but little studied from the fourth century till after the reformation from popery, should be much better understood under this trumpet; especially after the Turks had compleated those victories over the eastern Roman empire, A. D. 1672, which are predicted in the preceding verses. *And he* first majestically *set his right foot upon the sea*, out of which the first beast arose, chap. xiii. 1; *and* afterwards *his left on the earth*, out of which the second beast ascended, ver. 11, and to which, as a star, the pope descended, chap. ix. 1; thus keeping all his enemies by sea and land under his feet.

3, 4. *And* in this solemn attitude, so expressive of his boundless authority and dominion, he *cried with a loud voice, as lion roars. And when he had cried, seven thunders uttered their awful voices; and when the seven thunders had uttered their voices, I was about to write: And I heard a voice from heaven saying unto me, Seal up* in thy own breast *those things which the seven thunders uttered, and write them not:* Therefore it would be in vain to

conjecture

conjecture, whether they contained an explanation of the seven trumpets; or an account of seven grand and awful events which were to occur under this trumpet. Suffice it that the church of God, does, or shall know as much about them, as its all-gracious Head designed they should: And if any thing which these thunders uttered, would be useful for us to know at present, it is as certainly some other way revealed, as the substance of Christ's conversation with his disciples going to Emmaus, is found in other scriptures, *Luke* xxiv. 27. Yet as *thunder* is a loud voice of God in the heavens, *Psal.* lxxvii. 18; if the Lord should hereafter please to reveal by his *works*, what he has not here by his *word*, possibly the future church of God may be able to point out seven awful attacks made upon the man of sin, between A. D. 1672 and 1866: And to their consideration, I submit it, whether the expulsion of the Jesuits A. D. 1773, and the earthquake at Rome chap. xi. 13, may or may not be two of them.

5, 6, 7. *And the angel which I saw stand upon the sea and upon the earth,* in such a posture of majesty and grace, *lifted up his hand to heaven,* as he had done before in the sight of Daniel, when speaking of these times, *Dan.* xii. 7; *and sware by him that liveth for ever and ever, who created heaven and the things which are therein, and the earth and the things in it, and the sea and the things in it* ; thus calling his Father, as Lord of all to witness, *that χρονος ουκ εσται ετι, the time* so much desired, and so desirable, which was to put an end to Popery and Mahometanism *should not be yet* ; *yet the time* for concealing this mystery, *shall be no longer* than to the end of this trumpet: For *in the days of the voice of the seventh angel, when he shall be about to sound, the mystery of God,* which has so long amazed the world, whilst wrapt in awful darkness,

darkness, under the preceding trumpets even this mystery, that a being of every perfection, should suffer such infernal abominations as Popery and Mahometanism, to abuse his immortal creatures for so long a time *shall be finished*; according *as he hath declared* one part or other of it *to his servants the prophets*. When that trumpet sounds, every believing eye shall trace the riches and sovereignty of divine grace; when the Jews are brought back to their own land, according to the following prophecies, *Isa.* xi. 10—16. xxx. 19. xliii. 5, 6. xlix. 14—26. and lxvi. 6—16. *Jer.* xvi. 14, 15. xxxi. 4—12. and xxxiii. 23—26. *Ezek.* xvi. 53—63. *Joel* iii. throughout. *Amos* ix. 11—15. *Hof.* iii. 4, 5. *Zeph.* iii. 8, 19, 20. *Rom.* xi. 25, 26. When the numerous promises of the conversion of the Gentiles are fulfilled; and when the man of sin shall be destroyed, according to the following predictions, *Ezek.* xxxviii and xxxix. 2 *Theff.* ii. 6—10; the times of which had been before pointed out to the prophet Daniel, chap. viii. 13, 14. and xii. 7—12.

8—11. *And the voice which I heard from heaven*, ordering me not to write what the seven thunders had uttered, *spake with me again, and said*; *Go thy way, take the little book which is open in the hand of the angel, who is standing upon the sea and upon the earth*; that book, written in heaven, and so long concealed there, now lying open in his hand, tells thee that the time is come, when he will make known his secrets to his servants, that they may prepare to meet him, in the way of his vengeance and grace. By this order emboldened I went immediately to this angel (as we must now go to Christ, if we would know any thing to good purpose about the book of revelation:) And as I approached, a countenance of tenderness gave fresh courage to my heart; therefore *I said unto*

him,

him, give me the little book: And he said to me, Take and eat it up. Juſt ſo my ſervants will do under the ſixth trumpet; for though the Synod of Thoulouſe will deprive them of my word, A. D. 1228, yet when Wickliffe has publiſhed my honours to a gazing world, A. D. 1380; and when I have diſcovered to them the art of printing, A. D. 1450, *Prov.* viii. 12; like hungry men long detained from their neceſſary food, ſo will my humble followers ſeize this inſtrumental bread of life, when it is before them, eſpecially after I have, at the reformation from popery, A. D. 1517, reſcued the key of knowledge from the impious hands which had ſecreted it from them.

And I have appeared to thee with this little book open in my hands, after the account of the firſt *woe* of this trumpet is finiſhed, to aſſure thee, that after that time particularly; viz, A. D. 1672, I will hold this book open in my hands, for thoſe of my ſervants who deſire to read it. Yet this book will have this effect upon thee, and upon all my ſervants, who ſhall ever ſtudy it, before the things therein contained are accompliſhed; *it ſhall make thy belly bitter; but it ſhall be in thy mouth ſweet as honey.* But not diſcouraged by this, ſays our apoſtle, *I took the little book out of the angel's hand, and eat it up;* as others of God's prophets had done before me, that word which was given to them, *Jer.* xv. 16. *Ezek.* ii. 8. and iii. 1, 2, 3: *And* whilſt I was eagerly reading it, *it was ſweet in my mouth as honey; but when I had eaten it,* meditating upon its contents, *my belly was bitter.*

And he ſaid to me, Take care that neither the joy, nor the ſorrow of theſe diſcoveries, may drink up thy ſpirits; for, old as thou art, *thou muſt again propheſy,* or preach; which is in fact propheſying to every man that hears thee, what will be his own preſent and eternal ſtate, according as he does, or

does

does not receive the messages with which I send thee; so preaching was called *prophesying* here in England, in queen Elizabeth's days; and that word seems to signify the exercises of religion in general in 1 *Sam.* xix. 20. 1 *Chron.* xxv. 2, 3. and *Matt.* vii. 22.—Nor let the man honoured with my visits and revelation, shrink back from the service, or indulge to impious timidity; for my work must be done; and I will help thee to prophesy ἔτι to, *upon*, and concerning *many people, and nations, and tongues, and kings.* And this no doubt he did literally, in many parts of Asia, after he was returned to Ephesus from Patmos; where he had lain by to fit him for further service; and that whether he lived four, six, or twenty four years after this time, as is differently conjectured. He probably prophesied too, by writing his gospel the next year; viz, A. D. 97: And his three epistles, I apprehend, were written about the same time; at least nothing certain to the contrary appears.

And Christ's ministers in general have studied this book to purpose, if they are the more animated thereby, by every method within their reach, to spread the blessings of that gospel, which has been already testified to *many people,* (especially since A. D. 1672; when the first part of the woe of this trumpet was finished) and which these words, as falling under the sixth trumpet, assure us will be yet more testified to different *tongues* and *kings* before A. D. 1866; especially after A. D. 1816, if the conversion of the Jews should be then begun. God hasten the time when even sinners of the highest rank, shall hang upon the lips of those who bring the glad tidings of the gospel to them; and when these messengers of salvation, shall have no other ambition than that of guiding their feet into the way

of

of everlasting peace, under the eye and hand of the great shepherd and bishop of souls.

And that our apostle too might enter upon immediate work, though he was in Patmos, a visionary scene rose to his view, as of a church gathered out of those people, nations, tongues and kings, who were to be evangelized under this trumpet; **and**

IV. He is ordered to measure this future temple and its worshippers, chap. xi. 1, 2. *And there was given me a reed,* no doubt by the Lord Jesus; whom Ezekiel saw measuring the temple, which was afterwards to be built at Jerusalem, chap. xl. 3 : But this reed was short, *like unto a rod,* or the scepter of a governor. *And the angel* from whose hands I received the little book, stood saying, *Arise and measure the temple* ; not that at Jerusalem, which was long ago in ruins ; nor will there be any temple for God there all the time of this trumpet ; but measure the church of God, which is called his *temple, Zech.* vi. 12, 13. *Eph.* ii. 21. 2 *Theff.* ii. 4. *Rev.* iii. 12.—*And the altar* ; for the worship of my people, in all ages, must have a respect to a sacrifice of atonement : *And them that worship therein.* This measuring was to teach us, (1.) That the perfections of God will never so far connive at any degeneracy of the times, as to accept of any doctrines, persons or worship which fall short of the standard which himself has established ; for *I change not,* faith the Lord. And, (2.) This measure or standard, is to be estimated by the writings of the prophets and apostles, *Eph.* ii. 20. God help his ministers faithfully to regard this.

But *the court which is without the temple,* that *great* court, 2 *Chron.* iv. 9, the *outer* court, *Ezek.* x. 5, which was separated from the sanctuary, *leave out, and measure it not* ; *for it is given to*
those

those *Gentiles* who dwell in the environs of the
temple.   If this court had been to be measured,
a longer rod would have been given him: But
this court was only a passage to good men (who
will be measured when they come into the temple, and before the altar,) whilst carnal professors
of religion meet and stay there; and, as if they
had no business with the heavenly King, give that
honour to his supposed atetndants and courtiers
which is due to himself alone.   But, whilst they
are mutually applauding each others idolatries in
this court, the holy Ghost calls them *Gentiles*; and
this outer court is expressly *given to* them under
that name; see *Psal.* lix. 5, 8. *Luke* xxi. 24: And
how applicable this name *Gentiles* is to the Papists,
may be seen in Dr. *Middleton's letter from Rome*;
which shews the exact conformity between popery
and paganism, or that the religion of the present
Romans is derived from that of their Heathen
ancestors; see further on this subject at chap.
xiii. 2, and in *Delaune's Plea for the Nonconfor-
mists.*

How then can Protestants call those Christians,
who worship saints, angels and images? Are they
wiser, or will they be more charitable, than God
himself? Alas! such bastard charity is real enmity to God and men; (and such is also that charity which is now so resolutely demanded, for
those doctrines among us which lead over to
Rome) nor can popery come down, till we have
the piety, the zeal, and (I must add) the modesty
to think and speak of it, and its abettors, as
God himself has.

*And the holy city shall they tread under foot forty
two months*; that is, the Papists and Mahometans, having the outer court of the temple given
them, in the east and west; the former shall tread
down

down the weſtern church, that *city of God, Pſal.* xlvi. 4. and lxxxvii. 3. *Rev.* iii. 12, during the whole time of this trumpet; and the latter, viz, the Mahometans will tread Juruſalem, which is expreſsly called the *holy city, Iſa.* lii. 1. *Matt.* iv. 5, *under their feet,* for the ſame 1260 years; viz, from A. D. 606 to 1866; whilſt their own inhabitants are driven out into the wilderneſs for ſafety; the Jews by the juſt judgment of God, and Proteſtants by the unrighteous perſecution of their enemies.

Agreeable to ancient prophetic language, theſe 1260 years are called *forty two months,* ver. 2 : So thirty years before Iſrael's deſtruction by the Aſſyrians, the prophet Hoſea ſaid, chap. v. 7. *Now ſhall a month devour them with their portions;* unleſs thoſe words mean only, that their deſtruction will be thirty years in the effecting, before it is compleated. So thirty years before our Lord entered upon his public miniſtry, which was a dark *month* to the Jews, the Lord ſpiritually cut off thoſe *three ſhepherds,* the prince, the prieſt and the prophet, *Zech.* xi. 8; ſee ver. 12, 13, and ver. 3, of the preceding chapter : For there could be no legal Jewiſh *prophet, prieſt* or *king,* when Chriſt himſelf actually became all theſe to his people, except ſuch prophets only as himſelf ſaw proper to employ, to inform the world that he was really come. But whilſt many affected one or other of theſe characters, in thoſe days of general expectation; and ſome even procured a venal prieſthood, our Lord ſays of all theſe three ſhepherds. *My ſoul lothed them, and their ſoul alſo abhorred me.*

In like manner, the times here ſpoken of being called *months,* in oppoſition to the 1260 *days* of the two witneſſes, intimates the comparative darkneſs which will be both upon the Papiſts and

Mahometans

Mahometans all this time; whilſt the ſun of righteouſneſs continues to be a ſtranger to their wretched horizon, and they only enjoy ſuch different degrees of its reflected light, as their cruel leaders allow them: The conſequence of which muſt be, they will be morally cold, whilſt ſymbolizing with the ancient Jews, and eſpecially with the Heathens in their idolatrous worſhip; which will ſtill wax and wane as the Moon, notwithſtanding their vain boaſt of uniformity.

This 1260 years deſolation of the holy city, is the ſame length of time, as Daniel's *time, times and half a* time, chap. xii. 7. *Rev.* xii. 14, which is the time of the beaſt's continuance, chap. xiii. 5; and the ſame as the 1260 years of the two witneſſes; with which laſt they coincide, and therefore will end with them, A. D. 1866, as will be ſhewn under the next head—But this leads me,

V. To the account of the *two witneſſes,* ver. 3—12. And here it muſt be enquired, who are theſe witneſſes? What is their commiſſion and employment? The time of their miniſtry? And what is to befal them after they have finiſhed their teſtimony?

1. Who are theſe witneſſes? *Anſ.* They cannot be two individuals; for as no man was ever *ſuffered to continue* 1260 years *by reaſon of death, Heb.* vii. 23, ſo they are expreſsly called *two* diſtinct *candleſticks,* or churches, ver. 4. chap. i. 20. They cannot be the Jewiſh and Chriſtian churches, for there will be no Jewiſh church, properly ſo called, during the whole time of their prophecy: Nor can they be the Proteſtant churches only; for, however theſe may be diſtinguiſhed in other reſpects, they are all but one as a witneſs againſt popery: Yet Proteſtant churches in general are, no doubt, one of theſe candleſticks, or witneſſes; and, I apprehend, the Greek church

is the other; the former to witnefs againft popery
(as the many *people, nations, tongues* and *kings* do,
who are evangelized under this trumpet, chap.
x. 11.) and the latter againft mahometanifm.
Thefe are the two abominations which are exprefsly mentioned under this, and the preceding
trumpet; and againft which of them is it that the
Lord will leave himfelf without witnefs? fee
Gen. xxxi. 48. *Deut.* xvii. 6. *John* i. 7. *Acts* i. 8.
Heb. xii. 1. and if there are Chriftians, real or no-
minal, in the eaft, as well as in the weft, it is impoffible but that they fhould bear witnefs againft
the delufion that reigns there: And the woman,
the church, borne on the great eaftern and weftern wings of the Roman eagle, chap. xii. 14, who
is in different views, the fucceffor of thefe witneffes, and the fame with them under another
name, exprefsly directs us to look for them both
in the eaft and weft; over both of which it is
well known that eagle fpread its wings.

But to furnifh thefe churches to be witneffes
for God, they muft have their *minifters* to teach,
and *magiftrates* to guard them; and thefe are
here reprefented by *two olive trees*, growing by
the *two candlefticks*, and continually feeding them
with oil, that they may not go out, ver. 4: Such
were *Jofhua* the high Prieft and *Zerubbabel* the
governor, thofe *fons of oil*, who ftood *before the
God of the earth*, on the right and left fide of the
Jewifh church or candleftick, *Zech.* iv. 11—14.
Heb.

Here obferve, (1.) each of thefe two witneffes
is threefold; viz, the *church*, with its *magiftrates*,
and *minifters*, who are to fupply each candleftick
with oil; therefore in all the number is the fame
with the *three* who *bear witnefs in heaven and in
earth*, 1 *John* v. 7, 8; and (if I may without blafphemy name them together) the whole number
makes

makes a third *Twelve*, who testify the same thing as the *twelve* tribes of Israel, and the *twelve* apostles of the Lam

(2.) As God has said to his people, *All things are yours*, and *for your sakes*, 1 *Cor*. iii. 21, so ministers and magistrates then only answer their end, when in the discharge of their respective offices, they furnish the church with pure olive oil. And if either of them, either withholds this oil, or supplies the candlestick with the poisoned oil which results from a worldly carnal spirit, he shall bear his sin and shame whoever he is; for he is cruel as a man who puts out the fire of a light-house in a dark night, which may occasion the most fatal ship-wracks—But when these instruments are ever so faithful to God, lest they should think they can effect any thing saving without him, it was cried to them long ago, *not by* the *might* of the magistrates sword, or by any *army* he can bring into the field; *nor by* the *power* of the minister's learning, oratory, wealth or influence, is the work of salvation to be effected; *but by my Spirit, saith the Lord*, actuating them both for my own praise, *Zech*. iv. 6; see also 2 *Cor*. x. 4, 5: This is the oil they are to possess; that they may ministerially communicate it for the good of the church.

(3.) The Lord planted these two olive trees, as far distant from each other as possible, to answer their one end, which was that of supplying the candlestick with oil; and when ever the church and state come into contact, they neither of them, properly speaking, *stand before the God of the earth*, ver. 4; and if they do not speedily become as the trees of the wood, or poison-trees; yet, being planted too close together, neither of them, can possibly yield the same quantity of oil as they did before: Therefore the light of the candlestick must either go out, or be supplied with

offensive

offensive oil : The church of God will prosper as
soon as ever this is believed.

Thus, in some measure magistrates, ministers
and churches have united their testimony against
popery in the west; and in the east; the Greek
church too, with their ministers and magistrates,
testified against Mahometanism, till Constantinople was taken by the Turks, A. D. 1453: Nor
are any of these wholly wanting now in Russia.
And though the account which Sir Paul Rycaut,
Dr. Smith, and Mr. Sandys give of the eastern
Christians, shews them to be sunk in ignorance
and irreligion; yet in the times when they came
nearest to popish superstition and blindness, they
were still sufficient witnesses against Mahometanism. We know by what a contemptible instrument
God *rebuked the madness of* that *prophet* Balaam,
2 *Pet*. ii. 16: And to *the blind people who have
eyes, and the deaf who have ears*; even to those
who *had not called upon God*, but *been weary of
him*, he says, *Ye are my witnesses, saith the Lord*;
and especially so *my servant whom I have chosen*,
Isa. xliii. 8, 10, 22. And whatever the ministers or
members of the Greek church in Turkey are, the
money which they pay the grand Seignior, for liberty to be of that religion, is to this day a witness against
that shameful imposture : Nor are they less credi-
ble witnesses against it, than many Protestants in
England against popery; whose wicked principles and practices are hastening its return, while
they vainly testify against it.

Dr. Allix and many others have proved, that
in the darkest times of popery, the Lord never
left himself without witness against the different
parts of that grievous abomination : Nor can we
doubt of the same with respect to Mahometanism,
though the fair beams of science and literature
are now so beclouded in the east, that we cannot
trace

trace his witness there with the same exactness as in the west. Both of them have prophesied, and still continue, both *in* and *by* their *sackcloth.*

2. The commission and employment of these witnesses, ver. 3, 5, 6. *I will give* it; or, supplying a word from ver. 6, *I will give power to my two witnesses; and they shall prophesy* 1260 *days, clothed in sackcloth.* So professors of every name are called to witness for God, in **word and deed,** by their spirit and conversation; and even by their blood, when ever it becomes necessary. But though the life of every true Christian is a prophesy of heaven and hell to the righteous and the wicked, it is especially given to ministers amongst them to prophecy or teach; and to qualify them for this work, they are called to *stand before the God of the earth,* ver. 4: And when **they** do so, especially in conjunction with the **church** and their magistrates, they *have power,* by **their** prayers, *to shut heaven that it rain not in the days of their prophecy,* as Elijah did, 1 *Kings* xvii. 1; *and have power over waters to turn them to blood,* as Moses did, *Exod.* vii. 8—12; or over *peoples and nations* to counteract their designs, as far as is for God's glory, *Rev.* xvii. 15: *And to smite the earth with all plagues, as often as they will,* ver. 6. But good men only have this power; and they have it when God immediately gives it: Yet they might have it more frequently, if they walked more closely with God, ver. 3, 6. But, though we need no excitements to use those temporal powers which distinguish and dignify us; through their remaining corruption, God's servants need many arguments, to engage them to use their power with him by prayer, *Jam.* v. 17, 18.

It is *required of stewards,* and of those who are *witnesses* of eternal life and death to men, *that a man be found faithful,* 1 *Cor.* iv. 2: And if God's witnesses are so in word and deed, and will rather

yield

yield up their lives than his truths, or the fpirituality and purity of Chriftian difcipline and worfhip, they cannot but *torment them that dwell on the earth,* ver. 10; whofe unworthy attachment to feen things makes them unwilling, in thought and affection, to change their element: But as the Lord never fubpœnas witneffes, without bearing their expences in delivering their teftimony, and finally rewarding their unfhaken fidelity; fo *if any man will hurt them,* the *fire* of God's word, and particularly of his awful threatnings, *proceeds out of their mouth and devours their enemies,* as fire devours wood, *Jer.* v. 14; deftroying their prefent peace in the way of fin, and cutting off all their future hopes, while they perfift in their rebellion againft God: *For wickednefs,* which makes men as dry ftubble, *burneth as the fire; it fhall devour the briers and thorns* (that is, the wicked, 2 *Sam.* xxiii. 6,) and *kindle in the thickets of the forefts; and they fhall mount up,* like *the lifting up of fmoke,* to warn others, *Ifa.* ix. 18. They carry indeed no carnal weapons about them, though the magiftrate is ordered to ufe thefe for their defence; but *if any man will injure them,* let him look to himfelf, *he muft in this manner be killed,* that is, not temporally in common cafes, but fpiritually, according to, and by, that word of God to which he refufes to be in fubjection, ver. 5.

3. The time of their miniftry, which is 1260 *days,* ver. 3. The word *day* tells us that it is *day* with them, (for they teftify that which they have feen and heard;) whilft the nightly *moon* alone gives light to their enemies, for the fame length of time, ver. 2. There we took it for granted, but muft here prove, that thefe 1260 days fignify years—And, not to fay how improbable it is that the holy Ghoft fhould predict a teftimony of magiftrates, minifters, and vaft crouds of inferior witneffes

2

witnesses in the church, who were only to continue three years and a half; the very continuance
of these churches, to witness against Popery and
Mahometanism for so great a part of the 1260
years already, scarce leaves a doubt but that the
whole of that time was designed to be foretold.
And to this agrees the language of other scriptures,
Psal. xc. 12. *So teach us to number our days,* &c.
Numb. xiv. 34. *After the number of the days, in
which ye searched the land, even forty days; each
day for a year, shall ye bear your iniquity, even forty
years.* So Ezekiel was to *lie* on *his right* and
left side a day for a year, to bear the iniquities *of
Judah* and *Israel,* chap. iv. 4—8. After the same
manner are Daniel's 2300 days to be computed;
chap. viii. 14; his seventy weeks, chap. ix. 24;
and his 1290 and 1335 days, chap. xii. 11, 12.
When astronomy was but little understood, twelve
months, of thirty days each were reckoned for a
year: And it is generally apprehended that those
1260 days should be reckoned so many proper
years; though the real or Julian year is now found
to be 365 days, five hours, and 49 minutes;
which seems the more probable, as *times* signify
years, Dan. iv. 16, 23, 25. and xi. 13. Heb; and as
the holy Ghost calls a period of exactly the same
length as this, *a time, times, and half a time,* Rev.
xii. 14; that is a year, two years, and half a
year; or, in other words, 360, 720 and 180 days,
or 1260 in all. I see therefore no solid reason
for adding the eighteen years, which some have
proposed, on account of the different computation of the prophetic and the real year.

But we must further enquire when these 1260
years began, that we may know at what time they
will conclude. And here it would be easy to
prove, that the two witnesses prophesied before
A. D. 1281, when this sixth angel announced the

firſt *woe* of this trumpet, by looſing *the four angels*
who were *bound by the river Euphrates*, chap. ix.
14, 15 : And as the account of the witneſſes ſuc-
ceeds the account of the Turkiſh *woe* of this
trumpet ; ſo after that woe is concluded, our
Lord not only ſpeaks of his witneſſes as ſtill in
office, but particularly predicts' the power which
he will give them after, A. D. 1672, when that
woe concludes.   But though this ſtill leaves us
at a loſs when to begin their 1260 years, other
conſiderations offer themſelves to oblige us to begin them from A. D. 606, when the fifth trumpet ſounded, to open theſe two abominations,
Popery and Mahometaniſm, upon the world.

To prepare the way for the proof of this, obſerve, that the *woe* part of every trumpet ſtands
eſſentially diſtinguiſhed from that grace of God
on the hearts of men, which is diſplayed under
it : And if the firſt ſeal extends to the end of the
world ; and the *religious* part of the third trumpet, takes up more than the *ſecular* time of the
four firſt trumpets ; there can be no impropriety
in beginning the *religious* part of the ſixth trumpet, at the ſame time with the woe of the fifth :
So under the ſeventh trumpet we ſhall find, chap.
xii. 14, that the 1260 years of the woman's flight
into the wilderneſs, muſt neceſſarily be reckoned
far back into the times of the ſixth trumpet: And
as theſe witneſſes are only ſpoken of under this
trumpet, it is more reaſonable to go backward
into the 150 years of the fifth trumpet, (in which
time we are ſure they both lived and propheſied,)
than to advance 150 years forward into the time
of the ſeventh trumpet ; when we ſhall find them
raiſed up to heaven, ver. 12 ; which forbids us to
extend their times into the time of the ſeventh
trumpet.

We

We therefore reckon their times, not from A. D. 756 to 2016, but from A. D. 606 to 1866; For, (1.) It was not possible for good men to forbear testifying, both against Popery and Mahometanism, as soon as they discovered them: And the seal of God, which was first said to be set upon the saints in Constantine's time, chap. vii, and is mentioned again under the fifth trumpet, chap. ix. 4; viz, from A. D. 606 to 756, necessarily made them witnesses for God; though this name is not expressly given them till under this trumpet. (2.) Mahometanism, one of the things to be witnessed against, certainly began A. D. 606: And though we read of a *false prophet* under the seventh trumpet, yet not as a Mahometan; nor is there the least notice taken of Mahometanism under that trumpet; therefore the witness against that abomination, which began A. D. 606, must conclude A. D. 1866: And as they both lie dead together, consequently they must have begun together, A. D. 606: And the testimony, as well as the death and resurrection of them both, must conclude with this trumpet; for one of them does so.

And accordingly the church of God, was divided into the Greek and Latin churches, which are the two witnesses, near the beginning of the seventh century; See *Mosheim's Eccles. Hist. vol.* ii. *p.* 591. (3.) If the time of the witnesses had coincided with the 1260 years of the beast; viz, from A. D. 756 to 2016, chap. xii. 14. and xiii. 5; no possible reason can be assigned why they should not both have been described under the same trumpet: But nothing being said of the witnesses under the seventh trumpet, it is probable their times conclude before that is founded. (4.) Jerusalem seems to be intended by *the holy city*, chap. xi. 2; but in whatever sense we take that phrase, as *the holy city* cannot be said to be

trodden

trodden under feet, when the Jews are returned to their own land, and when the *kingdoms of the world* are become *the kingdoms of the Lord and of his Christ*; both which events will take place before A. D. 2016, chap. xi. 15, and xiv. 1—7; therefore the prophesying of the two witnesses, which synchronizes with the treading of *the holy city under feet*, chap. xi. 2, 3, must be finished before that year. (5.) The word *witnesses* supposes a cause litigated, and yet *sub judice* undecided in the court where they appear: But after the earthquake at Rome, chap. xi. 13; after the dragon is cast out of the church chap. xii. 9, and believing Jews and Gentiles are taken in, chap. xiv; and especially after the pouring out of the vials, chap. xvi. the cause between Christ and the beast will in no sense remain undecided: But all these things will occur before A. D. 2016; therefore the witnesses must be slain, and raised again before that time.

True, the world will be filled with glorious witnesses for God under the seventh trumpet; yet the grand events just now referred to, together with the numerous angel witnesses which we read of, chap. xivth, will afford such striking testimonies for God, that they will not under that trumpet be called *witnesses*; but be represented as a *woman clothed with the sun, having the moon under her feet, and upon her head a crown of twelve stars*, chap. xii. 1. (6.) As the witnesses will be slain by the first *beast, who ascended out of the bottomless pit*, chap. xi. 7. and therefore probably whilst he reigns alone; there is reason to believe they must be slain before A. D. 1866, as will appear when we come to consider the times of the second beast, chap. xiii. 11. (7.) Their enemies will have great power at the time when these witnesses are slain, so as to prevent their bodies being interred, and to stir up the world against them, ver. 9, 10; but

after

after the vials, and the rage of the ten horns have weakened them, they certainly can have no such power at or near A. D. 2016; which is the year of the beast's final fall chap. xiii. 5, and the grand Æra from which the millennium begins. (8.) The same hour as the witnesses ascend up into heaven, an earthquake will fall upon the court part of the city of Rome, and destroy 7,000 of their nobility and gentry, chap. xi. 13; but there will probably be no such city as Rome A. D. 2016, chap. xix. 3, 20—I only add, by that earthquake *the remnant* will be *affrighted, and give glory to the God of heaven*, chap. xi. 13; but at A. D. 2016, *the remnant* will be *slain* by the *sword of him who sitteth upon the horse*; *and all the fowls* will be *filled with their flesh*, chap. xix. 21.

From these considerations I conclude, that the 1260 years of the witnesses, which is the time of this trumpet, must be reckoned, not from A. D. 756 to 2016, but from A. D. 606 to 1866. They cannot be begun sooner, because Popery and Mahometanism did not begin till A. D. 606; and the above reasonings seem to necessitate us to conclude them by A. D. 1866.

But if it should be said, the time of this trumpet ought to be reckoned, not from the time of these witnesses, but from the time of the woe denounced in it; I answer, (1.) each of the three woe trumpets has both a *secular* and *spiritual* woe in it: And (2.) if one part of the *secular* woe of this trumpet was concluded A. D. 1672; see page 116, yet it has in it a *spiritual* woe too; viz, the slaying of the witnesses; whose resurrection is succeeded *the same hour* with another *secular* woe; viz, an *earthquake* at Rome, ver. 13: Therefore, whatever fixes the time of the death and resurrection of the witnesses, certainly fixes the real time of this trumpet; which we have heard will

be

be from A. D. 606 to 1866 ; therefore to return to the witnesses, let us see,

4. What is to befal them after they have finished their testimony, ver. 7—12. *When they shall have finished,* or are about to finish *their testimony,* (till then they are immortal!) *the beast which ascends out of the bottomless pit* ; see chap. xvii. 8, the same who opened the *well of the abyss,* while he was only a universal bishop, chap. ix 2 ; and who, when he had obtained the dominion of a beast, opened the mouth of hell out of the sea at Rome, chap. xiii. 1 ; this *beast shall make war against* both these witnesses, *and shall overcome them, and kill them.* Thus, I apprehend from A. D. 1862 to 1866 the pope will prevail against the Protestant and Greek churches; putting down and silencing both these witnesses, so that neither of them will be able to speak for God any more for three years and **a half** : But this time is certainly to be reckoned as **a** part of their 1260 years ; for, (1.) if the time they lie dead is added to their 1260 years, the same length of time must be added to the 42 months, in which the Gentiles are to tread down the holy city **ver. 2** ; for which we have no warrant. (2.) The phrase οταν τελεσωσι, *when they shall have finished,* or be about to finish *their testimony,* may mean the time while they are any way delivering their testimony, as well as the end of it ; see *Mat.* **x. 19.** Gr. (3.) Their dead bodies kept above ground, especially considered in connection with the inebriated state in which their enemies will stand exulting over them, will afford as clear and striking a testimony for God, as they had ever been able to deliver in their lives. (4.) 1260 years are so repeatedly mentioned under the sixth and seventh trumpets, that I cannot suppose **either** of those trumpets to continue longer than **that,** chap. xi. 2, 3. xii. 6. and xiii. 5.

To

To say nothing of the fatal tendency which there is, in every part of our depraved nature towards Popery; three things may assist our belief of the accomplishment of this dreadful work, by the above time; viz, (1.) The ten kingdoms into which the ancient Roman empire was divided, will continue to give their power to the beast, till long after that time, chap. xvii. 17. (2.) Though the second beast, (now the Mahometan chief) will not be actually risen out of the earth to support the pope; yet things will probably be openly preparing for his advent, about the time of this murder; which will inspire the first beast with fresh spirits and vigor, chap. xiii. 11. (3.) Things are already working towards so dire an event against the eastern and western churches: For as their sins and ours are sowing the fatal seeds of this destruction; so the Popish powers discovered a greater inclination to assist the Turks, in their late wars, than the Russians; which loudly tells the eastern churches what they are to expect in every future rupture, from that papal pride which effects universal sway, and cannot endure the least controul or opposition—And as to ourselves, as Arian and Pelagian errors in the fourth and fifth centuries, paved the way for Popery in the sixth and seventh; it will be nothing new under the sun, if the Arian and Arminian errors of the seventeenth and eighteenth centuries, introduce popery in the nineteenth and twentieth: And if these errors have already deluged our churches, Popery cannot be far off; for they have the very essence of Popery in them; and whoever promotes them is to all intents and purposes, advancing its interests, however sincerely and resolutely he may seem to himself to oppose it.

I am sensible the Papists (or Pappaists) deny that they are Arians; but they must cease to ad-

dress

dreſs the language of blaſphemy to the Virgin Mary, reſpecting her Son, &c. if they expect men of ſenſe to credit the aſſertion—And though proteſtant Arians can do but little, beſides what the pride of their hearers does for them, to promote their own cauſe; (—for it will be always, diſreputable for a ſinner openly to degrade his Saviour; beſides Arianiſm naturally inclines its votaries morally to doze, except when rage againſt the Trinitarians keeps them awake)—yet Arminianiſm, which is the gate into Arianiſm, being ever confident and noiſy, and putting on bewitching appearances of humility and holineſs, can eaſily effect great things unſuſpected, to promote it in the world; for *high thoughts of ſelf*, demand and produce *low thoughts of Chriſt*. And both theſe abominations lead directly to *profaneneſs* and *deiſm:* But if a thunder ſtorm, if ſickneſs, earthquakes or any awful providence befal the ſinner, he cannot ſtop in either of theſe; he muſt fly to *Chriſt* by faith and repentance; or *Popery* will become his laſt landing-place in his way to everlaſting burnings.

I have written the above, that I may be clear from the blood of all men, into whoſe hands theſe lines may fall; and eſpecially from that innocent blood of unborn poſterity, which Popery is now preparing to pour out, as a libation to the God of this world. In purſuit of this end, ſuffer me to add, if the ſcripture word *reward*, and the like, has emboldened ſome profeſſing Proteſtants, with an unbluſhing countenance, to defend the uſe of that Popiſh phraſe *the merit of works*; if *religious articles are ſigned* by many, who know at the ſame time their fixed intention to oppoſe them; if much of the modern religion conſiſts in miſrepreſenting the counſels of God, and the men whoſe conſciences oblige them to declare them; if the *names*

of

of some *of the reformers* are treated with the most spiteful contempt, by many who know not how to value the blessings they so painfully transmitted to them ; if *sable crouds* of pretended *witnesses* against Popery scarcely forbear avowing it, that they had rather fall into the *see of Rome*, than remove a hair's breadth further from it ; and the horror of Popery abates in the minds of the people, in proportion as the danger of it advances : If at the same time profaneness and dissipation increase, which even now call for the aid of pious tricks to satisfy the clamors of waking conscience: If—but why should I add any more ?—My tears shall tell the rest—But if this is in any degree a just portrait of the times, it surely cannot appear incredible to any man, that the above event should take place within eighty-eight years from this present A. D. 1778. *A prudent man foreseeth the evil, and hideth himself* ; *but the simple pass on, and* forge both moral and penal chains for their offspring . So did the good Jehoshaphat for his, even to the fourth generation, by his cursed complaisance to the idolatrous kings of Israel; see 2 *Chron.* xviii. and xxv. chapters.

If it is asked, what will become of the church, when the two witnesses are slain, and afterwards ? I answer, the mystical body of Christ is temporally, as every limb of it is spiritually, immortal ; see chap. xii : And probably when the witnesses are slain in the east and west, the church will find an asylum in America(—which would have been much more extensively poisoned by Popery, if the European nations had found it out some hundreds of years sooner) till after the vials are poured out A. D. 1942. From that time England, and the other horns of the beast, will probably hate the whore, and burn her flesh with fire, chap. xvii. 16. And if the children of the two witnesses fly thither,

soon

foon after A. D. 1866 to 1942, this will much
people the American waſte. I only add here,
when the goſpel came to England, it came to that
which was then reckoned *the end of the world:*
And when the ſon of righteouſneſs ſhone from
England to America, *his going forth was to the
end of heaven*; and perhaps from thence *his cir-
cuit* will be to all other *ends of it*; ſee *Pſal.* xix.
4, 6. *Rom.* x. 18.

But ſtep forward, and, in this prophetic glaſs,
ſee what a ſecond Judas will do againſt the bride
the Lamb's wife, ver 8, 9. Theſe witneſſes being
ſlain, *their dead bodies ſhall lie in the ſtreet of the
great city, which is ſpiritually called Sodom and
Egypt; where alſo our Lord was crucified.* Literal
Sodom is now the Dead ſea; but ſpiritual Sodom,
that *mother of harlots and abominations of the earth,*
is Rome, chap. xvii. 5 : At leaſt the unnatural
abomination denominated from Sodom, ſeems
not to have been publickly heard of in England,
till the prieſts were forbidden to marry; for the
firſt law here made againſt it was A. D. 1112.
Hiſt. of Popery, Vol. I. *page* 359. The Proteſtant churches will then lie dead in the Roman
ſtate, called *Sodom*; and the Greek church in that
which is ſpiritually called *Egypt*, for its ignorance,
baſeneſs, ſervility and theft; which will be eminently the reigning characters of the eaſt, while
theſe witneſſes lie dead there. The ſins of both
theſe places debaſed Jeruſalem when our Lord
was crucified there; and in theſe ſtates he is again
ſlain in his members. *And they of the people, and
kindreds, and tongues, and nations,* in the eaſt and
weſt, *ſhall view their dead corpſes three days,* that
is, three years *and a half; and not* even *ſuffer their
corpſes to be laid in graves.* Not ſo did the Jews
treat our Lord himſelf, he was buried; nor ſo
will they hereafter treat the Turks, they will bury
every

every bone they find, *Ezek.* xxxix. 11—16. But who that believes God, ever expected humanity from this beast? Rome had rather that the east and west should bear the stench of these dead, than not have the pleasure of looking upon them. Thus God's truths will be kept as it were dead above ground, perhaps under the hated name of Calvinism, to make sport for a scoffing world. But God's hand is in it, that they cannot bury these witnesses: However, this is not politic; for as long as they keep them within view, something which they have said will rise up in the consciences of men: Yet they resolve upon a triumph, and the joy is almost universal; for it is added,

Ver. 10. *They who dwell upon the earth*, a terræ—filial brood, *shall rejoice over them*; that is, the west over the Protestants, and the east over the Greek church χαρουσιν και ευφρανθησονται: And they will so *carouse*, that whole hecatombs of themselves will fall together at the shrine of Bacchus; and so *frantick* will their joy be, that if God was not soon to reanimate his witnesses, human nature could not long survive the wounds which it will then receive from its own intemperance; whilst they *make merry, and send gifts to one another*; *because these two prophets*, in word and deed *tormented them who dwell upon the earth*, ver. 3—6. Thus will Christ mystical *be wounded in the house of his* pretended *friends*, *Zech.* xiii. 6. But this *triumphing of the wicked will be short*, Job xx. 5; for

Ver. 11, 12. *After three days*; that is, three years *and a half*, *the spirit of life from God* (which had, in a great measure, awfully suspended its influences for the same length of time as the heavens withheld their rain, at the prayer of Elijah, 1 *Kings* xvii. 1. *Jam.* v. 17;) again *entered into them*; and immediately *they stood upon their feet*: And, in

in the midst of the forementioned dissolute ban-
quetings to which these hypocrites had abandoned
themselves, *great fear fell upon those who looked
upon them*, like that which seized Belshazzar, when
the fingers of a man's hand, writing against the
wall, announced his irrevocable doom, *Dan.* v.
6. *And,* whilst their enemies wished in vain to
turn their eyes from the terrifying sight ; *they
heard a great voice from heaven, saying to them,
Come up hither :* And thankful for so high a calling, immediately *they ascended up to heaven ; and
their enemies fixed their astonished eyes upon them.*

These phrases of the *beasts making war* against
the witnesses, and *overcoming* and *killing them* ; and
their dead bodies lying in the streets of the great city,
probably describe a literal slaughter which the
beast will make of the Protestant and Greek
churches about A. D. 1862.   Yet as the *witnesses*
may be said to be slain, as to their office, when,
through the power of a deep sleep falling upon
them, and the aboundings of a worldly spirit,
they cease to prophecy against these abominations ;
so their death will doubtless be *spiritual* before it
is *temporal* ; and the former more extensive than
the latter : For (1.) persecution alone, can never
reduce the church of God to so low a state as is
here described.   When men are *reproached for the
name of Christ, the spirit of glory and of God rests
upon them,* 1 Pet. iv. 14 ; (and this will make the
blood of the martyrs the seed of the church at
A. D. 1866 ; after that seed has lain three years
and a half under the clods :) But no such glory
awaits professors, when they are taken in the devil's net, and when *Balaam's* advice hast cast the
most fatal of all *stumbling-blocks* in their way, *to
eat things sacrificed to idols, and to commit fornication,* Rev. ii. 14. (2.) If but few magistrates
have now the oil of the spirit in them, to furnish
the

the candleſtick with light; and they have generally ceaſed to exert their power both againſt Popery, and that profaneneſs which leads to it: And
if at the ſame time, many miniſters and churches
(*proh dolor!*) virtually bear witneſs *for*, rather
than *againſt* Popery; whatever our ſucceſſors may
ſee, we already *behold* the *ſpiritual death* of many
of the witneſſes. (3.) If the reſurrection and aſcenſion of the witneſſes are to be underſtood ſpiritually or metaphorically, it will be the more
probable that their death ought to be underſtood
in part ſo too; but the following reaſons incline
me to underſtand their reſurrection and aſcenſion
to heaven ſpiritually; viz,

(1.) Becauſe this phraſe *the Spirit of life*, has
a ſpiritual meaning in otherplaces; ſee *Rom.*
viii. 2. *The law of the ſpirit of life in Chriſt
Jeſus, hath made me free from the law of ſin and
death*; and John vi. 63, *The words that I ſpeak
unto you, they are ſpirit and they are life.* (2.)
Standing upon the feet, in many places of ſcripture,
ſignifies, having ſtrength and courage for vigorous
exertion, *Ezek.* ii. 1, 2. iii. 24. and xxxvii. 10.
Dan. vii. 4. and x. 11. *Rev.* i. 17. And Chriſtians
are not only ſaid to be *raiſed up together*, but
made to ſit together in heavenly places in Chriſt Jeſus;
which was eminently and viſibly true of many
primitive believers, after the day of Pentecoſt,
Eph. ii. 6; ſee alſo *Heb.* xii. 22—24. (3.) If the
witneſſes ſhould be literally raiſed from the dead
A.D 1866, this would ſeem to be *the firſt reſurrection*; but *the firſt reſurrection* will not take place
till a hundred and fifty years after that time, and
that alſo will be ſpiritual; ſee chap. xx. 5. (4.)
The ſimilar phraſe of the *Man-child caught up to
God and his throne*, chap. xii. 5, ſeems to be underſtood ſpiritually; therefore the aſcenſion of theſe
witneſſes may be ſpiritually too. And (5.) if all
theſe witneſſes are caught up into heaven, as
Enoch

Enoch and Elijah (—not to fay, that fome who may witnefs againſt Popery and Mahometanifm, will be altogether unfit for fuch an honour—) there will be none left, that we know of, for God upon earth; yet a great work is to be done under the feventh trumpet, in which human inftruments will no doubt be employed. But if thefe witneffes attain unufual degrees of heavenly mindednefs, which feems to be meant by their *afcending up into heaven*, they will be the fitter inftruments of God's glory, under the feventh trumpet : And at the fame time their fpirituality will vex their enemies, more than if they had been taken to heaven out of their way.

VI. This trumpet concludes with an account of an earthquake, which will fall upon the court part of the city of Rome, ver. 13. *And* not only the fame year, month, week, and day, but *in the fame hour* in which the fpirit of God came, in fuch a fudden and moft extraordinary manner upon thefe witneffes, *there was a great* and violent concuffion, or *earthquake* felt at Rome : *And the tenth part of the city fell; and in the earthquake were killed feven thoufand* ονοματα ανθρωπων *names of men*; that is, men of figure and note ; who were unhappily, but, as it were, the *names* of certain ufelefs figures upon earth: *Vox et præterea nihil——And the remnant were affrighted, and gave glory to the God of heaven :* But this was no more than a legal or fervile act of worfhip ; as appears by the pouring out of the fifth vial upon the feat of the beaft fome years after ; fee chap. xvi. 10. (fo it is faid in *Pfal.* lxvi. 3, *Through the greatnefs of thy power, fhall thine enemies lie unto thee*, Heb.) And that Rome is the city here intended is certain, becaufe no other literal earthly city, then ftanding, is fpoken of in this prophecy, but that which at the time of this vifion, reigned over the kings of

the

the earth chap. xvii. 18. Such an earthquake Rome has not yet experienced; but will at the close of this trumpet, probably in the year 1866; see chap. xi. 13.

It is added ver. 14. *The second woe is past;* in the time of which notice has been given us of a most horrid abomination chap. xi. 7, which will not be finished till under the next trumpet; to which place a full account of its nature, and the time of his continuance is therefore delayed. *Behold,* though this woe did not come till many years after the first, yet *the third woe,* as a woe, *cometh* more *quickly* after it, than that came after the first; for such warnings have been given, both by the witnesses, and what has befallen them, and by the above earthquake, that there is no need of further delays: And accordingly a word is here used; viz, ταχυ *speedily,* which every where in the New Testament expresses an action immediately begun, or advancing from the time spoken of; see *Matt.* v. 25. and xxviii. 7, 8. *Mark* ix. 39. and xvi. 8. *John* xi. 29. *Rev.* ii. 16. iii. 11. and xxii. 7, 12, 20. Accordingly, I apprehend, that the Mahometan chief will be converted to papal Christianity A.D. 1866; will begin to call himself the apostle of Christ, within six years after that; and exert all the infernal powers attributed to the second beast by A. D. 1882, or at furthest by 1886; see chap. xiii. 11—17. But though the third woe comes so quickly after the former, and *the war* of the second beast is announced by sound of trumpet, as the two preceding woes had been; (see again *Jer.* iv. 19.)—yet

The seventh Trumpet

has this peculiar to itself, that, whilst the others begin with desolations and destruction, this sounds aloud the triumphs of divine glory and grace,

K   before

before any thing is exprefsly faid of the malicious rage of the enemy ; which gives us reafon to ex- pect fome very glorious difplay of divine grace (as well as of wrath) at the beginning of this trumpet ; and fuch will the return of the Jews to their own land be chap. xiv, 1—5, and the fub- fequent converfion of the Gentiles, ver. 6, 7.

15. And the feventh angel founded, and there were great voices in heaven, faying, The kingdoms of the world are become *the kingdoms* of our Lord, and of his Chrift ; and he fhall reign for ever and ever.

16. And the twenty-four elders, who fat before God on their thrones, fell upon their faces, and worfhipped God ;

17. Saying, We give thee thanks, O Lord God Almighty, who art, and who waft, and who art to come ; becaufe thou haft taken *to thee* thy great power, and haft reigned.

18. And the nations were wrath ; and thy wrath is come ; and the time of the dead, that they fhould be judged : And to give a reward to thy fervants the prophets, and to the faints, and to them that fear thy name fmall and great ; and fhouldeft deftroy them who deftroy the earth.

19. And the temple of God was opened in heaven ; and there was feen the ark of his covenant in his temple : And there were lightenings, and voices, and thunders, and an earthquake, and great hail.

The three laft trumpets contain an orderly feries of the moft interefting events, which are to
befal

befal the church and the world from A. D. 606
to the end of the world, and to all eternity ; the
times of which are partly marked by the trumpets under which they are defcribed ; but much
more by the years allotted to fome confiderable
events which are exprefsly defcribed under each of
thofe trumpets. Therefore, as this part of the
word of God will foon become as clear as any
other, fo thefe confiderations may well encourage
us to endeavour to develope thofe myfteries, which
yet lie concealed for unborn pofterity ; whom
we cannot fufficiently ferve, without warning them
of what we apprehend they are to expect.

We found the time of the fixth trumpet, by
the two 1260 years given under it ver. 2, 3 ; the
one for the Popifh and Mahometan *Gentiles,* and
the other for the *witneffes* ; whofe times we found
to coincide with each other from A. D. 606 to
1866 ; fee page 116—120. And as *the third woe
cometh quickly* after the fecond ver. 14; and the
word ταχυ *fpeedily,* there ufed, teaches us to expect fome melancholy events of the feventh trumpet, actually to commence from the time of this
warning; fee page 129, 130; therefore we conclude
that the feventh trumpet will found A. D. 1866—
May the Lord from his word open to us, by his
Spirit, its great event !

This trumpet fpeaks nothing of Mahometanifm ; but gives us a fuller explanation of that
greater abomination *Popery,* which is to furvive it
150 years. And ver. 18 gives us a fummary of
the contents of this trumpet, or a general account
of the things which will occur, from the time
when it is founded to the end of the world, and to
eternity.

Immediately after the Lord has reanimated his
dead witneffes, and after the earthquake at Rome
ver. 11—13, there will be *great,* numerous, and

K 2 moft

most earnest *voices* heard *in heaven*, that is, in the church; see chap. viii. 1, *saying, The kingdoms of this world* east, west, north and south, *are become* the kingdoms *of our Lord and of his Christ*; and men and babes of every tongue, now resign themselves up to his tender and faithful care; *and he*; viz, God and his Christ (who are *one John* x. 30.) *shall* display his saving power upon them, in such a manner as he had never done before; and *reign for ever and ever*, ver. 15.

And though no notice had been taken, in this prophecy of the *four and twenty elders*, who are the heads of the Jewish and Christian church, ever since that remarkable conversion of Jews and Gentiles in Constantine's time, chap. vii. 11, 13: Yet now at the beginning of this trumpet, the Jews are to be brought back to their own land; see chap. xiv. 1—5; therefore we hear again of these elders, ver. 16—18, who *sat on thrones* as kings, chap. 1. 6: And probably their being found on thrones before God when this trumpet sounds, may intimate, that their conversion will begin before A. D. 1866; though their return to their own land will not take place till that time, as this trumpet declares. These elders then being before the throne, and hearing this jubilee trumpet sound, they *fell upon their faces and worshipped God*; *saying, We give thee thanks, O Lord God Almighty*, whose glorious essence takes in past, present and to come, *that thou hast taken to thee thy great power, and hast reigned*. *And the nations* in general *were wroth*, particularly Gog and Magog, chap. xx. 8, at thy nearer approach to, and more dreadful exertions against them; therefore these briers and thorns will set themselves against thee for 150 years, under this trumpet; after which thou wilt put a period to their usurpations, and shake their Babel down: For *thy* long-predicted

dicted *wrath is come: And the time of the dead, that they should be judged*; *and* the set time *to give a reward,* not of debt but of grace, *to* the souls and bodies of *thy servants the prophets,* both on earth and in heaven; *and to the saints* in general, *and to them that fear thy name* both *small and great, and* that thou *shouldest destroy them who destroy the earth.*

The nearer our Lord comes to men, with the greater rapture will the saints contemplate his personal dwelling in our nature, that *temple of God, John* ii. 21; and see so much the more glory in his church which is *his body, Eph.* i. 23. *Rev.* xi. 1; and which exists partly in heaven, and partly on earth. But, besides the new views which will be given of these things under this trumpet, is is added ver. 19, *And the temple of God was opened in heaven; and there was seen in his temple the ark of the covenant*; which once contained the two tables of the law for the Jews, yet concealed them from them: So concealed too was the heavenly manna, after they came to Canaan, and the ever-budding rod of our great High-Priest which lay beside the ark; together with all other things which the holy of holies contained; see *Exod.* xvi. 33. *Numb.* xvii. 10. 2 *Chron.* v. 10; see also Mr. *Poole* on *Heb.* ix. 4. Once these things had been done in parables; and Uzzah the priest died for touching the ark, when he ought to have borne it on his shoulders; and the Bethshemites were smitten for looking into it, 1 *Sam.* vi. 19. 1 *Chron.* xiii. 10. and xv. 12, 13: But now the grace, represented by these material symbols, is laid open to the view of every believing worshipper, Jew and Gentile; for A. D. 1866 being come, the Lord hath bound up *the breach of his* Jewish *people,* and healed *the stroke of their wound*; therefore now, according to his promise, *Isa.* xxx. 26, *the light of the moon* of Jewish

K 3   shadows

shadows is *as the light of the sun, and the light of the sun sevenfold, as the light of seven days*; see at chap. iv. 5. Christ's death rent the vail of the temple, *Matt.* xxvii. 51; and under the seventh trumpet the Spirit of God will gloriously rend the vail which is upon our hearts, 2 *Cor.* iii. 16. *Hof.* vi. 3. Yet when the temple of God is opened and the ark seen, that ark of the covenant cannot be fully opened to the saints, till they come to heaven.——*And there were lightenings, and voices, and thunders, and an earthquake*: These were the usual attendants and indications of the divine presence, when he came to establish a new law, to reveal something before unknown, or to give a new discovery of himself in providence or grace, *Exod.* xix. 16. *Rev.* iv. 5. and viii. 5: And, as these dreadful signs will be repeated at the pouring out of the seventh vial, chap. xvi. 18, 21; so on this occasion too they demand attention, to preserve worshippers from irreverence, whilst admitted so near, as to look into these sacred mysteries: For even *our* new covenant *God* is *a consuming fire*, to all who trifle with his grace *Heb.* xii. 29; and he *will be sanctified in them that come nigh* him, *Lev.* x. 3.

CHAP. XII.

1. AND there was seen a great sign in heaven, a woman clothed with the Sun and the Moon under her feet; and upon her head a crown of twelve stars.

2. And

2. And being with child, she cried, travailing in birth, and pained to be delivered.

3. And there was seen another sign in heaven ; and behold a great fiery dragon, having seven heads and ten horns ; and upon his heads seven crowns.

4. And his tail drew down a third part of the stars of heaven, and cast them to the earth : And the dragon stood before the woman, who was ready to bring forth, that when she was delivered he might devour her child.

5. And she brought forth a masculine son, who was to rule all the nations with a rod of iron ; and her child was caught up to God, and his throne.

6. And the woman fled into the wilderness ; where she hath a place prepared of God, that they might nourish her there, a thousand two hundred and sixty days.

7. And there was war in heaven ; Michael and his angels warred against the dragon ; and the dragon fought and his angels.

8. And they prevailed not ; neither was their place found any more in heaven.

9. And the great dragon was cast out ; the old serpent called the devil and satan, who deceives the whole world, was cast out into the earth ; and his angels were cast out with him.

10. And I heard a loud voice, saying in heaven, Now is come salvation, and the

K 4　　　　　　　power,

power, and the kingdom of our God, and the authority of his Christ ; for the accuser of our brethren is cast out, who accused them before our God day and night.

11. And they have overcome him by the blood of the Lamb, and by the word of their testimony: And they loved not their lives unto the death.

12. Therefore rejoice ye heavens, and ye who dwell in them. *But* woe to those who inhabit the earth, and the sea ; for the devil is come down to you, having great wrath, because he knoweth that he hath but a short time.

In these verses we have an account (1.) of the church, under the similitude of a woman beautifully arrayed and pregnant ; (2.) of a great fiery dragon which stood before her, ready to devour her child : Yet (3.) she is safely delivered, and her child effectually guarded. (4.) She flees into the wilderness, for 1260 years. (5.) A war ensues in the church between Christ and the dragon ; in which the latter is routed and cast out. (6.) A triumph is sung on this occasion: And (7.) an alarm is sounded to the inhabitants of the earth, on account of the dragon's being cast out amongst them.

I. We have an account of the church under the striking similitude of a woman, beautifully arrayed and pregnant ver. 1, 2. At ver. 14, it will be proved that this is the same person, who had been represented at A. D. 756, as two witnesses prophesying in sackcloth chap. xi. iii; only *then* and *there* she appears without that conspicuous glory, here described, which John did not see the church arrayed with till under this seventh

3   trumpe

trumpet; nor may we therefore expect to see it generally diffused, till A. D. 1866. Yet observe, our author does not say of this woman, or of the dragon ver. 3, *I saw* them, which is the phrase used seven and thirty times in this book, but ωφθη *there* appeared or *was seen in heaven*; for these signs will be generally and universally seen by all, in their own times.

That the church militant is here described is plain; for the present is the only state in which this woman, the church can be pregnant, bring forth a man-child, or be annoyed by the dragon: Yet she is seen in heaven, both to intimate that the church of God is as much raised above the men and the enjoyments of the world, as the visible heavens are above the earth; and that grace is glory begun. In the present state even the genuine members of this heaven the church, are feeble, tender and delicate as a woman; but being taken out of the side of the second Adam, in the hour of his crucifixion, (See Gen. ii. 21, 22,) they all love him tenderly, and rely upon him with unreserved confidence: And these happy persons, living in a state of vital union with the Son of God, are even here said to be *clothed with the Son of* Righteousness, *Rom.* xiii. 14. *Gal.* iii. 27: For the bride the Lamb's wife, shines in the rays of her Husband, *(Uxor fulget radiis maritis.)* No doubt this phrase chiefly describes the spiritual glory of the saints, as it is seen by the eye of God, *psalm* xlv. 13; yet when their Lord is eminently with them, his glory is *seen upon them* by man too; and they diffuse around them that instrumental light, heat and fructifying influence which this metaphor expresses. Every age since A. D. 756, has produced here and there an instance of a person *clothed with the sun*; for whose sake the witnesses are called by the name of this woman, ver. 14.

But

But the church of God in general, never yet appeared with that conspicuous glory, and prolific spiritual power which this metaphor imports, but will when the seventh trumpet founds; at which time she will not only trample upon all sublunary things, but have *the moon* of Jewish ceremonies so *under her feet* as she has not at present, yet not to despise, but to use them as her stable ground to stand upon, *Isa.* i. 13, 14: *And upon her head a crown of twelve stars*, which are the twelve apostles of the Lamb, chap. i. 20. and xxi. 14: Therefore to despise their writings is not the spot of God's children; who on the contrary, especially at the time here specified, will as earnestly contend for their inspired epistles, as the princes of this world for their crowns, though in a far different manner.

Such *a great* and conspicuous *sign* will the church afford under his trumpet, and exhibit to the world a striking view of what it infinitely concerns them to be *Isa.* viii. 18; for it shall be then eminently cried to her from the word, *I have espoused you to one Husband, that I may present you as a chaste virgin to Christ*, 2 Cor. xi. 2; therefore *thy Makers is thy Husband, the Lord of Hosts, is his name Isa.* liv. 5. Heb. And as our Lord will then come, by his Spirit, to dwell with his church, *which is the mother of all believers*, she will *cry, travailing in birth, and pained to be delivered.* Christ brought forth the church meritoriously with travailing pains ωδῖνας *Acts* ii. 24; and churches and ministers must not hope to bring forth souls for God without pain even in these gracious times: We must *travail in birth*, if we expect to have *Christ formed in* any by our means, *Gal.* iv. 19.

II. A great red dragon stands before her ready to devour her child, ver. 3, 4. This enormous serpent is the devil, *that old serpent*, who *deceiveth the whole world*, ver. 9; but as it cannot be said of

the

the devil perfonally, that he has *feven heads, ten horns, and feven crowns upon his heads,* which is the well-known defcription of the *beaft* every where in this prophecy, chap. xiii. 1. and xvii. 3; therefore we muft neceffarily underftand what is faid of the dragon, ver. 3, of the pope to whom the Holy Ghoft has here given the devil's own name a dragon; the reafon of which may be well expreffed in the words of Jerom on *Dan.* viith; who, fpeaking of the ten kings who were to fhare the Roman world amongft them, adds ' an eleventh ' fhall arife, a little king, *in quo totus fatanas ha-* ' *bitaturus fit corporaliter,*' in whom ' fatan fhall ' wholly inhabit bodily;' fee *Dr. Halifax on Prophecy*, page 91. Obferve therefore, that that power at Rome, which had been called a *fallen ftar* under the fifth trumpet, chap. ix. 1, and a *beaft* under the fixth, chap. xi. 7, obtains under the feventh trumpet the devil's own name, a *dragon.* See an obfervation on this word near the end of the remarks on chap. xiii. In times paft fatan raged againft the church, as a dragon, by the Egyptians, *Pfal.* lxxiv. 13. *Ifa.* li. 9. *Ezek.* xxix. 3: But now his fury is to be exerted by a Chriftian Roman power, under whofe purple and fcarlet he conceals himfelf; and the felf-colour of his native cruelty is not altered, by thofe oceans of proteftant blood which he fheds, under this red flag of infernal war.

The time when the dragon will make this attack is alfo declared, both by the trumpet under which this defcription falls, and by the account here given of him ver. 3. He appeared *having feven heads*; which *are* both the *feven hills* on which Rome ftands, and the *feven* diftinct forms of *government* which fucceeded each other there, chap. xvii. 9, 10 : *And ten horns,* which are the ten kingdoms into which the Roman empire was divided,

ver.

ver. 12. of that chapter: *And seven crowns upon his heads,* that is, a crown upon each hill, as well as upon each of those seven forms of government which took place amongst them; viz, kings, consuls, dictators, decemvirs, military tribunes, emperors, and dukes say some: And if the dukedom of Rome, under the exarchs of Ravenna, was his seventh crown, he was degraded to this A. D. 566, which continued till A. D. 727; when this dukedom, threw off allegiance to the eastern emperor, and revolted from the exarch to the pope. Taking the words in this sense, the *beast* is *the eighth* form of government at Rome, chap. xvii. 11. But as a ducal coronet was not very worthy to be joined with his other six crowns, we may thererefore confider him as obtaining his seventh crown, A. D. 756, when the pope became a beast: In this sense he is *of the seven* forms of government, chap. xvii. 11; and then it was that *the dragon,* the devil, *gave his power, his throne, and great authority* to the beast, chap. xiii. 2. (which will be again renewed and confirmed to him, under the devil's own name a dragon, in the time of this trumpet, by means of the second beast,) chap. xiii. 11.

Taking the words in this sense, this event falls in exactly with the first visible flight of the woman into the wilderness, for *a time, times, and half a time,* ver. 14. But though his seven forms of government have been crowned so long ago, his seven *hills* have not yet been all crowned, or made the seat of royal residence; but these words inform us that they will be so by the time that this trumpet sounds: For observe, it is not said, chap. xvii. 9, 10, that his *seven heads are seven mountains* OR *seven kings,* but *seven mountains* AND *seven kings;* which obliges us to enquire for a time when his heads, taken in both these senses, will be crowned.

ed. The word occurs in both thefe fenfes, chap.
xiii. 1, 3, and muft have both here. Rome's feven
heads of government were all crowned by A. D.
756; but the feventh trumpet had not then founded, the church was not then clothed with the fun, or
eminently pregnant, nor was the dragon caft out
of the church foon after that time; but all thefe
things muft concur to mark the times here pointed
out. Befides the text fpeaks of the heads of this
dragon himfelf as crowned; and though the fix
crowns fet upon the heads of his heathen predeceffors, might, in a fenfe, be called *his* crowns
(as *his* both refembles, and derives honour from
each of *theirs*;) yet when his feven hills fhall be
crowned, it will then be more literally true, that
upon his own *heads* are *feven crowns.*

But who would have thought to find a dragon,
fo near this woman, or in the chuch of God! yet
the beaft had been nurfed up for many centuries,
where we fhould leaft have expected to find him:
And, though his nature feemed effentially contrary
to her's, he lived in actual peace with her, while
fhe was contented with the mere name of a Chriftian, and, under that abufed fignature, played the
harlot with him: But if the Lord Jefus muft dwell
with her by his fpirit; if fhe is with child, and
defires to bring forth fruit to her divine Hufband;
this will turn the beaft into a dragon, and as fuch
he here ftands before her, when fhe was about to
be delivered, that he may devour her offspring
(which he knew would fight againft him) and
fecure her for himfelf afterwards. Yet fee!

III. She is fafely delivered, and her child caught
up to God and his throne, ver. 5. *She brought
forth* υιον αρρινα *a mafculine fon*; *who* in a vital
union to the Lord Jefus, was not only to rule *the
nations* with which he had any immediate concern,
as it is promifed to every one *that overcometh*,
chap.

chap. ii. 26, 27; but as the spiritual empire of Christ was now become more extensive than ever, it is promised to this new-born heir of salvation, that *he shall rule all the nations in general with a rod of iron.*

This masculine son could not be Christ himself; for, not to say that his birth occurred above eighteen hundred years before these times; or that the characters here given of the church, as *clothed with the sun, having the moon under her feet, and upon her head a crown of twelve stars,* neither suited the Jewish church, nor even his own mother the Virgin Mary, at the time of his birth; though nature had given Rome seven hills from the beginning, at the time of Christ's birth it had not had its *seven kings,* nor its *ten horns,* nor *seven crowns upon its heads,* in either sense of that word. The same reasons in general also conclude against understanding this masculine son of Constantine the Great, of whom many expositors have understood this; and one or other of them will forbid us to apply the word to any person whatever, who shall be born before this trumpet sounds. Yet I cannot suppose that any individual only it intended by this masculine son; but rather the glorious instruments in general which the church will bring forth, under the seventh trumpet, to oppose popery (with the unanimity of one man;) and especially those of the Jewish nation: For when the Lord comes to perform that *good thing which* he *promised to the house of Israel, and to the house of Judah; in those days, and at that time, said the Lord, will I cause the Branch of righteousness to grow up unto David; and he shall execute judgment and righteousness in the land. And this is the name where with* the mother of this illustrious progeny, who is clothed with the sun, *shall* be called, *the Lord is our Righteousness, Jer.* xxxiii. 14—16. But

Isaiah

Ifaiah feems to fpeak yet more exprefsly of this
mafculine fon, chap. lxvi. 5—9; where, predict-
ing the Jews return to their own land, it is declared, ver. 7, 8. *Before fhe travailed fhe brought
forth, before her pain came fhe was delivered of a
man-child,* whofe exploits will make his name *remembered* as long as the world ftands, as the word
זכר a *man-child* imports: Therefore it is added, *who
hath heard fuch things? who,* even among Abraham's defcendants themfelves, *hath feen fuch things?
fhall the earth be made to bring forth in one day! or
fhall a nation to be born at once! for as foon as
Zion travailed fhe brought forth her children,* even
this mafculine fon, with whom the promifes had
been big for fo many hundred years. But now at
the beginning of this trumpet, Sion will bring
forth fuch an offspring, as will be adapted to give
a convincing, and almoft irrefiftible demonftration
of the excellence and glory of the gofpel. And
the above fcriptures, compared with this, feem
to give additional reafons to believe, that the
Jews will he brought home to their own land at
the beginning of this trumpet; fee chap. xiv. 1-5.

That the Lord might perform his word to
David, he preferved Joafh from the bloody Atha-
liah by Jehofheba, who *hid* him *fix years* in *the
temple,* 2 *Kings* xi. 1—3: So this mafculine fon,
who was inftrumentally to *rule all the nations with
a rod of iron,* ηρπασθη *was fnatched up* fuddenly,
haftily and powerfully *to God and his throne;* fee
Eph. ii. 6. *Col.* i. 13. Gr. And fome of thefe
fervants of God may perhaps be taken to dwell
with him at Jerufalem; others preferved by flight
into the wildernefs, ver. 6; whilft others are removed to heaven: But all will be fafe, as if
caught up to God and his throne; where they fhall
rule with the faints; and *take,* and *poffefs the kingdom for ever and ever. Dan.* vii. 18.

IV. The

IV. The woman, the church, flees into the *wilderness*; by which word, say the learned Ainſworth and Dr. Doddridge, is meant *uncultivated lands*, in oppoſition to thoſe which art and induſtry have made *fruitful:* But this was not her firſt flight into the wilderneſs; which is related in its proper place, ver. 14, where it is referred to as in a great meaſure paſt; and what remains of her 1260 years, there mentioned, at the time of the ſounding of this trumpet, will be fulfilled under it; viz, from A. D. 1866 to 2016. At the ſounding of this trumpet, neither *the holy city* Jeruſalem, nor yet the church of God in general will be *trodden under feet*; as they both had been during the whole time of the witneſſes, chap. xi. 2, 3 : Yet, freſh troubles ariſing againſt the woman under this trumpet, at A. D. 1866, ſhe will again obey that order of her Lord, *when they perſecute you in this city, flee ye to another Mat.* x. 23 : Therefore, leaving that part of the wilderneſs where ſhe had long been, (and which through the bleſſing of God on her induſtry, in a great meaſure, ceaſed to be a wilderneſs,) as Judea could not hold all God's out-caſts, at A. D. 1866 ſhe *fled*, probably *into the wilderneſs* of America; that there ſhe might peaceably wear her unfaſhionable celeſtial dreſs, ver. 1 ; to which the *corrupt eſtabliſhments* in her former neighbourhood were, alas ! too unfriendly. Here, pleaſed with her ſolar robes and ſtarry crown, her divine Huſband dwells with her ; and ſhe enjoys the place of her reſidence, as it was *prepared of God for her* ; that her magiſtrates and miniſters, yea that men and angels, under the eye and bleſſing of her own God, might *nouriſh her there a thouſand two hundred and ſixty days*, or years. It is the ſame length of time as the two witneſſes propheſied in ſackcloth ; called *forty two months*, as they will be to their enemies

enemies, chap. xi. 2, 3; and the same as the *time, times, and half a time,* ver. 14 of this chapter.

But the grand enquiry here is, From what period are these 1260 years to be dated?—And how earnestly I have studied, and besought the God of heaven, to enable me to give my reader satisfaction in this point, will appear when time is no more—I can think of but three periods from which the preceding and subsequent prophecies of this book will, in any sense, permit us to begin them; and they are all very remarkable in this vision; viz, A. D. 606, 756, and 1866—Let us consider what may be said of each of these, with respect to this her 1260 years flight.

It does not seem reasonable to begin them from A. D. 606; because (1.) As the holy Ghost had before informed us of the state of the church from A. D. 606 to 1866, by the account of the two witnesses, chap. xi. 2—12; in so short a prophecy, it is more honourable to the inspired author, to suppose him to go forward to some new matter, than to return, without necessity, to a subject which had been described before. (2.) This would be to describe a time which has no concern with this trumpet but as there are no other descriptions under this, or any preceding trumpet, but what, in part; at least, concern its own proper time, therefore this also must. (3.) This would make the woman's flight into the wilderness, as it were *from the face of the serpent,* 1410 years; but though she may be much longer than that in a wilderness, she is to *flee from* before *the serpent* only 1260 years, ver. 14. (4.) It would be absurd to begin the time of her flight from the Roman beast, or dragon, ver. 3, before the time that the Pope became such; but he was neither a beast, nor a dragon, at A. D. 606; therefore she could not then flee from him as such.

L.

Nor

Nor can her 1260 **years be** reckoned from A. D.
756; (1.) Becaufe this would make ver. 14, a
tautology, or needlefs reference to what had been
before defcribed; for there it will appear that her
flight *from the face of the ferpent*, exactly coincides
with his 1260 years from A. D. 756 to 2016; fee
chap. xiii. 5. (2.) Not one of the things which
are faid of this *woman*, or of the *dragon*, in thefe
verfes will agree to A. D. 756.

It remains therefore, that her 1260 years muft
be dated from A. D. 1866, when this trumpet
founds. They cannot, I apprehend, begin fooner,
(**1.**) Becaufe the church (which is reprefented as
God's *fealed* ones under the fifth trumpet; as his
witneffes under the fixth; and as the Redeemer's
bride under this trumpet) will be *clothed with fackcloth* from A. D. 606 to 1866, chap. xi. 3;
therefore fhe cannot be *clothed with the fun* till
fome time in that year: For that this *woman* and
the *witneffes* both reprefent the church of God,
will appear at ver. 14; and as the Lord cannot
have two different interefts in the world, fo his
church cannot be both *clothed with fackcloth*, and
clothed with the fun, at the fame time. (2.) It is not
till A. D. 1866 that it is faid, *The kingdoms of the
world are* become *Chrift's*, chap. xi. 15; therefore
till then the church will not eminently *cry, travailing
in birth*, or be in *pain to be delivered*, ver. 2. (3.)
As the Roman beaft will not have his *feven crowns
upon his heads*, in both fenfes of the word *head*, till
A. D. 1866; fo God has not given him the name
of a dragon, till under this trumpet, ver. 3. True,
at ver. 14, he is called a *ferpent* from A. D. 756 to
2016; but though every dragon is a ferpent,
every ferpent is not a dragon; nor is the pope
called fo till A. D. 1866. (4.) Though the witneffes, by their teftimony, *tormented them that
dwell on the earth*, chap. xi. 10, yet as witneffes
it was not their bufinefs to fight; but in thefe
                                                    times,

times, both *Michael and his angels fought against
the dragon,* ver. 7; which inclines me to date
these times after the 1260 years of the witnesses.
(5.) After this engagement the *dragon was cast
out into the earth, and his angels were cast out with
him; neither* could they find *their place any more
in heaven,* ver. 8, 9 : But the dragon was rather
taken into, than cast out of, the church at A. D.
756; nor was it likely that his sentence of excommunication should be even pronounced by the
court, till the witnesses had finished what they
had to say against him, A. D. 1866 : From A. D.
606 to that time, which is the whole time of the
sixth trumpet, the Pope sits in court unblushing
to hear what the witnesses testiy against him. And
when his sentence of expulsion is pronounced, it
must be executed by force of arms; for which purpose two swords will hardly be *enough* (unless we
understand them of the temporal and spiritual
sword); therefore he who said, *Put up thy sword
into his place,* when his own life was in danger, may
perhaps hereafter, in favour of his bride, visibly
lay by his providence, *He that hath no sword, let
him sell his garment and buy one,* Matt. xxvi. 52. *Luke*
xxii. 36, 38 : For now the dragon, who has never
yet been cast out of the church; (but is expressly
said to stand *before the woman,* when she was *ready
to be delivered,* ver. 4.) will be *cast out* after A. D.
1866, and *his angels with him.* (6.)

If the Pope in any sense *drew down the* political or
ecclesiastical *stars of heaven* at A. D. 756, I fear at
that time he drew much more than *a third part,* or
even two thirds of them : But while it fills me with
horror to hear, that after the resurrection of the
witnesses, and their ascent to heaven, his tail will
draw some of them out of the church, and *cast
them to the earth;* it is a pleasure to hear that he
will prevail but against one *third part* of them,
ver. 4: And the time when he will so prevail,

ſeems to be intimated in the word συρει *he drew* ;
for his drawing them down ſuppoſes his own de-
ſcent with them, which, we have before heard,
will not take place till after A. D. 1866. I only
add, (7.) This enemy, who had *accuſed* the witneſſes
before God day and night, cannot be ſaid to do it
ſo immediately *before God*, when he is caſt out of
the church into the earth : And the triumph ſung
on this account, will be more proper after A. D.
1866 than it had ever been before ; viz, *Now is
come ſalvation*, and *ſtrength, and the kingdom of our
God, and the authority of his Chriſt*, ver. 10 ; ſee
chap. xi 15.

If theſe reaſonings are juſt ; and if the things
which are here ſaid of the *woman*, of the *dragon*,
and of Chriſt's *victory* over him, will agree to no
year before 1866, the concluſion is unavoidable ;
viz, that her 1260 years, ver. 6, muſt be dated
from that time ; and conſequently they will end
A. D. 3126, which is the laſt account of time in
this book ; but I have reckoned it 3125, becauſe
the Pope was nearly a univerſal biſhop A. D.
605, as he became a beaſt A. D. 755 ; though
he is not commonly thought to have had full
poſſeſſion of a beaſt-like power till the year after.

I conſider therefore the words in ver. 6, as an
account of the ſtate of the church from A. D.
1866 to the end of the world ; and reckon her
1260 years the time of this trumpet, ſo far as time
reaches ; ſee chap. xx. 11—15, where the ob-
jections againſt ſuppoſing the time of the end of
the world to be given us in this prophecy, will be
carefully diſcuſſed.   At preſent it may favour this
thought to obſerve, (1.) That, as the time of both
the preceding woe-trumpets has been expreſsly
given us under each, it is the more reaſonable to
expect that of this ; eſpecially as the giving us
the time of this trumpet, aſſigns additional reaſons

of

of importance for giving us the times of the preceding. (2.) Separate from what is said in this verse, we have an account of 1150 years which will be spent under this trumpet; viz, 150 years at the beginning of it, which are the last times of the beast, in which the woman *flees from the face of the serpent*, properly so called ; viz, from A. D. 1866, to 2016, ver. 14; and the 1000 years in which satan is bound and cast into the bottomless pit, chap. xx. 1—5: After which he will be loosed out of prison for *a little season*, that is, for a part of the remaining 109 or 110 years.

(3.) There is an observable difference between what is said of the woman's *fleeing* and *flying* into the wilderness at ver. 6 and 14; which may incline us to make a very different estimate of them. At A. D. 756, when the beast was rising, and the holy city trodden under feet, chap. xi. 2 ; being the minority, and her enemies triumphant, the wilderness was this woman's *own place*, ver. 14; but at A. D. 1866 ver. 6, when the kingdoms of this world are become the kingdoms of Christ, it will appear that she deserves a more honourable place in the world : Yet being still forced to *flee* after A. D. 1866 from the same beast, *she hath a place prepared for her*, not of men, but *of God :* And if America is the wilderness here intended, where she is to be fed to the end of the world, by the time this trumpet sounds, it will appear by what methods God has been preparing this wilderness for her reception, ever since Mr. Robinson's flock settled there A. D. 1620—Again, at A. D. 756 she flies, for the whole of her 1260 years, *from the face of the* beast, that is, *the serpent*, ver. 14, chap. xiii. 11 ; but at A. D. 1866 ver. 6, there are but 150 years of the beast's time left, in which she can *flee* from him; and his chief exploits in that time will be confined to near the first half of

L 3

it; therefore it is not, nor could it have been said of this her second flight as of the former that she fled so long from him—At A. D. 756 she flew with rapid haste upon the *two wings of the* Roman *eagle*, ver. 14, which she saw were given her for her safety ινα πετηται that she might *fly into the wilderness*; where even this bird of prey foraged for her, as long as it had any use of its wings; but being off from these wings at A. D. 1866, when she is *cloathed with the sun*, &c. she will be more confident and daring; and, having stayed in her own place for perhaps two thirds of her month of thirty years, after her hard travail in bringing forth the *masculine son*, she will at length, probably at A. D. 1886, *flee* εφυγεν *into the wilderness*, because she sees it is the *place prepared of God for her*; not merely for safety, but ινα εκει τρεφωσιν αυτην *that they may nourish her there*, ver. 6: Accordingly, when this trumpet sounds, it is said in the present tense εκει τρεφεται, *she is nourished there from the face of the serpent*, ver. 14.

Having thus remarked the difference between her first flight A. D. 756 ver. 14, and her second after A. D. 1866 ver. 6, it may be asked, But why is the account of her second flight into the wilderness ver. 6, placed before her first ver. 14? I answer, in every short history, while the author is describing a regular series of events, it is common to reserve some grand incident, which will throw considerable light upon the preceding and subsequent parts of the history, to be produced when it becomes immediately necessary; and to which he will refer back in the plu-perfect tense. Just so the holy Ghost has done in this prophetic history: At ver. 6 and following, the events which will occur under the seventh trumpet, follow each other in a regular succession; but at ver. 14 he informs us, that there *had been given*

given to the woman (long before she was in that danger which he had mentioned in the verse before) *two wings of the* Roman *eagle*; *that she might fly into the wilderness from the face of the serpent* 1260 *years.* It was necessary to speak of this in the plu-perfect tense, as 1110 of these 1260 years were elapsed before this trumpet sounded; yet this was the properest time and place to mention it, just before that full account of the beast which follows chap. xiiith. The concinnity of the prophecy required it to be mentioned here; besides under this trumpet, the works of God are commonly described before those of the dragon.

Reviewing what has been said, I apprehend that the church, being found in a wilderness at A. D. 1866, will soon after that time be forced to flee into another, a different wilderness till A. D. 2016, from the dragon and the second beast. Yet if the second wilderness into which she flees should, in every view, resemble the first, it cannot be the same to her, when *clothed with the sun,* as the former had been, while she was clothed with *sackcloth*; for, after A. D. 1866, her solar robes will brighten every opening scene, guide her way, burn up the briars and thorns around her, fertilize the ground, and draw heavenly company down to her. But *clothed with the sun,* it is impossible that the most desirable place upon earth, should appear any otherwise to her than as a wilderness: Therefore, though she is only to flee from the dragon, in this her second flight, for a little part of her 1260 years; she is to be in the wilderness for the whole of that time, even in the millennium and afterwards: Yet, as her solar robes make the wilderness different to her after A. D. 8866, from what it had been before, so the grace bestowed in the millennium will make it yet more different. At that time the earth will

yield

yield an eminent temporal and spiritual *increase*, *Ezek.* xxxiv. 27; but, as some lands must from their own nature remain uncultivated to the end of the world, so those words will be conspicuously true to the end, *In the world ye shall have tribulation*, John xvi. 33; and *Who is this that cometh up from the wilderness, leaning upon her beloved? Cant.* viii. 5. Many miseries will be removed in the millennium; yet many will be left, to exercise and improve the Christian's graces. And as the dreams of sensual pleasure have, in every age, so abused the mind; if we have not mistaken the sense of these words, it seemed necessary to the holy Ghost to inform us, a little before the millennium began, that the world will be a wilderness to the church in its purest and happiest times: It cannot be otherwise to a sinful creature; therefore as the world was all of it a wilderness, in one view, at A. D. 756, when the woman flew into that which was emphatically called a *wilderness*; so it will be in her second flight into the wilderness, after A. D. 1866. *He that dwelleth in God* will always find the world a wilderness—But let us proceed to consider,

V. The war which ensues, after this woman's flight into the wilderness, between Christ and the dragon; in which the latter is routed and cast out ver. 7, 8, 9. *And there was war in heaven*, that is, in the church militant, the only heaven that can be made a field of battle: And here the combatants were *Michael and his angels, and the dragon and his angels.* Whether Michael, whose name signifies *Who is like God?* was a guardian angel of highest rank, or Christ himself is not universally agreed; see *Dan.* x. 21. and xii. 1. But if Michael's angels are *his*, in the same sense as the dragon's angels are *his*, then Michael is the Lord Jesus; who here fought, as the captain of the Lord's hosts,

hosts, at the head of those invincible Chieftains of war whom his grace raised up after A.D. 1866. *The dragon* also *fought and his angels*; but, the pope having been considered as Anti-christ ever since the tenth century (see bishop *Hurd* on prophecy, vol. II. p. 26,) and the servants of God having, in every succeeding age, treated him as such; when this main engagement began in the nineteenth century, the dragon and his army *prevailed not to keep their place any more* in the church, but were *cast* out *into the earth*.

To say nothing of the 338 Bishops whom the emperor Constantine Copronymus convened at Constantinople A.D. 754, to protest against the idolatrous practices of Rome; or of the resolute opposition made by the Emperors of the Greek church, and ministers of the gospel, in the eighth and ninth centuries, against worshipping of images, and praying to saints and angels; to say nothing of the attack made upon them by Wickliffe A.D. 1380; of the reformation A.D. 1517; or of the abolition of the Jesuits A.D. 1773 (whose order had been played off against the church ever since A.D. 1540,) as it is twice said ver. 9. that the *devil* is *cast out*, and also asserted that *his angels were cast out with him*, therefore we expect that, after this woman's second flight into the wilderness, in the time of this trumpet, both the devil, the pope and their angels will be so cast out of the church down to the earth, as they had never been before—God keep professors of religion from doing any thing, mediately or immediately, for that cause, against which he has thus resolutely set his face.

VI. A triumph is sung on this occasion ver. 10, 11, 12. *And I heard a loud voice saying in heaven, Now is come salvation and the power, and the kingdom, of our God; and the authority of his Christ* is difplayed : *For the accufer of our brethren*, whofe names are dear to us as our own ; *who accufed them*, not only in the prefence of their fellow men, but alfo *before our God day and night* (as long as he was permitted to ftand as before him) *is caft out* of the church, ver. 9; fee *Job* i. 9. And this triumph feems to be continued at ver. 10, through the millennium; when this accufer of the brethren will be *caft down* κατεβληθη into hell, fo as perhaps not to be permitted to accufe them before God, for that 1000 years. Long it had been faid, but faid in vain to many profeffors, *Be not railers, revilers* or *devils*, 1 Cor. v. 11, and vi. 10. 1 Tim. iii. 11. Gr. But now the lying tongue is put to filence in the church of God, and chiefly confined to the world : *And they overcame him by the blood of the Lamb*; which at once atoned for their fins, and conveyed to them the Spirit of all grace for their fupply. And this Spirit, which made the bleffings of the gofpel their own, taught and emboldened them to publifh *the word of their teftimony*, though with more than the rifk of their lives : *For they loved not their lives unto the death*; on the contrary the king of terrors wore to them the moft inviting charms, ‘ when endured in fuch a ‘ caufe and prefence.’ *Therefore rejoice ye heavens* above; *and ye who dwell in them*, ftrike your celeftial ftrings to yet higher ftrains of joy and praife, for what almighty grace has done for your perfecuted brethren below.

VII. The world is warned of their danger from the dragon, ver. 12. *Woe to the inhabitants of the earth*, which gave birth to the fecond beaft ; *and of the fea*, out of which the firft arofe, chap. xiii. 1, 11 : *For the devil* who had fo dreadfully poifoned, torne and mangled the church, as fcarcely to leave it one Chrift-like feature, wherever he had power, *is come down* out of the church *to you*,

having

having great wrath: And a defcending degraded devil is the moft horrible of all ; efpecially **as he** *knows that he has* now *but a fhort time* in which to exert his rage againft Chrift and precious fouls. He knows from the bible, that he is to be bound, and *caft into the bottomlefs pit* for *a thoufand years,* chap. xx. 2, 3 ; and probably underftands from this prophecy, better than we, when the time is : And if this will take place about A. D 2016, as foon as the feventh trumpet founds A. D. 1866, and he fees himfelf about to be caft out of the church, whilft the *kingdoms of the world* are efcaping from his cruel tyranny, and becoming the *kingdoms of the Lord and his Chrift* ; he will haften up the fecond beaft out of *the earth*, to oppofe thofe fwelling floods of falvation, which are going forth over the whole earth. Hear Chriftians, and for once learn of the devil, to haften your work as your time fhortens. *Fas eft et ab hofte doceri.*

13. And when the dragon faw that he was caft out into the earth, he perfecuted the woman who had brought forth the male-child.

14. And there had been given to the woman two wings of a great eagle, that fhe might fly into the wildernefs to her place ; where fhe is nourifhed there for a time, and times, and half a time, from the face of the ferpent.

15. And the ferpent had caft out of his mouth water as a river after the woman ; that he might caufe her to be carried away with the flood.

16. And the earth helped the woman, and opened its mouth, and drank up the river

ver which the dragon had thrown out of his mouth.

17. And the dragon was enraged againſt the woman; and went away to make war with the remainder of her ſeed, who keep the commandments of God, and who retain the teſtimony of Jeſus Chriſt.

In theſe words we have an account of the works of *God,* and of the *devil.* To begin with the latter of theſe;

I. The dragon makes a moſt ſpiteful attack upon the woman in the wilderneſs, ver. 13, 15, 16, 17. The beaſt has found ever ſince the *reformation,* that notwithſtanding his boaſted *holineſs,* he cannot preſerve himſelf from being treated by intelligent Proteſtants as a Heathen man and a publican; eſpecially on account of thoſe unpardoned, and for ever unpardonable, rivers of innocent blood which he has ſhed. But when he has ſlain the two witneſſes A. D. 1862, it will appear to every one, who has any moral uſe of his eyes, that he is the moſt terrene potentate upon earth: And after he has driven the woman into the wilderneſs the ſecond time, the war will viſibly appear to be betwixt Chriſt and the dragon, ver. 7—12: And when the witneſſes are raiſed from the dead, they will not touch him with thoſe light and gentle ſtrokes, by which ſome former heroes of the pen ſo loudly ſhewed their own duplicity and folly; but he will be univerſally and finally caſt out of the church: After which he will become more explicit in his hatred, and with the more fury *perſecute the woman, who brought forth the male-child,* ver. 13. He had ſtirred up many people againſt her ever ſince A. D. 1517; but when the ſecond beaſt ariſes, under this trumpet,

pet, speaking *like a dragon*, chap. xiii. 11, this serpent will *cast out of his mouth* yet more abundant *waters* than ever, that is, peoples, multitudes, nations and tongues, *as a river* to drown her; see chap. xvii. 15. When God speaks it is done; and this serpent must imitate the most high, in calling nations to his feet with a word; whom he may pour out, as easily as he can speak, filthy as they come from his mouth, *after the woman, that he may cause her to be carried away with the flood*; either to flow in the channel which he has cut out for her, or to be swept off the earth, ver. 15. *Prov.* xv. 28.

But as the more humane earth *had* in ages past *helped the woman*, and intombed the *Hildebrands*, the *Bonners* and the *Lawds* of the world; so now it more than ever *helped* her, and opening its *mouth* wider than common, it *swallowed up* that *flood* of people *which the dragon had cast out of his mouth*, ver. 16; some by desolating wars; others by the cruelty of their respective governors; and many more by the treading of the wine-press without the city, A. D. 1926, chap. xiv. 20; and by the grievous sores and plagues of the first and fifth vials A. D. 1936 and 1940; all of which fall within these times. *This is the Lord's doing*, and will be *marvellous* in the eyes of those who behold it. But when, in some of the first of these executions, the earth is made fat with the blood of its guilty sons, the dragon, *inraged against the woman*, and still thirsting for victory, will turn indignant from the sight of his own dead troops; and, with what forces he has left, *make war with the rest of her seed*; who, in spite of all his efforts, *keep* inviolate *the commandments of God*, and retain in heart and life unvarying *the* glorious *testimony of Jesus*, ver. 17. 1 *Cor.* i. 6. 1 *John* v. 10.

Thus

Thus we have feen what the Lord will do againſt that earth-born race, who inliſt themſelves under the banner of the dragon ; but let us fee,

II. What he does for the woman ver. 14. Her God had been before hand with this dragon ; for ' previous to his perſecution of her, and as a ' proviſion for her eſcape from him,' *to the woman there had been given* (in the time when ſhe was called the two witneſſes) *two wings of a great eagle, that ſhe might fly into the wilderneſs, to her place.* The Greek *Aoriſt* is, as that word ſignifies, *indeterminate* in its fenſe ; it is commonly rendered in the *preſent* or *imperfect* tenſe ; and the word εφυγεν *ſhe fled* occurs in this fenſe ver. 6, where we found no reaſon to depart from the fenſe in our tranſlation : But not to mention ετελεσεν *Matt.* xxvi. 1 ; or αλειψασα *John* xi. 2, the Aoriſt εδοθη feems to have at leaſt a *perfect* meaning in the following places ; viz, *Matt.* xxviii. 18. *John* i. 17. and xii. 5. 2 *Cor.* xii. 7. *Eph.* iii. 8. and iv. 7. 1 *Tim.* iv. 14. It has alſo a *plu-perfect* tenſe in our tranſlation, *Gal.* iii. 21. *If there had been a law given,* &c; and might have been rendered *had been given,* or *were given* in *Rev.* vi. 2, 4, 8. and viii. 2, and in moſt of the nineteen places in which it occurs in this book : And εδοθησαν muſt be ſo tranſlated, in the verſe I am now conſidering ; for if the *two wings of* the Roman *eagle* are given this *woman,* they muſt be given her at a time when both the eaſtern and weſtern empire was ſubſiſting. Theſe two wings had in fact been given her from A. D. 395, when the empire was divided into the eaſtern and weſtern ; but, though ſhe flew upon them from other enemies before, ſhe could not fly upon theſe wings from the enemy here ſpoken, till he became a ſerpent, a beaſt or a dragon A. D. 756. From that time the Proteſtants flew from him

upon

upon the western wing of this eagle, and the Greek church upon the eastern. But these wings could not be said to be given her A. D. 1866, when this trumpet was founded; for if the western empire still continues, and will till A. D. 2016, in the ten kingdoms into which it is divided; yet, whatever may be said of the eastern empire before A. D. 1453 when the Turks took Constantinople, it in no sense continued to be a wing of that eagle after that time; for the Turks have no such devotedness to the Roman spirit and manners as the Europeans. I conclude therefore, that these words refer us back to A. D. 756 when both these wings of the Roman eagle were given her. And this eagle, which is a bird of prey, was willing to protect her as a subject, though not for Christ's sake. Si *nostra* tueri non vultis, at *vestra* defendetis; *If you will not protect our things, at least defend your own.* The Lord himself bore Israel, as *the eagle* bears her young on *her wings*; which therefore cannot be pierced, but through her own body, *Exod.* xix. 4: And if he commits his treasure to this eagle, to carry it into the wilderness, he will be always with it himself; and whoever forages for his spouse in this wilderness, Christ alone can, and he will spiritually nourish her there all her 1260 days.

This view of things, both proves that we were right in seeking for the *witnesses* in the east and west; and that this woman is the same person with the witnesses, though that name is dropped at A. D. 1866, from which time the glory arrays her which is described ver. 1. And this also fixes the sense of the *time, times, and half a time,* so far as it concerns the beast to A. D. 756 and 2016; see *Dan.* vii. 25. and xii. 7. I only add, as ιβαλεν has necessarily a *plu-perfect* meaning ver. 16, it could not be improper to render it so ver. 15:

And

And the help which the earth affords the woman ver. 16, will be *paft*, yet eminently *future*, at A. D. 1866. And as the woman is *really* nou-rifhed, ver. 14, through every of her 1260 years, fhe will be *confpicuoufly* fo, after this trumpet founds A. D. 1866—But it is time to enter upon a more immediate defcription of the enemy, from whom this woman is even now flying.

C H A P. XIII.

1. AND I ftood upon the fand of the fea, and faw a wild beaft rifing up out of the fea; having feven heads and ten horns; and upon his horns were ten diadems; and upon his heads the name of blafphemy.

2. And the beaft which I faw was like a leopard, and its feet as thofe of a bear, and its mouth as the mouth of a lion: And the dragon gave him his power, and his throne, and great authority.

3. And I faw one of its heads as it were wounded to death; and his deadly wound was healed: And the whole world wondered after the beaft.

4. And they worfhipped the dragon who gave authority to the beaft: And they wor-fhipped the beaft, faying, Who is like the beaft? who is able to make war with him?

5. And there was given to him a mouth fpeaking great things, and blafphemies. And
authority

authority was given him to prevail forty-two months.

6. And he opened his mouth to blafphemy againſt God; to blafpheme his name, and his tabernacle, and them that dwell in heaven.

7. And it was given to him to make war with the faints, and to overcome them: and power was given him over every tribe, and tongue, and nation.

8. And all that dwell upon the earth ſhall worſhip him, whoſe names are not written in the book of Life of the Lamb, ſlain from the foundation of the world.

9. If any one has an ear, let him hear.

10. If any one leads into captivity, he ſhall go into captivity. If any one killeth with the ſword, he ſhall be ſlain with the ſword. Here is the patience and the faith of the faints.

11. And I ſaw another wild beaſt riſing up out of the earth; and he had two horns like a lamb; and he ſpake as a dragon.

12. And he exerciſes all the power of the firſt beaſt before him; and makes the earth, and thoſe who dwell therein to worſhip the firſt beaſt, whoſe deadly wound was healed.

13. And he doth great wonders, ſo as to make fire come down from heaven to earth before men.

14. And he deceives the inhabitants of the earth by the ſigns which it is given him to do before the beaſt; ſaying to the inhabitants of the earth, to make an image to

M the

the beaft, which had the wound by the fword, and did live.

15. And it was given him to give fpirit to the image of the beaft; that it might even fpeak, and caufe that as many as would not worfhip the image of the beaft, fhould be flain.

16. And he caufes all, both fmall and great, rich and poor, freemen and flaves, *to fubmit* that he fhould give them a mark on their right hands, or on their foreheads:

17. And that no one fhould buy or fell, except he who has the mark, or the name of the beaft, or the number of his name.

18. Here is wifdom. Let him who hath underftanding, count the number of the beaft; for it is the number of a man: And his number is fix hundred fixty-fix.

The word Θηριον a *favage* beaft, by which the ftoick philofophers ufed to exprefs our natural concupifcence, fignifies in prophetic language an idolatrous perfecuting empire: Such were the four monarchies defcribed, *Dan.* viith; viz, the Babylonian, Perfian, Grecian and Roman: And taking the word in the fame fenfe here, we have an account of two wild beafts; with refpect to each of which, let us endeavour to trace his *origin, character, operations,* and *times.* And

I. Of the firft wild beaft, ver. 1—10. *And I ftood upon the fand of the fea* in the ifle of Patmos, to take a view of thofe dafhing waves, which afford fo lively a reprefentation of the tumults and confufions of the world; and while I was gazing, wrapt in deep thought, *I faw a wild beaft rife out of the fea, having feven heads, and ten horns;* and

2   *upon*

upon his horns ten diadems, and upon his heads or hills *the* infamous *name of blasphemy*, ver. 1.

That this beast represents an empire subsisting at Rome is indisputable, and confessed by writers of every name; for the seven hills of that city which reigned over the kings of the earth, A. D. 96, are *the seven mountains on which this woman* sitteth, chap. xvii. 9, 10, 18. But in order to find the government here intended, we must enquire for such an idolatrous persecuting power at Rome as John could see rising; therefore it must not be risen before his time. It must also be a power which will continue, neither more nor less than 1260 years from its commencement; and must possess these seven hills, after that city has experienced seven different forms of government; for this beast is the eighth: And it must so resemble six of them as to be *of the seven*, chap. xvii. 11. It must also subsist after the Roman empire has been divided into *ten horns*, or kingdoms; and when the *ten diadems* which once adorned the Roman crown, are distributed among these ten kingdoms: None of which characters can possibly agree to Rome Heathen, but all of them concentre in Rome Christian or Papal; therefore there can be no rational doubt, but that the holy Ghost speaks of this. This is that power which the prophet Daniel has described, under the character of a *little horn* which arose among the ten, and *after* them; and was *diverse from the first* ten, being spiritual as they are secular; yet he shall *subdue three* of them, and *pluck them up* by the roots. He adds, this horn shall have *eyes like the eyes of a man; and a mouth speaking great things: For he shall speak great words against the most high, and shall wear out the saints of the most high; and think to change times, and laws: And they shall be given into his hands*, for the same

M 2   length

length of time as is here specified; viz, until *a time, times and the dividing of time,* chap. vii. 8, 24, 25. But as these characters can never agree to any other power but the pope, no wonder that he dares not suffer his dupes to read the bible, where he is so plainly characterized, and so awfully stigmatized, by the blessed God. But let us,

I. Enquire into the *origin* of this beast. He first proceeded out of *the well of the abyss,* under the character of a universal bishop, chap. ix. 1. Gr; then, as a beast, he proceeded from the abyss itself, up through that well, chap. xi. 7. and xvii. 8; see *Luke* viii. 31. But he made his first appearance in our world *out of the sea* at Rome, ver. 1, in a time of great tumult amongst the nations of the earth; which was, in a great measure, occasioned by the bloody manner in which the emperor Phocas gained, and administered the affairs of, the empire.

2. His *character.* As the Heathen Roman empire was diverse from the other beasts, and, having all the horrors of the three former concentred in itself, had no immediate hieroglyphic of its own, except its iron teeth, *Dan.* vii. 7; so the holy Ghost finds, no one hieroglyphic which could perfectly represent this beast: It had indeed the *mouth of a lion,* like the first Babylonian beast; and the *Feet of a bear,* like the second, or Persian empire; but upon the whole it most resembled the third, the Grecian empire, *Dan.* vii. 3—6; being *like a leopard,* with a *lion's mouth,* and a *bear's feet.*

Ver. 2. *And the dragon gave him his power, and his throne, and great authority;* that is, (1.) The devil, chap. xii. 9, who had reigned over Pagan Rome; and afterwards in the times of christianity, diffused the spirit of popery there, long before the Pope or the beast arose, 2 *Thess.* ii. 7; finding

things

things now more matured to his own hopes, when
this church and state monster arose, charmed with
his appearance, he came nigh to him A. D. 756,
and gave *him*, not the power and authority of another, but *his* own *power, and his throne, and great
authority*; see chap. xi. 2 : Therefore we do not
wonder to find, even in the churches in Rome
christian, the same kind of *incense, holy water,
worshipping of images, candles burning*, and *votive
gifts* as debased Rome heathen ; to say nothing
of their *images* of saints placed *on the roads*, of
their *crucifixes, holy days, processions, flagellants, &c.
&c.* See Dr. *Middleton's letter from Rome*. From
all which it appears that this grant from the devil
to the beast was subject to that condition of his
worshipping him, which our Lord had treated with
such infinite abhorrence, *Mat.* iv. 8—10; but to
which this pretended successor of St. Peter has
no objection, provided he can have his seven *heads*
or hills adorned with the *name of blasphemy*, ver. 1.
(2.) After A. D. 1866, when the second beast
arises *speaking as a dragon*, ver. 11, having *two
little horns* or kingdoms of his own, he will lay
them down at the feet of the beast ; and *give him*
that *power, throne*, and *authority* which himself
possesses ; which will both enable the beast to
take the devil's own name, style and title *a dragon*, and to speak and act accordingly, chap. xii.
3, 9; whilst his wretched votaries both worship
the dragon, who renewed this grant to him by the
second beast, and *worship the beast* himself, ver. 4.

Ver. 5, 6. *And* by means of this great power
which he had received, *there was given unto him a
mouth speaking great things and blasphemies :* And
having a mouth according to his own heart, he
opened it to blasphemy against God, even *to blafpheme his name ;* that is, his titles, attributes, or-

dinances

dinances, words and works: He blafphemes *his tabernacle* too, by anathematizing the true fervants of God, under the name of Hereticks and Schifmaticks; *and them that dwell in heaven*, both faints and angels; mifreprefenting their words and works, *Rom.* iii. 8. 1 *Cor.* iv. 13. and x. 30. 1 *Tim.* i. 20. 1 *Pet.* iv. 4. *Jude* 8. Gr. to oppofe their defigns; yet paying them undue honours, *Col.* ii. 8, 18; and at the fame time debafing their names with fabulous legends and lying miracles. And no wonder when he has opened his mouth *to blafphemy* againft God himfelf, Father, Son, and holy Ghoft; oppofing his worfhip, and arrogating to himfelf divine honours. But *words* are not all; let us fee,

3. His *works*, ver. 4, 5, 7, 8. *Power was given him* ποιησαι *to* practife and *prevail*, during his whole 1260 years; for it was *given him to make war with the faints, and overcome them*, as to this world, in which view only faints can be overcome: He alfo engages fome to worfhip him out of love, and others out of fear; the former even *worfhipped the dragon*, the devil, *who had*, mediately and immediately, *given* this *power to the beaft*; and both together *worfhipped the beaft, faying, Who is like the beaft? who is able to make war with him?* For unhappily he is the greateft being with whom they are acquainted; fee 2 *Kings* iii. 13, 14. 1 *Cor.* xv. 34.

Obferve, it is fix times faid that this *power was given* the beaft: The dragon's hand in it is afferted twice, ver. 2, 4; for after the devil has given him his power A. D. 756, he will renew the grant, and enlarge it by an acceffion of new power to the papal caufe, by the hands of the fecond beaft, who *fpeaks as a dragon.* Afterwards it is four times mentioned in general terms, that this *power was given him*, ver. 5, 7. As men had a hand in it, it, the four times may exprefs the confent of the four quarters of the world to it ; fee ver. 7, 8, or of the remnant of thofe *four horns,* the Baby-lonian, Perfian, Grecian and Roman empires which had *fcattered Judah and Ifrael,* Zech. i. 18—21 ; and whofe *lives* had been *prolonged for a feafon and time,* after their *dominion* was *taken away,* Dan. vii. 12 : But as it was difpofed by the uner-ring counfel of the Divine will, this repetition may inform us, that this power was given him by the Father, Son and holy Spirit, and by the God-man Mediator, to whom all judgment is committed : And if men will accept of a commiffion from the devil, it is juft in God judicially to allow them opportunities and abilities to execute it. But God's hand in this affair is a filencing thought to all our murmurings ; even while *his way* is in this Roman *fea,* and *his paths in* thefe *mighty* devour-ing *waters, Pfal.* lxxvii. 19.

4. The *time* of his continuance, ver. 5. *Autho-rity was given him to prevail,* in this war, *forty-two months,* that is 1260 years ; yet thefe times are not *days* to him but *months,* or like *moon*-light nights, in which to fport or fleep ; the holy city being trodden under feet the greateft part of this time, and the woman in the wildernefs through the whole of it ; fee chap. xi. 2. and xii. 6, 14. Thefe 1260 years, reckoned from A. D. 756 when the pope became a beaft, will end A. D. 2016 : But as there are 238 years of this time to come, from this year 1778, fo two other things are faid of the beaft, which are not yet accomplifhed ; viz, (1.) Something awful await him, which is taken no-tice of early in this account of him, in order to keep up the fpirits of good men, ver. 3. *And I faw one of his heads as it were wounded to death ; and his deadly wound was healed : And the whol: world wondered after the beaft.* His feven heads are

M 4

are *seven hills* on which the woman sitteth, and
seven kings or forms of government, chap. xvii. 9,
10. *Dan.* vii. 6. These *kings* might be called *his
heads*, as they were his predecessors, as he derives
glory from them all, and as his government par-
takes more or less of the peculiarities of each.
These Heathen heads had all of them the *name of
blasphemy* upon them, though not comparable to
himself, ver. 1 ; and one of these ; viz, the last
received such a wound with the sword, that it was
not probable that it should ever have had such an
eighth head as the pope is to succeed the *duke of
Rome*, in such pomp and power as he possesses—
But taking the word *head* in the other sense for a
hill, though one of the seven hills on which that
city stands cannot be really, yet it will hereafter
be *as it were, wounded by the sword*, when it is
taken out of the hands of the pope, by some enraged power : And such an event will seem to be
a *deadly wound* to *the beast* ver. 12, 14 ; from
which his recovery will for a time seem doubtful.

Without pretending to know certainly *when*, or
by whom, this wound will be given the beast, I
incline to believe it will be inflicted upon him by
the state of Rome itself ; for as his ten horns are
to *hate the whore*, chap. xvii. 16, I am unwilling
to suppose that the most injured of the ten, should
have no hand in executing the vengeance written : But after the vials are poured out, whilst the
other horns are making her feel their honourable
resentment, Rome will probably be a lake of
fire, chap. xix. 3 ; therefore if ever this state takes
vengeance, it must be either now, or when the
wine-press is trodden without the city ; see xiv. 20.
If this is the event intended in chap. xi. 13 ; if
the *earthquake* there spoken of represents a civil
commotion, as in chap. vi. 12, in which a *tenth
part*

part of the inhabitants of Rome will be slain, then
the time of this event must be A. D. 1866: But
as the similar phrase, chap. xvi. 19, *The cities of
the nations fell*, rather favours the literal sense of
the word *earthquake* in chap. xi. 13, we are left
uncertain when this disaster will befal the beast.
But if the angel flying through heaven with this
cry, *The hour of his judgment is come*, chap. **xiv. 7,**
refers to this event; this wound must be given
him soon after the resurrection of the witnesses,
near the beginning of this trumpet: And if his
wound is not healed before, it will be compleatly
healed by the second beast by A. D. 1886; then
will those words be fulfilled, *The whole world wondered after the beast*; which leads me to consider—
(2.) His glory after this, ver. 7, 8. *Power was given
him over every tribe, tongue and nation.* Observe,
pomp and universality are the characters of the
beast's, not of Christ's, kingdom: But these and
similar phrases, describe such an extent of influence as the beast has never yet obtained, but will
hereafter; see chap. v. 9. vii. 9. and xi. 9. Yet,
as if this had not sufficiently informed us of his
shameful glory, it is added, *All that dwell upon the
earth* east and west *shall* worship him, except the
elect who shall not be so deceived, *Matt.* xxiv. 24;
whose peculiar blessedness it is, that their *names
are written in the book of life of the Lamb*, who was
slain, in types and prophecies, *from the foundation
of the world:* And this his unbounded influence,
will take place, when the second beast arises to
exert his utmost power for his support.

But come and see what will be the end of this
beast, and of all such as he is, ver. 10. *If any one*
inslaves the souls or bodies of others, and *leads*
them into *captivity*, he is himself a slave, and
shall be further inslaved, and *go into captivity*,
under the power of satan; fastening on the chains
of

of others, he rivets on his own; fee *Matt*. vii. 2—
He that killeth any, and efpecially the faints, *with
the fword, muft be flain with the fword*; and this
will be the end of the beaft, as we fhall fee chap.
xiv. 20, and chaps. xviii. and xix.

Two things are further added to the account of
this beaft; viz, ver. 10. *Here is the patience and the
faith of the faints!* which were never fo glorioufly
difplayed fince the world began, as in the 1260
years of this beaft; fee chap. xiv. 12. *Heb*. vi. 12.
' Under heavy preffures, without faith, patience
' could not hold out : And under lively views of
' the future glory, without patience, faith could
' not hold in:' Faith fupports patience; and
patience prepares the foul for the further exercife
of faith, for God's glory and our own falvation.—
Again, ver. 9. *If any one hath an ear, let him hear*;
fee *Matt*. xi. 15. and xiii. 9, 43. At the clofe of the
epiftles to the feven churches in Afia, *Rev*. ii. and
iii. chapters, it is added to thefe words, *What the
fpirit faith unto the churches*; but thefe words are
addreffed to all, whether in or out of the church—
How dare then the fervants of the beaft to keep
God's word from the laity! And how can Proteftants fatisfy themfelves in their criminal inat-
tention to this part of God's revealed will? Do
they not pleafe the beaft by it?—But has not
God commanded, *In underftanding be ye not children*,
but men or *perfect?* 1 *Cor*. xiv. 20. Gr. Hear therefore I befeech you, that you may know what human nature is, even when it is externally chriftianized! What villainies have been, and will
yet be mafked under the name of Jefus! And
what abominations may be expected when ecclefiaftical men affect a monopoly of civil and facred
honours! Hear, that you may be preferved from
the damning arts of popery; and fee, with your
own eyes, how providence and grace will protect
the

the faints, when earth and hell are in arms againſt them—Hear for Chriſt's fake; for fee! a

II. Beaſt ariſes, ver. 11—18. The word θηριον *a wild beaſt*, muſt neceſſarily have the ſame ſenſe, ver. 11, as in ver. 1, and in the prophecy of Daniel; and ſignify an independent, idolatrous, perſecuting power: Therefore it cannot be underſtood of any of the religious orders among the Papiſts, or of eccleſiaſtical perſons now amongſt them, who are inveſted with temporal authority; who are neither *another*, nor a *beaſt*, being the creatures, members and dependents of the firſt beaſt. Nor can this ſecond beaſt, be nominally of any other religion than the Chriſtian; becauſe his whole authority and influence will be employed for the honour of the firſt beaſt. Let us then, as in the former, attempt to trace his *origin, characters, operations,* and *times.*

1. His *origin*, ver. 11. *And I beheld another wild beaſt riſing up out of the earth.* As the *ſea* out of which the firſt beaſt aroſe, ver. 1, is to be underſtood both literally and metaphorically; for our apoſtle ſays, that he ſtood *upon the ſand of the ſea,* and ſaw it *riſe out of* it; ſo the *earth* as oppoſed to it, is no doubt to be taken both ways; and probably the ſecond beaſt will ſpring up gradually and unobſerved, as a Papal beaſt, out of ſome inland country; as the other roſe out of the ſea at Rome.

2. His *character*, ver. 11. *He had two horns like a Lamb,* or like the Lamb, Chriſt: Theſe are two kingdoms, *Dan.* vii. 24. and viii. 3, 20. But though his horns are like thoſe of a gentle Lamb, his voice will give the lye to their inſidious appearance, when he *ſpeaks like the dragon* we heard of in the laſt chapter; for in him diſſimulation and cruelty will be carried to the utmoſt height they will ever attain on earth; whilſt he *works*

miracles

miracles before the other beaſt, with which he will amazingly *deceive them who dwell on the earth,* even all that receive the mark of the beaſt, and worſhip his image, ver. 14, 16. But this leads me,

3. To his *works,* which are two-fold, ver. 12— 17; for firſt as a beaſt, *he exerciſes* all that *authority* which the firſt beaſt had ever aſſumed over the ſouls and bodies of men *before him;* and *makes the earth* in general, *and them that dwell therein to worſhip the* firſt *beaſt, whoſe deadly wound was* ſo recently healed, about the time of this beaſt's riſing. Beſides this, *he doth great* ſigns and *wonders;* for the holy Ghoſt had told us, that his coming would be *after the working of ſatan, with all power, and ſigns, and lying wonders; with all deceivableneſs of unrighteouſneſs in them that periſh,* 2 *Theſſ.* ii. 9, 10. Accordingly, that he may not ſeem to come behind Elijah in power with God, *He maketh fire to come down from heaven to earth before men;* as if to teſtify God's diſpleaſure againſt thoſe who oppoſe his infernal deſigns, 2 *Kings* i. 10—12. But whatever pretended miracles are wrought in ſupport of falſe doctrines and worſhip, they muſt be from the devil; ſee *Deut.* xiii. 1—3. However, having forged the broad ſeal of heaven, his end is anſwered, *he deceives them that dwell on the earth,* or earthly minded creatures, *by thoſe miracles which he hath power to do;* not in the ſight of God, or for his praiſe, but *in the ſight of the beaſt;* by theſe miracles, *ſaying to them that dwell upon the earth, that they ſhould make an image to the beaſt, which had* ſo lately *a wound by the ſword, and did live,* ver. 14.

We have heard that heaven will open under this trumpet, chap. xi. 15, 19, therefore hell will certainly ſtrive to open; for the laſt years of the beaſt will be buſy years to the devil, before he is
confined

confined to the bottomless pit : And as in this period the faints will have *the name of God in their foreheads*, chap. **xiv. 1**, fo this beaft *causeth all* of **every** rank and condition, *fmall and great, rich and poor, bond and free to receive a mark on their right hand*, the hand of action and of honour ; *or on their foreheads*; as flaves wore their mafters marks, and the votaries of Heathen idols had fome impreffion of their Gods on their flefh, ver. 16.

In thefe days there will be upon *the bells of the horfes*, as upon Aaron's mitre, *Holinefs to the Lord*; yea, *every pot in Jerufalem and Judah, fhall be Holinefs to the Lord of hofts*, Exod. xxviii. 36. Zech. xiv. 20, 21. On the contrary, befides his *mark*, his *name*, or the *number of his name*, which the votaries of the beaft muft receive, he will caufe them to have *an image* or picture of the beaft in their houfes, or on their furniture and the veffels they ufe ; and command that a ftatue of the beaft fhall be fet up in every town, and perhaps at the corner of every ftreet ; and compel every wretched paffenger to pay homage to it, ver. 14, 17. Yea he will *have power to give fpirit to the image of the beaft* ; thus imitating, in order that he may infult, him who only *giveth breath to the people upon earth, and fpirit to them that walk therein*, Ifa. xlii. 5 : *That the image of the beaft might* even *fpeak*; either as the Heathen oracles ufed to do, by the lying artifice of the priefts ; or by the power its votaries have to reward, or revenge what is done to this image : *And caufe that as many as would not worfhip the image of the beaft fhould be flain* ; for now again is their *hour*, and the *power of darknefs*. Obferve, this image breathes nothing but death ; temporal death to its defpifers, but eternal death to its admirers, ver. 16. Yet the beaft prevails fo far, that *no man may buy or fell, except he who has the mark, or the name of the beaft, beaſt, or the number of his name,* ver. 17. The firſt beaſt had iſſued ſuch an order ; but his authority was chiefly confined to ſome parts of Europe ; but now the people of *every tribe, tongue, and nation,* ver. 7, are forbidden to exerciſe their trades, or enjoy the comforts of life, except under an avowed ſubjection to theſe two beaſts ; who are in fact one in their operations and deſigns.

This ſecond beaſt may perhaps be the perſon who uſed to be called the Mahometan chief, who will probably become a Papal Chriſtian ſoon after the firſt beaſt has ſlain the eaſtern witneſs, the Greek church ; for, (1.) I can ſee no other method by which the beaſt can be ſo likely to attain that extent of influence and authority *over all kindreds, tongues, and nations,* which he is to poſſeſs, ver. 7, 8, 12—17. (2.) It is ſaid of the grand Turk, *Dan.* xi. 44. *He ſhall go forth with great fury to deſtroy, and anathematize many,* Heb. This phraſe deſcribes a religious war, which he will make between A. D. 1866 and 2016, probably under the ſixth vial, A. D. 1941 ; ſee chap. xiv. 5. and xvi. 12—16 : And his *anathematizing* many, ſeems to intimate that he will become a Chriſtian before that time ; for he certainly will not embrace the Jewiſh religion ; ſee *Godwyn's Moſes and Aaron,* page 201. (3.) Every character of this ſecond beaſt ſuits the Mahometan chief : He is called a *falſe prophet,* chap. xvi. 13. xix. 20. and xx. 10, which is the name by which Mahomet is known in every part of the Chriſtian world, eaſt and weſt. True, he wrought no miracles whilſt he was a Mahometan ; but it has been proved that Mahometaniſm will expire by the year 1866 ; ſee chap. xi. 3 : And after that year we read here of a beaſt, *a falſe prophet* who wrought *miracles before the firſt beaſt* ; by which he ſo far tricked men out of their reaſon that, like beaſts,

they

they tamely fubmitted to receive any mark he pleafed : And who can this be but the Mahometan chief, turned a Popifh Chriftian, and amufing himfelf with that fuppofed miraculous power, by which Rome had long infulted the underftandings of deluded Europeans ? His defcription alfo as a beaft agrees to Mahomet, who literally *came up out of the earth*, ver. 11, when he left his cave near Mecca, which was in the inland part of Arabia ; fo that the fecond beaft, both literally and metaphorically, rofe *out of the earth*, as the firft rofe *out of the fea*—And *he had two horns* or kingdoms ; and if thefe are fecular, they probably refer to the two kingdoms of Arabia and Syria, which Mahomet perfonally conquered : And, though it is well known the Turks were never able to reduce Ifhmael's defcendents in Arabia into a ftate of fubjection, nor will they be long fubject to any foreign power whatever ; yet by the year 1866 the grand Turk's dominions may be reduced to two little inland horns or kingdoms, though we know not which they will be.

But as the beaft and the Mahometan chief have always agreed in this, to unite in themfelves an abfolute fecular and fpiritual power ; fo thefe two horns may poffibly refer to the temporal and fpiritual government which the fecond beaft will continue to claim ; for he *exercifes all the power of the firft beaft before him*. Accordingly it is faid of thefe his *two horns*, that they were *like thofe of a Lamb*, or of *the Lamb* Chrift ; whofe temporal and fpiritual government are both of them reprefented by his *horns*, chap. v. 6. *Hab.* iii. 4. *And he fpake as a dragon* ; and if literal dragons exift now any where they originated from the eaft ; which inclines us the more to underftand this fecond beaft of the Mahometan chief. The following accounts reprefent him as powerful, yet meanly
giving

giving up all his glory to the firſt beaſt; *before whom* he is contented to ſtand propheſying, charmed with that pretended power of working miracles, with which his new religion has furniſhed him. And probably he will be ſo degraded in the eaſt before A. D. 1866, as may heartily incline him to change his ſituation, and come and work miracles before the firſt beaſt at Rome. Thus Popery will ſurvive Mahometaniſm; and appear in the end to have been a more maſterly engine of the devils kingdom, than ever that had been. But we are yet to conſider,

4. The *times* of this beaſt; of which nothing being ſaid, we are naturally led, with all others, to look for him in the 1260 years of the firſt beaſt; and what has been already offered, directs us in what part of that time to expect his advent. As nothing is ſaid of Mahometaniſm in this prophecy after A. D. 1866, probably the Mahometans will become Papiſts about that time, and join the ſtandard of that power which had ſlain for them the Greek church. And as Mahomet began to call himſelf the apoſtle of God A. D. 612; as the Mahometans date their hegyra from A. D. 622, when he fled from Mecca; and the ſun in the firmament gave notice of that infernal abomination upon earth, by withdrawing much of its light A. D. 626; ſo 1260 years after theſe different times, probably the grand Turk will advance towards the height of his papal power. If he is a temporal prince, with two horns or kingdoms at A. D. 1866, by A. D. 1872, he may perhaps call himſelf an apoſtle of Chriſt; enter upon his full reign temporal and ſpiritual A. D. 1882; and go to work miracles before the beaſt at Rome A. D. 1886; ſee chap. ix. 5, 10. And from this time to A. D. 1936, when I expect the firſt of the vials to be poured out, will probably

be

be the darkest fifty years the world ever faw:
But for the elect's fake those days will be shorten-
ed. And though this ignoble pair of brothers
will reign together from the above time to A. D.
2016, yet the vials will reduce them to a state of
great imbecillity; and the last of them, however
filently it may fall upon *the air*, in the calm ear
of reflection and thought, will invite exulting nature to attend their funeral.

But though fuch a particular notice is here
given us of this fecond beast, it was not neceffary
that the prophet Daniel should have any account
of him, as he only rifes for the fupport and honour of the first beast in his last times.

It is added, ver. 18. *Here is wifdom*; for he is
divinely wife who can detect and guard against the
fpirit of popery, in every form, in himfelf and
others: *Let him that hath* a mind or *underftanding
count the number of the beeft*. The word ψηφιςω
fignifies to *count* the number of white or black
ftones, by which votes had been given in any
affair, *Rev.* ii. 17; fo if we add the numeral figni-
fication of one letter of his name to another, we
shall find the number of the beast; *for it is the
number of a man*; therefore I do not feek the number in thofe three Greek words Ξυλον ςαυρου χριςου
the wood of the crofs of Chrift; though it cannot
be improper for Proteftants or Papifts to obferve,
that the initials of thofe words give us the number
666. But of what *man* is it *the number?* I anfwer,
It cannot hurt the French king, who is the Pope's
first-born, to obferve that *Ludovicus* or Lewis will
give us the above number; yet to find the perfon whom the holy Ghoft immediately intends,
we muft look for a man, who may be denominated from the country where the beaft reigns,
whofe capital city is fo vifibly pointed out in this
prophecy, chap. xvii. 18; that is reckoned by

numeral

numeral Letters, as the Greeks and Hebrews
ufed to count the names of their idols, or of famous perfons amongft them.   Iræneus therefore juftly judged that the name muft be Λατεινος

Λ	30
α	1
τ	300
ε	5
ι	10
ν	50
ο	70
ς	200
	666

the Latin man emphatically fo called ; and the
Hebrew word Romiith, *a Roman*, gives us exactly
the fame number; viz, 666: And about that
year the Latin fervice began.   Chrift's accufation
was *written in Latin, Greek, and Hebrew* letters,
Luke xxiii. 38 : And though we are not to expect to find the number of the beaft in the Roman word *Lateinos*, (for the Latins ufed but few
of their letters as numerals,) yet this word being
originally written the fame way in Latin and
Greek, the number of the beaft is virtually announced in all thefe three languages; though it
is really defcribed only in the two laft of them ;
in which this way of numbering by letters was fo
commonly ufed.   But whilft the Roman word
Lateinos (for fo it was anciently fpelt) teaches us
that he will fpiritually tyrannize by means of his
Latin fervice, his name thus publifhed in Greek
and Hebrew, ftrengthens our affurance, that as
he will practife his tyranny upon the weftern
churches, who are one of the witneffes, fo alfo
upon the other of them the Greek church.

The Jews alfo, who ufed to number by alphabeti-
cal letters as well as the Greeks, muft feel his iron
teeth

teeth when they are brought home to their own
land; fee chap. xiv. 1—5. *And his number is six
hundred sixty six:* The firft beaft no doubt is
chiefly intended, who will continue the whole
1260 years; and who is, in every fenfe of the
word *Lateinos,* a Latin man, a man of Italy, and
a Heathen man, notwithftanding his vain pretenfions to Chriftianity; yet the word, and the
number agrees to both thefe beafts, who are fo
one, that one word will defcribe them both; for
their religion and language being the fame, they
will latinize and tyrannize together. At the fame
time, as their greateft exploits againft the Jews
and Greeks, will fall in the fhort time of the fecond beaft, their common number, which is defcribed in the numeral letters of thofe two languages, is given us in his time.

Thus in various ways the Lord has defcribed
thefe two beafts, that the little flock of Jefus may
know from whom to flee. But obferve, Though
the beaft was a *ferpent* from the beginning, and
exprefsly fo called through the whole of his 1260
years chap. xii. 14, yet he will not be a *dragon*
till A. D 1866, ver. 3. of that chapter; where
however, the regular feries of the times of the feventh trumpet, required that he fhould be defcribed as a *dragon,* before he is defcribed at full
length as a beaft in this chapter; in which all the
abominations of his character are gathered into
one point of view, as they will be feverally difplayed in the times of thefe two laft trumpets—But
whilft chriftianized men are appointing the
fheep of Jefus for the flaughter, fee! their great
Shepherd advances! JEHOVAH is his name! And
his abounding grace to Jews and Gentiles, which
is fo loudly announced in the next chapter, will
fill my reader's heart with joy, if it is at all attuned to celeftial ftrains of love and praife.

CHAP.

C H A P. XIV. 1—5.

1. AND I looked, and behold, a Lamb
standing on the mount *called* Sion;
and with him a hundred and forty-four
thousand, having the name of his Father
written on their foreheads.

2. And I heard a voice out of heaven, as
the voice of many waters, and as the voice
of great thunder; and I heard the voice of
harpers, playing on their harps.

3. And they sung, as it were, a new
song before the throne, and before the four
living creatures and the elders : And no one
could learn the song, but only the hundred
and forty-four thousand, who are redeemed
out of the earth.

4. These are they who had not been defiled with women, for they are virgins; these
are they who follow the Lamb whithersoever he goeth : These were redeemed from
among men, the *holy* first-fruits to God, and
to the Lamb.

5. And in their mouth was found no
guile; for they are without blame before
the throne of God.

Under this trumpet we have already heard of
the *four and twenty elders*, who are the heads of
the Jewish and Christian church, see chap. iv. 4;
and

2

and of the temple opened in heaven, chap. xi. 16, 19 : And I cannot but confider thefe words as an account of the Jews return to their own land ; the proofs of which will open in the words them-felves : For fays our apoftle, ver. 1, after I had feen the former vifion, ftruck with horror at the depredations of the two beafts, *I looked* round, and lo! a moft relieving fight met my view ; for the Lord Jefus Chrift, as *a Lamb* who had made atonement with his blood, chap. v. 5, 6, *ftood on the mount Sion;* which fhould feem to be taken literally here, as fuch things are faid of it, ver. 3, 4, as do not agree to the ftate and circum-ftances of the church of God in general : And we know that *all Ifrael fhall be faved*; *as it is written, There fhall come out of Sion the Deliverer, and fhall turn away ungodlinefs from Jacob,* Rom. xi. 26.

Yet our Lord will no more *come* corporally to *mount Sion,* than he will literally *ftand* there *as a Lamb* ; for the heavens muft *receive him* till the times of the *regulation of all things* ; fee *Doddridge* on *Acts* iii. 21.——*And with him a hundred and forty four thoufand* ; the fame number as the Jewifh converts in the time of Conftantine the Great, in the fourth century, chap. vii. 3——8 : And it is the more reafonable to underftand this of the fame people, as both *here* and *there* they are contra-diftinguifhed from the converted Gentiles, who were *there* faid to ftand before *the thorne and be- fore the Lamb,* ver. 9, as the bleffed company *here* ftand with him on mount Sion : *Having his Fa- ther's name written in their foreheads,* to intimate the notoriety of their refolute and avowed fub-jection to him. Their anceftors had been *fealed in their foreheads,* chap. vii. 3 ; but, like epiftles of Chrift lying wide open, thefe carry his Father's name upon their foreheads ; in oppofition to the idolaters of that age who have the *mark, the name,*

of

or *the number* of the beast on their *right hands,*
where they might conceal it, or on *their fore-*
heads where they could not, chap. xiii. 16, 17.

2. *And I heard a voice from* that *heaven* the
church, loud and solemn *as the voice of many*
waters, or people, chap. xvii. 15; who were gathered together to gaze upon this blessed phæno-
menon in the world, the return of the Jews to
their own land; for *the receiving of them will be as*
life from the dead to the church, *Rom.* xi. 15:
And their settlement in Canaan will be as the return of Lazarus, and the widow of Nain's son
to their own habitations, out of which they had
been carried dead—*And as the voice of a great*
thunder ; see *Exod.* xix. 16; for this is a kind of
new dispensation of divine authority and grace,
which fills the believing nations with transporting joy—*And I heard the voice of harpers playing*
on their harps; an instrument of Jewish worship
with which the four animals, and the four and
twenty elders praised God, when our Lord took
the sealed book into his hands, chap. v. 8. *Psal.*
lxxxi. 2—5.

3. And this exulting croud of Abraham's descendents *sung,* not really but, *as it were a* NEW *song;*
for though their renowned progenitors had believed and gloried in a Messiah to come, their
nation had shamefully slighted him for about
1500 years: However, recovered by his grace,
they now *sing before the throne, and before the liv-*
ing creatures, and the elders : But there were such
peculiar strains in *that song* that *no one could learn it,*
but only the 144,000 *who were redeemed from the*
earth, that is, from the different countries in
which they had been dispersed; for converted
Jews will have a song peculiar to themselves, in
which the vaster crouds of gentile converts cannot

not join, as it is predicted, *Jer.* xvi. 14. 15, and
xxiii. 7, 8.

4. *These are they who had not been defiled with
women,* either in corporal, or in the spiritual un-
cleanness of indulged idolatry ; *for they are virgins,* returned to that blessed Husband to whom
their ancestors had been so long ago espoused,
Hos. ii. 7 : And whatever adulterous ideas had
once debased their fathers, who had been converted in the different countries where they lived,
A. D. 1816 (see chap. xi. 16, and a remark on
Dan. viii. 13, 14. at p. 193) and whom grace had
brought back again to virgin purity, as the woman of Samaria, *John* iv. 29; these their more
favoured descendents, to whom the honour of
returning to their own land is indulged, had never *been defiled with women—These are they who*
know the power and grace of *the Lamb* so well;
and have such an affection to, and confidence in
him, that they chearfully *follow* him, even through
giants, terrors, and temptations, to the land
which the Lord gave their fathers for an everlasting possession, *whithersoever he goeth*; as their
ancestors in the wilderness, going to Canaan,
never refused to follow the leading pillar of cloud
and fire ; which was long afterwards remembered
to their honour, *Jer.* ii. 2—*These were redeemed,*
with a strong hand and out-stretched arm, out of
the nations *from among men,* being *the first fruits*
(blest earnest of a vaster harvest of their own nation at hand ! And as such they are presented) *to
God and to the Lamb,* whom they declare to be
their God; for he is the *Lord* and *God* of every
believer, *John* xx. 28.

5. *And in their mouth was found no guile*; for
these ransomed of the Lord do not compass him
about with lies, as many of their fathers had done :
And as the Jewish first-fruits were the most ex-

cellent

cellent in their kind, so these happy persons, like the sacrifices chosen out of the fold or the stall, *were without* blame or *blemish* αμωμοι, *before the throne of God*'s grace here; as they shall soon be *without spot or wrinkle, or any such thing* in the presence of his glory above, *Eph.* v. 27; for grace and glory differ only in degrees.

Thus honoured inwardly and outwardly will be the descendents of that long, and now again favoured people: and the words *virgins* and *first-fruits*, may perhaps intimate, that the young among them will shew an exemplary zeal to return to their own land.

Now probably the time is come for those words to be fulfilled, *Dan.* xi. 44; where, speaking of the grand Turk, it is said, *Tidings out of the east,* either of the Persians coming against him, or of the Jews returning from thence to their own land; *and out of the north*, of the assistance which Russia gives them towards their settling there, *troubled him*; *therefore he shall go forth with great fury*, particularly under the sixth vial, *to destroy and anathematize many*, Heb. after the manner of the beast; whose religion the Turks will probably imbrace after the beast has slain the Greek church; see p. 174.

Many things incline me to expect this long-predicted event about A. D. 1866; not sooner, because the seventh trumpet will not be sounded till then, or the kingdoms of this world fall into the extended arms of Immanuel, chap. xi. 15: And as the account of their return falls under this trumpet, it is not reasonable to expect it before that sounds; unless any previous intimations had been given of that event under the sixth trumpet; as there were implicitly of the woman's flying into the wilderness, and explicitly of the beast; the accounts of both of which were begun
under

under the former, and ended under this trumpet; see chap. xi. xii. and xiii: But, nothing of
this nature occurring with respect to the Jews
return, I cannot expect it before A. D. 1866—
But it is not probable that it should be deferred
beyond that year; (1.) Because their conversion
will be begun before that time; for at the founding of this trumpet the four and twenty elders,
who are the heads of the Jewish and Christian
church, chap. iv. 4, are before God, chap. xi. 16:
And the number is never more than twelve when
the tribes of Israel, or the apostles of the Lamb
are spoken of distinctly and separately; see chap.
xii. 1. and xxi. 12, 14, 21. And if they return to
God fifty years before the end of the sixth trumpet,
this will prepare for their return to their own land
by the time this trumpet founds.

(2.) As this trumpet begins differently from
any of the preceding; viz, with an account of
the triumphs of Christ's kingdom in the world,
chap. xi. 15; so, as soon as the holy Ghost has
finished, chap. xii. and xiii, what he had begun to
say under the preceding trumpet of the woman's
flight from the beast, he resumes the same subject
with which this trumpet began, by giving us this
account of the Jews return. And though their
return, and the conversion of the Gentiles, will
be nearly co-temporary events, yet the favour
shewn to the former, is both here and in Constantine's time, spoken of before that indulged to the
latter; see chap. vii. 8, 9; and ver. 6, &c. of
this chapter; which inclines me to place this
event at, or near the beginning of this trumpet;
for the holy Ghost has spoken of it before all those
great events which are predicted from ver. 6. of
this chapter to the end of chap. xixth: Therefore it must not only precede the general conversion of the Gentiles, but the pouring out of the
vials,

vials, and the destruction of the two beasts; with whom the Jews, as well as Gentiles, will be called to struggle through the whole time of the second beast, that is, from soon after A. D. 1866 to 2016: But they will receive the storm near their Redeemer's side, and as *before the throne of God,* against whom it is raised, ver. 1, 5. (3.) When the sixth trumpet sounded, the Gentiles were to tread the *holy city* Jerusalem *under feet* for no longer time than the 1260 years of *that* trumpet; which coincided with the times of the two witnesses, and which it has been already proved will end at A. D. 1866; see chap. xi. 2, 3 : Therefore the Jews must return to their own land about that year.

If we should find that the prophecies of Daniel point out the same time for their return to Judea, the conviction will be the more clear and satisfying. Observe therefore, As the atonement of Christ is the grand hinge of every gospel hope, so the daily sacrifice which typified it, is mentioned in three of the four visions which were given that prophet; and the time of its ceasing is given us in most of them. It ceased

By Manasseh	684	years before
By Nebuchadnezzar	584	Christ's Time.
By Antiochus Epiphanes	168	

And finally by the Romans A. D. 70. We read of its ceasing four times in Daniel's prophecy, by means, or on account of the *transgression,* or *abomination of desolation*; viz, chap. viii. .13, 14. ix. 27. xi. 31, and xii. 11 : And the chief difficulty is, to determine to which ceasing of the sacrifice each phrase refers, and in ascertaining the time of it. If the holy Ghost takes no notice in this prophecy, of any one of these times of its ceasing, it will probably be that which Antiochus Epiphanes occasioned; because it continued at the furthest but three years and ten days, 1 *Macc.*
i. 54,

i. 54, 59, and iv. 52—54. But whatever may be said of its ceasing by Manasseh (whose abominations laid a dreadful foundation for the destruction of the Jewish nation, 2 *Kings* xxi. 4, 5. and xxiv. 4;) to have judged before hand, we should certainly expect that some notice should be taken of its ceasing by the Babylonians; and especially of its final conclusion by the Romans: And it is so; for our Lord has explained, *Dan.* ix. 27, of the final ceasing of the Jewish sacrifice by means of Titus, which took place A. D. 70; see *Matt.* xxiv. 15. And the same event seems to be referred to *Dan.* xi. 31; where, having spoken of *the ships of Chittim*, or the Roman power, (see bishop Newton on prophecy, vol. 1. page 147—151) which should come against Antiochus Epiphanes, who reigned in the *latter time* of the Grecian empire, *Dan.* viii. 23, 168 years before Christ's time, ver. 30; it is said ver. 31, ממנו *after him* (so Sir Isaac Newton reads it,) *arms*, or the Roman power *shall stand up; and they shall pollute the sanctuary of strength; and they shall take away the daily sacrifice; and place the abomination that maketh desolate* on the once holy ground.

Antiochus indeed had *indignation against the holy covenant* and *intelligence* with those profligate Jews *who forsook* it, as it is mentioned, ver. 30; and forbad the offering of burnt-offerings and sacrifices in the temple, 1 *Macc.* i. 11—15, and 45—54; But his profanation of the temple was but a prelude to the greater devastation of the Romans, who came against him, ver. 31, took away the *daily sacrifice* A. D. 70; and at A. D. 132 erected a temple to Jupiter Capitolinus where the temple of God had stood.

And it is the more probable that ver. 31 speaks of the Romans, because ver. 32—35 contain such an exact description of the state of the Christian world, for the first five or six centuries, viz, *And such*

such profeſſing Chriſtians *who do wickedly againſt* that *covenant* of God, which they vainly pretend to take hold of, *ſhall He,* the Roman, *corrupt by flattery;* but *the people who* really *know their God ſhall be ſtrong, and do* ſuch *exploits* as will amaze the empire. *And they that underſtand among the people, ſhall inſtruct many,* by their activity in ſpreading the goſpel, and by their holy lives; *yet,* beneficent as they are to human nature, *they ſhall fall by the ſword, and by flame, by captivity and by ſpoil* in the ten Heathen perſecutions; in which they will however, be more than conquerors over death in its moſt frightful forms. *And when they ſhall fall* in Dioclefian's ten years perſecution, *they ſhall be holpen with a little help* by Conſtantine the Great, who will eſtabliſh Chriſtianity in the empire; but then *many ſhall cleave to them with flatteries :* And afterwards *ſome of them of underſtanding ſhall fall* by the Arian perſecutions, *to try them, and to purge them, and to make them white even to the time of the end;* when the Arian hereſy will iſſue in that popery to which it viſibly tends; *becauſe it is yet for a time appointed.* Then follows an account of the depredations of popery, ver. 36—39; ſee page 37.

But the deſolations to be made by the Babylonians ſeem to be intended by this phraſe, *Dan.* xii. 11; where, ſpeaking of the power of the beaſt, which is to continue 1260 years, ver. 7, our author is informed, that *from the time* when *the daily ſacrifice ſhall be taken away,* to the time when *the confounding abomination ſhall be given,* Heb. *ſhall be* 1290 *days* or years. Arias Montanus reads it, *Ad dandum abominationem obſtupefacientem;* and תת doubtleſs ſignifies *giving;* this is its uſual and moſt natural ſignification, though it is rendered to *place* in *Dan.* xi. 31, which I have juſt conſidered; and the word שמם which is uſed in all theſe four places in Daniel (and which ſounds in Engliſh *ſhame 'em*) ſignifies *ſtupifying* or *confounding;* and eminently
ſuch

such is the abomination spoken of, *Rev.* xvii. 2, 6. If we reckon these years from Antiochus's profanation of the temple; and much more if we date them from A. D. 70, when the Romans put an end to their sacrificing, the 1290 years will carry us far beyond the time when popery was set up: . They must therefore necessarily refer to the time of Nebuchadnezzar's conquests, who destroyed the temple at Jerusalem, says Dr. Prideaux, 588 years before Christ's time; yet two or three months after the temple was burnt, offerings were brought to the house of the Lord, *Jer.* xxxix. 2. and xli. 1, 5; as they were also presented on the altar, seven months before the foundations of the second temple were laid, *Ezra.* iii. 1—8.

And though they were not to sacrifice in Heathen lands, charity must suppose that a people who had been used to offer sacrifices time immemorial, and whose ancestors had practised this sacred rite, by the divine order, before they had either a tabernacle or temple, would continue this sacred custom as long as there were any devout people left in Judea, who had any cattle; for they knew, that *without shedding of blood* there was *no remission of sins.* Accordingly, says the fore-mentioned author, ' Though the temple was destroyed, the people ' that were left continued to offer sacrifice and ' worship there on the place where it stood ;' And he reckons they did so for four years; which brings the ceasing of the sacrifice to 584 years before Christ's incarnation. Add these 1290 years to the year 584 before Christ, and it brings us to A. D. 706: And as the text speaks of something voluntary *given* to the pope or the church, without force of arms, such were the *patrimonies* of which history speaks, (see *Universal Hist.* vol. xix. page 652—654) which were so liberally bestowed upon the Romish church, especially at the beginning of the eighth century, and particularly at

A. D. 706: For as liberal donations to the church were about this time fuppofed to make atonement for fin; fo fays Mofheim, 'Emperors, kings and ' princes fignalized their fuperftitious veneration ' for the clergy, by invefting Bifhops, churches ' and monafteries in the poffeffion of whole pro- ' vinces, cities, caftles and fortreffes; with all the ' rights and prerogatives of fovereignty that were ' annexed to them under the dominion of their ' former mafters.' *Eccles. Hift.* vol. I. page 349. He adds, page 351, 'The barbarous nations ' looked upon the bifhop of Rome, as the fuccef- ' for of their chief druid, who under the dark- ' nefs of Paganifm enjoyed a boundlefs authority; ' and, upon their converfion to Chriftianity, they ' thought proper to confer upon the chief of ' Bifhops,' who was fhamefully ready to claim, as well as accept, 'the fame honour and authority as ' had formerly been vefted in their arch-druid.' Accordingly the *elegance* of kiffing the pope's toe came in fafhion in this century. But though this *confounding abomination* of fpiritual and fecular power was *given* the pope A. D. 706, he could not *fet it up* as *a beaft* till A. D. 755; when Pepin king of France, by force of arms, gave him the exarchate of Ravenna, and fome time after the Roman dukedom.

Or if by this *confounding abomination* is meant Mahometanifm, which is thought to be fpoken of in this chapter as well as popery; fee chap. xvi. 12—16, and which, as well as that, unites in itfelf a fpiritual and fecular power; this will require us to date the ceafing of the daily facrifice from 684 before Chrift's time, when it ceafed by Manaffeh; to which year add the 1290, and it points out A. D. 606, which was the time when that abomination was given as an infernal prefent, to the world; fee chap. ix. 1: Of which nothing being

being said under the seventh trumpet, we have before heard that its 1260 years will conclude A. D. 1866.

What has been here offered on Daniel's prophecy thus far, serves to illustrate some preceding and subsequent parts of this; but we have yet to consider *Dan.* viii. 13, 14, which will throw further light on the present subject; and at the same time shew the necessity of introducing what has been already said on Daniel's prophecies. Observe therefore, *in the third year of Belshazzar*, ver. 1. Daniel had a prophetic view of the three great beasts which were to succeed the Babylonian empire then standing ; viz, (1.) The Medo-Persian, represented by a *Ram* with two Horns; the one *higher* than the other, and the *highest* came up last; viz Darius and Cyrus ver. 3, 20. (2.) The Grecian, represented by a *He-goat*, which had a *noble Horn* between his eyes; viz, Alexander; and when this was broken, for it came up four *notable Horns*, or kingdoms towards the four winds of heaven, ver. 5—7, 21, 22. (3.) The Roman empire, represented by a little horn *Dan.* vii. 24, 25 ; which came *after* that particular *one of the* four preceding *Horns*, into which Alexander's kingdom had been broken ; viz, Syria which had been so troublesome to the Jews in the person of Antiochus Epiphanes, ver. 9; Heb. see a remark on *Dan.* xi. 31. page 187. This seems to be the power described, ver. 23—25, which stood up *in the latter time of* the *kingdom* of the four Horns *when the transgressors*, amongst the Jews and Gentiles *were come to the full*. He shall be *a king of a fierce countenance* ; *understanding dark sentences*, by means of his priests and augurs. *And his power shall be mighty, but not by his own power*: And he shall *destroy wonderfully, and shall prosper, and practise* ; *and shall destroy the mighty and the holy people*. *And through his policy also he shall cause craft to prosper in his hand*; and

be

he shall magnify himself in his heart, and by peace shall destroy many. He shall also stand up against the Prince of princes the Messiah; *but he shall be broken without hand.* This is the power which *waxed exceeding great, toward the south, and toward the east, and toward the pleasant land* of Judea, ver. 9.—12 : *And it waxed great even to the host of heaven,* in the Jewish world; *and it cast down some of the host and of the stars to the ground, and stamped upon them. Yea he magnified himself even to the Prince of the host; and by him the daily sacrifice was taken away,* A. D. 70; *and the place of his sanctuary was cast down. And an host was given him against the daily sacrifice, by reason of transgression; and it cast down the truth to the ground; and it practised and prospered.*

Hearing this, a holy one asks the Lord Jesus, ver. 13. *For how long a time shall the vision last, the daily sacrifice be taken away, and the transgression of desolation, to give both the sanctuary and the host to be trodden under feet;* so Mr. Lowth translates the words, agreeable to the Hebrew, the LXX, the Arabic version, and the vulgar Latin; See *bishop Newton :* And the answer is ver. 14, *Unto* 2300 *evening mornings,* Heb. that is, to so many *days* or years; (see ver. 26, and *Gen.* i. 5 : The phrase seems to be of the same import as the apostle's νυχθημερον *a night and a day,* 2 *Cor.* xi. 25 ;) or *to* 2400 *evening morning days,* as the LXX read it. And as the daily sacrifice was to cease for the greatest part of the time of this vision, probably the holy Ghost expressed these sacrifices by the times in which they might have been offered, awfully to remind us, That they who live without prayer, and without applying to a sacrifice of atonement, have, as it were, no *mornings* or *evenings;* but are *dead in trespasses and sins.*

If we date these years from the beginning of the Grecian empire with which this vision began,

gan, Dr. Prideaux fays exprefsly that Cyrus took
Babylon 539 years before Chrift's time; and
allowing him five years to compleat his conqueft
of that vaft empire, this brings us to 534 years
before Chrift; to which time add the 2400 years
of this vifion, and it points out A. D. 1866 as the
time for the cleanfing of the fanctuary, as we
found before: And this is probably the proper
folution of this difficulty: At leaft I can find no
interpretation of this prophecy whatever, that
will either allow us to underftand thefe 2300 or
2400 days of natural days, that is, of fix years,
and 140 or 240 days; or that will admit of 2300
or 2400 years to intervene between any ceafing
of the daily facrifice whatever, and the literal
cleanfing of the temple. If we think of its ceafing by Antiochus, or by the Romans (who are
fpoken of in the two preceding verfes) to add
only 2300 years to the firft, and efpecially to the
laft of thefe times, would bring us far into the time
of the millennium, before which the fanctuary
muft be cleanfed. And if the ceafing of the facrifice by the Babylonians, 584 years before Chrift,
had been intended, this would end the 2400 years
at A. D. 1816; at which time many of the Jews
may be converted; but the fanctuary cannot be
cleanfed, nor will the church of God in general
be purged, till about the time of the Jews return
to their own land; which will not take place till
the beginning of the feventh trumpet. Yet poffibly the fanctuary may be *fpiritually* cleanfed
2400 years after the year 584 before Chrift; that
is, by A. D. 1816.

But I have the lefs hope of living to fee this
text compleatly developed, becaufe the Angel-
interpreter added, ver. 17. *At the time of the end
fhall be the vifion:* Till that end comes, *many fhall
run to and fro, and knowledge fhall be increafed,*

O   *Dan.*

Dan. xii. 4 ; and who would not enquire into thefe things, who has ever read the words which follow there, ver. 10. *None of the wicked fhall un- derftand, but the wife fhall underftand ?*

I only add here, That as the *confounding abomi- nation* is connected with the removal of the *daily facrifice,* in all the above places ; fo it is impoffi- ble that a *finner* fhould do any thing more hateful to God, or mifchievous to men, than to talk or print any thing againft Chrift's true and proper atonement for the fin of the world ; without which the gofpel is a medley of inconfiftencies, and falvation a painted dream.

6. And I faw another angel flying in the midft of heaven, having the everlafting gof- pel, to preach the glad tidings to them that dwell upon the earth ; and to every nation, and kindred, and tongue and people.

7. Saying with a loud voice, Fear God, and give glory to him ; for the hour of his judgment is come : And worfhip him that made heaven and earth, and the fea, and the fountains of waters.

As the converfion of the Gentiles immediately followed the fealing of the twelve tribes of Ifrael, chap. vii. 9 ; fo here, after the gathering in of the Jews to their own land, a glorious harveft fprings up in the gentile world, by means of the *angels of the churches,* chap. i. 20 ; for though only one *angel* is mentioned, more muft be employed in preaching to every *nation, kindred, tongue* and *people.* The inftruments of the Jews converfion in Conftantine's time ; are fpoken of both in the fingular and plural number, chap. vii. 2, 3 : But minifters in the nineteenth century will fo refemble

ble angels in their unanimity, as well as in their purity and zeal, that they may fitly be called one : And this *angel flying* through *the midst of heaven,* as Mr. Whitefield lately did through the British dominions, intimates the rapid progress of the gospel, after the Jews are returned to their own land.

With a very different message another angel had posted through heaven, A. D. 566, &c. to give warning of the three woe-trumpets, chap. viii. 13 ; but *this* bears no *flying roll* of vengeance, *Zech.* v. 2 ; but has that *gospel,* which is *everlasting* in the purpose, contrivance and blessed fruits of it, *to preach to every nation* upon earth ; *saying, with a voice, loud* enough to rouse the animal soul, *Fear God* ye sinners of every name, *and give glory to him*; *for the* long appointed *hour of his judgment* of the great whore *is come*; as though he had said, You have already seen Rome judged by the *earthquake* there, chap. xi. 13 ; and as one of its seven hills is now taken out of the hands of the beast, chap. xiii. 3 ; so this double attack made upon him, assures you that all the vengeance written against him will be speedily executed. Judgment also even now begins again at the house of God, by means of the second beast, who is rising out of the earth. Sin and satan too, yea and your own souls are now to be *judged,* by that gospel which is preached to you ; which both sets you over to a judgment to come, and shews, that judgment very near : And with such a day in his eye, with what ardor will he cry, Oh ! *worship him that made the heavens,* which beam every day with his various glories, *and the earth,* his humble footstool, which supports you ; *the sea* from which vapors arise to fertilize the land, *and the fountains of water* which quench your daily thirst ! He made your *progenitors* too, from whom you severally sprang, through all their successive ge-

nerations

nerations, chap. xvii. 15. *Ifai*, xlviii. 1. Come
therefore, fall down and adore him in his works
of nature, providence and and grace.

The return of the Jews to their own land will
be very fpeedy; for that *nation* will be, as it were,
born in a day : And as there is no time mentioned
as intervening between the fcaling of the tribes
of Ifrael, and the converfion of the Gentiles
in Conftantine's time, chap. vii. 8, 9 ; fo we have
reafon to believe this angel will begin his flight
through heaven at, or foon after A. D. 1866;
for as foon as Zion has *travailed* and *brought forth*,
her breafts will be full of the fincere milk of the
word; and *the Gentiles fhall fuck, and be fatisfied*
with thefe *breafts of her confolation :* And God will
*extend peace to her like a river, and the glory of the
Gentiles as a flowing ftream,* Ifa. lxvi. 6—12. And
when thefe events take place, *the hearts* of Sion's
friends *fhall rejoice,* and their *bones fhall flourifh as
an herb,* Pfal. cii. 3, 5. *Prov.* xv. 30. and xvii. 22.
*And the hand of the Lord fhall be known towards his
fervants, and his indignation towards his enemies ;
for by fire and by his fword will the Lord* afterwards *plead,* not only with the Turks, but *with
all flefh,* till the man of fin is confumed ; *and the
flain of the Lord,* amongft the fervants of the two
beafts, *fhall be many ;* efpecially by means of the
feven vials, ver. 14, 15, 16. See further of the
calling of the Jews and Gentiles in the feven laft
chapters of Ifaiah.

8. And another angel followed faying, It
is fallen, it is fallen, Babylon, the great
city ; becaufe fhe made all the nations drink
of the wine of the rage of her fornication.

9. And a third angel followed them faying, with a loud voice, If any man worfhips
the

the beaft, and his image, and receives the mark on his forehead, or on his hand;

10. Even he fhall drink of the wine of the wrath of God, which is mixed, yet not diluted in the cup of his wrath: And he fhall be tormented with fire and brimftone, in the prefence of the holy angels, and in the prefence of the Lamb.

11. And the fmoke of their torment afcendeth for ever and ever; and they have no reft day nor night who worfhip the beaft, and his image, and whofoever he is who receives the mark of his name.

12. Here is the patience of the faints! here *are* they who keep the commandments of God, and the faith of Jefus!

13. And I heard a voice from heaven, faying unto me, Write, bleffed are the dead who die in the Lord *even* henceforth. Yea faith the fpirit, that they may reft from their labours; and their works follow them.

Obferve, the fervants of God in this period are not called witneffes, but *angels*, which was the name eminently given to gofpel minifters in the firft century; fee chaps i. ii. and iii; and now the ftrength, wifdom, purity, activity, fimplicity and fervour of the primitive times, begin again to beautify and adorn the churches of God: Accordingly thefe two angels follow the former, into every nation, and to every kindred, tongue, and people, loudly and folemnly denouncing God's Judgments againft the Papifts: Which implies that the two beafts have poifoned the whole earth with

their

their infernal doctrines, which is also afferted, ver.
8. *She made all nations drink of the wine of the
rage of her fornications.* The firft of thefe angels
declares, that Rome is a mere babylon of pride,
idolatry, perfecution and lafting infamy; He an-
nounces her fall as the ancient prophets did that
of literal Babylon, and in the fame words, *Ifa.*
xxi. 9. *Jer.* li. 8; faying, *Babylon is fallen, is
fallen* to the earth, chap. xii. 13, and fhall
be foon fhaken out of it; and indicts her in God's
name for having banifhed fobriety and modefty
from the earth: *She hath made all nations drink
of the wine of the rage of her fornications*; particularly in the 'ftews licenfed by the Pope, which
' are no inconfiderable branch of his revenue;' fee
chap. xvii. 4; which the Lord certainly would not
have fuffered, if he had not been greatly provoked by the wickednefs of the world.

After this, ver. 9, 10, 11, a third angel follows
the former; preaching as earneftly as he, and
faying with a loud voice, *If any man,* high or low,
*worfhips the beaft and his image, and receive the
mark* which he appoints, *on his forehead or in his
hand*; whatever excufes of fecular advantage, or
fear of perfecution he may plead for fuch an infult upon the Divine throne and government;
even He, whoever he is, *fhall drink of the wine of
the wrath of God, which is mixed* by every abufed
attribute of Deity, *without* fuffering any one alle-
viating ingredient to foften the terrors of that
dreadful *mixture, in the cup of his indignation* which
his enemies muft drink; who *fhall be tormented
with* fuch *fire and brimftone,* as it never was in
the power of the beaft to kindle againft God's
fervants; though he could once madly amufe
himfelf, by making *fire come down from heaven in
the fight of men,* chap. xiii. 13: And this torment
fhall be inflicted upon them, not only before thofe
angels

angels who pour out the seven vials, but *in the presence of the holy angels* in general : For at certain seasons at least, through eternal ages, their ' torments will become a spectacle to the inhabi- ' tants of the blessed worlds above,' see *Luke* xiii. 28. and xvi. 23—*and in the presence of the Lamb*, to whom all judgment is committed : And now that long merciful and compassionate High-Priest, will for ever *laugh at their calamity, and mock when their fear cometh*, *Prov*. i. 26—and the *smoke of their torment ascends up for ever and ever* ; and besides their eternal torments, even here upon earth, especially in this period, they *have no rest* who continue to *worship* this infernal *beast and his image, and whosoever receives the mark of his name.* And ' I heartily wish that all those, who connive ' at such things in the discipline and worship of ' Protestant churches, which they, in their own ' consciences, think to be sinful remains of Popish ' superstition and corruption, would seriously at- ' tend to this passage, which is one of the most ' dreadful in the whole book of God, and weigh ' its awful contents, that they may keep at the ' greatest possible distance from this horrid curse, ' which is sufficient to make *the ears of* every one ' *that hears it to tingle.* Compare *Jer*. xxv. 15, ' 16,' Dr. Doddridge.

Ver. 12. *Here is the patience of the saints*, which will be more tried and honoured in the times of the second beast, than when the first reigned alone, chap. xiii. 10—*here are they who keep the commandments*, not of the beast but *of God*; and in the face of every danger, *preserve the faith of Jesus*, and their own inviolable fidelity to him.

Ver. 13. But as the happiness of the saints in heaven immediately after death, is a point of the highest importance to be established, for its greater confirmation, ' it is announced to our author by

' two

' two different ways of inspiration at once; viz,
' by a voice from heaven, and the secret irradiation
' of the spirit;' for says he, *I heard a voice from
heaven, saying, Write, blessed are the dead that die in
the Lord,* Martyrs and others, even *henceforth,*
from the time of their death, by which they escape many calamities which will terrify these
times; and they are now known to enter into
glory, without having any thing to fear from the
feigned fires of purgatory: *Yea saith the spirit,*
using his own well known voice in my heart; that
Sperit which is in all the saints, which brought them
into a vital union with their Lord, and taught,
quickened, and sanctified them; *for they rest from
their labours; and their works,* so much despised
by men, though they do not go before to procure
their admission into heaven, yet *follow;* not a
thousand years after, but μετ' αυτων *with them,* as
the certain witnesses of the sincerity of their faith
and love; which are to be rewarded with immediate glory.

14. And I saw, and behold a white cloud,
and on the cloud one sitting like the Son of
man; having on his head a golden crown;
and in his hand a sharp sickle.

15. And another angel came out of the
temple, crying with a loud voice to him that
sat on the cloud, Put forth thy sickle and
reap; for the hour is come for thee to reap,
for the harvest of the earth is ripe.

16. And he that sat upon the cloud, thrust
in his sickle on the earth; and the earth was
reaped.

The general harvest for heaven and hell will
be at *the end of the world, Matt.* xiii. 39; but before

fore that, we have here an in-gathering to heaven, as the next verses give us an account of one for hell: And as the last of these signifies the cutting off the wicked out of this world, as grapes thrown into a wine-press; see ver. 17—20, so the same phrase of *putting in the sickle* to reap his wheat, doubtless designs God's removing his children out of the way of danger; for I cannot recollect that the word *sickle* is ever used, where only a gathering into Christ is intended; see *Matt.* ix. 37, 38. *Luke* x. 2. *John* iv. 35—38: Nor does the grace of God cut men off from the earth, or remove them from the society of their fellow-men.

Ver. 14. *I saw and behold a white cloud,* the usual emblem of God's gracious presence in the temple; *and upon the cloud one sat,* conspicuous to my view in the most serene splendors, *like the Son of man,* on whose bosom I had leaned in his incarnate state; *having on his head a golden crown;* for he was now going about an important act of his kingly office, chap. i. 18: *And in his hand a sharp sickle;* which was sharpened to make the stroke of death the more quick and easy.

Ver. 15. *And another angel* or minister, perhaps of Jewish extraction, *came out of the temple,* chap. xi. 19; and seeing this sickle in the hands of his Lord, he knew it was intended for use: Therefore, though the complexion of the times assured him that many of the saints would be cut off by *sharp persecutions,* as the word *sickle* intimated; leaving the methods of their removal with secure confidence in *his* hands, without *whom* he knew none of them could be cut off; he cried *with a loud voice to him who sat on the cloud, Put in thy sickle and reap;* for thy servants have been sowing the good seed of the word over all the earth, and now *the time is come for thee to reap;*
for

for the harvest of the earth is ripe or dried, Gr.
And as thou canst not leave out thy wheat
through all the cold and storms of winter ; so thy
late declaration of the blessedness of those who died
in the Lord, was certainly designed to reconcile
us to those bereaving providences, which await
the church and the world. And perhaps at this
period, peculiar reasons may appear to vindicate
such a prayer as this ; which intimated ' a high
' degree of holiness, and a great desire to be with
' God,' in those who offered it. *And* accordingly
our Lord answered their request, ver. 16. *He that
sat on the cloud put in his sickle on the earth :* So
just before the following desolations, perhaps
from about A. D. 1920 to 1925, there will be a
glorious in-gathering of the saints to heaven,
though by a sharp persecution ; for it is God's
way to house his saints when a storm is coming,
Isa. lvii. 1 : But the world has every thing that
is horrible to expect when they have slain God's
people.

17. And another angel came out of the
temple which was in heaven, he having also
a sharp sickle.

18. And another angel came out from
the altar, having power over fire ; and he
called with a loud cry, to him who had the
sharp sickle, saying, Put forth thy sharp
sickle, and lop off the clusters of the vine of
the earth ; for her grapes are fully ripe.

19. And the angel thrust in his sickle
upon the earth, and gathered the vine of
the earth ; and cast it into the great wine-
press of the wrath of God.

20. And

20. And the wine-prefs was trodden without the city; and blood came out of the wine-prefs even unto the horfes bridles, from a thoufand fix hundred furlongs.

David faid, *Evil doers fhall be cut off*; and *yet a little while and the wicked fhall not be. The Lord fhall laugh at him, for he feeth that his day is coming*, *Pfal.* xxxvii. 9—13: Accordingly, when the Lord had removed his faints to heaven, *another angel* comes *out of the temple which is in heaven*, which manifefted that he was a heavenly angel; *he alfo having a fharp fickle*, ver. 17. Obferve Chrift reaped his wheat himfelf, ver. 16; and though wicked inftruments were employed, there is only a kind of tacit notice taken of them in the word *fickle :* But in the deftruction of the wicked, an angel is employed, as againft Sennacherib and his army, *Ifa.* xxxvii. 36.

Ver. 18. *And another angel came out from the altar, which had power over the fire*; and if the fire of the altar is intended, we may fuppofe this angel to be Chrift, as in chap. viii. 3, 5 : But if fire in general is meant, fo reftrictive an idea does not feem fufficiently honourable to our Lord; but rather defcribes an honour proper to fome of his fervants, who have that power over fire which the fecond beaft vainly pretended to, chap. xiii. 13; as others of them have εξουσια *power* (the fame word as here ufed) over waters, chap. xvi. 5. And he *called* upon this celeftial minifter of vengeance *with a loud voice*, as David called upon the angels to praife God, *Pfal.* ciii. 20, *faying*, the time is come; therefore now exert thy *excelling ftrength*, that the church of God may fee thy power: Hafte, *put forth thy fharp fickle*, with which God has intrufted thee, *and lop off*, and gather *the clufters of the vine of the earth* ; *for* it is
the

the vine of Sodom, and *her grapes are fully ripe.*
So cried the Prophet *Joel* iii. 13, againft the enemies of Ifrael, *Put ye in the fickle, for the harveft
is ripe: Come, get you down for the prefs is full,*
and, under your powerful feet, *the fats overflow*;
for their wickednefs is great: So Edom's deftruction is reprefented by treading a *wine-prefs*, *Ifa.*
lxiii. 3; fee alfo *Ifa.* xviii. 5. It is natural to reap
wheat with a fickle; but the ufe of this inftrument in cutting off grapes, feems to intimate that
thefe finners fhall be hurried out of this world
with violence, as well as in anger—But God muft
be glorified—

Accordingly, ver. 19, 20, though this angel had
no orders to cut down the tree itfelf, which was
referved for future perdition, *He thruft in his fickle
into the earth*; *and gathered* the prefent fruit of
this vine, which was wholly *of the earth,* and fup-
ported by it; and, to prepare a dreadful libation to Divine juftice, *he caft* the grapes he had
out off *into the great wine-prefs of the wrath of
God*; *and the wine-prefs was trodden without the
city* Rome; *and blood came out of the wine-prefs
even to the bridles of the horfes*; a ftrong metaphor
to exprefs the moft horrid flaughter made by fome
hoftile power, (fee bifhop Newton on the place)
from, or at the diftance of *a thoufand fix hundred
furlongs,* or 200 miles; which, fays Mr. Mede,
is the exact length of Stato della Chiefa, or the
ftate of the Roman church, moft *abfurdly* called
St. Peter's patrimony; viz, from the walls of
Rome to the river Po; fee Acts iii. 6.

This awful carnage, a little time before the
vials are poured out, may probably be made about
A. D. 1926: For as 'the Babylomifh captivity
' was accomplifhed by two or three different tranf-
' portations, and its feventy years concluded by
' two or three different returns, fo the 1260 years

' of popery may be reckoned to begin differently;
' viz, at the several very remarkable steps it took
' towards its full power; as at A. D. 606, when
' the Pope became a universal bishop; at A. D.
' 666, about which time his Latin service begun;
' and at A. D. 756, when he became a temporal
' prince: So popery will have a remarkable blow
' when Jews and Gentiles are gathered in A. D.
' 1866; and we expect the next attack upon it,
' A. D. 1926, before that by the vials; which
' will be succeeded by his total overthrow A. D.
' 2016.' But as this stroke will fall without the
city, it must be different from, and the account
here given represents it as some considerable time
after, that which will befal the first beast, when
one of his seven hills are taken from him by the
sword; see chap. xiii. 3.

This vengeance will probably be occasioned
by some daring act of wanton cruelty and oppression perpetrated by the two beasts; which
will rouse such an indignation as will produce
blood up to *the horses bridles*; a phrase which occurs no where else in scripture. But we are uncertain whether to look in the east, or west for
the instruments of this destruction; as the united
power of the two beasts will, before this time,
have imitated Christ himself, and set its *right foot*
on the sea, and its *left on the earth*, chap. x. 2.
Possibly this sword of God may come down upon
the whole length of the Pope's territories, by
some friends of the Greek church; against which
the Popish powers have already begun to shew
their rancour and impertinence: Or if *the words*
which *God* has spoken about this beast, may be
said to *be fulfilled*, when the second beast has attained the full height of his power (which he certainly will by A. D. 1926; see chap. xvii. 16, 17.)
perhaps this vengeance may be executed upon
them

them by the ten Horns of the beaſt: But whoever are the inſtruments, this truth will be written plain to every eye in their blood, *He that killeth with the ſword, muſt be ſlain by the ſword,* chap. xiii. 10.

C H A P. XV.

1. AND I ſaw another ſign in heaven, great and wonderful, ſeven angels having the ſeven laſt plagues; becauſe in them the wrath of God is filled up.

2. And I ſaw as it were a ſea of glaſs, mingled with fire; and thoſe who *had eſcaped* conquerors from the beaſt, and from his image, and from his mark, and from the number of his name, ſtanding on the ſea of glaſs; having the harps of God.

3. And they ſung the ſong of Moſes the ſervant of God, and the ſong of the Lamb; ſaying, Great and marvellous are thy works, Lord God Almighty; juſt and true are thy ways, O King of ſaints;

4. Who would not fear thee, O Lord, and glorify thy name! becauſe thou only art holy; becauſe all nations ſhall come and worſhip before thee; becauſe thy righteous judgments are made manifeſt.

5. And after theſe things I looked, and behold the temple of the tabernacle of the teſtimony in heaven was opened.

6. And

6. And there came out the seven angels, who had the seven plagues, from the temple; clothed with pure and shining linnen, and were girded about the breasts with golden girdles.

7. And one of the four living creatures gave to the seven angels seven vials, full of the wrath of God, who liveth for ever and ever.

8. And the temple was filled with smoke from the glory of God, and from his power; and no one was able to enter into the temple, till the seven plagues of the seven angels were finished.

Sinners of every name must *turn* or *burn*; for God *can* and *will* be glorified in all his reasonable, as well as in all his other, creatures : And when he begins, as here, with the man of sin, he will make an end : The beloved apostle saw this in vision; happy they, who see, believe and flee from the wrath to come !

Our author had before seen a sign of the glory and conflicts of the church, in the *woman clothed with the sun*, &c. chap. xii. 1, 2; and another sign of the rage of satan, in the person of the second beast, ver. 3. of that chapter : After which he saw here *another sign*, *in* that earthly *heaven* the church, (where God has represented every thing, which will ever be interesting to human nature to observe, in this world;) a sign of the day of judgment, *great and marvellous*; viz, *seven angels*, the same who stood before God, chap. viii. 2; and who, *having* in many visits studied, in the church, the nature and effects of the great salvation, *Eph.* iii. 10. 1 *Pet.* i, 12, were now the

3   willing

willing inftruments of Divine vengeance on thofe hypocrites who had fo fhamefully oppofed it, under the fpecious pretence of regard to it.

As to the times of the vials; the order of this prophecy inclines us to believe that they are not poured out; for the great things predicted, chap. xivth are none of them yet accomplifhed. It is alfo manifeft that the firft vial has not been poured out; for it is to fall on the men who have *the mark of the beaft, and worfhip his image,* chap. xvi. 2; but we do not hear of the mark of the beaft, or of his image, till in the times of the fecond beafts, who is not yet rifen, chap. xiii. 14, 16. The vials are alfo called *the laft plagues; for in them is filled up* that *wrath of God* againft the man of fin, which began to be publickly teftified by the *earthquake* at Rome A. D. 1866, chap. xi. 3; was confirmed foon after by the taking of one of his *hills* from the beaft, chap. xiii. 3; and awfully fealed in blood again, by the treading of the wine-prefs of his wrath about A. D. 1926: Therefore it is not reafonable to expect them very long before A. D. 2016. And accordingly, though the woe of this trumpet, fo far as it declares the *fpreading of fin,* began with it; fee chap. xi. 14, yet as it fignifies the *punifhment of thefe tranfgreffors,* it is not exprefled till after all the vials are poured out, chap. xviii. 10. Gr. But the woe which God has denounced againft the wicked, falls upon them, both in the *fuccefs,* and in the *punifhment* of their works, *Ifa.* iii. 11.

But before our apoftle was allowed to take any farther notice of thefe fhining minifters, or the feven-fold vengeance they were commiffioned to execute, his eye is drawn away to a triumphant company who had conquered the two beafts, ver. 2, 3, 4; *I faw,* not a real, but *as it were a fea of glafs* (alluding to that great vafe, in which the priefts

priests of the Lord washed their hands and feet;
see chap. iv. 6.) ' large enough for all these con-
' querors to stand upon', and transparent; which
was also *mingled with the fire* of persecution, to
make gospel truths and hopes yet more purifying:
So says David, *We went through fire and through
water, Psal.* lxvi. 12; see *Numb.* xxxi. 2, 3.

And, though they meant not so, even their enemies were Christ's *fire in Zion,* and his *furnace in
Jerusalem,* to purge his gold and silver, *Isai.* xxxi.
9. *Mal.* iii. 3—*And those who* had escaped *victors,*
εκ του θηριου *from the beast, from his image, from
his mark and from the number of his name*; *standing* επι *upon* this *sea of glass*; from which neither
flattery nor force could remove them as they
came along in life: And now, having gained the
victory, this sea furnished a transparent pave-
ment for, and reflected a glory upon their feet;
whilst they stood exulting as having preserved
the most valuable of all possessions their integrity.—*Having the harps of God in their hands;
and they sung,* Jews and Gentiles together, *the
song of Moses the servant of God*; who in such
exalted strains praised him, *Exod.* xv, for the
great deliverance wrought out for his people
from the oppressing Egyptians; *and the song of
the Lamb,* both that which his grace inspired,
and which his example had taught them; when
he said, *I beheld Satan as lightning fall from heaven:* And again, *Father I thank thee, Lord of
heaven and earth, that thou hast hid these things
from the wise and prudent, and hast revealed them
unto babes; even so Father, for so it seemed good in
thy sight, Luke* x. 18, 21. Thus they praised
God for mercies temporal and spiritual, which
distinguished themselves and others; *saying, Great
and marvellous are thy works* of nature, providence and grace, *Lord God Almighty; just and*

P

true

true are thy ways, O King of faints : Who should
not, who that has the reafon of a man, *would not,
fear thee, O Lord, and glorify thy name ? becaufe
thou only art holy* in a fenfe peculiar to thyfelf;
and whatever others do, *at the remembrance* of
this we *give thee thanks, Pfal.* xcvii. 12 : *Becaufe all nations,* as nations, *fhall come and worfhip before thee* ; *and becaufe* the *righteous judgments,* both of *thy* word and fword *are* now *made
manifeft,* fo as they never were before : And as
furely as thy papal foes are now to be made thy
footftool; fo fhall every finner receive his awful
doom from thy lips, at the day of judgment,
Rom. xiv. 11, 12.

Refrefhed with the view, and with the mufical
harps of thefe conquerors; *I looked,* fays our author, ver. 5, 8. *and behold the temple of the tabernacle of the teftimony in heaven was opened,* that is,
the moft holy place, for the whole tabernacle
was called the *tabernacle of witnefs,* or teftimony,
Acts vii. 44; and the *temple* of this tabernacle
muft be the place of the oracle, where the Lord
manifefted himfelf to the High Prieft : And this
was left open, after *the feven angels came out* of
it in folemn proceffion, ver. 6, 8.   But when our
apoftle began to enjoy the hope of having an
immediate difcovery of God's grace and glory,
behold the flames of Divine juftice burnt hot and
ftrong there for the prefent ; and *the temple was
fo filled with fmoke from the glory of God, and from
his power, that no one was able to enter into* this
inmoft part of *the temple, till the feven plagues of
the feven angles were finifhed* ; for God will have
his people meditate terrour, and confider what
themfelves have deferved as finners, whilft they
fee his vengeance upon the workers of iniquity.
Yet as this holy oracle ftill lay open, he doubtlefs conceived hopes, that believing Jews and
Gentiles

Gentiles should soon have an abundant access to this dwelling-place of the Most High, and share his hitherto-unequalled grace.

This prophecy is in every part highly figurative; and, if I could have conceived of any thing in it analogous to the paintings which are cast around a picture, merely to decorate the piece of which they are no part, I might have considered what is said of this temple as such: But however obscure our views may be, it is most honourable to the inspired author, to suppose every word big with an important literal, or metaphorical meaning; therefore I ask, What temple is here intended?—It cannot be the temple of Christ's body, *John* ii. 21, from which angels could not come out; nor could it be filled with smoke, ver. 6, 8.—It cannot be a temple in heaven properly so called, for John *saw no temple therein,* chap. xxi. 22; nor can God's dwelling place in heaven be so *filled with smoke from* his *glory and power,* as to preclude the entrance of the celestial worshippers: Nor have we any idea of the saints in heaven giving the vials into the hands of the angels there; but a gospel minister may give the vials to these seven angels, as they come out of some earthly dwelling of our God, ver. 7.—Yet it is not probable that all the churches of God should be so filled with his glory at this period, that no worshippers can enter into them, during the whole time of the pouring out of these vials; though such a glory of God would increase the reverence, as much as it interrupted the usual forms, of worship.—But if a sacred building of vast dimensions should be erected at Jerusalem about this time, both these words, and those in chap. xi. 19, may have a literal accomplishment—Unborn ages will clearly shew our

P 2   successors

successors many things which we know not—But
certainly,

When the Jews return to their own land, with
an ardour which can neither be described or ima-
gined, they will most devoutly. adore .the God
of their fathers; and having put away for ever
all those traces of Mahometan and Popish delusions, which had disgraced their country, they
will rebuild their long-desolated city, and divide
their land by lot among themselves, and the
strangers who come up to Jerusalem with them:
And this may well be effected in seventy years after
their return; viz. by A. D. 1935 or 1936. And
being now again *precious in the sight* of God, they
will be *honourable in* the eyes of the nations, *Isai.*
xliii. 4; and especially of those who *keep the truth*;
multitudes of whom will, no doubt, visit them
to be witnesses of the grace bestowed upon them:
And as *the Lord of Hosts* will now, more literally
than he had ever done before, *In this mountain,*
Jerusalem *make unto all people a feast of fat things,*
Isai. xxv. '6, so redeemed Jews and Gentiles
will doubtless enjoy this feast in their united
worship; in which the strains of praise which are
peculiar to the Jews, chap. xiv. 3, will but add
new fervour to the devotion of converted Gentiles, when they fall in again with them, in the
loud triumphs of one universal chorus.

Those words are yet to be accomplished, and
why may they not be literally so? *There shall be*
one fold, and one shepherd, John x. 16. But when
the inclement sky forbids them to sing redeeming
love in the open air, *where* can they worship together, unless a spacious edifice is erected for this
purpose at Jerusalem, which will now again be
made the head-quarters of salvation? And if
such a temple should be compleated just before
the vials are poured out, and the glory of God
take

take and keep possession of it, the whole time they are pouring out; this will be taking possession in the same glorious manner, as he entered the ancient tabernacle and temple, which the Lord filled with his glory, *Exod.* xl. 33, 35. 1 *Kings* viii. 10, 11. 2 *Chron.* v. 14. *That* entrance was designed to typify the incarnation of the Son of God; and *this* will loudly announce both the certainty of the thing, and the manner in which God will for ever dwell in the souls of saints and sinners, by his vengeance or grace.

In these happy days greater light will certainly beam out upon the now obscurest parts of scripture; among which some may be ready to reckon the nine last chapters of Ezekiel, which predict the second temple, and the division of the land. Many things may indeed be said in favour of the literal sense of that prophecy; which was doubtless designed to assure the captives in Babylon of their return to their own land, and that their temple should be rebuilt. That temple is described, chap. xl. and xli; and afterwards sacrifices are appointed. In chap. xliii. 16—18, an altar is ordered twelve cubits square; which was a medium size between that of Moses in the wilderness, which was five cubits square, *Exod.* xxvii. 1. and that of Solomon, which was twenty, 2 *Chron.* iv. 1: at this altar the seed of Zadock was to minister; and therefore certainly at a time while their genealogies remained to distinguish that family, chap. xliii. 19. And the *five hundred* square reeds which the temple, its out-buildings and courts occupied, some reckon a space something less than a mile square; and so it must be if the cubit and hand breadth, chap. xl. 5, is only twenty one inches; for then the reed of six cubits long, is 126 inches, or 3 yards and an half; and the

500 reeds

500 reeds square makes 1750 yards square; see chap. xlii. 20, and xlv. 2.

By the measures given in this prophecy, perhaps Jewish builders may hereafter be able to develope the mysteries of this description, better than we can at present: And, as there is more obscurity in this vision than in the account of the Jewish ritual by Moses, and the division of the land by Joshua; it is natural to suppose, that the light which is *sown for* the church, will hereafter more irradiate this part of inspiration. But those words were more than once accomplished literally, *Out of Egypt have I called my son,* Hos. xi. 1. *Matt.* ii. 15; and as the land of Israel is yet to be divided a third time to Abraham's descendants, it is not impossible but that a third temple, here described, may be erected at Jerusalem; though no worship can be performed in it, but such as is adapted to gospel times. If such a building should be raised, whether its *breadth* does, or not, still *increase upwards,* chap. xli. 7; and even if the worshippers in it should not literally *go out* at a gate of the temple, *opposite* that at which they entered, chap. xlvi. 9; yet they will possess that growing spirituality, and make those advances in religion, which seem, to have been the chief design of these orders. And if what is said of the holy waters, chap. xlvii. 1—12, which proceeded from *under the threshold of the house,* should be no more literally realized in such a future building, than it was in the second temple; yet when the saints in the twentieth century, see the *holy waters* of salvation fructifying every barren spot, except the *miry* and *marshy places,* and spreading wide the most glorious spiritual fertility; will they not confess, with grateful joy, that they are to them become *waters to swim in,* in comparison of what they were to the patriarchs and prophets;

I

in whose times they were only *ankle,* or *knee* deep, or, at the furtheft, up to the *loins?* And will they not fay with rapture, Happy the fpiritual *trees* which now grow on the banks of this river !

These are fome of the *fpiritual* ufes which God's fervants have made of this part of the word in gofpel times, while ftill they are waiting for thofe clearer difcoveries of its meaning and grace, which may poffibly be referved for the times we are now confidering ; in which certainly the fpiritual dangers which invade men, when they return from worfhip to their own abodes, will be much lefs than in times paft ; for *the name of the* whole *city from that day fhall be* Jehovah Shammah, *the Lord is there,* chap. xlviii. 35.

But it may be enquired, What time will the vials take up ? and how long will the glory of the Lord fill his temple?—I anfwer, there is an obfervable difference between what is faid of the trumpet-minifters, and the language addreffed to thefe minifters of divine vengeance; *To them were given feven trumpets ; and they prepared themfelves to found :* But to all thefe together it is faid, *Go, and pour out the vials of the wrath of God upon the earth,* chap. xvi. 1 ; which inclines me to believe that the vials will make much quicker difpatch than the trumpets : And as they will not be poured out till after the treading of the wine-prefs A.D. 1926 without the city, which is defcribed in the clofe of the preceding chapter; fo they muft conclude foon enough before A.D. 2016, to leave room for the publick wailing, &c. expreffed, chap. xviii. and xix; which will be fucceeded by the final rout of the two beafts, chap. xix. 11—21.

But to come yet nearer to the times, It is probable the plagues of Egypt were not more, if fo long as a month apart from each other, as the Jews conjecture; poffibly fome of them might

be

be only a week, *Exod.* vii. 25, and others not so
long: But the following confiderations incline
me to fuppofe, that the feven vials may probably
take up feven years, (1.) Becaufe Jerufalem was
fo long in deftroying by the Romans; viz, from
A. D. 66 to 73. So fix or eight years before that
time, the apoftle faid of them, *Rom.* ix. 27, 28.
A remnant only *fhall be faved: for the Lord is fini-
fhing and cutting fhort his account in righteoufnefs,*
Gr; and one awful week fettled it: And *in that
week* God *confirmed his covenant with many;* viz,
with the Gentiles, *Dan.* ix. 27. See *Mr. Blayney
in loc.*

So probably by another feven years deftruction upon the kingdom of Anti-Chrift, he will
again confirm his covenant with the Jewifh
and Gentile church; for the following words of
the apoftle ftand yet in the bible for a further
accomplifhment, *The Lord will make a fhort account upon the earth;* and if we afk, How fhort?
the preceeding hiftory feems to anfwer, Seven
years, (2.) Probable reafons will be adduced under the fixth vial, both why we may expect that
vial to be poured out, A. D. 1941, and that it
will take up one year; which may give fome colour of reafon to fuppofe that the other vials will
take up the fame time. (3.) The nature of fome
of thefe judgments, as immediately in God's
hands; fee chap. xvi. 8, 9, feems to forbid the
thought of their being of long continuance; for
if a *noifome* and *grievous fore* on the bodies of men;
if the *fea* and *rivers* becoming *blood;* and the
fun's fcorching men with burning heat, fhould continue long, who then could be faved?—True,
the fame judgments metaphorically underftood,
under the trumpets, in which men were employed
as inftruments, might be expected to be of longer continuance; as is plainly fuppofed in the
choice allowed David of *three years famine, three
month's*

month's defolating *war*, or *three day's peftilence*,
1 *Chron.* xxi. 12.   But when they are immediately
in God's hands, he will probably make as *fhort*
an *account upon the earth*, as he made with Jerufalem by the Romans : Nor is it any objection to
the fhortnefs of the time here allowed for the
vials, that upon this fuppofition, they poffefs a
difproportionate part of this prophecy ; for we
could certainly have formed no idea of the time
which the deftruction of Tyre, Babylon, Egypt,
or Jerufalem would take up, from the number
of words ufed to defcribe, or bewail, that of
each.

On the contrary, it feems needful to allot them
fo much time, that the fervants of the beaft may
hear of one another's miferies from each vial, in
the different places where they live.   And if thefe
plagues are brought upon them by any natural
means, a year will both afford fufficient time for
the operation of thefe fecond caufes, which may
produce them round the world ; as for the fun's
fcorching men with heat, &c. and at the fame
time give us reafon to believe, that they probably
may not continue fo long upon any one fpot ;
but each move gradually from one place to another, to the end of its year—But to return—

Thefe *feven angels, having the feven* laft *plagues*,
ver. 6, 7, being called to offer a dreadful facrifice to the juftice of God, were *clothed* in robes of
‘ more than bare innocence ;’ viz, *with pure and
fhining linen, and having their breafts girded with
golden girdles*, to denote the firmnefs, dignity and
fplendour with which they will perform this
dreadful work ; fee chap. i. 13.   And, that it
might appear, what power God's minifters have
with him over their enemies, and that the work
which thefe angels were going about was the
avenging of his perfecuted fervants, *one of the four
living*

living creatures—(But, left any of them should, through unbelief, suppose himself incapable of such an honour, the Lord has not informed us whether it was he who resembled the lion, the ox, the man, or the eagle—) *gave to the seven angels seven vials,* that is censers, cups, or bottles *full of the wrath of God, who liveth for ever and ever* ; the unchanging enemy of every impenitent immortal, who has dared to take up arms against him and his Christ, chap. viii. 5 : So David, by his prayers, gave the angels those vials which they poured upon his enemies, *Psal.* xxxv. 5, 6 ; and Isaiah and Hezekiah gave that vial to the angel which he poured upon the 185,000 Assyrians, *Isa.* xxxvii. And when these vials are to be poured out, God will put it into the heart of some gospel minister, or of a sett of ministers of similar dispositions, firmly to believe, and therefore to desire of God by prayer, the execution of this vengeance ; which may properly be called their giving the vials to the angels, though we have no reason to suppose that these angels will visibly appear to him or them, when they are going about this work.

Observe, (1.) God bottles the tears of his saints, not only to be witnesses of the sincerity of their love to him, but also to make them vials of his wrath on the heads of their enemies, *Psal.* lvi. 8. For *shall not God avenge his own elect, who cry day and night unto him ? I tell you that he will avenge them speedily, Luke* xviii. 7, 8 ; as he promised to the souls under the altar, chap. vi. 10. 11. Yet, (2.) all that sinners can endure in this world, is no more in comparison with what they shall suffer in eternity, than a cup or bottle to the ocean : And slighting, and much more despising Christ, merits all that Divine vengeance can eternally inflict upon a sinner.

CHAP.

C H A P. XVI.

1. AND I heard a great voice out of the temple, saying to the seven angels; Go away, and pour out the vials of the wrath of God into the earth.

2. And the firſt went, and poured out his vial upon the earth; and a malignant and grievous ſore, fell upon the men who had the mark of the beaſt, and them who worſhipped his imaged.

3. And the ſecond angel poured out his vial upon the ſea; and it became blood, like that of a dead *man*; and every living ſoul *that was* in the ſea died.

4. And the third angel poured out his vial on the rivers, and on the fountains of waters; and they became blood.

5. And I heard the angel of the waters ſaying, Righteous art thou, O Lord, who art, and waſt, even thou holy One; becauſe thou haſt judged theſe things;

6. Becauſe they have poured out the blood of ſaints and prophets; and thou haſt given them blood to drink; for they are worthy.

7. And I heard another from the altar ſaying, Yea, O Lord God Almighty; true and righteous are thy Judgments.

8. And

8. And the fourth angel poured out his vial upon the fun; and it was given to it to fcorch men with fire.

9. And the men were fcorched with great heat: And they blafphemed the name of God who had power over thefe plagues; and repented not to give glory to him.

The four firſt feals, trumpets and vials, fo far differ from the three following, that the three laſt of each, are either more extenfive or more awful than the preceding.

The refemblance between the four firſt trumpets and the four firſt vials, is remarked by every writer on this fubjeɛt; each of them refpeɛtively affeɛts the *earth*, the *fea*, the *rivers* and the *fun*, chap. viii. 7—12; folemnly to remind us of the time when *the elements fhall melt with fervent heat; and the earth alfo, and the works that are therein fhall be burnt up,* 2 *Pet.* iii. 10: But there is this difference; thofe trumpets affeɛt but the third part of each of thefe things; viz, the Roman empire; thefe vials are not fo reſtrained, but fall upon the fervants of the two beaſts where ever they are. There is alfo a ſtriking refemblance between the three laſt trumpets and the three laſt vials, which will be remarked as we come to each of them.

The four firſt trumpets fhook down the weſtern Roman empire from A. D. 395 to 566; and thefe four vials make fucceffive attacks upon the beaſt; whofe kingdom, however fpiritually it may be faid to be adminiſtered, is in every view of it, as much of this world as the ancient Roman or any other kingdom ever was.

1. *And* after the *feven angels* had received the vials from one of the four animals, chap. xv. 6,

7, *I heard a great voice out of the temple*, which declared the will of God, and the united defire of his people, *faying to them, Go away*; *and pour out the vials of the wrath of God*, with which you are charged, *into the earth*. Obferve, God is *long-fuffering*, but he will not be always-fuffering; and he that *defpifes the riches of his goodnefs and forbearance*, leffens that flock which will be expended upon himfelf every moment.

2. *And the firft went, and*, probably in the prefence of the other fix angels, chap. xiv. 10, *poured out his vial upon the earth*; *and* prefently either the food which the fervants of the beaft eat, (who were become very dainty, chap. xviii. 14.) was impregnated with a multitude of noxious animalcula ; or by fome other means *a maglinant*, epidemic *and grievous fore fell*, not upon God's fervants, but *upon the men who had the mark of the beaft, and* upon *them who worſhipped his image*. This plague will be worfe than the *hail* and *fire* of the firft trumpet. chap. viii. 7 ; and refemble the fixth plague of Egypt, which was boyls breaking forth with blains, *Exod.* ix. 10. Lazarus died partly by his fores, *Luke* xvi. 20—22, Gr; and thofe fpoken of here being *malignant, grievous* and inflicted in anger, no doubt multitudes will die of them ; though probably fome will languifh under them till the time of the fifth vial, ver. 10, 11 ; that is, four or five years, if each vial fhould take up fo long time as a year.

3. *And the fecond angel* performed his allotted fervice, and *poured out his vial upon the fea*; and immediately the briny flood, which had fo long rolled from fide to fide in the fpacious hand of infinite goodnefs, arrefted by Divine juftice, not only forgot to flow with wonted rapidity, *but became* black and putrid *blood, like that of a dead* man ; *and every foul that had* animal *life in*, and

3

upon those seas which washed the territories of the
beast, presently *died*; for they would not worship
him that made the *sea* and the *fountains of waters,*
chap. xiv. 7. *Exod.* vii. 20. Yet they still remained incorrigible; therefore,

4. *The third angel* advanced forward, and *poured out his vial on the rivers, and on the fountains
of waters; and they became blood.* And, though it
is not for us to know, how long time this angel
would take in visiting all the rivers and fountains
against which he has a commission, a year will
certainly afford a full sufficiency of time for this
purpose; if indeed his pouring his vial on one of
each, does not instantaneously affect all the rest;
as *ashes of the furnace,* sprinkled by the hand of
Moses, became a *boyl with blains upon man and
beast, throughout all the land of Egypt, Exod.* ix. 8—
10.

5. *And* as soon as he had done this, *I heard
the angel* who had power over the *waters* in general, salt and fresh (as another of them had power
over fire, chap. xiv 18.) under whom probably
this minister of vengeance was ranked and ranged, in the wise order of the angelic hierarchy,
Col. i. 16; I distinctly heard him *saying, Righteous
art thou O Lord, who art and wast, even thou* holy
One (for many copies instead of ὁ ἐϛομενος read ὁ
οϛιος thou *holy,* or *gracious* One; see acts xiii. 34,
35, compared with *Psal.* xvi. 10. Heb. and both
these characters were designed to be eminently
displayed to saints and sinners in the vials) —*because thou hast thus judged*; *for,* in defiance of
all thy gracious warnings, *they have* wantonly *shed
the blood of saints and Prophets*; *and* in return *thou
hast given them blood to drink:* For, suffering no
guilt upon earth to equal their own, *they are* most
conspicuously *worthy*; they have merited their
portion at God's hands, which cannot be said of
the

the saints, though they also are said to be *worthy,*
chap. iii. 4. *The wages of sin is death* ; *but the gift
of God is ternal life, through Jesus Christ our Lord,*
Rom. vi. 23. Sinners are worthy, in and of themselves, of the destruction to which the broken
covenant of works dooms them ; but saints are
only worthy, in and by Christ, according to the
tenor of the covenant of Grace which saves
them.

7. *And I heard another* angel, who came out
from the altar ; the place of him who had power
over fire, chap. xiv 18. (of which the next
vial speaks) *say, Yea, O Lord God Almighty* ; *true
and righteous are thy judgments*—So under the second and third trumpets, a burning mountain
turned the sea to blood, and a burning star made
the rivers and fountains bitter as wormwood,
chap. viii. 8, 10. And this spiritual Egypt is
judged, as that literal house of bondage had been,
Exod. vii. 19.

8, 9. *And the fourth angel poured out his vial
upon the sun, and it was given to it to scorch the
men with fire,* no kind cloud daring to interpose
to mitigate the flaming day : *And the men were
scorched with great heat,* which would naturally
inflame their sores, ver. 2 ; *and* casting their fain-
ting eyes upwards, *they blasphemed the name of God,
who* they knew *had power over these plagues :* Yet
unconcerned about the more dreadful fire which
awaited their removal out of life, their hearts
still hardened, whilst their animal moisture was
consuming away, *they repented not to give him glory :*
For it is not in the sinner to give God any willing
glory ; nor is it even in hell-fire to abate the
enmity of the carnal mind against him : It is *the
grace,* not the wrath, *of God that brings salvation,*
Tit. ii. 11—14. *Rom.* viii. 24.—See the fourth
trumpet :

trumpet: And when the vials are poured out, the trumpets will be better underſtood.

Reaſons were aſſigned under the four firſt trumpets, for underſtanding them metaphorically; but I incline to take the vials literally, as the plagues of Egypt, 1. Becauſe the two laſt muſt be taken literally. 2. That phraſe, ver. 5, *The angel of the waters*, inclines me to the literal ſenſe; as we know of no created angel who has power over *peoples, multitudes and nations* in general, chap. xvii. 15. 3. I ſee nothing in the account of the vials which confines them to a figurative ſenſe, as in the trumpets. 4. The order to *render to her according to her works*, is not given to the ſaints till after the vials are poured out, chap. xviii. 6; nor will the kings, ſignified by the ten horns of the beaſt, recover from their drunkenneſs, ver. 3, to effect any great things againſt her before, A. D. 1926, or perhaps before A. D. 1942; ſee chap. xvii. 16. Beſides, 5. By giving theſe vials to the angels, this earthly miniſter teſtified that neither himſelf, nor any of mankind were to be employed in pouring them out, chap. xv. 7; yet the ſixth vial will bring crouds of the human race upon the ſtage to fight againſt God; ſee ver. 12—14.

Parhaps many of the ſaints may be removed to heaven, juſt before the pouring out of the vials, *Iſa.* lvii. 1; as many of them had been houſed in glory, a little before the wine-preſs was trodden without the city, chap. xiv. 14—20. But whether they are or not, as the firſt part of this fourfold vengeance is expreſsly reſtricted to the ſervants of the beaſt, ver. 2; ſo probably will the remainder of it: At leaſt providence will as certainly make all neceſſary diſtinctions in their favour, as it did for the Iſraelites in Egypt, and for the Chriſtians in Jeruſalem's deſtruction by the Romans.

10. And

10. And the fifth angel poured out his vial upon the throne of the beast; and his kingdom was darkened: And they gnawed their tongues for pain;

11. And blasphemed the God of heaven, for their pains and their ulcers; and repented not of their works.

A literal *darkness* that might *be felt* was one of the plagues of Egypt, *Exod.* x. 21, 22; and as Popery and Mahometanism, like the smoke of a great furnace, wrapt the east and west in dreadful moral night under the fifth trumpet, chap. ix. 2. So, as the temple at Jerusalem was destroyed in the fifth year of the Roman war; viz. at A. D. 70, when this fifth vial is poured out, *the throne of the beast* at Rome, whatever it may be of literal, will probably *be* as *full* of metaphorical, *darkness* as Jerusalem was when their temple was burnt by the exulting Romans: And if every one of the seven hills of Rome, should have been made by this time the seat of royal residence, the whole city may well be called *his throne:* Accordingly I expect that the papal *kingdom* will be *darkened*, A. D. 1940, as the great lights of the Roman empire had been under the fourth trumpet, chap. viii. 12: And at the same time, such *pains* and *ulcers* will invade the man of sin, as will leave him no present ability, to catch at those reins of government which are now snatched from him. Now also the dependents of the beast, not knowing what to do, in great confusion and anguish, even *gnaw their tongues for pain*, see ver. 2; thus proudly taking vengeance on themselves when they cannot on God's servants, and anticipating the torment of everlasting burnings. Yet still unhumbled, they *blaspheme the God of heaven for*

Q   *their*

their pains and their ulcers; which were much inflamed by the grievous heat of the fourth vial, ver. 8, 9: It is added, *And they repented not of their works*; for it Chrift does not give repentance, *Acts* v. 31, no temporal, or even eternal torments will, in the leaft, move the inflexible difpofitions of God's enemies.

12. And the fixth angel poured out his vial upon the great river Euphrates; and its water was dried up, that the way of the kings from the eaft might be prepared.

13. And I faw, *leaping* out of the mouth of the dragon, and out of the mouth of the beaft, and out of the mouth of the falfe prophet, three unclean fpirits like frogs:

14. For they are the fpirits of devils, working miracles; which go forth to the kings of the earth, and of the whole world, to bring them together to the battle of that great day of God Almighty.

15. Behold I come as a thief: Bleffed is he that watcheth, and keepeth his garments; that he may not walk naked, and they fee his fhame.

16 And He gathered them together to a place called, in the Hebrew tongue, Armageddon.

The river Euphrates muft be underftood literally under the fixth trumpet, which took off the reftraint from the four Turkifh principalities, who had long been confined near it, chap. ix. 14: And no reafon appears for underftanding it otherwife under this vial, which is poured upon the fame river, to *dry up* its *water*; not its *waters* in the

the plural number, or the *people* who dwelt on its
banks; the Holy Ghost has sufficiently notified
his meaning, where ever he has used the word
waters in that sense, as in *Isa.* viii. 6, 7. *Rev.*
xvii. 15: Yet it will make no great difference in
the sense, whether we understand the word metaphorically or literally; for either way the *water*
is *dried up,* previous to the mighty convulsions
which the next vial will occasion; *that the way of
the kings from the east might be prepared,* who are
marching from India, Persia and other eastern
parts towards *Judea:* For the river Euphrates
which lies in their way to Jerusalem, as well as
the Hebrew word, *Armageddon,* sufficiently informs us that their design is against that place;
and that they are coming in hostile forms is very
visible from ver. 14, 16: Therefore we cannot by
these eastern kings understand the Jews, who returned to their own land seventy five years before
this, as we have seen, chap. xiv. 1—5.

There will be nothing remarkably tempting
to these kings in Judea, till the smiles of providence upon Abraham's descendents, have made
it again *a delightsome land.* But it appears from
Ezekiel, chapters xxxviii. and xxxixth, that after
they are brought back to their own land, the
Turks and eastern nations will come upon them,
in dreadful swarms, to plunder and destroy; *to
carry away silver and gold, to take away cattle and
goods; to take a great spoil,* chap. xxxviii. 13. But,
instead of succeeding in this design, they shall
themselves return no more out of the land of
Israel, but find their graves there: And the Israe-
lites will be *seven months* in burying them; and
(in that warm climate where fewel is not much
wanted) *seven years* in burning their weapons,
chap. xxxix. 9—15. This seems to be the grand
event for which the sixth vial prepares the way:

For

For the *three frogs* here spoken of, go forth to gather these kings to fight against God, ver. 14, 16 : And as the literal drying up the river Euphrates, will give them an opportunity to follow their avaricious hopes ; so probably these croaking advocates for the dragon and the two beasts, will represent the drying up of that river, as a token from God of their certain success. Thus many of the Jews, mistook the prodigies which preceded Jerusalem's destruction by the Romans, for certain prognostics of their deliverance. *Josephus's wars*, &c. B. vii. chap. xii. But in fact the drying up of this river will, in the event, be as real a plague from *the wrath of God* to these enemies of his people, chap. xv. 1, 8 ; as the dividing the sea and Jordan was to the Egyptians and Canaanites, which were such eminent mercies to Israel. Yet when that river, which so long fertilized the banks of ancient Babylon, is not only *divided* as the Red-sea and Jordan, but *dried up* ; this may be afterwards a great mercy to the nations, who desire to come and worship God at Jerusalem.

Probably this is the host of which it is said, *Dan.* xi. 45. He *shall*, with much strength and confidence, *plant the tabernacles of his palace between the seas*, that is, between the sea of Galilee and the dead sea ; see page 236, *in the glorious holy mountain: Yet* in the midst of his vain hopes, *he shall come to his end, and none shall help him* : For after *the Lord of Hosts* has made *in this mountain unto all people a feast of fat things, he shall bring down* the *pride* of their enemies, *together with the spoils of their hands, Isa.* xxv. 6, 11.

The prophet Zechariah seems to speak of the same times, chap. xiv ; from which we may further learn the following particulars ; viz, That this war will continue *one day* or year (which inclines me the more to allow the same length of time for the
other

other vials :) *And it shall come to pass in that day,
that it shall not be clear nor dark ; but it shall be one
day,* or year, and no more, and unlike any other
they ever saw ; yet *known to* the honour *of the
Lord* ; *not day nor night* separate and alone : *But
it shall come to pass that at evening time it shall be
light,* ver. 6, 7. The morning of that day will indeed be dark ; for *the nations* gathered *against
Jerusalem to battle,* will *take the city, rifle the
houses, ravish the women, and* take *half of the City
into captivity,* ver. 2. For God will visit his returning people, for that Laodicean lukewarmness
into which there is reason to believe they will be
sunk, some years after their return to their own
land (notwithstanding their building a temple at
Jerusalem) through the fatal influence of the dragon, and the two beasts ; who have extinguished
Light divine, and quenched celestial fire where ever
they could.

Yet *the residue of the people shall not be cut
off from the city :* And before this day or year
concludes, *the Lord shall go forth, and fight against
these nations ; as when he fought in the day of battle* against the Midianites, *Judg* vii. 22 : Those
children of the east fell upon, and destroyed one
another ; and so shall *these,* ver. 13. *Yea their flesh
shall consume away, while they stand upon their feet ;
and their eyes shall consume away in their holes ; and
their tongue shall consume away in their mouth,* ver.
12. *In that day* the Lord *shall stand upon the
mount of Olives,* which will *cleave in the midst,* and
remove to *north and south,* ver. 4 ; which certainly
hath not yet been accomplished. At that day
*Judah shall fight at Jerusalem ; and the wealth of
all the Heathen round about shall be gathered together,
gold, and silver, and apparel in great abundance,*
ver. 14 ; which will of course fall into the hands
of the Jews, when they who brought it thither are
dead. After this *every one that is left of all the na-*

tions

tions that *came up against Jerusalem,* shall *come and worship the King the Lord of Hosts*; whose worship to the end of the world will be a spiritual *keeping the feast of tabernacles,* ver. 16. And this judgment shall be inflicted upon those nations who will not keep this feast, *Rain shall be withheld* from them; and the heavens, becoming hard as brass over their heads, will declare to every one their impiety and impudence, ver. 17, 18, 19. Thus things will go on till the Spirit is poured out in the millennium. But as to the Jews, *after this there shall be no more destruction*; but *Jerusalem shall be safely inhabited* to the end, ver. 11, in great purity and peace, ver. 20, 21.

The time also when this event will take place may be conjectured, with considerable probability, from *Dan.* xii. 7, 11, 12. To explain which, observe, That it is universally agreed that the *time, times and half a time,* ver. 7, are the 1260 years of the beast; and so we have considered them, *Rev.* xii. 14. These years, dated from A. D. 756, will end A. D. 2016: But after that it is added, ver. 12, *Blessed is he that waiteth, and cometh to the* 1335 *days* or years; that is, to 75 years after A. D. 2016, or to A. D. 2091; at which time probably some unknown glorious event will fill the church of God with transporting joy: And at that time we expect the great things which are predicted in the six last chapters of Isaiah, will be fulfilled in all their glory to Jews and Gentiles. But this cannot be the victory mentioned above, for popery will be concluded before A. D. 2091; and we know of no wars which will disgrace the millennial state then begun. We must therefore enquire whether the words will not admit of, and may not even oblige us to begin the 1260 years at an earlier date: And observing that, after what is said of the beast in Daniel's vision, chap. xi.

36—39, the Saracens and Turks are spoken of, ver. 40—43; our ablest expositors have justly considered these 1260 years as the time of the Mahometan, as well as of the Papal delusion. But as we hear nothing of the Mahometans, as such, in scripture under the seventh trumpet, or after A. D. 1866, though the Turks are mentioned under this vial, and in those old testament prophecies which relate to the same subject; so far therefore as the 1260 years relate to the Mehometans, we are necessitated to begin them from A. D. 606, when Mahomet retired to his cave. How *Dan.* xii. 11. is to be understood agreeable to this sense, we have shewn before at chap. xiv. 1—5; viz, by adding 1290 years to the year 684 before Christ, when the daily sacrifice ceased by Manasseh; which points out A. D. 606 for the setting up of Mahometanism. So far then as concerns the Jews, whose country is now in the hands of the Mahometans, these 1260 years, ver. 7, are to be dated A. D. 606, and will end A. D. 1866.

And though popery as reckoned from the time of the beast, must be dated from A. D. 756, yet we have seen under the sixth trumpet, that that monster, *a universal bishop* upon earth, will tread the holy city, and the outer court of the temple under feet, for the whole 1260 years of the two witnesses, chap. xi. 2, 3; and that these years are to be reckoned from A. D. 606 to 1866. Dating therefore the above 1335 years from that time, they will lead us to 75 years after 1866; that is, to A. D. 1941; at which time probably the church will experience the *blessedness* spoken of *Dan.* xii. 12; viz, the defeat of those eastern nations which Ezekiel has predicted will come up against Jerusalem, and which this vial shews will be inlisted under the banner of the dragon and the two beasts. To effect this we have before heard that the Mahometans will become Papifts, after the beaft has flain the Greek church, A. D. 1862, and after they are raifed again A. D. 1866; and that the grand Turk will be the fecond beaft. And this vifion itfelf tells us, that as thefe eaftern nations muft be under the fatal influence of a moft avaricious fpirit, to be fo ready to come upon this fhameful expedition againft the Jews: So, if they had not favoured the fee of Rome before A. D. 1941, thefe croaking emiffaries of the beaft would fcarcely have invited them to fhare this expected plunder of Judea; and, if they could have been prevailed upon to fall upon the Jews in the manner here defcribed, they would not have been fo ready to inlift under the banner of the beaft, in this war againft God.

In explaining the above fcripture, perhaps the text might have allowed us to add the whole 1335 years to the 1260 years of the beaft, or the Pope; but this would have carried us beyond the end of the world; therefore the fulfilment of the prophecies obliged us to add only 75 years to the 1260. But fee a conjecture about the length of the day of judgment, founded upon adding the whole 1335 to the 1260 years, at the clofe of the xxth chapter;

The prophet Daniel adds, chap. xii. 1. *At that time*; viz, A. D. 1941, *fhall Michael ftand up, the great prince which ftandeth for the children of thy people.* Chrift had ftood upon Mount Sion, A. D. 1866, chap. xiv. 1—5; and now he will both ftand up himfelf, and employ his holy angels to put an everlafting end to the troubles of his people, as a nation; which will make this a moft *bleffed* time, ver. 12. *But* long before this bleffed Æra, in the time of the Roman empire (which has been already fpoken of in this vifion, chap. xi. 30, 31; and whofe ten horns will continue to be

be an important subject of this prophecy, even
beyond A. D. 1941) *there shall be a time of trouble*
to thy people; *such as never was since there was a*
nation, to that same time; our Lord adds, *no, nor*
ever shall be, when he expresly applies thefe words
to the deftruction of Jerufalem, *Mat.* xxiv. 21,
which occurred A. D. 70.   *And at that time* particularly, as well as in other of their fubfequent
troubles, *shall thy people be delivered*; even *every*
one that shall be *found written in the book.   And,*
as an emblem and earneft of the general refurrection at the great day, *many of them that* now
sleep in the duft of the earth; and feem as unlikely
to return to Judea, as the dead are to rife from
their dufty beds, *shall awake* and come as out of
their graves.   But, as all the Jews who return to
their own land will not favingly return to God,
therefore I add, *some* of them shall awake *to ever-*
lasting life; *and some to shame and everlasting con-*
tempt, ver. 2. *And* as the church will now refemble a woman clothed with the fun, &c. *Rev.* xii.
1; fo efpecially in thefe times, *shall they that be*
wise shine as the brightnefs of the firmament; *and*
they that turn many to righteoufnefs, as the ftars
for ever and ever, ver. 3—But to return—

   I faw, fays our apoftle, ver. 13, 14, *three un-*
clean spirits like thofe impudent and loquacious
creatures which have their dwelling in fens,
marfhes, ditches and filthy places, the *frogs—*
coming, after their own frightful manner, *out of*
the mouth of the dragon the devil, chap. xii. 9;
and out of the mouth of the firft *beaft*, chap. xiii. 1;
and out of the mouth of the fecond, ver. 11; who,
when the power of his temporal horns failed him,
refolved to act as a *false prophet*; not only working miracles like the firft beaft, and before him,
but perhaps alfo keeping up his own peculiar pre-
eminence as a *prophet*, by uttering falfe predic-

I   tions

tions to promote their common cause; that he
might one way, when he could not another, deceive and damn immortal souls; see chap. xix.
20. and xx. 10. These frogs, which are spawned and
bred in the mouth of the devil, the beast and the
false prophet, from their corruptions, (and which
had been rolled as a sweet morsel under their
tongues) are certainly human spirits, though the
holy Ghost calls them *the spirits of demons, working* pretended *miracles*; *which go forth*, with more
than common human activity and wickedness, *to
the kings of the earth* papal and pagan; *even of
the whole world*, east, west, north and south, see
Ezek. xxxviii. 2, 5, 6, 13, 15, *to bring them*, as
they design, to the assistance of their three prin-
cipals; but in fact to gather them *together to the
battle of the great day of God the Almighty*. Beware therefore, ye kings; and, if you design to
be the loyal subjects of JEHOVAH, look carefully
down and watch your palace gates at this season
against these croaking vermin.

But whilst our author was contemplating these
frogs, he to whom all judgment is committed,
said to him, ver. 15, as these frogs will enter
unobserved; so *Behold I* also *come as a thief*, suddenly, unexpected, and in the night; yea with
great surprize and dread I come, to take away all
that the sinner hath: But the Christian can lose
nothing by my coming, to whom I AM All in All—
Lord bring thyself to me, then take away what
thou wilt from me!—Yet adds our Lord, as this
time will be dark and trying to my servants,
Blessed is he that watcheth; *and keepeth his garments*, that heavenly dress which I gave to cover
him, *Isa.* lxi. 10; *that he may not walk naked, and
they see his shame*. Every Christian is at least a
watchman over himself.

But come, and in devout thought, attend the
funeral of these anti-christian powers, ver. 16.

And

And He, the Lord Jesus, *gathered them together.*
' They were the *dragon's army*, yet God assembled
' them. Such oblique intimations of the inter-
' position of *providence*, are wonderfully instruc-
' tive, and they are scattered up and down in
' many places of the sacred writings,' see *Dod-*
dridge in loc. He gathered them *to a place*, to
which the present possessors of that country have
given a different name; but *which is called in the*
Hebrew tongue, Armageddon, that is, the mountain
of Megiddo in the tribe of Manasseh, *Josh.* xvii.
11; which had a well watered valley lying under
it, famous for the slaughter made there in times
past, *Jud.* v. 19. 2 *Chron.* xxxv. 22. *Zech.* xii. 11:
And, if the derivation of words is regarded, this
eminence will be differently to God's people and
to their enemies, *a mountain of delight*, and *a*
mountain of destruction: For the enemy being gathered thither, a dreadful slaughter will ensue, as
is described by Ezekiel.

Probably the prophet *Joel* speaks of this slaughter, chap. iiid; where, to give us a striking representation of the future judgment, *the valley of Jeho-*
shaphat is called a *valley of decision*, ver. 2—17.
Hear the summons, ver. 11—14. *Assemble your-*
selves and come, all ye heathen; and gather your-
selves together round about: Thither cause thy mighty
ones to come down, O Lord. Let the heathen be
wakened, and come up to the valley of Jehoshaphat;
for there will I sit to judge all the heathen round
about. Put ye in the sickle, for the harvest is ripe:
Come, get you down for the press is full, the fats over-
flow; for their wickedness is great. Multitudes, mul-
titudes in the valley of decision! for the day of the
Lord is near in the valley of decision! We heard
before that at first the enemy will seem to have
the

the day; but when they have taken *half the city captives, Zech.* xiv. 2, probably they will not go away with them out of the land; but ftaying as they expect to compleat their conqueft, the men who took them captive, will fell *the children of Jerufalem* to thofe who follow the camp for gain. And give *a boy for a harlot*; and fell *a girl for wine that they may drink, Joel* iii. 3, 6 : But before the night of that day comes, the fcene is changed ; death feizes on them, and they go down quick into the pit, from *the valley of Jehofhaphat,* that is, either from a valley which lay between Jerufalem and Mount Olivet, or from Engedi fo famous for Jehofhaphat's victory there, 2 *Chron.* xx.2; both of which were in the tribe of Judah, *Jofh.* xv. 62.

These fcriptures therefore compared teach us, that thefe enemies will *plant the tabernacles of their palace between* thofe two *feas,* the fea of Galilee and the dead fea, which are inland feas of Judea, *Dan.* xi. 45 : That their camp will extend about fixty miles in length; (and we know not how far in breadth) viz. from Megiddo in the tribe of Manaffeh, near the fea of Galilee, almoft to Jerufalem; and that an eminent flaughter will be made at both ends of it; viz. at *Armageddon,* and in *the valley of Jehofhaphat,* which is the valley of Cedron. See *Dr. Wells's Geography of the Old and New Teftament, vol.* 3. *page* 79, 80.

Now will thofe words of Balaam be fulfilled again, as they had been by the deftruction of the devoted nations of Canaan, *The ftar of Jacob fhall deftroy the children of Sheth,* or of men, *Numb.* xxiv. 17. *Gen.* iv. 25. And, as providence had made Saul *king* of Ifrael, *higher than Agag,* the king of the Amalekites (fee 1 *Sam.* xv. chapter;) fo *the kingdom* of Jefus *fhall* now *be exalted above Gog,* as the LXX read that word, *Numb.* xxiv. 7. *And it fhall come to pafs in that day,* that, befides the great fertility
of

of the earth, *the mountains*, or the princes of Judea *shall drop down* refreshing *new wine*, *and the hills shall flow with* nutritious *milk*; *and all the rivers of Judah*, or the common people *shall flow with* fructifying *waters*; *and a spiritual fountain shall come forth of the house of the Lord*, *and shall water* that *valley of Shittim*, on the borders of Canaan, in which Ifrael had committed abomination with the daughters of Moab, *Numb.* xxv. 1. *Joel* iii. 18.— But the time is not yet come for the beaft and the falfe prophet finally to fall; fee chap. xix. 20.

17. And the feventh angel poured out his vial into the air; and there came forth a great voice from the temple of heaven, from the throne, faying, It is done.

18. And there were voices, and thunders, and lightnings; and there was a great earthquake, fuch as there had not been from the time that men were upon the earth, fuch an earthquake, and fo great.

19. And the great city was divided into three parts; and the cities of the Gentiles fell down: And Babylon the great came into remembrance before God, to give her the cup of the wine of the fierceness of his anger.

20. And every ifland fled away, and the mountains were not found.

21. And a great hail, as the weight of a talent, fell down from heaven upon the men, and the men blafphemed God for the plague of the hail, for the plague of it was exceeding great.

When

When the seventh trumpet founded there were *great voices*, as well as *lightnings and thunders* in the air, chap. xi. 15, 19; and the seventh vial is poured into *the air*, which the devil, as the prince of the power of it, had so often employed against God and immortal souls, *Job* i. 19. *Eph.* ii. 2: But now, divested of its healing virtue, and impregnated with the seeds of death (except that part of it in which God's servants breathed) *there came forth a great voice from the temple of heaven*; that is, from the temple which had been filled with smoke, while the vials were pouring out, chap. xv. 5, 8; *from the throne* of grace which is erected there, *saying, It is done*; my servants may now live at peace; for the scene is concluded, and *the words of God* in a sense *fulfilled* which he has spoken against the man of sin, chap. xvii. 17, though he is not yet absolutely destroyed—

For what can his enemies do, when God withdraws breath from them, or poisons those floods of air which once refreshed their lungs? *And there were* hideous sounds, *voices and thunders* in the terrified air. (And if this vial should be poured out on *the air*, A. D. 1942, this will be about 1260 years after the time that the pope established the use of organs in the church, which was a returning to judaism; but they will be used no more after A. D. 1866, when the church has *the moon under her feet*,) It is added, And vengeful *lightnings* flashed the wrath of heaven in the face of impenitent sinners; whilst the air itself, striving to hide itself from the wrath of God in the bowels of the earth, added unusual horrors to such *earthquakes* as the world had never trembled under before. *And the great city* Rome, (see chap. xi. 8. xiv. 8. xvii. 18. and xviii. 10.) *was divided into three parts*—Come hither, ye murdering beasts, and see what ye have done upon the affrighted earth, and against your

own

own city !—*And the cities of the nations* in general, and especially those who were in friendship with the beast, *fell down*; which ministered an occasion for the reduction of the vast empires and monarchies of the world, to a less enormous, that is, to a more rational size; see chap. xx. 4. *And* that *great Babylon* of tyranny and persecution, *came in remembrance before God, to give her the cup of the wine of the fierceness of his wrath*; yet all that she can endure here is no more to hell, than a cup to the ocean, as we observed before. *And every Island*, which had proudly reared its head amidst the swelling floods, *fled away*; either sinking down, or removing to another place : *And the mountains were not found* where they used to stand, ' What ' an awful change will this be upon the terraque- ' ous globe ! yet the end of the world is not ' come'—The chapter concludes with an account of a *great hail* of the *weight of a talent*, some stones sixty, some a hundred pound weight, which fell upon the servants of the beast ; yet the few whom it missed, or who found caverns of the earth strong enough to shelter them from it; as well as those on whom it fell, so as not to kill them immediately, unhumbled still, *blasphemed God* so much the more *for the plague of the hail*; *for the plague of it was exceeding great*, ver. 21.

The vials are said to be *the last plagues, for in them is filled up the wrath of God*, which had been begun before, chap. xv. 1 : Yet, as the destruction of Pharoah and his host in the Red Sea, was not reckoned among the ten plagues of Egypt, which are here referred to ; so I apprehend the final destruction of the two beasts, described in the close of the nineteenth chapter, is not to be reckon- ed a part of this last vial, (1.) Because the vials are predicted at such a distance from the account

of

or the final deſtruction of the two beaſts, chap. xix. 19, 20. (2.) As the preſent reign of mercy will ſhorten God's judgments, as much as is conſiſtent with his glory; ſo no man's being *able to enter into the temple, till the plagues of the ſeven angels were fulfilled,* chap. xv. 8, inclines me to ſuppoſe them ſpeedily concluded. (3.) If the laſt vial concludes A. D. 1942, as all of them together will, for a time at leaſt, have broken the ſpirits of the ſervants of the beaſt, this gives us a pleaſing hope of the partial and comparative reſt which the church may probably enjoy from A. D. 1942 to 2016; and at the ſame time allows the enemy ſufficient opportunity, in theſe ſeventy-four years, to recruit their ſtrength and ſpirits again, for that laſt attack which they will make upon the Lamb, A. D. 2016: For Divine vengeance will no more *immediately* fall upon them after the vials; till their final overthrow. Yet now probably is the time for the ten horns of the beaſt to *hate the whore,* to make *her deſolate and burn her fleſh with fire*; for now *the words of God* againſt her are *fulfilled,* and all that remains is his *work,* in executing the ſentence written; ſee chap. xvii. 16, 17.

C H A P. XVII.

1. **A**ND there came one of the ſeven angels, who had the ſeven vials, and talked with me, ſaying, Come hither, I will ſhew thee the judgment of the great whore, who ſitteth upon the many waters.

2. With

2. With whom the kings of the earth have committed fornication; and the inhabitants of the earth have been made drunk with the wine of her fornication.

3. And he carried me in ſpirit into the wildernefs; and I ſaw a woman ſitting upon a ſcarlet beaſt, full of names of blaſphemy; having ſeven heads, and ten horns.

4. And the woman was covered round with purple and ſcarlet, and adorned with gold and precious ſtone, and pearls; having a golden cup in her hand, full of abominations and uncleannefs of her fornication.

5. And upon her forehead a name written MYSTERY, BABYLON THE GREAT, THE MOTHER OF HARLOTS, AND OF THE ABOMINATIONS OF THE EARTH.

6. And I ſaw the woman drunk with the blood of the ſaints, and with the blood of the martyrs of Jeſus: and I wondered, ſeeing her, with great amazement!

7. And the angel ſaid unto me, Why didſt thou wonder? I will tell thee the myſtery of the woman, and of the beaſt which carries her, which hath the ſeven heads and ten horns.

8. The beaſt which thou ſaweſt was, and is not; and will aſcend out of the bottomleſs pit, and go away into perdition: And they who dwell on the earth ſhall wonder, (whoſe names are not written in the book of life, from the foundation of the world) ſeeing the beaſt who was, and is not, though he is.

R   9. Here

9. Here is the mind that hath wifdom. The feven heads are feven mountains, where the woman fitteth upon them.

10. And they are feven kings : Five are fallen, and one is; the other is not yet come; and when he cometh, he muft continue a little time.

11. And the beaft that was, and is not, even he is the eighth; and is of the feven, and goes away into perdition.

12. And the ten horns which thou faweft, are ten kings, which have not yet received their kingdom; but receive authority as kings, one hour with the beaft.

13. Thefe have one mind; and will give their power and authority to the beaft.

14. Thefe will make war with the Lamb; and the Lamb fhall overcome them, becaufe he is Lord of lords, and King of kings; and thofe that are with him, *are* called, and chofen, and faithful.

15. And he faith unto me, The waters which thou faweft, on which the whore fitteth, are people; and multitudes, and nations and tongues.

16. And the ten horns which thou faweft upon the beaft, thefe fhall hate the whore, and fhall make her defolate, and naked, and fhall eat her flefh, and burn her with fire.

17. For God hath given it into their hearts, to effect his defign, and execute one purpofe; and to give their kingdom to the beaft, till the words of God fhall be fulfilled.

18. And

18. And the woman which thou sawest is that great city, which hath dominion over the kings of the earth.

We have here a more particular account of that persecuting power which had been described before, and will be perfectly known when the vials are all poured out, A. D. 1942; nor is even now unknown, except to those who are given up to *strong delusions, that they should believe a lie,* 2 Theff. ii. 11.

Ver. 1, 2. *And there came one of the seven angels, who had had the seven vials,* (see the note on chap. xxi. 9.) *and talked* in such familiar forms *with me,* as precluded every degree of terrour; *faying* unto me, *Come hither, I will shew thee the judgment of the great whore, who sitteth,* in pomp and power, *upon the many waters; with whom the kings of the earth,* through many long infamous ages, *have committed* spiritual and corporal *fornication;* in circumstances of more aggravated guilt, than those in which it was committed at Tyre, in times past, *Ifa.* xxiii. 17. *And the* meaner *inhabitants of the earth,* in every quarter of it, *have been made* spiritually *drunk with the wine of her fornication;* and intoxicated with a false zeal, have as chearfully parted with their reason for her, as if it had been a useless incumbrance to, or the disgrace of their nature.

Ver. 3—6. *And he carried me in spirit into the wilderness,* where I might, more composedly contemplate this execrable delusion, which has in fact reduced the country about Rome to a comparative wilderness. *And I saw a woman sitting upon a scarlet beast;* for cities and countries are often represented by a woman (as *Britannia* our mother, on some of our coins:) *full of names of blasphemy; having seven heads, and ten horns,* as

we

we heard, chap. xiii. 1. *And the woman,* which repreſented the city of Rome, ver. 18, *was array-ed,* or *covered round* περιβεβλημενη, like the Roman emperors and ſenators in a time of peace and war, *with purple and ſcarlet;* and adorned, Gr. *golden over with gold, and* precious ſtone (without leav-ing out one of that name, which the earth could furniſh;) *and pearls;* ſuch as St. Peter never re-commended; ſee 1 *Epiſt.* iii. 3; but it was no part of her deſign to engage the heart, or attract the eye of Deity, *Cant.* iv. 9: *Having* however with theſe ornaments caught the vulgar eye, like other harlots, ſhe holds out *a golden cup in her hand, full of* impure ingredients, here called *the abominations and filthineſs of her fornication;* that with theſe philtres or love-potions, ſhe may af-ſimilate all that approach her to her own brutal diſpoſitions, *Jer.* li. 7.

And, as ſome ſhameleſs proſtitutes had their names written over their doors, ſo, in order that ſhe might appear as much as poſſible un-like the ſervants of God, who have his name in their foreheads, chap. xiv. 1; *upon her forehead was a name written,* which in fact announced the crimes for which God will puniſh her; viz. MYSTERY; ' this very word was inſcribed ' on the front of the pope's mitre, till ſome of ' the reformers took public notice of it,' ſays Mr. John Weſley; but *biſhop Newton* in loc: only ſpeaks of it as a point highly probable, though much controverted. BABYLON THE GREAT, THE MOTHER, the nurſe and patroneſs OF HARLOTS, AND in ſhort of all THE ABO-MINATIONS, corporal and ſpiritual, which fill the different regions OF THE EARTH. —God forgive and humble thoſe, who will not read this character of Rome papal, which is written, (not on her hand where ſhe might conceal it, but) ſtands conſpicuous on her forehead, ſo that no man
can

can look her full in the face without seeing it, unless
God *has given him eyes that he should not see*—ver. 6.
*And I saw the woman drunk with the blood of the
saints, and with the blood of the martyrs of Jesus.*
' To be drunk supposes the draughts to have been
' frequent, large and pleasant: No body chuses
' to be drunk with what is unpleasant to the pa-
' late.   And what a palate must that be to which
' blood is pleasant, but cruelty itself? And as
' people when they are drunk talk nonsense, and
' do extravagant things; so this woman, having
' by cruelty and blood intoxicated herself with
' the grandeur thereby attained, she says, and in-
' sists upon it, That number one is number a thou-
' sand; that an inch is as long as five or six feet;
' that she never did, nor can, tell a lye in her life,
' nor do any thing amiss; and she raves at every
' one that does not believe all this, and vows to
' be the death of them, when she gets them in her
' power.'   See *Dr. Grosvenor's* sermon, p. 29,
30, in the *sermons against popery*, vol. 2d. She also
calls the Protestants *hereticks* and *dogs*; but God
has called some of them *saints:* Therefore says our
author, *Seeing her* in such a state, by such a poti-
on, *I wondered with great amazement*, to see even
a Christian power outdo all that Heathen rage itself had ever meditated against the name of Jesus.

    Ver. 7, 8. *And the angel said unto me*, Grieved
as thou mayest well be at this horrid ruin of thy
own nature, *Why didst thou wonder? John* iii. 7:
Knowest thou not, that all the wickedness of devils will be acted out by inhuman, though nominally Christian hands, against thy Lord that bought
thee? But that thou mayest point out to the future church of God their enemies and dangers,
I will tell thee the mystery of the woman, or of
Rome; and of the beast, or the papal state *which
carries her, which hath the seven heads and ten*

R 3   *horns;*

horns; and by whose means she rages and triumphs
10.   *The beast*, that temporal persecuting power
which thou sawst, and which bears the woman,
was in being long before thy time ; *and* yet *is not*
now, in the manner in which he will be hereafter;
for being an infernal power, he *will ascend out of
the bottomless pit*, to torment the earth a while, *and*
then *go away into* temporal and eternal *perdition :
And they who dwell* soul and body *on the earth*,
shall wonder at this monstrous prodigy; (the in-
sincere professors I mean, whom thou wast forbidden to measure, chap. xi. 2, *whose names are not
found written in the book of life, from the foundation of
the world*, chap. xiii 8. xx. 15. and xxi. 27.) when
they *see* in the outer court *the beast who was, and*
yet *is not*; *though* in fact *he is* now in the spirit of
Diotrephes, and of those *false apostles, deceitful workers* who want to have *the pre-eminence* themselves
in the church and world, instead of giving it to
Christ; see 2 *Cor.* xi. 13. *Col.* i. 18. 3 *John* 9, 10.

Ver. 9—11. It is in vain to pretend to wisdom,
if men will not endeavour to discover and avoid
such a beast as this ; therefore, as it had been
said before, chap. xiii. 18. *Here is wisdom ;* so,
whilst the servants of the beast stand wondering
at him, this angel adds again, *Here,* fixed in cau-
tionary attention, *is the mind that hath wisdom* in
it ; for he is truly wise who can detect the spirit
of this beast in others, and guard against it in
himself.   But that you may know his place, *The
seven heads are seven mountains where the woman,*
the city *sitteth on them* ; viz, the Palatine, Capi-
toline, Quirinal, Cælian, Æsquilian, Viminal and
Aventine hills on which Rome stands; every one
of which will probably be honoured, as three or
four of them have already been, to have a royal
palace erected upon it, by some pope or other, before this abomination is swept down into hell.
                                                    And

And they are seven kings, or seven different forms of government, which are to take place at Rome, see *Dan.* vii. 17, 24, of which the holy Ghost saw proper to take no other notice in this prophecy, than merely to inform us of their number; that we might the more certainly know the beast which is the eighth: But their own historians have given us their names; viz, kings, consuls, dictators, decemvirs, military tribunes, emperors, and dukes. The *five* first of these *are fallen,* and passed away before this A. D. 96; *and one,* the sixth; viz, emperors now *is: the other*; viz, dukes *is not yet come; and when he cometh, he must continue a little time,* that is, from A. D. 566 to 727, says bishop Newton; which was but a short space compared with the preceeding *imperial* power, which continued above five hundred years; and especially with the *papal* which followed it, and will continue 1260 years. *And the beast* described before, *that was and yet is not, even he is the eighth:* But as the dukedom of Rome, subject to the exarchs of Ravenna, under the Greek emperors, scarcely deserves to be named as a different head of Roman government; therefore it is added, the beast *is of the seven,* and must accordingly be reckoned with the other six heathen forms of government, which have taken place in that city: Yet a heavier doom awaits him than them; *they* only landed themselves in something not utterly unlike themselves, but he *goeth away into* compleat, final and irrevocable *perdition.*

Ver. 12—14. *And the ten horns which thou sawest are ten kings,* that is, *kingdoms* or distinct governments, (for so the holy Ghost has explained the word, *Dan.* vii. 17, 23;) *which have not yet received their kingdom,* being only at present members of the Roman empire; and so they continued till about A. D. 456; see chap. viii. 10, 11;

R 4 when

when the empire was crumbled into ten kingdoms, three hundred years before the time of the beaſt; who at his riſing, finding theſe ten horns in full poſſeſſion of their reſpective thrones, inſiduouſly ſupplanted three of them, and pulled them up by their roots, *Dan.* vii. 8. But it is not the deſign of the holy Ghoſt to ſpeak of theſe ten kingdoms, conſidered as fragments or remains of the Roman empire, but only as they are the *horns* with which *the beaſt* puſhes at the church of God: And as horns of this beaſt, *they receive authority as kings* μιαν ωραν, both at the ſame time, and for the ſame length or time as the beaſt. When his head is broken, his ten horns can do nothing; and to in-timate both the ſhort continuance of his reign, and of their abject ſubmiſſion to him as his horns, they are ſaid *to receive* royal *authority with him* but *one hour :* Yet in the review, when they become the kingdoms of the Lord and of his Chriſt, they will think that *hour* long in which they accepted authority with him, and puſhed at the church of God under his infamous direction.

The three kingdoms which this little horn the beaſt acquired, are generally reckoned to be the exarchate of Ravenna, gained for the pope A. D. 755; the kingdom of the Lombards, A. D. 774; and the ſtate of Rome gained ſoon after; on which account the pope wears a triple crown. The other ſeven, biſhop Newton reckons thus in the eighth century, when they were properly conſidered as horns of the beaſt; viz, the *Huns* in Hungary, the *Alemans* in Germany, the *Franks* in France, the *Burgundians* in Burgandy, the *Sa-racens* in Afric and Spain, the *Goths* in other parts of Spain, and the *Saxons* in Britain : But all agree that *Britain* is one of theſe ten kingdoms; for, from fifty five years before Chriſt's time, Britain felt the valour of the Roman arms, for about

about five hundred years: And that she has been a horn of this beast is too notorious.

It is added, ver. 13, 14. *These* kingdoms, intoxicated with the wine of this harlot's fornication, however their interests or inclinations may clash in other respects, *have* all *one mind* in this point; *and will give their power and authority to the beast*, in an offensive and defensive alliance: Therefore *they will all make war with the Lamb* in his followers; *and the Lamb* from one age to another *shall overcome them, because* he is in truth, what the beast vainly pretends to; viz. *Lord of lords and King of kings; and those who are with him*, as all his saints are, even in his hand, *are called, and chosen, and faithful*: And as such they will joyfully fight under his banner; for they love not their lives unto death, when the honour of their Lord calls for it.

Ver. 15, 16, 17. *And he saith unto me, The waters which thou sawest on which the whore sitteth, are people, and multitudes, and nations and tongues*; whom the holy Ghost taught the ancient prophets to compare to *waters*, for their multitude, instability and turbulence; see *Isa.* viii. 6, 7. and xxviii. 2. *Jer.* xlvii. 2. *And the ten horns which thou sawest upon the beast, these*, when they recover from their drunkenness, *will* mortally *hate the whore* after A. D. 1942; *and* observing the command which succeeds the vials, *Reward her as she rewarded you*, chap. xviii. 6; in obedience to God they will *make her desolate, and naked, and eat her flesh, and burn her with fire*. And as such a doom awaits her, though the time of it, which makes haste, is not yet arrived, it is the sin and shame of modern Protestants, and of some true Christians, that they do not now feel indignation against her, more proportioned to that which will hereafter dignify their more illuminated successors. At the same

time

time let no man be ſtumbled, either at our luke-
warmneſs, or the future indignation which will be
conceived againſt her; for the righteous hand of
God is in the one and other of theſe things: *For
God hath given it* both *into* our, and *their hearts,
to effect his* awful *deſign, and execute one* fixed *pur-
poſe: And,* as the Lord frequently puniſhes one
ſin by leaving men to commit others which are
more dreadful; ſo, in righteous vengeance, he
has left theſe deluded kings *to give their kingdom
to the beaſt; till the words of God,* which he has
ſpoken on this ſubject, by one and another of his
prophets, *ſhall be fulfilled.* When the beaſt is
deſtroyed thoſe words will be compleatly fulfilled: But as theſe horns cannot turn upon the
whore, to make her *naked and burn her with fire*
when ſhe is not; *his words* muſt be conſidered as
fulfilled, either when the ſecond beaſt has attained
the height of his power, A. D. 1886, chap. xiii. 17,
or a little before A. D. 1926; ſee chap. xiv.
18—20; or rather when the vials are poured out
A. D. 1942, at which time our Lord will probably *tread the wine-preſs alone, and of the people* there
will be *none with him, Iſa.* lxiii. 3: But after this,
his ſervants will certainly deſire to come in and
teſtify their duty to him; for now his *words* are
fulfilled, and the only *work* that then remains is
the final execution of the beaſt, chap. xix. 20. But
the above words aſſure us, that theſe ten horns of
the beaſts will give their power to him, at leaſt
till after the ſecond beaſt is come, and has attained the height of his power.

‘ General prophecies, ſays Biſhop Newton, like
‘ general rules, admit of limitations and excep-
‘ tions;’ but nothing of this nature can take place,
when the Lord is deſcribing the ſinful conduct of
his creatures, as in the preſent caſe, and drawing
up accuſations againſt them for violations of his
law;

law; here every thing muft be fyllabically true; nothing can be exaggerated here, or protracted beyond its real time: Therefore, as the holy Ghoft fpeaks of all thefe ten horns without diftinction, as *giving their power* to the beaft, till *the words of God are fulfilled*; how many individuals foever there are, or have been in thefe ten kingdoms, who never confented to the unworthy deed, if *the words of God* are not yet *fulfilled*, (and indifputably they are not;) the *ten kingdoms* do all of them to this hour, in fome degree or other, *give their power to* him.

Hear my dear countrymen, and tremble at this word of the Lord—It is the honour of the Britifh horn that it does not now bow down to the beaft, as in ages paft, or as others of them continue to do: Yet this fcripture afferts that England now gives its power to the beaft; for *the words of God* are not *fulfilled*. If it is demanded, *How?* I anfwer, To fay nothing of bowing to the eaft, or at the name of Jefus; of the fatal confidence in baptifmal regeneration with which life is begun; of the impoffibilities, with refpect to themfelves, which the fponfors then promife; or of the fign of the crofs in that ordinance—To be filent about the office of confirmation; at the confequences of which good men, *whatever* they *have figned*, cannot but fhudder; as well as at fome things in the vifitation of the fick, and in the burial fervice—To pafs over *holy-days* appointed merely by the will of man; an uninftituted *liturgy*, which militates againft that love of variety which is effential to the foul of man, and fo wonderfully provided for in God and in his word; and the manner in which that liturgy is chanted in cathedrals, and repeated in common churches; neither of which are at all adapted to the purpofes of devotion—To wave the thought of the people's being deprived of their
unalienable

unalienable right to choose their own ministers, and such frequently obtruded upon them as are no way morally adapted to promote their everlasting interests; and that such a door is left open to the Lord's table, as cannot but fill good men with horror at the company they sometimes meet with there. These, and similar things, awfully *established* the dissenting interest, A.D. 1662, (when more than 2000 ministers were ejected for not submiting to the *spiritual ordinances* of men) before it was *tolerated* in 1689—But to say nothing of these things, my grand objection against the church of England arises from what this concluding book of scripture suggests under the word *beast*; which signifies such an unlawful combination of civil and sacred power as intoxicates the minds of church-men, whilst it invades the prerogative of the Son of God, and in part at least obstructs the ends of his incarnation.

King Henry the viiith assumed to himself that ecclesiastical supremacy which the pope had long so shamefully usurped; and, as might be expected, his children walked in the same steps. And is that supremacy to this hour restored to the Son of God, if still the state maintains, That ' the church has power to decree rights ' and ceremonies, or authority in matters of ' faith?' See article xxth. Alas! the simple laws of Jesus are thought insufficient for the government of his church, without the superadded decorations of human inventions; and the state insists upon being Christ's coadjutor, to establish some things which it seems he omitted. True, it does not ' enforce' its peculiar requisitions, as things ' to be believed for the necessity of salvation;' but those who will call no one *master* but the Lord Jesus, are not permitted to exercise their ministry among, or to commune with, them; which

3   is

is a direct invasion of Christ's government, who *opens and no man shuts*, and *shuts and no man opens*.

David indeed was both a prophet and king; but if any king now becomes a preacher, as he cannot be inspired to give any new revelation to the world, the New Testament gives him no more authority than the meanest of his subjects, to alter, or make any additions to, the established constitutions of that kingdom of grace, of which he has the honour to become a subject—And as to the priesthood, among the ancient Heathens the same person was often king and priest, as *Anius :*

Rex Anius, Rex idem hominum Phœbique sacerdos.
                                          VIRGIL.

But among the Jews, when the priesthood was settled upon Aaron's family, and royalty upon David's, these offices were of course kept sufficiently distinct from each other: And after the captivity, by planting the two olive trees, which represented the magistracy and ministry, on the right and left hand of the Jewish church or candlestick, the Lord forbad the latter to grow under the shade of the former; see chap. xi. 4. *Zech.* iv. 3, 11: For to be *a priest upon his throne* was an honour reserved for *Immanuel* only, *Zech.* vi. 13: And when James and John requested to have these characters united in themselves, our Lord's answer was clear and peremptory, *It shall not be so among you, Matt.* xx. 20—28. *Mark* x. 35—45. Oh! that professing Christians had considered his decision as definitive to themselves! But the Pope, as well as Mahomet, has set up his will in this respect against the will of God, which ruined the church of Rome; and England can never recover its spiritual glory till it knows but *one Lord* in
                                          spiritual

spiritual things.   There is one *Lord Bishop* of
souls, and but one; and as he did not at first, he
never can build his church upon hierarchical or
prelatical ground; for his plan is incapable of
improvement; and as such will be universally
adopted in the millennium, when there *shall be one
Lord* in the church, *and his name one*, *Zech.* xiv. 9 :
Nor have we now, as Christians, any concern with
any other officers or offices in the house of God,
but such only as our great Lord appointed; for
one is our master, even Christ.   And by the time
the church of England has sat three hundred
years from the reformation, or from A. D. 1562,
when the thirty nine articles were first produced
in a convocation of the clergy; or two hundred
years from A. D. 1662, deliberating upon it
whether she shall be *more reformed*; there is
reason to fear that heaven, earth and hell will say,
It is time for her to be *more deformed*, by that popery which she never would wholly extirpate—
True, the *worldly sanctuary*, both at Rome and in
England, preserves a *unity*; but it is a unity of
sound, not *of the faith*; a unity which has wounded ten thousand consciences, for the sake of ecclesiastical gain; while many pretended followers of
St. Paul, almost avow the maxim which he detest-
ed; viz, of *doing evil, that good may come*; *whose
damnation is just*.

Alas! signing religious truths or constitutions
which are not believed, is a crying sin, which
tends to destroy all tenderness of conscience.   At
the same time, in men of no conscience, the vain
trammels of orthodoxy, confine nothing but the
tongue and pen, and that only for an hour.   But
is satan in jest too? And has his servant the levia-
than, who is playing in these *waters*, no other
design but to amuse himself?—*Credat Judæus
appella* !

2

To

To explain ver. 17, fo far as it concerns the British *horn*, was my chief defign in what I have written above: And I befeech my epifcopalian reader, to read Mr. *Flavel's Tidings from Rome*, or *England's Alarm* ; and prove to himfelf at leaft, the improbability that the words of a Mr. *Reeves*, and others there quoted, fhould ever be fulfilled againft our dear native country, before or after A. D. 1866, before he fuffers himfelf to decide againft the literal fenfe of this 17th verfe ; or takes upon him to affert that the command, chap. xviii. 4, *Come out of her, my people*, does not concern him—The church, I apprehend, is then only built on fcriptural ground, when God's minifters neither claim, nor accept any precedence, but what arifes from their fuperior age, gifts, graces or ufefulnefs; for Chrift is to be exalted, and not men.

The diffenters indeed have *no power* of the *horn* to give the beaft ; yet fome of them too are vifibly ferving his interefts, by degrading *the Lord* who *bought them*, and indulging to that Arminian pride and deceit which are popery begun.

But that no man may plead ignorance of the enemy we are here warned againft, the holy Ghoft, by this angel, points out the fpot whence all this mifchief was to arife, ver. 18. *And the woman which thou fawest* riding upon the fcarlet beaft, *is that great city* Rome ; *which hath* now, and will long continue to have, *dominion over the kings of the earth*. This is the execrable fpot where hell opened its mouth, chap. ix. 1 ; to fend out the firft beaft, chap. xiii. 1 ; the Sodom and Babylon of the world, chap. xi. 8. and xviii. 10. And this woman or city now rides in pomp and pride, upon that papal power which at prefent fupports her ; but foon fhe will find her beaft too low ; and when he ftumbles and throws her, fhe will fink

l ke

like lead in the mighty *waters*, on which she now sits, as secure as if they had been everlasting mountains, ver. 1.

CHAP. XVIII.

1. AND after these things, I saw an angel coming down from heaven, having great power; and the earth was enlightened with his glory.

2. And he cried in *his* might, with a loud voice, saying, It is fallen, it is fallen, *even* Babylon the great; and it is become the habitation of devils, and the hold of every impure spirit; and a cage of every unclean and hateful bird.

3. Because she hath made all nations drink of the wine of the wrath of her fornication: And the kings of the earth have committed fornication with her; and the merchants of the earth have been enriched by the power of her luxuries.

When Ezekiel saw the glory of the God of Israel, *the earth shined with his glory*, chap. xliii. 2; which makes it the more probable, that the angel who here *enlightened the earth with his glory*, was the Lord Jesus; who suddenly darted himself down from heaven to the view of his apostle, as he will be seen by every eye at the great day. *And he cried in* his *might with a loud voice*, to awake attention, *saying*, in the same language which had

announced

announced the fall of the Old Testament Baby-
lon, (*Isa.* xxi. 9, and *Jer.* l. and li. chapters) *It is
fallen, it is fallen; Babylon the great:* And as
Isaiah, chap. xiii. 21, 22, had predicted, *The wild
beasts of the desert shall lie there, and their houses
shall be full of doleful creatures; and the owls shall
dwell there; and satyrs,* or demons, supposed to
take the shape of goats (see LXX) *shall dance
there; and the wild beasts of the islands shall cry in
their desolate houses, and dragons in their pleasant
palaces;* so this New Testament Babylon *is become
the habitation of demons, and the* φυλαχη the cage,
the hold, *the prison-house of every impure spirit;*
the place where *every unclean and hateful bird* is
confined. ' Suppose then Babylon to mean Hea-
' then Rome, what have the Romanists gained;
' seeing, from the time of that destruction which
' they say is past, these have been, and are to
' be its only inhabitants for ever?'

The cause of this follows, ver. 3. *For she hath
made all nations* from pole to pole, *to drink* into
her principles and practices; which have overcome them like *wine,* morally disturbed their
understandings, and heated them into rage and
fury against God and men: But as this wine sti-
mulated the vilest lusts of the heart, it became
the wine *of the wrath of God* against those whom
he permitted to drink of it.   Yet, see with horror! *the kings of the earth have committed fornication
with her; and the merchants of the earth,* who
took out their licences to trade from her office,
chap. xiii. 17; and particularly the Romish clergy, who deal in her trinkets and special commo-
dities, *have been enriched by* the abundance of
those *her luxuries* της δυναμεως του στρηνους, which
cherish wantonness, and dispose to acts of uncha-
stity; see *Doddridge in loc.* which yet have had
sovereign and the most fatal *power* over her.

S

4. And

4. And I heard another voice from heaven, saying, Come out from her, O my people, that ye may not be partakers of her sins, and that ye receive not of her plagues :

5. Becaufe her sins have followed *one another* up to heaven, and God hath remembered her unrighteoufnefs.

6. Render to her as fhe hath rendered to you ; and double to her double according to her works : In the cup which fhe hath mingled, mix for her a double quantity.

7. As much as fhe hath glorified herfelf, and lived in luxury, fo much torment and grief give her : Becaufe fhe faith in her heart, I fit a queen ; and am not a widow, and fhall not fee forrow.

8. On this account, in one day fhall her plagues come, death and mourning and famine ; and fhe fhall be confumed with fire : For ftrong is the Lord who judgeth her.

9. And the kings of the earth who have committed fornication, and lived luxurioufly with her, fhall bewail her and lament for her ; when they fee the fmoke of her burning:

10. Standing a far off, for fear of her torment, faying, Alas, alas, thou great city Babylon, the ftrong city ! for in one hour thy judgment is come.

11. And the merchants of the earth fhall wail and lament over her ; becaufe no man buys her wares any more.

12. The *fhip*-lading of gold and filver, and precious ftone, and pearls, and fine linen,

nen, and purple, and filk and fcarlet; and all odoriferous wood; and every ivory vef-fel; and every veffel of moft precious wood; and of brafs, and of iron, and of marble;

13. And cinnamon; and perfumes; and ointment, and incenfe, and wine and oil; and fine flour, and wheat, and cattle, and fheep; and horfes and chariots, and flaves, and fouls of men.

14. And the fruits which thy foul lufted after, are gone from thee; and all thy deli-cious and fplendid things are gone from thee; and thou fhalt never find them any more.

15. The merchants of thefe things, who were enriched by her, fhall ftand a far off, for fear of her torment, weeping and wail-ing;

16. And faying, Alas, alas! the great city, which was clothed with fine linen, and purple and fcarlet, and adorned with gold, and precious ftone, and pearls!

17. For in one hour is fo great wealth de-folated. And every fhip-mafter, and every company in the fhips and the mariners, and all that labour *upon* the fea, ftood afar off,

18. And cried, when they faw the fmoke of her burning; faying, What *city is* like the great city!

19. And they caft duft upon their heads, and cried, weeping and lamenting; faying, Alas, alas! the great city, in which all who had fhips in the fea were enriched, through her expenfivenefs; for in one hour fhe is made defolate.

20. Rejoice

20. Rejoice over her, O heaven, and ye holy apostles and prophets; for God hath avenged *her* judgment of you upon her.

As Jehu took care, that none of God's servants should be slain with the worshippers of Baal, 2 *Kings* x. 23; and the angel hastened Lot out of Sodom when it was going to be destroyed, *Gen.* xix. 15; so *I heard a voice from heaven,* says our author, *saying* to the saints scattered amongst them, *Come out from her my people*; *that ye be not partakers of her sins, and that ye receive not of her plagues*; for none but God's enemies and yours will now dare to promise you safety in her communion: And this order will be duly regarded after A. D. 1942; though alas! at present, for the sake of gain, many professors choose to build their houses in the suburbs of Rome, and, entangle themselves in the skirts of this whore's garments; see chap. xvii. 17. But there is no room for trifling or duplicity now, *for her sins,* ripe for judgment, *have followed* one another like mountains piled *up to heaven*; *and God* will at length prove that he *hath remembered her iniquities.* And as men are to be the instruments of this vengeance, so I command my people, ver. 6, 7, 8, *Render to her* for her sins, *as she hath rendered to you* for your faithfulness to God: And as the thief found with stolen goods was to restore double, *Exod.* xxii. 4, so *double unto her double*; for this will be but *according to her works*: Yea, no temporal punishments you can inflict upon her, can compensate the everlasting injury she has done the souls and bodies of men: But though she cannot in this life suffer a full retaliation, yet *in the cup which she hath mingled, mix for her a double quantity* in terrorem, and as a warning to others. She has robbed me, and sunk my glory in in the whirlpool of felf; therefore *as much as she hath glorified herself, and lived in luxury* ϵϛρηνιαϲϵ **Gr.** as the minifters of my vengeance, *fo much torment and forrow give her*; for even now, going down into the jaws of ruin, fwelled with pride, fhe faith *I fit a queen* to be adorned, *and am no widow, and shall fee no forrow*, Ifa. xlvii. 7—10. Say, delufion, couldft thou have done more than this on a race of thinking immortals! But *on this account, in one* yet future *day, shall her plagues come* from God and men; viz, *death and mourning, and famine, and she shall be* burnt *with fire*, like Sodom, till fhe is *confumed; for strong is the Lord who judgeth her*, and fhe muft feel the power fhe would not fear.

It is impoffible that the followers of Jefus fhould be men of cruelty and blood; yet you fee the order which God has here given his fervants, with refpect to Babylon's fall: Therefore, with whatever horror the view fills me, I'll give up the unmeaning name of a Chriftian, when I am afhamed to avow my joy in the profpect of our Lord's future triumph over her, and the glorious fpreading of his kingdom.

But her death warrant being thus figned, here follows the wailing of her friends over her, ver. 9—19. *The kings of the earth, who have committed* corporal or fpiritual *fornication, and lived luxurioufly, with her*, efpecially after the rife of the fecond beaft; and all the merchants, and trading people of every name, who had been enriched by *her magnificent expences*, in the moft paffionate ftrains bewailed her ruin; ftanding afar off *for fear of her torment*, when they faw *the fmoke of her burning; cafting duft on their heads*, wringing their hands, *crying, weeping, wailing* and faying, Ουαι, ουαι, Woe, woe, *Alas, alas! that great city Babylon! that mighty city!* whofe royal mandates once controlled the fou's and

bodies

bodies of men; *for in one* long predicted *hour is
thy judgment* **come:** And now, this mart of pleasure being shut up, the world itself looks like a
desolated wilderness to those different persons; for
the bills which these beasts had drawn upon heaven
and hell, being now returned, with a vengeance,
both upon the drawers of them, and upon many
of the kings of the earth who had indorsed them,
no man buys their merchandise any more; nor can
her lying currency any more procure any one of
the following twenty-eight articles, in which she
had long traded, ver. 12, 13; viz. *Gold, silver, precious stone, pearls, fine linen, purple, silk, scarlet,
odoriferous wood; ivory-vessels, and vessels of most
precious wood, and of brass, of iron, and of marble;
cinnamon, perfumes, ointment, incense, wine, oil, fine
flour, wheat, cattle, sheep, horses, chariots, slaves,
and souls of men.*

Many of these bounties of providence, from
the respective climes which produced them, had
been brought to Tyre for sale; but when the
second beast has spread popery over the whole
earth, Rome will far exceed Tyre in the extent
of her commerce, and in the abundance of her
delicacies; and especially in her cruelties. Did
Tyre trade in the *persons* of men? (*Nephesh*, Heb.
ψυχαις LXX, *Ezek.* xxvii, 13.) to the Romish
market too are brought, not only *slaves*, but *the
souls of men*, to be sold there; to work in the
smoke of that *furnace*, where adamantine chains
are forged for immortal minds; and where the
dupes of this infernal delusion, are contented to
yield to the will of Rome their civil and religious
hopes. But behold! *in one hour* she is irreparably
desolated; see *Isai.* xxiii. 1, 7, 14, and *Ezek.*
xxviith throughout.

But amidst all this hopeless wailing, here is
no sorrow for the dishonour done to God, no
penitent

penitent confeffions of their guilt and fhame in fupporting her fo long; no cries to heaven for mercy for themfelves; no compaffionate warnings flow from the lips of thofe kings and traders of the earth; no intreaties are addreffed to the votaries of the beaft, already brought low by the vials, fo fave themfelves from that future vengeance which ftands ready to blaft them forever.—Thefe would have been fubftantial proofs of love to God, to men, and therefore to themfelves.—But alas! theirs was the *forrow of the world which worketh death,* 2 *Cor.* vii. 10; or perhaps worfe than fo.—It is well if it did not arife from the difappointment of their lufts; and if there was not anger burning in their breafts againft God, for fpoiling their fhameful markets, by taking this juft and neceffary vengeance on the treafons of men.—Alas! they give the beaft their tears, when they have nothing elfe to give him. They had iron eyes in the day of God's difhonour; but when he takes to himfelf his mighty power and reigns, they can weep aloud.—Rebellious wailings thefe, which quarrel with the righteoufnefs of God! for pride, avarice and defpair can furnifh their plenteous tears, as well as repentance and faith.

But turning from thefe unheeded wailings of the kings and merchants of the earth, the angel adds, ver. 20, *Rejoice over her,* O *heaven;* the Father, Son, and Spirit rejoice at her fall, and fo muft you; *And ye holy apoftles and prophets,* who predicted her ruin, and have been yourfelves fo fhamefully difhonoured by her idolatrous and fuperftitious rites, *rejoice over her; for God hath judged,* or avenged *her* impious *judgment of you upon her;* and dafhed that Babel down which had fo long dared his vengeance, by difcharging its artillery againft his precious family.

21. And

21. And a mighty angel took up a ftone, like a great milftone, and caft it into the fea; faying, Thus fhall Babylon the great city be hurled away, and never be found any more.

22. And the found of harpers, and muficians, and of pipers, and trumpeters fhall be heard in thee no more; and no artift of any art whatfoever, fhall be found in thee any more; and the found of a milftone fhall be heard no more in thee.

23. And the light of a lamp fhall fhine in thee no more; and the voice of the bridegroom, and of the bride fhall be heard no more in thee; becaufe thy merchants were the grandees of the earth; becaufe all the nations were deceived by thy forceries.

24. And in her was found the blood of the prophets, and of faints, and of all who were flain upon the earth.

When that *quiet prince* Seraiah, who was fent as an envoy *from* Zedekiah to the court of Babylon, had finifhed reading the book which Jeremiah had written againft that place, he was ordered to bind a ftone to it, and caft it into the midft of Euphrates; faying, *Thus fhall Babylon fink, and fhall not rife from the evil that I will bring upon her,* Jer. li. 59—64. But Euphrates was now dried up, chap. xvi. 12; and when this *mighty angel took up a ftone, like a great milftone,* he *caft it,* not into a river but, *into the fea;* faying, *Thus fhall Babylon the great city,* not merely fall by its own weight, but, with the ftrength of an all-avenging arm, *be violently hurled away, as* a milftone into the fea; *and never be found any more.*

more. For Rome being firſt burnt, ver. 18.
Dan. vii. 11, may probably afterwards become
a lake of fire and brimſtone, chap. xix. 3; and as
ſurely as God has taken from the ancient Babylon *the voice of mirth, and the voice of gladneſs,
the voice of the bridegroom, and the voice of
the bride; the ſound of the milſtones,* preparing,
bread for the hungry, *and the light of the candle,*
Jer. xxv. 10; ſo ſurely ſhall the ſame things,
here predicted, ver. 22, 23, befal Rome, whoſe
temporal and ſpiritual *candle* ſhall be *put out;*
eſpecially thoſe which they have ſet up at noon-
day on their altars, and before their idols: But
now a general vengeance ſhall blaſt her, becauſe
under the lying pretence of ſeeking a better
country, her ſpiritual *merchants* were not contented to be any thing leſs than μεγιϛανες *the
grandees of the earth;* becauſe ſhe hath *deceived all
the nations with her ſorceries;* and becauſe, (as if
ſhe had obtained a patent from hell to be the only
murderer upon earth) in this ſlaughter-houſe of
the Redeemer's ſheep, *was found the blood of the
prophets, and of ſaints, and of all who were ſlain
upon the earth,* ver. 24; where no murder was
ever perpetrated, but under the influence of ſome
or other of thoſe principles, which have found
ſanctuary at Rome.

C H A P. XIX.

1. **A**ND after theſe things, I heard a loud
voice, as of a great multitude in heaven, ſaying, Hallelujah; ſalvation, and glory,
and honour, and power to the Lord our
God:

2. For

2. For true and righteous are his judgments; for he hath judged the great whore, who corrupted the earth with her fornication; and hath avenged the blood of his servants at her hand.

3. And again they said, Hallelujah; and her smoke ascends for ever and ever.

4. And the four and twenty elders, and the four animals, fell down and worshipped God who sat on the throne, saying, Hallelujah.

5. And a voice came out from the throne, which said, Praise our God, all ye his servants, and ye that fear him, both small and great.

6. And I heard, as *it were*, the voice of a great multitude, and as the voice of many waters, and as the voice of mighty thunders, saying, Hallelujah; for the Lord God omnipotent reigneth.

7. Let us rejoice, and exult, and give glory to him; because the marriage of the Lamb is come, and his wife hath made herself ready.

8. And it was given to her, that she should be cloathed in fine linen, pure and resplendent; for the fine linen is the righteousness of the saints.

9. And he saith unto me, Write. Blessed are they who are called to the marriage supper of the Lamb. And he saith unto me, These are the true words of God.

10. And I fell before his feet to worship him. And he said to me, See, not; I am a fel-

a fellow servant with thee, and with thy brethren who have the testimony of Jesus. Worship God; for the testimony of Jesus is the Spirit of prophecy.

It was commanded, chap. xviii. 20, *Rejoice over her, O heaven, and ye holy apostles and prophets*; and accordingly, says our author, ver. 1. *I heard a loud voice, as of a great multitude in heaven, saying, Hallelujah,* praise ye the Lord: This word occurs four times in this paragraph, ver. 1, 3, 4, 6, to the glory of the Father, Son, and Spirit, and of the God-man Mediator—yea let the *salvation* wrought, and all the *glory* and *honour* of it, and the *power* by which it was effected, be ascribed *to the Lord our God*; *for true and righteous* are the *judgments* both of his word and his hand; and his righteousness, long concealed under a cloud of popish darkness, is now manifested, by his judging *the great whore, who corrupted the earth with her fornication;* and by avenging *the blood of his servants at her hand,* as the souls under the altar long ago requested him to do, chap. vi. 10, 11. *And again they said,* ver. 3, *Hallelujah.* And *her smoke ascends for ever and ever:* For from about A. D. 2016, to the end of the world, Rome will probably become a lake of fire and brimstone: So, at least, the Chaldee paraphrase understands those words, *Isai.* xxxiv. 9, 10, which were never verified in the literal Edom; *The streams thereof shall be turned into pitch, and the dust thereof into brimstone, and the land thereof shall become burning pitch; it shall not be quenched night nor day; the smoke thereof shall go up for ever:* And it is the more probable that Rome may be intended in those words, because the enemies of God's people in general are judged, in that chapter, under the name of

2   Edom;

Edom; see ver. 1, 2, 8: And under the same name we have the doom of those enemies of Israel, chap. lxiii. 1—6, who will come up against them, after they are returned to their own land; see that chapter throughout. And it is well known that the soil about Rome is sulphureous and bitumi- nous, ready to be kindled by the breath of God; see Bp. Newton.

If Rome should be made a lake of fire and brimstone from A. D. 2016, to the end of the world, it will be a yet more conspicuous emblem of hell to the men of that generation, than Sodom in old times was, and still is, to the Gentiles, and the valley of the son of Hinnom to the Jews; (where they burnt the children to Moloch, and consumed the filth of the city) which is called Gehenna *hell* in *Matt.* v. 30, Gr.

Ver. 4—8, *And the four and twenty elders*, who stood furthest off from the throne, as well as *the four animals* who were nearer to it, chap. iv. 4, 6, and v. 8, 14; seeing this great work of God, which had delivered them from this blood-thirsty enemy, *fell down and worshipped God, who sat on the throne, saying, Hallelujah. And a voice came out of the throne*, though I saw not the person who spake; *saying, Praise* and magnify *our God all ye his ser- vants; and ye that fear him, small and great*, though you dare not call yourselves by this honourable name his servants, yet prove your- selves such by joining in this blessed work : And this voice was no sooner uttered, but immediately *I heard* a sound, *as the voice of a great multitude, and as the voice of many waters, and as the voice of mighty thunders; saying, Hallelujah, for the* Lord ὁ παντοκρατωρ, *the Omnipotent reigneth*; and as Christ will reign and judge at this time, so He applies this word to himself, chap. i. 8; see chap. iv. 8: And he is that Lord God Almighty
who

who will fight the battle of the sixth vial at Armageddon, chap. xvi. 14, 16. Besides, creating all things out of nothing, which is said of him, is an incommunicable character of Deity, *Rom.* i. 20; for a mere creature could not have received into himself those Divine perfections, from which alone creation could originate: Therefore they add, ver. 7. *Let us rejoice, and exult; and give glory to him.* If Christ had not been Almighty, he would not have had power to redeem us from the wrath of God, and the tyranny of Satan; or love sufficient to make us his spouse. If he had not been man, our spiritual marriage with him had been impossible; and if he had not been God, it had been unlawful, *Psal.* cx. 3. *Eph.* v. 25—32.

But as his ministers have been long *espousing* souls to him, by the aids of his own Spirit, *2 Cor.* xi. 2; so now, say this exulting throng, *The marriage of the Lamb is come,* and he is come down for this purpose: And as Jacob kept a feast seven days upon his marriage both with Rachel and Leah, *Gen.* xxix. 27, 28. *Judg.* xiv. 10, 12; so now the seventh day, or the seventh thousand years begins to dawn, which will compleat the Redeemer's marriage with the Jewish and Christian church; *and his wife,* knowing well, at this season, the time when she is to be brought unto the King in the glorious millennium, *hath made herself ready. And,* whilst she was stirring up her graces to meet her Lord, as some royal bridegroom bestows a costly array on his bride, so *to her it was* now eminently *given, that she should be* arrayed περιβαληται (not like the idolatrous harlot we heard of, chap. xvii. 4, in *purple and scarlet,* to catch the vulgar eye; but) *with fine linen, pure and resplendent,* fit for the Lamb's wife; *for the fine linen is* δικαιωματα *the righteousnesses of*
the

the faints, both of juftification and fanctification ;
and efpecially thofe amiable, triumphant and
glorious robes of holinefs, which fhall adorn the
church of God, when her Divine Hufband has deftroyed the man of fin, by the breath of his
noftrils, and by the brightnefs of his appearing.

Ver. 9. *And he,* that kind angel who had been
talking with me, chap. xvii. 1, *faith unto me,* as
the time draws near, *Write ;* and fend the folemn
meffage round the world ; faying, Inexpreffibly
bleffed are they who are honoured fo far as to be
called to this marriage fupper of the Lamb ; which
will be folemnized about midnight between the
fixth and feventh day, or the fixth and feventh
thoufand years ; or at leaft not half an hour after,
Matt. xxv. 6 ; fee chap. viii. 1. and xxi. 1—6. And
though the Jewifh day began at fun-fet ; yet their
polity being deftroyed, and our apoftle now a
Roman prifoner, I can fee no improbability in
fuppofing him to underftand the artificial day as
beginning at the time, at which it will be univer-
fally reckoned to begin, when thofe great events
take place. This will be a feafon of fignal, and
hitherto unequalled, grace, the glory of which will
make faints as confpicuous, as if they wore pure
and fhining linen ; for now the Lord's *people* will
be willingneffes, (as Bp. Reynold's renders the
word) or *willing offerings in the day of his power.*
Pfal. cx. 3. Heb. And in that day *they fhall not
teach every man his neighbour, and every man his
brother, faying, Know the Lord ; for all fhall know*
him, *from the leaft to the greateft, Heb.* viii. 11.
And he faith unto me, Let not thy unbelief ftagger
at the greatnefs of this grace ; for *thefe are the
true words of God,* and the *fcripture cannot be
broken.* John x. 35.

Ver. 10. Greatly enraptured with this account,
which I was enabled to underftand and feel, *I*
fell,

fell, says our author, *at the feet* of the angel who
shewed me the great things mentioned, chap.
xviith, and stood by me whilst I heard the things
spoken in chap. xviiith, and in this *to worship him*:
And immediately *he said unto me*, with a haste and
eagerness which was very striking—*See! not! I am*
only *a fellow servant with thee, and with thy brethren who have the testimony of Jesus; worship
God; for the testimony of Jesus is the Spirit of prophecy*, whether given to saints or angels. And
though *prophecies will* be *rendered useless* in heaven, when the glorified bodies and souls of the
saints predict every thing to them, which they can
want to know, with respect to themselves; and here
on earth these holy waters *will fail* from the fountain of Israel, when the sacred canon is closed;
see 1 *Cor.* xiii. 8, 10, 11, Gr; yet good men to
the end of time will be enabled to see, and declare
from the written word, whatever it will be necessary for the saints to observe and do, for the
honour of their Lord; see *Amos* iii. 7.

That this celestial courtier could not affect his
Lord's appearance; and that John could not de-
liberately design to worship an angel, are both
indisputable; and yet that such an act of worship
was performed as creatures have no right to receive, the angel's answer to him loudly declares.
But we may well suppose that our author was not
perfectly composed, but overpowered as Daniel,
chap. vii. 28. viii. 27. and x. 8—11, 15—19; and
therefore mistook the angel for Christ, though
he appeared only in his own proper glory. But
is there no sin in such weakness? at least it was
occasioned by sin; and in the present case a re-
prehensible action resulted from it: Nor will all
danger of *worshipping angels* be eternally past,
with respect to any of us, till all remains of a
fleshly mind are for ever removed, *Col.* ii. 18.
                                        Therefore

Therefore let us be satisfied, though angels don't appear to us, as to our apostle: And, as there is such weakness in human nature, let no man *glory in man*, on their own account, 1 *Cor.* iii. 21; and let us learn to beware of church-idols, and heavenly idols; when we think we have shaken off those of the world. *In many things we all offend*, says the apostle James, chap. iii. 2, and to suppose himself perfectly free from sin, is a mistake which a child of God can scarcely make. *If we say we have no sin* in us, *we deceive* (probably not others, but certainly) *ourselves*, whilst we tell the world that *the truth is not in us*, 1 John i. 8.

11. And I saw heaven opened; and behold a white horse, and he that sat upon him was called faithful and true; and in righteousness he judges and makes war.

12. But his eyes *were* as a flame of fire; and upon his head many diadems; having a name written which no man knows but himself.

13. And he was covered round with a garment dipped in blood; and his name is called The Word of God.

14. And the armies which are in heaven followed him upon white horses, clothed in fine linen, white and clean.

15. And out of his mouth goeth a sharp sword, that therewith he might smite the nations; and he shall rule them with a rod of iron: and he treadeth the wine-press of the indignation and wrath of Almighty God.

16. And he hath on his garment, and on
his

his thigh, a name written, KING of
KINGS, and LORD of LORDS,

17. And I faw one angel ftanding in the
fun; and he cried with a loud voice; faying to all the birds which were flying in
the midft of heaven, Come and gather yourfelves to the fupper of the great God;

18. That ye may eat the flefh of kings,
and the flefh of generals, and the flefh, of
the mighty; and the flefh of horfes, and of
thofe who fit on them; and the flefh of all
men, *both* free and bond, both fmall and
great.

19. And I faw the beaft, and the kings
of the earth, and their armies gathered together, to make war with him who fitteth
upon the horfe, and with his army.

20. And the beaft was taken; and with
him the falfe prophet, who wrought figns
before him; by which he had deceived
thofe who received the mark of the beaft,
and thofe who worfhipped his image. Thefe
two were caft alive into the lake of fire,
burning with brimftone.

21. And the reft were flain with the
fword of him that fitteth on the horfe,
which proceeded out of his mouth; and all
the birds were fatiated with their flefh.

We have feen Rome, which had burnt the
martyrs of Jefus, itfelf burnt with fire, ver. 3,
kindled by the breath of God; but the beaft is
ftill alive, to make this laft vain attempt againft
the Lamb and his followers. The *words of God*
on this fubject, have been in a great meafure

T   *fu filled*;

fulfilled; but one dreadful *work* yet remains:
And see! the long-expected A. D. 2016 is come;
at which time *the Lamb* will *overcome* the powers
who are confederate againſt him, for he is *Lord
of Lords*, and *King of Kings*; *and they who are
with him are called, and choſen, and faithful*, chap.
xvii. 14, 17. Accordingly, ſays our author, ver.
11. *I ſaw heaven opened* in a way of vengeance,
which had ſtood open long, beaming in vain
with neglected grace to men; ſee chap. iv. 1.—
And behold, a white horſe, the emblem of ſtrength,
dignity, purity, beauty, triumph, joy and glory;
that ſame white horſe *the goſpel*, on which John
ſaw his Divine Lord taking the field, A. D. 96.
chap. vi. 2; which he ſtill keeps, and will till all
his enemies are driven thence: For the deſtruction
of Anti-Chriſt will not only be a fulfilment of
goſpel threatenings, but it is an eſſential conſti-
tuent part of the goſpel of Jeſus; for it is mentioned as one of its peculiar bleſſings, that by it
the prince of this world is judged, both perſonally
and in his ſervants, *John* xvi. 11. And as *white*
reflects all the colours of the rain-bow, ſo the
goſpel of Chriſt, both as it ſaves believers and
deſtroys their enemies, reflects the full glory of
the Father of lights to every well-prepared eye:
And our Lord comes on this horſe with purity,
dignity and ſplendor, whether he comes to ſave
or to deſtroy: And when he comes on this awful
expedition, in the light of his judgments, every
eye ſhall ſee that he is *faithful and true*; and
that *in righteouſneſs he judges and makes war.*

Ver. 12. *But on this occaſion his eyes were as
a flame of fire*, to conſume his enemies, chap. i.
14. *And on his head were many diadems*; which
our victorious David had taken from the heads
of his enemies, 2 *Sam.* xii. 30. 1 *Chron.* xx. 2.
and which had been voluntarily ſurrendered to
him,

him, by the numerous nations and individuals
whom his grace had conquered, especially under
this seventh trumpet, *Cant.* iii. 11. *Rev.* xi. 15. and
xxi. 24, 26. *Having* that *name*, expressive of his
nature and designs, *written* in each diadem, *which
no man knows but himself*, and the Father, who
are *one*, *Matt.* xi. 27. *John* x. 30; for there are
mysteries in the nature and mediation of the Son
of God, which confound the most prying eye of
creatures.

Ver. 13, 14. *And he was* clothed *with a garment dipped in blood*, as when he returned from
the slaughter of the Edomites, *Isa.* lxiii. 1; for he
had been at war with popery from its earliest in-
fancy; both by his witnesses, and by the repeated
exertions of his own immediate power against it.
And his name, that wonderful name which I just
now spoke of, *is called*, *The* Reason, Wisdom,
Sentence, Speech, Oracle or *Word of God*, *John*
i. 1. *And the armies* of angels *in heaven*, and of
saints in the church below, most joyfully *followed
him*, to share in the triumphs and joy of their Lord;
riding *upon white horses*, and animated by that peculiar Spirit which, according to the prophecy, in
chap. xvii. 16. shall influence the saints from A. D.
1942, to 2016; yet, to intimate their purity in
the part they were now taking against the beast,
their dress corresponded to the appearance of
their horses; they were *clothed in fine linen, white
and clean*.

Ver. 15, 16. *And* (to say nothing more of the
armies, who followed our Lord, rather as witnesses of his triumph, than as instruments of his
victory) *out of his mouth goeth a sharp sword*, the
word of God, *Eph.* vi. 17; whose edge they had
refused to feel when it was sharpened against their
corruptions; but our Lord has now taken up
his despised words, as a sword in his own mouth;

that

that therewith he might fmite the nations, who had been confederates with the two beafts, and as devouring wolves to his fheep and lambs: Thefe, as well as others, were the fheep of his general pafture; therefore he who would have fed them as a gentle fhepherd, now *rules them* ποιμανει *with a rod of iron*; which they can no more refift than a potter's veffel, *Pfal.* ii. 9. *Rev.* ii. 27. and xii. 5. *And he treadeth the wine-prefs of the indignation and wrath of almighty God*, into which his enemies are caft, with as much eafe and pleafure as men burft grapes under their feet, *Ifa.* lxiii. 2, 3. *Rev.* xiv. 19, 20. *And he hath upon his garment, and upon his thigh*, that feat of his natural and federal military ftrength, (*Gen.* xxiv. 2, 3. *Pfal.* xlv. 3. *Jer.* xxxi. 9.) that *name written* which the Eaftern monarchs fo infolently affect, and which the Pope arrogates; viz. KING of KINGS and LORD of LORDS, chap. xvii. 14. 1 *Tim.* vi. 15. This is he who cometh forth for this final victory over the beaft, and over the kings of the earth, whoever of them fhall then be found confederates with him.

And as he invited the beafts of the field, and the fowls of the air to his facrifice, when he flew the nations which broke in upon the land of Ifrael, under the fixth vial; fee chap. xvi. 12. *Ezek.* xxxix. 17—21; fo fays our apoftle, ver. 17, 18. *I faw one angel ftanding in the fun*, whofe fiery beams had no manner of influence upon this celeftial Warrior; *and he cried with a loud voice, faying to all* the *birds* of prey, *which were flying in the midft of heaven*, in queft of food; Hither, hither wing your way; *Come, gather yourfelves to the fupper of the great God; that ye may eat the flefh of kings, of generals, and of the mighty*, who have long feafted themfelves for this day of flaughter, *James* v. 5; or, if *the flefh of horfes* is
more

more grateful to you, you will find it here in a
dreadful plenty, lying mingled *with the flesh of
all* forts of men, both *free and bond, both small
and great*; and what you cannot devour, muft
remain as dung to fatten the earth, 1 *Sam.* xvii.
44, 46. *Jer.* ix. 22.

Ver. 19, 20. This order had no fooner iffued
out of the lips of this angel, but *I faw the wild
beaft, and the kings of the earth, and their armies
gathered together; to make war with him who fitteth upon the horfe, and with his army*: But whether any of thofe nations, which have long been
called the ten horns of the beaft; and who have
mortally hated the whore ever fince A. D. 1942,
will now fo far repent of their vengeance upon
her, as to join their forces in this final war
againft Chrift, we are not told; fee chap. xvii.
14—17. However, in fpite of every warning,
fee! many are gathered together, as if they
hoped to outbrave Omnipotence: But what can
created force do againft God? therefore, faying
nothing of the engagement, it is only added, *The*
firft *beaft was taken, and with him* the fecond, who
had both pufhed at the church of God with his
two little horns, chap. xiii. 11, 12, and, as a *falfe
prophet*, wrought *figns before the* firft *beaft; by
which he had deceived thofe who received his mark,
and thofe who worfhipped his image*. *And thefe
two beafts*, who were the laft of their name and
rank, *were caft alive into the lake of fire, burning
with brimftone*; which doubtlefs is to be underftood of hell, whither Satan is caft, chap. xx. 1,
3, 10, 14: And they defcended thither foul and
body together, as the moft diftinguifhed monuments of Divine vengeance; to teftify to damned
friends what their own refurrection bodies fhall
be; as Enoch and Elijah had been long ago
caught up into heaven, to witnefs there what fu-

T 3 ture

ture glory shall array the saints at the resurrection. But as hell is a state invisible to us, and the place of it unknown, as this battle will probably be fought in the heart of the pope's territories; if Rome should be at that time a burning furnace, and these two beasts should be cast alive into this lake of fire, in their way to eternal burnings, they will then perish in some respects like Korah and his company, *Numb.* xvi. 32, 35; and, like Sodom and Gomorrah, be *set forth as an example suffering the vengeance of eternal fire,* *Jude* 7: Yet their doom will be more compleat at once, than that of Korah, or of Sodom.

But after our Lord has gained this victory, if his attending angels should be employed in casting them into this lake, this will be similar to their future *binding the tares in bundles* to be burned, *Matt.* xiii. 30. And if any of the ten horns of the beast should have any concern in this destruction, those words will then be literally fulfilled, They *shall burn her with fire,* chap. xvii. 16.

Ver. 21. *And the rest* of this confederate army, *were slain with the sword of him who sat on the horse;* which *proceeded out of his mouth,* and mowed down their ranks with infinite ease; which inclines me to believe that there will be no literal fighting of men on either side, in this last engagement; whether they are or not employed, after the victory, in casting the two beasts into the lake of fire. *And all the birds* of every wing, which could relish such provisions, *were satiated with their flesh.*

And now we have heard the last of this beast and his army; for at A. D. 2016, the world will have for ever done with that which is called Popery; which had been virtually concluded ever since the pouring out of the seventh vial, chap. xxi.

17; though

17; though all remains of this abomination will not be eradicated from human nature, till it is made perfect in heaven.

CHAP. XX.

AND I saw an Angel coming down from heaven, having the key of the bottomless pit, and a great chain in his hand.

2. And he seized the dragon, that old serpent, who is the devil, and satan; and bound him a thousand years.

3. And cast him into the bottomless pit, and shut him up, and set a seal upon him; that he might deceive the nations no more, till the thousand years were finished: And then he must be loosed for a little season.

4. And I saw thrones, and they sat upon them; and judgment was given to them. And *I saw* the souls of those who had been beheaded for the testimony of Jesus, and for the word of God; and who had not worshipped the beast, nor his image, and had not received his mark upon their forehead, or in their hands; and they lived and reigned with Christ a thousand years.

5. But the rest of the dead lived not again, till the thousand years were finished. This *is* the first resurrection.

6. Blessed and holy is he who hath part in the first resurrection, on these the second

death

death hath no power; but they shall be priests of God and of Christ; and shall reign with him a thousand years.

In six verses we have here a prophetic history, of far the most important thousand years which the world will ever know: But so short a description of it was surely designed to remind us, that a thousand years is nothing, when compared with that vast eternity which awaits our immortal nature! As a thousand sabbatical years, out of seven thousand, is nothing to the interminable *sabbatism* of the saints in glory, *Heb.* iii. 9. Gr.

We have already seen the dreadful end of the two beasts; beheld the stable burnt in which they lay down; and marked the vengeance which blasted them as the vengeance of the gospel: And now the dragon, the devil, who had instigated this earth-born and sea-born monster, to all the outrages they have severally and together committed, comes himself to be dealt with: As an immortal spirit he has no hope of dying; yet his rage is restrained to the bottomless pit.

It had been given to the pope to open *the well of the abyss,* A. D. 606, chap. ix. 1, to fetch assistance from thence in framing his deceits, and sheets of infernal darkness to cover his impious design: And in that darkness *the angel of the bottomless pit* had come out, at the head of his Mahometan and Roman locusts, and raged and reigned even in the church, from that time till he was cast out after A. D. 1866, chap. ix. 11. and xii. 7; soon after which the Mahometan chief, as he used to be called, forsook the prophet of the east, to become himself a *false prophet,* working miracles before the first *beast* at Rome. But observe, as the earth could not support the wickedness and misery of hell without becoming itself a hell, there-

therefore the Lord had never suffered either of those beasts immediately to open the abyss itself, any other way than through its well, chap. ix. 1: And now the key of that well being wrested out of the hands of the beast, and both the beasts cast into the lake of fire; not only that well itself is shut up, but the dragon the devil is seized, and *cast into* his fiery den, *shut up*, and a *seal set upon him* for a time, by the Captain of our salvation, of whom these words indisputably speak; for He was manifested to destroy the works of the devil; and he only has *the keys of death and hell*, chap. i. 18.

1. *And I saw an Angel*, for Christ will wear that name till he has made all his people *equal to the angels*, *Luke* xx. 36; even he who cast the dragon and his angels out of the church, chap. xii. 7, 9—*Come down from heaven*, from the immediate presence and glory of the Father; *having the key* not only of the well of the abyss, but *of the bottomless pit* itself; as he has also the keys of the kingdom of heaven, *Matt.* xvi. 19: Yea *he opens* (the human heart, the mouth, and heaven and hell) and *no man shuts*; and *he shuts and no man opens*, chap. iii. 7. *And a great chain in his hand*; which this proud spirit will find too heavy for his utmost strength to support.

2, 3. The apostle Jude tells us, ver. 6, That the *angels, who kept not the government of themselves,* under their own head Christ, he *hath reserved in everlasting chains under darkness* (see Doddridge *in Loc.*); but Satan's chain had been awfully lengthened from A. D. 606 to 1866; in which time the outer court worshippers had been *delivered unto him*, by a spiritual kind of excommunication from God, chap. xi. 2: But soon after A. D. 1866, the devil having been cast even out of the outer courts of the temple *into the earth,*

chap.

chap. xii. 12; and having from that time to A. D.
2016, moſt dreadfully raged there, the time is
now come in which Divine mercy will, more glo-
riouſly than ever, exert its gracious power for a
long enſlaved world: *And* accordingly, all judgment being committed to the Son, *he ſeized the
dragon,* whom nothing but force could cauſe to
ungraſp his prey; *that old ſerpent, who is the devil
and ſatan;* whoſe names and accuſations are here
ſolemnly publiſhed, juſt before he is caſt into
prifon: *And bound him a thouſand years;* which
are mentioned three times, ver. 2, 3, 7, for the
greater certainty both of the thing, and of the
length of the time; as well as perhaps to inform
us, that this reſtraint will be laid upon him,
about the beginning of the third thouſand years
from Chriſt's incarnation. *And caſt him into the
bottomleſs pit;* which will be his eternal priſon,
ver. 7, 10, to which ſatan intreated our Lord not
to command him to depart, in the days of his
fleſh, Luke viii. 31. *And ſet a ſeal upon,* over
or above *him;* as the Jews had done on Chriſt's
dead body, *Matt.* xxvii. 66; and the heathens
on Daniel in the lions den, chap. vi. 17, but as
this ſealing will neither deſtroy the activity, nor
the wickedneſs of his nature, I am ready to aſk,
Will he not ſtill be the prince of this world,
though his power is much limited? Or will all
thoſe ſcriptures be rendered uſeleſs in the millennium, which now warn us againſt this adverſary?

Poſſibly theſe phraſes may not predict the total
ſuſpenſion of his temptations; this *ſhutting him up*
may chiefly refer to that *opening* of the well of
the abyſs, mentioned chap. ix. 1, 2, in which
ſatan came out, ver. 11, at A. D. 606; as he
alſo greatly exerted his power, A. D. 1866; ſee
chap. xii. 9. By popery and mahometaniſm he
had long abuſed the nations; but now he is ſhut

up,

up, *That he might DECEIVE the Gentiles* or nations *no more*, as he had before, *till the thousand years were finished*; *and then he must be loosed for a little season*, to renew his efforts against Immanuel: But, blessed be God, he will not be *loosed* for Bengelius's *Chronos* of 1111 years, nor for near so long a time; see ver. 7—10.

4. When the dragon is thus cast down to hell, the church will prosper, as Daniel predicted, chap. vii. 27. *And the kingdom, and dominion, and the greatness of the kingdom under the whole heaven, shall be given to the people of the saints of the Most High; whose kingdom is an everlasting kingdom, and all dominions shall serve and obey him.* In every age the Lord's people have been *kings and priests unto God and his Father*, chap. i. 6; and eminent saints have conspicuously *reigned on the earth*, chap. v. 10, *in* and by that divine *life* which they have received from *Jesus Christ*, *Rom.* v. 17. But in this blessed time says our author, *I saw thrones* prepared for living saints, *the thrones*, not of Heathen kings, but *of the house of David*, *Psal.* cxxii. 5; which were placed over all those nations which satan had so long deceived, ver. 3. And as the saints will in general be of a princely spirit in this period, so the particular notice here taken of these *thrones*, inclines me to believe that they will be very numerous in the millennium. Christ has always fed *his flock as a shepherd*, *Isai.* xl. 11, who knows the name and state of all his sheep: And the dominion of these princes will probably be no larger than they can personally superintend and judge; which will greatly contribute to make civil and religious liberty compleat, in these thousand years.—*And they sat on them*, as lords over their own power and glory, not vassals to them; therefore these thrones neither rival, nor envy each other. *And judgment was*

given

given to them to determine wisely, and execute vigorously. But though the saints will have dominion over their enemies in the morning of the seventh millennary, and execute upon them all the judgment which is written, *Psal.* cxlix. 5—9; yet when the scale is turned, they will not treat the few wicked who are left amongst them, as themselves were treated, when they were the minority. At the same time, God's people will not be so free from sin, sorrow and afflictions, as either to render their bibles useless to them, or supersede the need of ministers, ordinances and magistrates: But as they will be all righteous, so will their officers and exactors be; and the saints will be so generally qualified to *judge* of one another's matters, 1 *Cor.* vi. 2—5, as will gloriously preclude vexatious law-suits.

    ' Thou bright celestial Day begin;
    ' Dawn on these Realms of Woe and Sin.'

And I *saw the souls of those who had been beheaded for the testimony of Jesus, and for the word of God; and who had not,* in any form whatever, paid their senseless homage to the *beast; and they lived and reigned with Christ,* in such different circumstances as infinite wisdom saw fit to mark out for each of them, for that *thousand years* in which satan was so restrained: And this thousand years of their reign with Christ, as well as of satan's confinement, is also mentioned three times, and for the same reasons as the other; see ver. 4, 5, 6.

    5, 6. *But the rest of the dead,* who died in enmity and arms against God; for of such this word οἱ λοιποι the rest or *remnant,* who were, as it were, the *caput mortuum,* of human nature is to be understood, chap. ix. 20. xi. 13, and xix. 21, *lived not again, till the thousand years were finished.*

2

This

This is *the first resurrection:* Truly *blessed,* and in every sense of the word *holy, is he who hath part in the first resurrection;* on *these the second death,* which will be inflicted in the lake of fire and brimstone, ver. 14, *hath no power* or authority εξουσια; *but they shall be,* not only kings and priests *to* God and Christ, chap. v. 10, who will be the united object of universal adoration in the millennium; but, to express their personal excellencies and accomplishments, they shall be *priests of God and of Christ; and they shall reign with him a thousand years.*

For a long time I understood this first resurrection literally; viz. of the martyrs rising out of their graves, to reign with Christ in heaven, a thousand years before the other dead arose; but as this book every where abounds with figures, and the two witnesses arose only figuratively or spiritually, so the following reasons now incline me to the figurative sense here. (1) Because it seems as if their reigning with Christ must be upon earth, though it is not asserted: For as Christ's binding satan, ver. 2, and his deceiving the nations, ver. 3, 8, and his troops incompassing the camp of the saints, ver. 9, must be upon earth; so it may be doubted, whether the saints can properly be said to be *priests of God and of Christ* in heaven, ver. 6, and to have *judgment given to them* there before the great day of God, ver. 4. (2) This phrase, I saw *the souls of them who had been beheaded, &c. and they lived and reigned with Christ,* ver. 4, is not a natural or common description of raising men from the dead. (3) The rest of the dead are represented as living again immediately after this thousand years, ver. 5, 7; but the general resurrection certainly will not take place, till more than a hundred years after the millennium; in which time another effort will be made, by the God of

th:s

this world to regain his loft power; fee ver. 7, 8, 9: Therefore the refurrection of thefe martyrs, and the living again of the wicked muft be both of them figurative. (4) To fay nothing of the improbability, that glorified faints fhould return to live in animal bodies upon earth again; if the martyrs are raifed to reign with Chrift, either on earth or in heaven, it would feem very flat and low, to fay of thofe who had been fo eminently with God for fo long a time, *The fecond death had no power over them,* ver. 6: But if living faints upon earth, attain fuch purity and peace, as to have no fear of eternal perdition, the fecond death may well be faid to have no power over *them,* in whom *perfect love has caft out fear.*

(5) After the account of the dignity of the faints, as living and reigning with Chrift, ver. 4, it feem-ed reafonable to expect a proportionable charac-ter of them; and what more glorious could be faid of them, than to reprefent them by thofe illuftrious chieftains of our David's war, who adorned the line of falvation in the primitive ages, and in the times of the fharpeft papal perfecution? And if in fcripture, perfons and places eminent for wickednefs, are frequently defcribed by the names of their fimilar predeceffors, who flourifh-ed before them, we cannot wonder that John the Baptift is called Elijah, in whofe *fpirit* and *power* he came, *Luke* i. 17; or that the return of Ifrael to their own land is thus expreffed by *Ezek.*xxxvii. 3, 12—14, *I will open your graves, and caufe you to come out of your graves, and bring you into the land of Ifrael:* To the fame purpofe Dr. Whitby quotes the following fcriptures; viz. *Ezra* ix. 8, 9; *Pfal.* lxxi. 20. lxxx. 18. lxxxv. 6. *Ifai.* xxvi. 19, *The earth fhall caft out the dead. Hof.* vi. 2, 3, and xiv. 7, and *Zech.* x. 8, 9; fee his *Treatife on the Millennium.* The primitive chriftians and martyrs, were

were defigned to be a kind of *firft-fruits of his creatures*, who were to arife in every fucceeding age, *Rom.* xvi. 5. *Jam.* 1. 18; and the general gofpel harveft being now come, I faw, fays our apoftle, *the fouls* which refembled thofe who had been *beheaded* (which was a Roman punifhment) *for the witnefs of Jefus, and for the word of God*, in the days of Nero; and thofe whom no allurements or terrors, could tame into a compliance with the views of the beaft; either to *worfhip him*, or his image, or to *receive his mark* on their *foreheads*, or in their *hands*.

And though thefe men will have no beaft to conflict with in the millennium; yet it will be eminently for the glory of their Lord that they fhould, by a princely fpirit, *reign in life* over their own corruptions within, and over temptations from fatan and the world without : *And* accordingly men who refembled thefe ancient worthies *lived and reigned with Chrift*; ' and therefore certainly not in ' fenfual pleafures,' *a thoufand years*; and the *Lord alone* was *exalted in that day, Ifai.* ii. 11. But *the reft of the dead*, who had the fpirit of Sodom, of Babylon and Egypt in them, *lived not again*, that is, they had none to fucceed them in their fpirit and views, *till the thoufand years were finifhed*; for the few wicked who will be found in thofe times, will be greatly awed by that glory of the divine perfections which will beam forth from his fervants.—In fupport of this fenfe, I only add, (6) That the living again of the reft of the dead is not, nor could it properly be called a refurrection, becaufe their wickednefs will originate from their indulging the natural propenfions of their own depraved hearts; and as their living again after the thoufand years, will not be in confequence of any literal refurrection of wicked perfons before the day of judgment, it is the more

2 reafon-

reasonable to suppose that that resurrection of the saints, with which it is contrasted, will not be a literal resurrection ; but only an appearance of persons of similar dispositions, with the eminent heroes of ancient times.

When man was become *dead* to the original ends of his being, if mercy will save him, that *resurrection* which is *first* in God's design, in nature, as well as in the order of dignity and precedence, must be the resurrection of the soul from the death of sin, which (will afterwards secure a glorious resurrection for the body ; as it) was the grand design of the Redeemer's incarnation ; see *John* xi. 25. *Eph.* i. 19, 20. So *this resurrection* in the millennium, which is analogous to it, though it is not strictly speaking the first instance of a resurrection which our Lord had ever shewn, taken either literally or figuratively ; yet being both spiritual in its nature, and eminent and unparalleled in its kind, it is properly called the *first resurrection* ; to intimate that all that he had wrought before, was as nothing in comparison of this ; which will afford as striking a display of his power and glory, as his raising the dead in general at the day of judgment. *Happy and holy* are they *who have part in this resurrection,* or partake of that spirit of glory, which actuated the primitive christians, and the confessors and martyrs of succeeding ages ; for *the second death* will have *no power* on such even to terrify them ; they shall live in the full assurance of faith ; and as the *priests of God and Christ*, arranged in spiritual royalty, they shall minister to him, in such a manner as will raise them much above the mean glories of the earth, *Hos.* xi. 12, *Rom.* v. 17. Haste then reader! so live as to teach unborn ages how to live for God ; then live thyself in similar suc-

If

cessors in the millennium. He that aims high,
will fly the higher.

If the Holy Ghost had designed that we should
compute this thousand years, in the same way
as the 1260 years in chap. xii. 6, 14, he would
probably have called these, as he did them, *days*
or *times*; viz. 360,000 days or times : But though
days, weeks, months and *times* are used in prophetic language to represent years, as the seven
days of the week adumbrate the seven thousand
years of the world's age ; yet, if a *year* signifies
360 years in chap. ix. 15, I do not recollect any
place in scripture, where *years*, in the plural
number, are put for years, in the manner they
must be here, if these 1000 signify 360,000 *years* ;
much less where they are so used, without any
annexed circumstance necessarily fixing them to
that meaning, as may perhaps be the case in
chap. ix. 15. And if Christ should reign so long
upon earth, how then can his people be called a
little flock, and a *remnant?* Besides, though we
know but little of spiritual bodies, if Christ reigns
so long spiritually upon earth, probably the new
Jerusalem would have been larger than it is described, chap. xxi. 16. Again, it is said that
*Christ appeared in the end of the world, to put away
sin, Heb.* ix. 26, (for as Christ's crucifixion, near
the beginning of the gospel dispensation, would
seem to be improperly called the *conclusion of the
ages* in general, as Dr. Doddridge reads it ; therefore I read αιωνων *the world*, as our translators do
here, and in 1 *Cor.* ii. 7. and x. 11.) and his appearing *in the end of the world*, supposes that the world
had passed the meridian of its age, at the time of
his appearing : Accordingly the Lord is said to
have *spoken to us by his Son, in these last days, Heb.*
i. 2 ; and the gospel is the *last time*, 1 *John* ii. 18 ;
which seems to give us reason to believe, that the

U   world

world will not continue so long after Christ's time, as it had before. Dr. Owen indeed underſtands, *Heb.* i. 2, of the *laſt days* of the judaical ſtate; but 1 *John* ii. 18, was written after the judaical ſtate was deſtroyed: And as this phraſe *the laſt days*, in *Gen.* xlix. 1. *Iſa.* ii. 2. *Mich.* iv. 1, ſtill predicts what is yet to befal the Jews, after their return to their own land; ſo the days of the goſpel are expreſsly called *the laſt times*, 1 *Pet.* i. 20, reckoned from the foundation of the world; and *the laſt times*, abſolutely conſidered, ſeem to ſuppoſe the world to have continued more than half its time, when theſe words were written.

It is acknowledged, that we ſometimes ſpeak of the *laſt days* of any government, or any affair, without adverting to the proportion, which the time we ſpeak of bears to the preceding: But if a reign continues fifty one years and a half, or a book has ſo many pages, if we call all thoſe years or pages, except the firſt, *the laſt*;—(and this is nearly the proportion between the two ſuppoſed times of the world's continuance; viz. 367, 125, and 7,125 years), we plainly intimate that we do not intend to inform the world any thing about the time of that reign, or the length of that book. If the Holy Ghoſt had ſpoken in this manner, 1 *Pet.* i. 20, this phraſe *the laſt times*, would only ſignify that the goſpel, was the laſt diſpenſation of grace to the world; and if ſo, his meaning would have been clearer if he had uſed the word *diſpenſation*, inſtead of *times:* But *the laſt times*, in connection with what he had *fore-ordained before the foundation of the world*, probably both points at the time, and at the grace diſplayed in it.

Beſides, believing Jews and Gentiles never apprehended, that the world was to ſtand much more than 7000 years: And as I cannot, without proof

of

of it, confent to the thought of the faints being
confined to their graves fo many additional thoufands of years, beyond what living faints in general have ever expected; fo the account of the glory
of the church in *Ifa.* lx. 15, 21. and lxi. 7, 8, does
not neceffarily imply any fuch continuance; for
the *eternal excellency*, the *everlafting covenant*, and
the *everlafting light* and *joy* there fpoken of, are
of the fame nature, and expreffed by the fame
word, as the *everlafting priefthood* given to Phi-
nehas, *Numb.* xxv. 13; neither of which can be
fully accomplifhed, any where but in heaven.——
I might have added, that if this 1000 years is not
a part of the 1260 years of the feventh trumpet,
chap. xii. 6, both the proofs of that there adduced, muft be annulled; and the futility of the
fuppofed fcriptural illuftrations of the times of the
day of judgment, which are mentioned after ver.
15th of this chapter, muft be demonftrated; till
both thefe points are effected, 1 muft underftand
thefe words of a *thoufand* literal years.

We may further obferve, as a concluding
thought on this fubject, That this revelation proceeds in every thing by fevens; and accordingly
beginning the Chriftian æra at A. M. 4000, the
preceding prophecy fhews us, that this thoufand
years will be the feventh thoufand of the world's
age: and, as it is generally apprehended that we
are ftill under the fixth trumpet, at this A. M.
5,778; and there will be at leaft a 1000 years under this feventh trumpet, therefore the world will
indifputably continue near 7000 years; and may
probably remain fomething longer. Accordingly
the *Talmud* fpeaks to this purpofe, ‘ *This world*
‘ *is to laft* 6000 *years*, in its prefent ftate; *and*
‘ *after one* millinary more, *it fhall be deftroyed; as*
‘ *it is faid, And the Lord alone fhall be exalted in*
‘ *that day*, that is in the feventh millinary.’ See

the

the bishop of Clogher's *Enquiry into the Time of the Messiah's Coming*, p. 37.

And perhaps the thousand years of which I am speaking, may be mentioned six times, ver. 2—7, to establish an expectation, that this glorious period will begin after six thousand years are past. *In six days the Lord made heaven and earth, and rested on the seventh day*; and after six days labour, *a seventh is* to us *the sabbath of the Lord our God*; so the seventh thousand years will probably be the Lord's rest and ours. All believers, live spiritually and eternally, in consequence of Christ's living two or three *days* or years upon earth, *Luke* xiii. 32: And as this reign of the saints with Christ is mentioned three times, so we expect that *that after two days*, or two thousand years from Christ's time, *he will revive us*; in the *third day*, or third thousand years, the great restorer Jesus *will raise us up, and we shall live in his sight, Hos.* vi. 2: For the words *we* and *us*, may be used here with as great propriety, as David said of Israel's passing through the Red-sea: *There did we rejoice in him, Psal.* lxvi. 6.

This rest will be glorious after six days, or six thousand years of labour: And, though the saints will not then be free from sin, tempters or temptations, there will probably be the same difference between the millennium and the present time, as to the spirituality of it, as between our present Lord's days and common days; for now satan being much restrained, Christ will reign among his saints; and his word will come to them, as at first, *in power, in the Holy Ghost, and in much assurance,* 1 *Thess.* i. 5: And this will produce a truly divine spirit in men, when that seed of God, the *word,* more gloriously opens and expands its immortal life in their exulting powers, than it had in the preceding ages, 1 *Pet.* i. 3. At the same

3

time,

time, the wicked of former times will, at present, have none to succeed to their impudence, however wicked their hearts may be; for now *the Lord shall be King over all the earth:* And *in that day there shall be one Lord, and his name one,* Zech. xiv. 8, 9.

Reckoning this seventh thousand years as a sabbath day, which was typified by the ancient sabbatical seventh year (in which servants were released, and the land rested, *Exod.* xxi. 2. and xxiii. 10, 11;) suffer me to add, that, comparing the millennium with the six preceding days, or 6000 years of labour, we are entered upon the last quarter of the sixth millennary, and are at near seven o'clock on the saturday evening of the sixth thousand years; for if a day shadows forth a thousand years, an hour, the twenty-fourth part of that day, must be forty-one years and eight months; (see the half hour's silence, chap. viii. 1); therefore the night is already begun with us, John xi. 9: And as the last quarter of the fourth and fifth millennary, was remarkably dark to the church, so probably will the last quarter of the sixth thousand years be. But when the two beasts are cast alive into the lake of fire, A. D. 2016, chap. xix. 20, this prophetic day will begin; and the night itself, while it continues, will *shine as the day,* and *the darkness* resemble the *noon,* after the vials are all poured out, A. D. 1942; see *Psalm.* cxxxix. 12: *Isai.* lviii. 10.

It is no objection to this prophetic sense of the *hour,* or of the half hour, chap. viii. 1, that the word occurs, chap. xvii. 12, and in many other places, in no such determinate sense; for it is well known, in sacred and common language, that both *a day* and *an hour* are used in a determinate and indeterminate sense; and the subject or circumstances only can fix their meaning; see John

U 5   iv. 21.

iv. 21. 1 *Cor.* iv. 11. and viii. 7, where a *day* reprefents a *year*, as in chap. ix. 15, the twenty-fourth
part of that day muſt be fifteen days; but if it
here refembles a thoufand years, an hour of fuch
a day muſt be forty-one years and eight months.

If it fhould be further objected to this fcheme,
that I ' affign no lefs than three different fignifi-
' cations to prophetic time; fometimes it is quite
' literal, as in the thoufand years of the church's
' glory; fometimes a day ſtands for a year; and
' fometimes, as in this inftance, for a thoufand
' years.' I anfwer, at chap. xi. 2, I have endea-
voured to prove that a day is put for a *year* in
Hof. v. 7, and *Zech.* xi. 8; befides which, whoever reads thefe two prophecies through, efpecially that of Zechariah, will fee that a day is alfo
taken both *literally* and for a *feafon*; which fufficiently vindicates our taking the word *day* for
different lengths of time in this prophecy, as it
is ufed both in facred and common language.
True, it is this prophecy only, which feems to
conſtitute a thoufand years a *feafon*; but, as every
thing in this book is difpofed and ordered by
fevens, if the faints in the feventh millennary, fee
that as a kind of fabbatical year, it will be impoffible for them to avoid confidering the feven
thoufand years of the world's age, as adumbrated
by a week of fix days labour, fucceeded by a
fabbath of facred reſt.

7. And when the thoufand years are
ended, fatan fhall be loofed out of his prifon.

8. And he fhall go forth to deceive the
nations, which *are* in the four corners of
the earth, Gog and Magog; to gather them
together

together to battle, whose number *is* as the sand of the sea.

9. And they went up over the breadth of the earth, and surrounded the camp of the saints, and the beloved city: And fire came down from God out of heaven and devoured them.

10. And the devil who deceived them, was cast into the lake of fire and brimstone, where the beast and the false prophet *are*; and they shall be tormented day and night for ever and ever.

Notice had been given in the above thousand years, that satan would be loosed from his prison for a little time, when they were finished, ver. 3; for our most durable pleasures upon earth, are attended with the alarms of future danger. Accordingly A. D. 3016 being come, the restraint which had been laid upon this immortal enemy of men will be taken off; and his nature not being at all changed, only exasperated by the torment which his interdiction occasioned, he will *go forth to deceive*, (not only individuals, but) *the nations* in general; especially those of them who are *in the four corners of the earth*, most remote from Jerusalem, that centre of the world and of salvation; whom he can no way ruin, but by deceiving them either by a repetition of some of his former *methods*, or by some new *devices* which he has studied in the last thousand years. Now also the impious dead of every name, who had had none to succeed them in their spirit and views in the millennium, *live again* in their similar successors, ver. 5: Yet satan will not now be able to make such inroads upon the purity and peace of the church, as the beast had done in his times;

U 4   for

for the *camp of the saints* in thefe happy times, is
kept diftinct from the devil's camp : And *the beloved of the Lord dwell by him*, as little Benjamin
of old, *Deut*. xxxiii. 12 ; and are with our David
in fafeguard, 1 *Sam*. xxii. 23 ; keeping a fpiritual
feaft of tabernacles before him, *Zech*. xiv. 16,
18, 19.

But as the three frogs out of the mouth of the
dragon, the beaft and the falfe prophet, affembled the kings of the eaft againft the Jews, under
the fixth vial, chap. xvi. 12—16; fo now, for
the laft time, the devil will once more *gather his
hofts together to battle againft God*; *whofe number*
will be immenfe, *as the fand of the fea*; fee *Gen*.
xxii. 17. *Jofh*. xi. 4. *Pfal*. cxxxix. 18. *Rom*. ix.
27 : And this hoft will go up, from eaft to weft,
over the breadth of the earth; perhaps attacking
every church of God, every *camp of the faints*, in
their way, till they come to *the beloved city* Jerufalem, fo called, *Eccluf*. xxiv. 11; where many
of the Jews and Gentiles will be gathered together.

Thefe confederate troops, who all turn out
volunteers againft God, are called by the name
of that enemy who, eleven hundred years before,
broke in upon the land of Judea; viz. Gog and
Magog; the former the Prince, and the latter
the kingdom which ftands devoted to deftruction,
Ezek. xxxviiith and xxxixth chapters. Yet thefe
are not the identical hofts whofe doom is there
read, though they came from the fame country;
for, not to repeat all the arguments mentioned,
chap. xvi. 12—16, to prove that the deftruction
predicted in thofe chapters of *Ezekiel* will be accomplifhed A.D. 1941, after the Jews are returned to their own land, and before the millennium begins; there are things faid of that flaughter of the enemy which do not agree to this; as
(1) That

(1) That pestilence and the sword were employed against the former enemy, as well as fire from heaven, chap. xxxviii. 21, 22; against this it is only said, *Fire came down from God out of heaven and devoured them*, ver. 9. (2) *A sixth part* were left after that destruction, chap. xxxix. 2; but we have no account of any thing left in this. (3) After that destruction the Lord resolved to be eminently glorified in the Jews, from A. D. 1941 to the end of the world, chap. xxxix. 22—29; but we have no account of any thing after this but the day of judgment. I might add, (4) the former enemy came up only against the Jews; these *surround the camp of the saints* in general, Jews and Gentiles, ver. 9. We conclude therefore, that this enemy is the successor of those hardy Scythians, who came up against the Jews eleven hundred years before, as they came from the same country, and probably with the same cruel and avaricious views. But they were not Scythians only, for *they overspread the surface of the earth*, as Mr. Worsley reads those words; and *encompassed the camp of the saints, and the beloved city:* But weapons, and the hands which might have used them, are now become useless; for *fire came down* immediately *from God out of heaven and devoured them*, before the general conflagration began.

And now those words in *Isai.* lxvi. 24, are verified a third time, as they had been once in the 185,000 Assyrians slain, *Isai.* xxxiii. 11—14, and afterwards in the destruction of the kings in the land of Israel, under the sixth vial; (see chap. xvi. 12—16, and *Ezek.* xxxviiith and xxxixth) *They shall go forth, and look upon the carcasses of the men who have transgressed against me; for their worm shall not die, neither shall their fire be quenched: And they shall be an abhorring unto*

a.l

all flesh. And, to strike the deeper terror into the minds of sinners, *the devil who deceived them,* and who had been only restrained by the Redeemer's chain in the millennium, ver. 1, 2; may now probably, in his way to the hell prepared for him, in some visible form be *cast into that lake of fire and brimstone,* which will continue burning at Rome, *where the beast and the false prophet are* before him; *and they shall* all *be tormented* together *day and night for ever and ever,* without any possible hope of escape.

From the close of the millennium, A. D. 3016, to the end of the world, A. D. 3125, we have 109 years; but in what part of that time, this great head of the apostacy will be cast into this lake, and his army destroyed by fire from heaven, we know not: But as these events are spoken of before the account of the day of judgment, in the following verses; probably they may occur some years before it: For if that day begins with this execution, how then can the saints *judge angels,* the good and evil, before they are judged themselves? And if it occurs only a few days or months before that day, how then can the world, so soon after, be sunk again into that supine security, which will, notwithstanding every warning, disgrace human nature at the coming of Christ? *Matt.* xxiv. 37—51. But whenever it occurs between A. D. 3016 and 3125, the world's sinking afterwards into that brutish insensibility which our Lord has most surely predicted, even when a tempting devil is cast into the lake of fire, will probably afford such an awful view of human nature, as had never been given before.

As the sixth trumpet continued 1260 years, chap. xi. 2, 3; viz. from A. D. 606 to 1866, so will this, chap. xii. 6, that is, from A. D. 1866 to about 3125, which is the furthest account of

time

time we have in this book ; all beyond that is
vaſt eternity. And poſſibly ſome may think it
remarkable, that if we add the three numbers
together which occur in *Dan.* xii. 7, 11, 12; viz.
1260, 1290 and 1335, they make 3885, which is
the number of years from the time when Iſaiah
began to propheſy, who firſt ſpoke of many of
theſe great things, to the end of the world; for
he began to propheſy 760 years before Chriſt's
time, which added to A. D. 3125 makes 3885;
and this ſeems to ſtrengthen the evidence, that
the end will be about the time here ſpecified.

But as we have now done with the hiſtory of
Time, I call upon my reader moſt devoutly to adore
the WONDERFUL, COUNSELLOR, who in ſo
ſhort a compaſs (as leſs than fifteen chapters, and
in leſs than 255 verſes,) has given us the civil and
religious prophetic hiſtory, of near half the time
of the world's continuance; viz. from A. D. 96
to 3125. It was indeed *expedient that* our Lord
ſhould *go away*, to receive this revelation for us
chap. i, 1; as well as to ſend us the Comforter.
And the writings of the four Evangeliſts, ſcarce
yield ſo bright a diſplay of his power and glory,
as this book contains; which, under the Divine
bleſſing, will not fail to excite the moſt devout
awe in every pious heart at every attentive peru-
ſal. Yet ſuch is our native blindneſs and unbelief, that it was neceſſary to diſtinguiſh this book
with the following preface ; viz. *Bleſſed is he that*
readeth, and they that hear the words of this pro-
phecy; and keep thoſe things which are written
therein: for the time is at hand, chap. i. 3. And what
can be more adapted to beget reverence, and kindle
affection to Jeſus, and to the word of his grace,
than the concluding accounts here given of things
the moſt intereſting to us! We are however not
yet come to the concluſion ; for though time is

no more, the great day of judgment is to be described, and the everlasting blessedness of the
saints in heaven; which makes this seventh an
eternal trumpet.

11. And I saw a great white throne, and
him who sat thereon; from whose face the
earth and the heaven fled away, and there
was found no place for them.

12. And I saw the dead, small and great,
stand before God; and the books were
opened, and another book was opened, which
is *the book* of life; and the dead were judged
out of the things written in the books, according to their works.

13. And the sea gave up the dead which
were in it; and death and the invisible state
gave up the dead which were in them: and
they were judged every one according to
their works.

14. And death and the invisible state were
cast into the lake of fire. This is the second
death.

15. And if any one was not found written in the book of life, he was cast into the
lake of fire.

That day is now come, which every preceding
day had predicted and prepared for, the day
which will fix every one of us in infinite bliss or
irremediable woe. It is come! And *the Lord is
revealed from heaven in flaming fire, taking vengeance on them who know not God, and obey not the
gospel of our Lord Jesus Christ*; *who shall* not only
feel the pain of loss, by *absence* from the grace *of
the Lord*, but *be punished with everlasting destruction
from*

from his immediate *presence, and from the glory of his* *power :* At the same time he comes *to be glorified* *in his saints, and to be admired in all them that be-* *lieve.* See! for these purposes the *Lord himself* *descends from heaven wi.. a shout, with the voice of* *the Arch-angel, and the trump of God* ; and before him *the heavens pass away with a great noise, and* *the elements melt with fervent heat ; the earth also,* *and the works that are therein are burnt up.* So the apostles had predicted to Jews and Gentiles, 1 *Thess.* iv. 16. 2 *Thess.* i. 7—10. 2 *Pet.* iii. 10— 12.

And accordingly, says our author, *I saw a great* *white throne* ; *great* to contain the far-extended splendors in which the Judge appears; and *white* to reflect the glories of every Divine attribute, chap. vi. 2. and xix. 11. *And him who sat on it,* *from whose face the earth and heaven fled away ;* *and there was no place found for them,* that is, in their present form and appearance ; which is suited to a mixed state of goodness and wrath, but must be essentially altered if grace or vengeance reigns alone in them. ' Here the Son of the eternal God ' appears only, and all nature is alarmed : Nor ' heaven nor earth can keep their standing ; they ' flee away like the affrighted roe—How grove- ' ling are the loftiest flights of the Grecian and ' Roman muse, compared with this magnificence ' and elevation of the prophetic spirit !

' It is not said, a few herds of the forest, a few ' kings, or armies, or nations ; but the whole ' system of created things—It is not said, They ' were thrown into great commotions, but they ' fled entirely away ; not, They started from their ' foundations, but they fell into dissolution ; not, ' They removed to a distant place, but there was ' *found no place for them*—And all this, not at ' the strict command of the LORD JESUS ; not at ' his

' his awful menace, or before his fiery indigna-
' tion, but at the bare presence of his majesty,
' sitting with serene but adorable dignity on his
' throne.'   Mr. *Hervey.*

But affrighted as the earth is, it cannot flee
away, till it has given up the living and the dead
which were upon and in it, each in his own time
and order, 1 *Cor.* xv. 23; it cannot carry off, or
conceal the bodies of the righteous or the wicked,
to defraud grace or vengeance of its own.   As
radiant stars, the righteous shall *ascend out of the
earth*, 1 *Sam.* xxviii. 13; arrayed in glory, far
exceeding that of a royal bride on the day of
her coronation: On the contrary, the blackest
horrors of despair deform the impious race, who
died in arms against God; and are now dragged
to his tremendous bar.

The apostle speaking of the resurrection of the
righteous, says, 1 *Thes.* iv. 16, 17. *The Lord himself shall descend from heaven with a shout, with
the voice of the Arch-angel, and with the trump of
God: And the dead in Christ shall rise first*: And as
their graves are opening, the saints *which are
alive and remain, shall be snatched up* suddenly and
powerfully, *together with them, in the clouds to
meet the Lord in the air.*   This change upon their
bodies will be effected *in a moment, in the twink-
ling of an eye, at the last trump*, and as the Judge
descends to that lower region of *the air*, where
they are *to meet* him, 1 *Cor.* xv. 51, 52.   And
when all the saints are caught up to him in the
air, that near approach of the returning Judge
may perhaps so convulse this globe of ours, as
to throw the waters of the sea over all the land;
and possibly the earth may continue in this chaotic state, with the bodies of the wicked in it, all
the time that the saints are judged: Afterwards
the wicked shall be raised; therefore our author,
who

who is indisputably speaking of the general resurrection, taking no notice of the *land*, only says,
ver. 13. *And the sea gave up the dead which were
in it*; see the concluding remark on these verses
—He adds, *And death and hades gave up the dead
which were in them*, their spirits returning from
heaven and hell, to reanimate their now immortal bodies. Then I saw them, says he, *small and
great stand before God*; every eye fixed, with
unutterable joy, or overwhelming horror upon
him : *And the books* which God had written *were
opened*; the books of natural and revealed religion; the book of the law and the gospel; the
book of God's omniscience and remembrance;
and the book of conscience, the now deepened
characters of which appear all of them written as
with a pen of iron, and with the point of a diamond : *And another book was opened, which is* the
book *of life*; which contained the names, and
described the characters of all those whom the
Father gave to Christ, *John* vi. 39 and xvii. 6: *And
the dead were judged out of those things which were
written in the books*; *according to* the nature, origin
and ends, as well as according to the number,
and the different degrees of good or evil which
were found in *their works*; whether they died
under the covenant of works, or of grace : And
now it appeared visible to every eye, who were
really in Christ, and who were only nominally
and in profession so. And to preclude every
possible hope or fear of any future disunion, or
dissolution of their two natures, *Death* which had
once devoured their bodies; and the *separate state*,
which had furnished an abode for their spirits
when parted from it, *were* themselves swallowed
up in *the lake of fire*; for the joy or torment of
an unbodied spirit, will neither of them be
enough

enough for that ſoul when it is reunited to its
(body: And this *lake* of fire, which will probably
be typified in a lively manner by that lake at
Rome, which continues burning from A.D. 2016
to the end of the world, chap. xix. 3, 20) *is that
ſecond immortal death*, of which Chriſt has pro-
miſed that they who *overcome ſhall not be hurt*,
chap. ii. 11.

But, leſt our pride ſhould ſwell with the thought
of being judged *according to our works*; to point
out the celeſtial origin of all works which are ſpiritually good, and trace up our ſalvation to its
fountain head in God; it is added, ver. 15. *And
whoſoever, or if any one* Gr. *was not found written
in the book of* life; (by which cannot poſſibly be
meant a book of external church privileges,) *he
was caſt into the lake of fire*, chap. xiii. 8: For *there
ſhall in no wiſe enter* into heaven any *εἰ μὴ but they
which are written in the Lamb's book of life*, chap.
xxi. 27. *Matt.* xx. 16, 23. *Rom.* viii. 29—33. and
ix. 11—16. *Eph.* i. 4—6. 2 *Theſ.* ii. 13. 2 *Tim.* i.
9. 1 *Pet.* i. 2. Pride may rage itſelf into a fever
at this; but God's counſel will ſtand, and he will
do all, and only his pleaſure.

Profound awe certainly becomes us, if we pre-
ſume to think of the time when this day of the
Lord will *begin* or *end*; yet of the former there
can be no doubt, if we have not miſtaken in
computing the time when the world will end
(under the preceding verſes, and at chap. xii. 6);
for the day of judgment will begin at *the end of
the world, Matt.* xiii. 49, 50: And if the world
ends A.D. 3125; ſee ver. 7—10, judgment will
then begin: And if ſo the time of it will bear
ſome analogy to the time of ſome important things
which are mentioned in the old Teſtament, as
well as of one or two of the moſt intereſting
events

events, which the world ever saw; viz, the resurrection of Chrift, and the gift of the Spirit at
the day of Pentecoft.

The rib which was made into a woman, was
probably taken out of the fide of Adam, on the
eighth day of the world's age; at leaft the particular hiftory of it fucceeds the account of the
fabbath day, and the command given him not to
eat of the tree of knowledge of good and evil,
Gen. ii. 18—25. Having fpent that firft fabbath
alone with God, probably at the clofe of it, the
brute creatures paffed in review before Adam
(after the fabbath had fanctified them to God;)
that, as their Lord, he might give each of them
names. After this, the third hour of the eighth
day might be a probable time for that deep fleep
to fall upon him, which is mentioned, ver. 21—
But whatever may be thought of this, it certainly
was not without fome myftery, that all the following things were fixed to, or concluded the
eighth day; viz, circumcifion, *Lev.* xii. 3; the
prefenting the young of the beafts to God, *Exod.*
xxii. 30; cleanfing of the leper, and of the perfon who had an iffue, *Lev.* xiv. 10, 23. and xv.
14, 29; the confecration of the priefts, *Lev.* viii.
35. and ix. 1, &c; the holy convocation at the
clofe of the three annual feafts of the Lord, *Lev.*
xxiii. 39; and the dedication of Solomon's temple, 2 *Chron.* vii. 9, which was finifhed the eighth
year, 1 *Kings* vi. 1, 38.

But to come to the New Teftament—Every
week affords a lively emblem of the 7000 years
of the world's age: And after the conclufion of
that week, which introduced the moft interefting
paffover the Jewifh nation had ever kept, our
Lord rofe from the dead early in the morning of
the next day, which began another week; and
which was, with relation to that remarkable week,

X   an

an eighth Day; which our Lord has made the Christian Sabbath. We have indeed no certainty at what hour he returned to life; nor could the time of his leaving his grave inform us of it, if that could be ascertained. Gilbert West, Esq; supposes that he arose, that is, left the grave, some time between the dawning of the day, and the sun-rising; but as *Mark* xvi. 2, first part, might have been read in a parenthesis, so the λιαν πρωι *very early*, seems to describe an earlier hour than fifty-nine minutes after three o'clock, at which time, says Mr. S. Reader, the day broke at Jerusalem in N. Lat. 31° 50', April 25th, A. D. 34, the Friday before which Sir Isaac Newton seems quite positive was the day of Christ's Crucifixion; as the sun rose 30 minutes after 5 o'clock that morning.

But at whatever time the women came first to the sepulchre; the earthquake, and the descent of the angel to roll away the stone, which ministered to his coming forth from the tomb, had nothing to do with our Lord's return to life: And as he was crucified at the third hour of the Jewish day; viz. at 9 o'clock, the time of the morning sacrifice, *Mark* xv. 25, so probably he revived at the third hour of the Roman day; viz, at 3 o'clock in the morning; for whilst our Lord's body was a Roman prisoner, his day must be reckoned to begin at their time; viz, at twelve o'clock at night; and so all the Evangelists expresly reckon his rising day; see *Matt.* xxviii. 1. *Mark* xvi. 2. *Luke* xxiv. 1. *John* xx. 1. Very early that day our Lord returned to life; and as his soul, like all other human spirits, was created with a propensity to its own body, returning to it, he probably for a time contemplated with pleasure the scars of his wounds, and the future glory which should soon array his body in heaven: And having in that body bowed before his

eternal

eternal Father, and turned his sepulchre into a *proseuche,* or house of prayer for a time; and having also created new garments for his body, in which to appear in the world, when he saw proper to leave the tomb, at his solemn nod the earth quaked, and the angel descended to roll back the stone, and to fright the guards away, perhaps at break of day—So if the great decisive day should begin at 3 o'clock in the morning of the eighth thousand years, this will fall at A. D. 3125, or A. M. 7125, (that is, reckoning the Christian Æra to commence at A. M. 4000;) for an hour is forty one years and eight months; see ver. 1—6, and three hours is 125 years.

But the *day,* as opposed to *night,* begins at sunrising, or at 6 o'clock in the morning; and the fiftieth day from the passover was the Christian sabbath, and consequently an eighth day with respect to a Jewish week: And at the third hour of that day, the Spirit was miraculously poured out upon the apostles and others, *Acts* ii. 1—15; which, reckoning a day for a thousand years, after the above manner of computing, symbolizes with A. M. 7125, or A. D. 3125—Thus probably about the same time as our Lord rose from the dead, and the Spirit was poured out on the eighth day, the eternal joys of the saints in soul and body, and the eternal woe of the wicked, may begin in the eighth thousand years.

Obj. But did not our Lord say, *Mark* xiii. 32. *Of that day and hour knoweth no man; no not the angels which are in heaven; neither the Son, but the Father?* Answer 1. Even the *Man* Christ Jesus could *receive nothing, except it was given him from heaven,* *John* iii. 27: And perhaps his human soul knew not why his Father *hid the gospel from the wise and prudent, and revealed it unto babes;* which yet his perfect purity chearfully referred to his Father's good pleasure, *Matt.* xi. 25, 26,

as

as we alfo fhall, if led by his Spirit. As the God-head communicated to him, fo he *increafed in wifdom, and in favour with God and man, Luke* ii. 52; and *all things* neceffary to our falvation, *which he had heard from the Father, he made known* to his difciples before he left the world, *John* xv. 15; which he afterwards explained by his Spirit from heaven. And after his afcenfion, this fur-ther revelation was *given him,* chap. i. 1; which he fent and fignified by his angel to his fervant John, A. D. 96. But if Chrift received know-ledge gradually, it would be great pride in us to expect to be informed of every thing at once: Yet,

2. Our Lord might at that time know about the *year,* though he knew not the *day* or *bour,* of judgment: At leaft, if the *year* was known in all thofe adumbrations by which our Lord reprefents the day of judgment, though the *day* and *bour* was not; this both fets this thought above con-tempt, and feems to affure us that the facred canon would not conclude, without informing us of the *year* of the general judgment; for what rea-fon can be affigned for pointing out the *year* of Noah's flood, and Jerufalem's deftruction, but what will equally hold for pointing out the year of judgment?

Noah knew not, till within a few days of the deluge, the *day* or *bour*; but he knew the *year* when it would come; and gave warning, that it would be in 120 years, *Gen.* vi. 3. and vii. 4. 2 *Pet.* ii. 5: But they faw in vain his affiduity in preparing the ark, therefore their unbelief drown-ed them; for, inftead of repenting of their fins, *they were eating and drinking, marrying and giving in marriage, until the* very *day that Noah entered into the ark; and knew not,* becaufe they would not know, *till the flood came and took them all away;*

away; *so shall also the coming of the Son of man be*, *Matt.* xxiv. 37, 38. Our Lord had also in that chapter, been speaking of Jerusalem's destruction; from which he seems to make a transition, at ver. 36, and in *Mark* xiii. 32, to the great day of the Lord: Now, though no man knew the *day* or *hour* of Jerusalem's destruction, yet Daniel had predicted, chap. ix. 25—27, that after *seventy seven weeks, and threescore and two years*, that is, 601 *years* after the 536th year before Christ, when Cyrus gave forth the decree to rebuild Jerusalem; or by A. D. 66, *Messiah* would *cut off from belonging to him both the city and the sanctuary*; to which if we add the *week*, or seven years which their destruction took up, ver. 27; it will bring us to A. D. 73, by which time Jerusalem was utterly desolated, as Mr. Blayney understands that prophecy: But Jerusalem would not know the day of their visitation; therefore the day of the Lord came upon them *as a thief in the night:* And whilst they were saying, *Peace and safety, sudden destruction* came *upon them*, for that contempt of Christ which was indulged amongst them; *as travail upon a woman with child, which they cannot escape. But ye brethren*, who are taught of God, *are not in darkness, that that* great *day* of which the apostle is speaking, *should overtake you as a thief*; *ye are all the children of the light, and the children of the day*, which shines into every well prepared eye; *we are not of the night, nor of darkness*, 1 *Thes.* v. 3—6.

Two other illustrations of this point our Lord makes use of; viz, by a *housholder* and a *servant*; of both of whom such things are said as incline us to suppose, that about the *year* of judgment will be known, though not the *day* or *hour*; see *Matt.* xxiv. 42, 43. If a *housholder* is only informed in general, that an enemy has a design upon his house, whatever other precautions he may ufe, he cannot himfelf fit up every night; but if he knows the night when *a thief cometh*, though he *knows not in what watch* he will come, he is unworthy of the name of *the good man of the house*, if he will not *watch*; but *suffer his house to be broken up. Watch therefore, for ye know not what hour your Lord doth come.* The fame fubjeft is reprefented in *Mark* xiii. 34, 37, under the charafter of a *fervant*, who knowing within a few hours, when his mafter will return; (for that is fuppofed in what is required of him,) it is ex- pefted that he be not found *fleeping :* So, if we know that our Lord will come about A. D. 3125, He may well expeft the world to watch; though they know not whether he will come at *the even- ing* of that year; *at midnight*, at the clofe of it; or *at the cock crowing, or in the morning* of the next year—And to us who know neither the day, the hour, nor the year OF OUR *death*, well might our Lord add; *What I fay unto you, I fay unto all, Watch.*

From thefe confiderations it feems more than probable, that the concluding year of the world will be known before it arrives; to which the faints of thofe times will look forward with the moft rapturous and joyful awe; whilft the wicked are fhut up in unbelief about it. I might add on this fubjeft, If the Lord does *nothing without re- vealing his fecret to his fervants the prophets, Amos* iii. 7; it is probable he has fomewhere revealed the time of the day of judgment, as well as of events of lefs importance: And if the Lamb's wife was informed by this prophecy, of the time cf her Divine Hufband's coming, and therefore made herfelf ready for him juft before the millen- nium, chap. xix. 7; will not her Lord give her the fame advantages to prepare for her great and final prefentation to him? This at leaft we are

certain

certain of, that towards the clofe of the millennium, and afterwards, when the prophecies are
fulfilled, the fcene of things will as vifibly announce the approach of the great day, as the
opening buds of fpring predict the coming fummer, *Mark* xiii. 28—Happy they who now know
Chrift's near approach to remove them to glory,
by the leffening of their own *fpots*, and the fmooth-
ing of their moral *wrinkles, Eph.* v. 27.

But feeing ye look for fuch things, be diligent
profeffors, *that ye may be found of him in peace ;—*
What meaneft thou, O fleeper ! Up, and be doing !
The judge ftandeth before the door ! What thou doft,
do quickly—Hafte ! hafte ! thou haft no time to
loiter—Flee for thy life ! Stay not ! *There is no*
device to efcape ruin in the grave, or in hell !

OH ! THE JOYFUL ! DOLEFUL DAY !
—We have feen its beginning ! Will my reader indulge me in (I hope at leaft) a harmlefs conjecture
about the time of its ending ?—It is called the
work of *a day, Acts* xvii. 31. 1 *Thef.* v. 2 ; but furely not of one day only, nor even of a prophetic
day, that is, *a year.* The word *days*, in common as
well as fcripture language, fignifies the times of any
perfon or work ; as the *days of Noah* and *of Chrift*
—Accordingly the words *times* and *feafons* are applied to this great event, 1 *Thef.* v. 1 ; which inclines me to believe that it may be a work of
many years.

We found the end of the world, and confequently the beginning of the day of judgment,
by adding the 1260 years of the fixth, and of the
feventh trumpet, to the year 606, when the fixth
trumpet began : And by a like method we may
guefs at the time of the judgment from *Dan.* xii.
chapter ; where, after popery has reigned 1260
years, ver. 7, it is added, ver. 12. *Bleffed is he that*
waiteth, and cometh to the thoufand three hundred

and

and five and thirty days; that is, to A.D. 1941, when
the kings of the eaſt, who come up againſt Judea, will be ſlain there; ſo we explained the word
under the ſixth vial, chap. xvi. 12—16. p. 230—
233.   But that accompliſhment of theſe words,
certainly does not preclude the poſſibility of another.   In the former explication, beginning the
1260 years, ver. 7, at A.D. 606, and adding only
75 years more, they brought us to A.D. 1941.
But beginning them at near the ſame time; viz,
A.D. 605, we may add both theſe numbers to
them; viz, 1260 and 1335; which will bring us
to A.D. 3200. that is, to about ſeventy five years
after the end of the world: And if the judgment
of the great day ſhould continue ſo long, this
will be half as many *years* as the waters prevailed
days, upon the earth in Noah's flood, *Gen.* vii. 24:
And as all the creatures muſt have been drowned
in much leſs time than that, it is probable the
Lord had ſome other end beſides that, in ſuffer-
ing the waters to prevail ſo long; which he had
ordered to deſcend in ſuch a manner, and in ſuch
degrees, as not to endanger his covenant treaſure
in the ark.

But the abomination which maketh deſolate was
not fully ſet up till A.D. 755, or 756: Add to
that year the above 1260 and 1335, and it brings
us to A.D. 3350 or 3351; that is, to about 225
years after the end of the world: And about ſo
many days the Lord took in judging the old
world by the flood, before the tops of the mountains were ſeen, *Gen.* viii. 1—6.   We can indeed
have no abſolute certainty of theſe things, as the
Holy Ghoſt has not ſeen proper to inform us,
what is the bleſſedneſs to be expected at the end
of the 1335 years.   But if the day of judgment
ſhould continue the above 225 *times* or years; and
the firſt ſeventy five of them ſhould be taken up
in

in judging faints and angels, and the remaining *feafon*, in judging the wicked; as the righteous and the wicked will ftand before God, in their refurrection bodies, ftriking fpectacles of glory and of horror to each other, well may it be faid, *Bleffed is he that waiteth, and cometh to the* 1335 *days*, which will conclude this final judgment. For then the righteous will be removed from the fight of the wicked, and enter with Chrift into his glory; to behold the beatific vifion of God, and join the everlafting hallelujahs of exulting feraphs—At the fame time the glory of their re-furrection bodies, and the perpetual influx of Di-vine love upon their fouls, will preclude all anxious uncertainty, whilft they ftand *waiting* be-fore the judgment feat.

At that great day of which I have been fpeak-ing, *We muft all appear before the judgment feat of Chrift*, 2 *Cor*. v. 10: But as *the dead in Chrift fhall rife firft*, 1 *Thef*. iv. 16, perhaps they may be judged before the wicked are raifed to life; and poffibly the earth, after the bodies of the faints are fnatched up from it, may lie in that kind of chaotic ftate fuppofed in ver. 13, with awful marks of God's vengeance upon it, for feventy five years, whilft the faints are judged: But then the wicked will be raifed; and *fmall and great*, ftand together before God, as it is afferted, ver. 12. But when the righteous appear before the judgment feat, it will not be either in the place, or with the appearance of criminals: Yet, whe-ther they are judged in the prefence of the wicked, or before they are raifed, their appearing before the judgment feat feems to intimate that their fins will be mentioned; though it will be only to in-hance the riches of that grace, and glorify that fcheme of redeeming love, which has faved them. Neither God nor themfelves can fimply forget
their

their fins to all eternity; but as they will not be
mentioned againft them as matters of judicial accufation, fo their carnal felf-love being now fwallowed up in a regard to God's glory, it will rather give them pleafure than pain, however publickly they are mentioned; whilft gofpel finners
with horror fee in them what they have loft, for
want of applying to the blood of fprinkling.

C H A P. XXI.

AND I faw a new heaven and new earth,
for the firft heaven, and the firft earth
was paffed away; and the fea was no more.

2. And I John faw the holy city, the
new Jerufalem, defcending from God out of
heaven; prepared as a bride adorned for her
hufband.

3. And I heard a great voice out of heaven, faying, Behold the tabernacle of God
is with men, and he will dwell with them;
and they fhall be his people, and God himfelf fhall be with them, *even* their God.

4. And God fhall wipe away every tear
from their eyes; and there fhall be death no
more, nor grief, nor crying, nor fhall there
be any more *painful* labour; for the former
things are paffed away.

5. And he that fat upon the throne faid,
Behold, I make all things new! And he faid
to

to me, Write; for thefe words are true and faithful.

6. And he faid to me, It is done; I am ALPHA and OMEGA, the BEGINNING and the END: I will give to him that is athirft, of the fountain of the water of life freely.

7. The conqueror fhall inherit all things; and I will be to him a God, and he fhall be to me a fon.

8. But to the fearful and unbelieving; and to the abominable, and to murtherers, and whoremongers and forcerers, and idolaters, and all liars, their part *fhall be* in the lake which burns with fire and brimftone; which is the fecond death.

Time was concluded when the day of judgment began, and that alfo is now paft; all therefore that remains is vaft boundlefs eternity— We have feen, in this prophetic glafs, a reprefentation of that lake of fire, where the wicked are to be tormented for ever; and have now only to view the blefsed eternal abodes of the righteous, and devoutly attend the parting admonitions which conclude this prophecy, and the facred canon.

It is not probable, that infinite power and wifdom fhould ever remand any part of the material creation into its primitive nothing; yet the hofts of heaven will be difbanded, and *the heavens themfelves*, which have feen and covered our crimes, *fhall pafs away with a great noife; and the elements*, which compofe the material creation, *fhall melt with fervent heat; the earth alfo, and the works which are therein fhall be burnt up*, 2 *Pet.* iii. 10: For there is to be a grand *reftitution*, or reftoration *of all things*, αποκαταστασις, *Acts* iii. 21; called

called the *regeneration*, *Matt.* xix. 28; by which God will *reconcile all things in heaven and earth*, to his own delightful enjoyment; as he has already so far reconciled them, by the blood of the Redeemer's crofs, as to employ them for his ufe and praife; whilft ftill the earth and the vifible heavens, wear the confpicuous marks of his difpleafure againft fin upon them, *Col.* i. 20. There can be no reconciliation of fouls without regeneration; of which though Chrift is incapable, his people may be faid to *follow him in* it, when they begin from their hearts to trace his holy fteps. But polluted matter cannot be reconciled, without diffolving its fubftance by fire, taking it all to pieces, and glorioufly changing every thing which has been either defiled by fin, or an occafion or inftrument of, or any temptation to it: This therefore will be done; and after this was effected by the power of God, fays our author,

1. *I faw* that *new heaven and new earth*, which had been typified by the purity and glory of the Jewifh nation, after they were brought back to their own land, *Ifa.* lxv. 17—25; and in which the Holy Ghoft will continue to the end of time to *promife* the faints a fhare, when the prefent material creation is *diffolved*, 2 *Pet.* iii. 11—13: *For the firft heaven, and the firft earth were paffed away*, and had loft their former appearance and pollution, in the penetrating fire through which they had paffed. And now, purged by fire, perhaps the earth refembles fome refplendent diadem, reflecting from every part the various glories of its maker; at leaft, it labours no more to bring forth food for its now immortal inhabitants; whofe animal life is fwallowed up in fpiritual glory.

The former earth, (let us look back a little upon it!) had been *founded upon the fea*; had

trembled

trembled with its motions, and could not rest, *Pfal.* xxiv. 2. and xlvi. 3 : And time was when that fea, preffed with the unwieldy load, fo refented an affault made upon it by the four winds of the earth, that it caft out four beafts upon the earth ; viz, the Babylonian, Perfian, Grecian and Roman empires, *Dan.* vii. 2, 3 ; and when the earth had intombed thefe, it fent forth a fifth more mifchievous than all of them together, *Rev.* xiii. 1. But to be revenged, the earth afterwards fent out another beaft ; which, joining with the former, fufficiently tormented both fea and land, chap. xiii. 11. But fee ! the general conflagration has now drank up all the waters of the deep ; therefore in this new earth *there is no fea*; nor any turbulent and unquiet fpirit, to excite commotions in this new-made world of grace.

It is not for us to know, in what part of illimitable fpace the new heavens and earth will be fituated ; but as they are to *remain before God,* *Ifa.* lxvi. 22, no doubt they will be inhabited ; for he makes *them not in vain, Ifa.* xlv. 18. And as they will be inhabited by rational, yet not by miferable beings, fo the following verfe informs us particularly of their inhabitants.

2. *And I John,* who add my name again to this part of the prophecy, which refpects another world, as I had before when fpeaking of the affairs of this chap. i. 1, 4, 9—*faw the holy city, the new Jerufalem, coming down from God out of heaven*; *prepared as a bride adorned for her hufband.* If this city was not to be inhabited by the human race, why is it called *the holy city, the new Jerufalem?* If the inhabitants had been changed, no doubt the name would have been different. And as this city appears in the fplendor of a royal bride, it may be afked, Who, befides

2   fides

sides believers of Adam's family, were ever the
bride adorned for this *Husband?* And when the
first earth was removed, to what *great and high
mountain* could John possibly see this *city descend-
ing, as a bride out of heaven from God,* but to a
mountain of that new heaven and earth, of which
he had just spoken before; and to which *the
angel* had *carried him away in spirit,* ver. 10 ?
Besides, it has been remarked before, that the
Spirit of God promised every believer a share in
this new heaven and earth, 2 *Pet.* iii. 13.

At judgment the saints were caught up to
meet the Lord in the air; and that day being
concluded, they must *inherit the kingdom prepared for them, from the foundation of the world.*
But alas! wrapt in sense, we are ready to con-
ceive of a meer local heaven, where the Divine
glory beams with inexpressible, yet confined radiance; but this confinement of God's glory,
is all self-created and therefore contemptible:
Wherever God reveals his glory, there is heaven; and if this *bride adorned for her Husband,*
goes from the seat of judgment to the new earth,
she will find him here to receive her, and to continue eternally with her—But oh! how is she
altered!—When the Gentiles were represented to
Peter in vision, in a sheet let down from heaven,
*four-footed beasts of the earth, wild beasts, creeping
things, and fowls of the air* were the natural and
striking hieroglyphics of all of them, *Acts* x.
12, 28; and when the Father drew them to
Christ, they were all over *wounds,* and *bruises,*
and *putrifying sores:* But now, besides the regularity and glory which reigns in all their souls,
their bodies are fashioned like Christ's glorious
body, which had ascended, with so much ease,
from Mount Olivet to heaven, *Acts* i. 12; and
being spiritual, they are active, quick in their
motions,

motions, incorruptible, and impaffible; and need neither food, phyfic nor fleep, nor know they any fear of decay. Yea, they fhine *as the brightnefs of* a beaming *Firmament, and as the ftars for ever and ever*; and may perhaps with as much eafe vifit other parts of God's dominions, as light travels from the fun to us.

The foul now often wants to fly, and looks wifhfully upwards in vain; for the body has no wings like itfelf; but hereafter it fhall have a body to its own mind; for the wide extremes in our nature will come nearer together, when the terrene part is made *fpiritual*, as *light* and *air*: And when this immortal bride is fully *adorned*, fhe *fhall walk with* her Divine Hufband *in white*, chap. iii. 4; and who will fet bounds to her walk? or *feperate* her from him, *Rom.* viii. 35— The Spirit which fometimes tranfported the prophets, and particularly Philip in the fight of the eunuch, through the air, feemed by this to predict the future flights of all the redeemed; fee 1 *Kings* xviii. 12. 2 *Kings* ii. 16. *Ezek.* iii. 14. *Acts* viii. 39. And as the faints will be *caught up to meet the Lord in the air*, 1 *Theff.* iv. 17, they certainly cannot be afterwards confined to one place; unlefs it is moft for God's glory, and their own good to be fo: But if it is their prefent imperfection, that they can only view the diftant glory of many of God's works, in one part of their nature; when *that which is perfect is come, that which is* only *in part fhall be done away*, 1 *Cor.* xiii. 10. The wicked too will have fpiritual bodies, as well as the righteous, to capacitate them to fuftain eternal torments; but having fpiritual bodies adapted for flight, it will probably be an additional circumftance to heighten their mifery, that they will be confined for ever in the lake of fire and brimftone.

I may

I may add here, that *the new heaven* and *new earth*, being only mentioned once, and this holy city being reprefented as coming down from the third heaven, as it were, to them both; this may intimate, that there will be a free communication and intercourfe, between this heaven and earth for ever and ever.

3. *And I heard a great voice*, following this royal Bride *out of heaven*; and *faying, Behold the tabernacle of God is* now, and will be for ever *with man*; and, as really as the Divine glory fills the human nature of the Son of God, *Heb.* viii. 2; fo furely *will he dwell with them*, and entertain their fouls for ever, with the different and fucceffive rays of his glory; *and they shall be* owned and treated as *his people*; *and God himself*, no more fending to them by heavenly or earthly angels, *shall be with them*, as *their* own *God:* And this threefold declaration, that God will dwell with them, be with them, and be their God, both afcertains the hope; and may perhaps be defigned to feal the grace of each perfon in the adorable Trinity to them for ever.

Ubi uxor, ibi domus; *Where* Chrift's *fpoufe* is, *there* is *his home:* And if we take the word *men* emphatically, this phrafe *The tabernacle of God is with* MEN, may intimate that the glory of God, and particularly of the God-man Jefus, will take up its refidence in this new heaven and new earth; other worlds being probably fo placed around this new earth, as that his glory, reflected from it, may fhine through them all. At the fame time, as a *tabernacle* or tent is eafily removed, poffibly this word may intimate, that, in fome unknown point in eternity, (to afford the wider fcope for the Divine power and goodnefs) this fcene of things may give place to another, or others; while ftill every fuch fuppofed new fcene, has in
it

it all the splendor, durableness, ease and dignity, which our Lord ever intended to express
by this phrase, the *mansions in* his *Father's house,*
John xiv. 2.—It is added,

4. *And God* the Father, Son and holy Spirit,
shall wipe away all those *tears from their eyes,*
which he left in them here, to wash the dust of
earth out of them; *and death shall be no more*
natural nor moral, *nor grief, nor crying;* nor *shall*
there be any more painful *labour* for soul or body;
for the former things are eternally *passed away.*

5—8. *And* when I had gazed on this rapturous
scene for a time, *he that sat upon the throne;* viz,
the Father, chap. iv. 3, and Christ, chap. xx. 11,
said, In order to secure that glory which thou
hast seen, and preclude all creature decays, *Be-*
hold I make all things new. Then he said unto
me his honoured Amanuensis, *Write,* that every
man may read; *for these words are true and faith-*
ful; and all my *words* shall soon be *works:*
Yea *he said unto me, It is done;* the scene is concluded in eternal glory: And now by my own
name I sign it; *I am Alpha and Omega,* that is,
the Beginning and the End, chap. i. 8, 11. and xxii.
13. Go therefore and tell my servants, that,
whatever reserves I may now see proper to make,
while sin keeps them at a partial distance from
me; when they are come to this blessed world,
I will give to him who is now *a thirst,* as much
of the fountain of the water of life as his soul can
hold; while, through eternal years, he confesses
that I give it *freely.* Yes, *the conqueror,* and
every thirsty soul bears that honoured name, *shall*
inherit all things, which I either am myself, or
have made in this new creation: These are the
holy men, who as new creatures, are made without fear of any thing but offending me; and of
every such person, I am not ashamed to say,
I will be the *God; and he shall* stand eternally con-

Y   fessed

feſſed as *my Son. But to the fearful and unbelieving*, who choſe their lot out of God, and turned their backs on heaven to ſecure the ſmiles of their fellow-men; *and to the abominable, and to murtherers, and whoremongers, and ſorcerers* φαρμακευσι thoſe temporal and ſpiritual *poiſoners; and to idolaters;* and (to comprehend all ſinners under one name, I add) *to all liars,* to every one of theſe I have very different language to addreſs; a language adapted to convulſe their hearts with infinite horror, while I aſſure them, upon the immutable word of a God, that *their part* ſhall be *in the lake which burns with fire and brimſtone; which is the ſecond death,* the due wages of ſin, *Rom.* vi. 23. He that turns from God's grace, only runs into the hands of his flaming juſtice! Hear, ſinners, tremble! and flee for your lives!

9. And there came to me one of the ſeven angels, who had had the ſeven vials full of the ſeven laſt plagues; and ſpake with me, ſaying, Come hither, I will ſhew thee the bride, the wife of the Lamb.

10. And he carried me away in ſpirit to a great and high mountain; and he ſhewed me that great city, the holy Jeruſalem, coming down out of heaven from God;

11. Having the glory of God; and its luminary *was* like a moſt precious ſtone, as a Jaſper-ſtone, clear as cryſtal.

12. Having alſo a great and high wall; having twelve gates, and at the gates twelve angels, and names written, which are *thoſe* of the twelve tribes of the ſons of Iſrael.

13. On the eaſt three gates; on the north three gates; on the ſouth three gates; and on the weſt three gates.

14. And

14. And the wall of the city had twelve foundations; and in them the names of the twelve apoftles of the Lamb.

15. And he that talked with me had a golden reed, that he might meafure the gates thereof, and the wall thereof.

16. And the city lieth four fquare, and its length is the fame as its breadth; and he meafured the city with the reed, *amounting* to twelve thoufand furlongs. The length, and the breadth, and the height of it are equal.

17. And he meafured its wall, a hundred forty-four cubits, after the meafure of a man; which is *that* of the angel.

18. And the ftructure of its wall was jafper, and the city pure gold, like tranfparent glafs.

19. And the foundations of the wall of the city *were* adorned with every precious ftone; the firft foundation, a jafper; the fecond, fapphire; the third, chalcedony; the fourth, emerald.

20. The fifth, fardonyx; the fixth fardins; the feventh, chryfolite; the eighth, beryl; the ninth, topaz; the tenth, chryfoprafus; the eleventh, hyacinth; and the twelfth, amethyft.

21. And the twelve gates *were* twelve pearls; each of the gates was of one pearl throughout; and the ftreet of the city pure gold, like tranfparent glafs.

22. And I faw no temple in it; for the Lord God Almighty is the temple of it, and *fo is* the Lamb.

23. And

23. And the city had no need of the sun, nor of the moon, that they should shine therein; for the glory of the Lord enlightened it, and the Lamb *was* its light.

24. And the nations of those who are saved shall walk in its light; and the kings of the earth bring their glory, and their honour into it.

25. And the gates of it shall not be shut by day; for night is not there.

26. And they shall bring the glory and honour of the nations into it.

27. And there shall in no wise enter into it any thing that is common *(or unclean)* and that worketh abomination, and a lye; but those only who are written in the Lamb's book of life.

Our apostle had seen the holy city, the new Jerusalem, come down from heaven; and heard this rapturous exclamation, *The temple of God is with men*, &c. But he must see more of it, for our consolation and refreshment; for who that has read the former verses, would not wish for a further account of this city? Therefore *one of the angels who had had the seven vials, full of the seven last plagues, came and spake with him*. Observe, this angel had not now this vial, for he had poured it out; nor could it be poured again, for *the first earth*, which had received it, *was passed away*, ver. 1: Therefore, though εχοντων and γεμουσας are both of them participles of the present tense, the sense obliged me to render it, that he *had had* the vial; see the following similar instances, in which the present participle refers to something past; viz, *Mark* vi. 44. and viii. 9. *John* ix. 25. *Phil.* iii, 4. *Rev.* xv. 2.

Saying,

Saying, Come hither, I will shew thee a sight, which will make all the glories of time sicken upon thy view, and fire thy heart with more abundant, Christian and ministerial, ardor; I will shew thee, as far as thou canst bear the sight, *the bride, the wife of the Lamb,* in her celestial dress.

10, 11. *And* he had no sooner spoken the word, than *he carried me in spirit* away from things about me, *to a great and high mountain* of that new heaven and earth, to which the holy city was come down; for the new Jerusalem will be more eminently *a city set upon a hill which cannot be hid,* than the church on earth had ever been, *Matt.* v. 14. And now those words are to be fully verified, *God is not ashamed to be called their God; for he hath prepared for them a city, Heb.* xi. 16. Accordingly, *he shewed me* again *that great city, the holy Jerusalem,* which as before, ver. 2, still appeared as *coming down out of heaven from God;* to assure me of the constant unremitting intercourse, which the new heaven and earth will perpetually enjoy with the blessed God; which was further proved by the glory which I saw upon this city, for it appeared *having the glory of God,* or the beauty of all his perfections, shining with united and the most vivid rays in every part: *And her luminary* φωϛηρ *was like a most precious stone, as a jasper,* κρυϛαλλιζοντι, *clear as crystal;* or perhaps it communicated the transparency of crystal to every thing on which its holy beams fell; see ver. 23. At least every thing in that world, will be as much adapted to reflect the Divine glory, as the most precious stones here, to reflect the splendors of a beaming noon.

12, 13. This city had also *a wall great and high,* to denote its security; *and twelve gates, and at the gates twelve angels,* watchers, as centinels on duty; *and names written* thereon, *which are* those of

the

the twelve tribes of the sons of Israel; who had represented the church of God on earth, *Gal.* vi 16; and been the means of introducing the Gentiles into it. It will appear in the millennium, that none of these tribes have been lost, *Ezek.* xlviii. 1—34; and after their return to their own land, when their glory there has given the world a striking representation of the eternal blessedness of the saints in heaven, as we have seen, ver. 1; the names of every one of them shall be transferred to the twelve gates of the celestial city; and written three on the *East* side, and the same number on the *North, South* and *West*, ver. 13. For *as the new heavens and new earth, so shall their name remain* for ever, *Isa.* lxvi. 22; and, whilst the names *of the wicked rot, the righteous shall be in everlasting remembrance, Psal.* cxii. 6. *The name* of this *city* had been written upon their hearts here, *Heb.* xi. 13—16. *Rev.* iii. 12; and now their names are written on its gates, yea *I have graven thee,* saith the Lord, *on the palms of mine hands, Isa.* xlix. 16.

14. And this building, being either suspended in the air, or at least its foundations being perfectly transparent; our author observed, that its *wall had twelve foundations,* lying one under the other; (alluding to the strata of different and durable materials, which were anciently laid upon each other, to make the foundations of the walls of large and opulent cities)—And as the church of God on earth had been *built upon the foundation of the apostles and prophets, Jesus Christ himself being the chief corner* stone, *Eph.* ii. 20; so in the foundations of this city wall, were written *the names of the twelve apostles of the Lamb*; who had been employed in laying the foundations of heaven in the hearts of men. And this account is here given us, to beget in us the highest veneration for their inspired writings, which no traveller to this

this city can with safety neglect; as well as to engage us to an ardent imitation of their spirit and
views.

15, 16. *And,* as our author was to report the
size of this city to the saints below, the angel
who *talked with* him, *had a golden reed to measure*
it, *and its gates and wall*; as the Lord Jesus had
measured Jerusalem in the sight of *Ezekiel,* chap.
xl. 3 : And upon measuring, it appeared to be a
perfect square of *twelve thousand furlongs,* that is,
fifteen hundred miles *long, high* and *broad.* If
this city had been designed for the habitation of
pure spirits only, nothing need to have been said
of the size of it : And though such a city as this
would not be fit for animal bodies, who cannot rise
fifteen hundred miles high, it is perfectly adapted
to the spiritual bodies who are to inhabit it; who
will ascend to these heights, and go these lengths,
with much greater facility, than we now advance
to the usual heights, or move through the comparatively trifling lengths of our earthly cities.

The circumference of the present earth is about
24,000 miles; but it is well known how fire re-
duces the size of things : And though we have no
account of the size of the new earth, whatever
that may be, from the glory of the city which descends to it, we conclude, that it can have no un-
inhabited waste upon its surface; nor any such
hidden, and comparatively useless bowels in it as
the present earth; but probably it will shine
throughout with a transparent glory, suited to the
dazling, yet serene splendor of that new Jerusalem
which comes down to it. This city being a square
of fifteen hundred miles, (and consequently six
thousand miles in circumference) the largest cities
upon earth sink into mere villages, when compared with this city of the great king; in which
there are many blissful habitations, and one for

the

the man who is reading this, if he will turn his back on the vanities of time, and run for his life to JESUS the Bridegroom of this resplendent bride.

17. *And*, to satisfy us that no possible danger can ever invade this new-made world of grace, *he measured* the thickness of *its wall*, at one of the gates, *a hundred forty-cubits*, or seventy two yards ; *according to the measure of man*, who reckons it a cubit from his elbow to the end of his middle finger ; and *the angel* who talked with me had, in appearance, assumed a body of the same size ; that he might not draw off my attention from the city he designed to shew me, any more by his extraordinary dimensions, than by his overwhelming glory—But haste ! haste ! thee, my reader, for as thy life itself never was half a cubit long ; so perhaps thou hast not half *an inch* further to travel, before it will be decided whether thou shalt ever inhabit this city.

18. *And the* pile, the structure, or *building of* this *wall was* one solid *jasper*, red, green and white, to delight every enraptured eye ; *and the city* was *pure gold*, without any alloy of a baser metal ; yet it was unlike that thick clay which puts out the eyes of deluded mortals here, being *clear* as *refined glass*.

19, 20. We heard before of *the twelve foundations of the wall of* this *city*, which had the names of the twelve apostles of the Lamb in them, ver. 14 ; but the holy Ghost saw fit to add, that these *foundations were adorned with precious stones* of *every* name, which are here mentioned. Come hither then, ye vain and gay, who are so often put besides yourselves by the fatal glare of sensual enjoyments ; come and see how mean those dying splendors are which captivate your hearts, when compared with the solid glory reserved for those men, whom you are now so ready to scorn.

The

The names of the twelve tribes of Israel had been set, in Aaron's breast-plate, in twelve precious stones; which the learned Ainsworth takes to be the same with the twelve stones here mentioned; see *Exod.* xxviii. 10, 17—20. There they were placed according to their birth; but no such order is observed here, for the account of these foundations begins with the jasper, which belonged to the tribe of *Benjamin*, (out of which the apostle Paul sprang; and so *the last is* first, *Matt.* xix. 30,) and ends with the amethyst the stone of *Gad*; for the order of nature is not the order of grace or glory.

The first foundation (reckoned from the lower part, which first met the apostle's eye in its de-icent from heaven) *was* a white, green and red *jasper*; *the second*, a sky-blue *sapphire*, streaked with gold; *the third*, *chalcedony*, like red hot iron; *the fourth*, a beautiful grass-green *emerald*; *the fifth*, a red *sardonyx*, streaked with white; *the sixth*, a deep red *sardius*; *the seventh*, a deep yellow gold-coloured *chrysolite*; *the eighth*, a sea-green, or waterish sky-coloured *beryl*; *the ninth*, a pale green gold-coloured *topaz*; *the tenth*, a green and gold *chrysoprasus*; *the eleventh*, a red purple *hyacinth*; *the twelfth*, a violet purple *amethyst*.

These bright and durable foundations of the heavenly city, may well remind us of the following twelve perfections of the Divine nature, which God himself has laid at the foundation of our eternal hopes; viz, self-existence, infinity, eternity, immutability, sovereignty, omnipotence, omniscience, omnipresence, holiness, justice, goodness and truth—These, Christians, are the blessed foundations of that wall of your defence, on earth and in heaven, which you may well call *salvation*, *Isa.* lx. 18; which have the names of the
twelve

twelve apoftles of the Lamb in them, ver. 24; and
fhine to believing eyes, with a beauty and glory
far exceeding that of the moft precious ftones.

It is added, ver. 21. *The twelve gates* in this
wall, at which twelve angels attended, and on
which the names of the twelve tribes of Ifrael were
written, ver. 12, *were twelve pearls ; each of the
gates*, with its pillars, arches, mouldings and
cornifhes, *was of one* undivided *pearl throughout :
And* as Solomon *overlaid the floor of the* temple
with gold within and without, 1 *Kings* vi. 30, fo
the ftreet of this holy *city* was *pure* polifhed *gold;*
yet *tranfparent as glafs.*

But though our darknefs cannot at prefent fupport the dazling light of celeftial fcenes, or our
earthly powers bear the radiance which thefe gates
emit; that we may hereafter enter this city, let
us often meditate upon the following great gofpel
truths; which we may call *twelve gates*, which
inftrumentally lead into the city of our God
below ; viz, Man is mean, yet important, as a
creature—but ruined as a finner.—His God fovereign, yet gracious—Lays a wonderful plan for
his falvation—fends his equal Son to teach, to
die a ranfom, and to reign—This is to be teftified in due time to all—The Spirit makes this
teftimony efficacious to whomfoever he pleafes—
They who receive his teftimony, are united to
Chrift—And live by faith in him—This produces univerfal holinefs in heart and life—God
keeps them by his power—And finally, makes
both parts of their nature happy together in
heaven.—Thefe are fome of the truths by which
the Lord *fanctifies* his people, *John* xvii. 17;
which have the names of the twelve tribes of
Ifrael in them, and more than twelve angelic
guards ftand over to defend them; whilft they
make the man who fpiritually receives them, one
of

of God's *jewels, Mal.* iii. 17. If God will lead me into the practical knowledge of these things, I will not doubt his bringing me to glory.

After this account of the wall, the foundations, and gates of this city, it may well afford the humble Christian, a devout pleasure to observe; that the glorified bodies, who are to inhabit this city will, no doubt, as much exceed the city where they dwell in glory, as their present bodies excel the appearance, and the nature of the streets and walls, of our earthly cities: If the *brightness of the firmament,* excels the diamond which reflects its light, how much more will spiritual bodies excel these pearley gates and walls!

Our author adds,

Ver. 22, 23. *And I saw no temple in it,* where worshippers were to assemble for the more immediate acts of devotion; *for* the whole city was sanctified, to the highest possible degree, by *the Lord God Almighty,* who *is the temple* in every part of it; *and* so is *the Lamb,* though his human nature is now no more their way to God. *And the city had no need of the sun, nor of the moon, that they should shine therein;* for these instruments of the Divine goodness, which had ministered to the saints in their minority, are now for ever removed; and the blessed inhabitants of that world, being fitted for an immediate intercourse with God, have no such dependence on intervening creatures and means as we; for his *glory enlightened* this city, *and the Lamb* is *its light*; whose body beams with the most delightful splendors, whilst still it wears the marks of that atonement, which is the foundation of all their blessedness. But besides the glory of his human nature, if Christ had not been God by nature, and had a subsistence in some sense, distinct from the Father; it surely could not have been said of him,

after

after he had given up the mediatorial kingdom, as it is of the Father, that he is the *Temple* and the *Light* of heaven ; see chap. xxii. 5.

24. *And the nations of those who are saved, shall walk in its light* ; for their bodily eyes are adapted to it ; and their glorified understandings now possess all that spirituality, clearness, capacity, sanctity, strength and fixedness which they had so earnestly desired in this world. *And they* saved *kings of the earth* ; (for that is the idea to which the preceding clause of the verse restricts this,) *do bring their glory and honour into it* ; viz, those kings who had been evangelized towards the close of the sixth trumpet, chap. x. 11; and whose thrones had made such a distinguished figure in the millennium, chap. xx. 4; at which time, as it were, whole *nations* together had been *saved*, as the former part of this verse intimates. These are the only kings who can bring their glory and honour into the new heavens and the new earth ; and they do so, (1.) As the dominion intrusted in their hands, answered its Divine design, and became a means of peopling heaven with blessed inhabitants ; (2.) As all the wisdom and goodness which had dignified their government, shall be fully compleated in that world of regularity and blessedness, and (3.) As all its blessed inhabitants shall appear arrayed in splendor and glory, far superior to that of courtiers. But the wicked kings of the earth in every age have been the vassals of the devil, led captive by him at his will ; and the vain glories of such men would not suit the millennial, much less the heavenly state—But see ! these redeemed kings, who have washed their robes, and made them white in the blood of the Lamb, move off from the place of judgment, each at the head of his saved nation ; and in the solemn joyful throng, methinks I see

every

every minifter of Chrift, at the head of that large or lefs number, in whom Divine grace had wrought favingly by his means—See! all triumphant they enter thefe pearly gates ; and go, in joyful ranks, to inherit the kingdom prepared for them from the foundation of the world.

25, 26. *And the gates of it fhall not be fhut by day,* the only time that world knows ; *for night,* natural or moral, *is not,* cannot be *there* ; where what had been predicted of the millennial ftate, which typified this, *Ifa.* lx. 19, 20. muft be fully accomplifhed, *The fun fhall be no more thy light by day, neither for brightnefs fhall the moon give light unto thee ; but the Lord fhall be unto thee an everlafting light, and thy God thy glory. Thy fun fhall no more go down,* &c.—*and the days of thy mourning fhall be ended—And they,* the Father, Son and Spirit, or the holy angels, *fhall bring* (the faints ; and in and with them) all that which true wifdom had ever efteemed *the glory and honour of the nations into it* ; where every thing that had been truly excellent upon earth, fhall attain its higheft and moft durable perfection.

But as thefe pearly gates will remain, after all the glory of the nations is brought into it ; I am ready to afk, What purpofes can they anfwer after the faints are entered, unlefs they ferve for the ad-miffion of guefts from the other worlds ; who, if they come to vifit this new Jerufalem, will cer-tainly enter orderly into it ; agreeable to the eftablifhed regulations of wifdom and rectitude, which will eternally govern every happy being ? —If the church is the angel's ftudy now, *Eph.* iii. 10. 1 *Pet.* i. 12, no doubt it will be fo here-after, wherever it is found : And if the faints fhould be permitted to vifit different worlds after the refurrection ; (when their bodies are perfectly fuited to the difpofitions of the immortal mind ;)

fee

fee ver. 2, they will go forth through thefe twelve
gates. And as happy beings, from different
worlds, had become intimately acquainted with
each others perfons and hiftories, whilft they ftood
rejoicing together at the right hand of their
Judge; nothing but the Divine will, and their
refpective natures, can fix any limits to thofe
expreffions of joy in each others bleffednefs, to
which their ardent love to God and each other,
will for ever and immutably prompt them. Ever
fince the fall of man, for their fafety, they had
been all gathered together, in one common head
of prefervation CHRIST, *Eph.* i. 10, though they
did not all need redemption : And having been,
in the fullnefs of time, affembled all together at
the feat of judgment, they will probably be
ftrangers to each other no more ; but fall in, at
certain feafons at leaft, in the moft animated
ftrains of one univerfal CHORUS; whether they had,
like us, defcended from one common parent, or
been, as the angels, created all at once. And if
the inhabitants of the new heaven and earth,
fhould be adapted to fuch an unbounded fociety
with other worlds, no doubt their joy in each
other will be inexpreffible, whether they look
back on what grace has done for each other here,
or forward to their mutual interminable glory.

Reviewing what has been faid of this city, we
muft confefs that the moft magnificent ideas, and
the boldeft images of nature, have done their
utmoft ; yea have been even put upon the rack,
to give our too-fenfual minds fome proper con-
ceptions of the celeftial glory. *Lord, increafe our
faith* of thefe glorious, though yet invifible rea-
lities ; and efpecially imprint upon every heart the
all-important declaration with which this chapter
concludes, ver. 27 ; viz, that this city is unlike
the pureft focieties we ever faw upon earth ; for

there

there shall in no wise, or under any pretence whatever, *any thing enter into it that is common,* or unclean; *and that worketh abomination* of any kind, or
that sets up any thing above God in their heart ;
and that frames *a lie,* to screen that abomination
from their own or others eyes ; *but* ει μη *those only
who are written in the Lamb's book of life* ; whose
characters and difpofitions, the reverfe of the
others, refulted from, and were the accomplifhment of, God's gracious purpofe in their favor,
2 *Theff.* ii. 13.

C H A P. XXII.

1. AND he fhewed me a pure river of
water of life, clear as cryftal, pro-
ceeding out of the throne of God, and of
the Lamb.

2. In the midft of the ftreet of it, and
of the river, on the one fide and the other,
was the tree of life ; producing twelve
fruits, every month producing one *kind of*
fruit : And the leaves of the tree *are* for
the healing of the nations.

3. And every curfe fhall be no more : And
the throne of God and of the Lamb fhall be
in it ; and his fervants fhall ferve him.

4. And they fhall fee his face ; and his
name fhall be on their foreheads.

5. And

5. And there shall be no night there: And they have no need of a lamp, nor of the light of the sun, because the Lord God enlightens them; and they shall reign for ever and ever.

The angel is still speaking of the celestial city, which God has prepared for his servants; and of which such *glorious things* are here, and elsewhere *spoken.*

When the body is animal, and therefore thirsty, no more, there must be such a thirst in the glorified soul, as to welcome and endear all further Divine discoveries: *And* accordingly, as a river proceeded out of the ancient Eden, to water that garden of God, and quench the thirst of its happy inhabitants, *Gen* ii. 10; so *he shewed me a pure river of the water of life, clear as crystal;* which was adumbrated by the living *waters* which *issued* from *under the threshold* of Ezekiel's temple, and came out from *the right side of the house, at the South side of the altar,* chap. xlvii. 1 *John* vii. 37: But these waters proceeded immediately *out of the throne of God and of the Lamb;* for the Lamb could say, ' *All that the Father hath is* ' *mine,* even to the throne of his glory :' And if the Father and Christ communicate of their grace here, how much more will they in heaven?— *There the glorious Lord* will be unto his people, *a place of broad rivers with streams, wherein shall go no galley with oars; neither shall gallant ships pass thereby,* Isa. xxxiii. 21.

In the midst of the street of this city, *and of the river,* which branched itself out into glorious streams; *on the one side and on the other,* both of the street and the river, *was* that *tree of life,* in the midst of the Paradise of God, of which our Lord promised those who overcame, that
they

they fhould for ever *eat*, chap. ii. 7. fee *Gen.*
iii. 22—*Producing twelve fruits* for the twelve
tribes of Ifrael; and *yielding one* kind of *fruit*
every month; which fpeaks the enjoyments of
heaven various, progreffive, yet ftill the fame,
though ever new and young.

This tree of life reprefents Jefus Chrift, who,
when wounded with the fword of Divine juftice,
bled out the only balm which could ever heal a
dying world; and when as thus wounded, he is
caft into our bitter waters, called *Marab*, he
makes them both fweet and purifying, *Exod.*
xv. 25. The faints *fit under the fhadow* of this
tree of life in this world *with great delight*; *and*
his fruit is *fweet to their tafte, Cant.* ii. 3, particularly thefe twelve; viz, Spiritual *Life, Wifdom,*
and *Faith; Strength, Repentance* and *Love; Pardon,*
Sanctification and *Adoption; Patience, Heavenly-*
mindednefs and *Perfeverance;* fruits which no other
tree, but the Tree of Life can ever yield to fallen
men—But who can venture even to guefs at the
fruits which this Tree will yield in heaven?—Mr.
Cafe (on *mount Pifgah,* part 3. page 50.) mentions ten ingredients, which make up that enjoyment which the faints have in heaven, viz, *Sui-*
tablenefs, Fulnefs, Prefence, Propriety, Poffeffion, In-
timacy, Frefhnefs, Fixednefs, Reflection and *Compla-*
cency; to which if we add *Company* and *Immutability,*
we fhall have twelve ingredients of the heavenly
Bleffednefs: But thefe are properties of the fruit
which this Tree will yield every month of their
eternal years, not *twelve* different kinds of *fruits.*
Every power of the foul will however have new
delights, and new pleafure in them, though *it*
doth not yet appear what we fhall be; but *we know*
fays this apoftle, that *when* Chrift *fhall appear*
we fhall be like him, for we fhall fee him as he
is, 1 *John* iii. 2.

Z

And

And the leaves of the Tree have been, are, and shall be, (as the verb is not mentioned, we may read it either way) *for the healing of the nations, Pfal.* i. 3. The leaves of a tree shew both the reality and the species of the life which is in its root; so that *good confession* which our Lord *witnessed before Pontius Pilate, John* xviii. 37. 1 *Tim.* vi. 13; and the gracious affurances which he gives in the word, of his willingnefs to help and save every returning finner, have been, and shall, to the end of the world, be for the healing of the nations; particularly of this dreadful malady, their unbelief; and for this they are preferved in the word, as in spirits, publifhed by minifters, and applied to the finner's bleeding wounds by the Spirit of God. And in heaven too, the unceafing declarations which our dear Lord will make, of his unabating and everlafting tendernefs to them, will for ever preclude all decay of that affection and duty to him, which might otherwife take place, through the natural defectibility of all creatures as fuch; for faints and angels in heaven know nothing of felf-fufficiency: But whilft they fee their everlafting bleffednefs refulting from the mediation and the guardian care of the Son of God, his continued demonftrations and communications of love to them, will make it impoffible that their duty or blifs fhould ever decay.

3, 4, 5, And, though the effects of the firft curfe had been long written in the duft of the faints in the grave, now after the faints are raifed, are publickly acquitted, and placed in this new heaven and earth, *every curfe fhall* ceafe, and *be no more*; nor fhall there be any appearance of it left, either on foul or body, or in their fituation, connections, or circumftances; *for* on the contrary, *the throne of their* now perfectly

reconciled

reconciled *God, and of the Lamb shall be* in the
city they inhabit, and fill every part of it with
the moft tranfporting joy : *And his fervants shall
ferve him*, in fuch animated and tranfporting miniftrations before him, as God himfelf and they
defire. *And they shall*, not as here behold his
back parts, or the fkirts of his garments, but *fee
his face* unclouded, without an envious veil between. *And his name*, which had here been their
truft, fhall there be their everlafting boaft *on their
foreheads* ; as Aaron had holinefs to the Lord on
the fore-front of his mitre, *Exod.* xxviii. 36, 37, and
as they had worn his name *on their foreheads* in
this world, chap. xiv. 1. And as that world will
know no fcenes of inward or outward mifery,
darknefs, forrow or fear, to be covered up in a
fable gloom ; fo *there shall be no night there*, to
fnatch the very diffetent fcenes of that bleffed
ftate from view, but perfect, unclouded, eternal
noon ; and this not occafioned by any external
or created light ; for there *they have no need of a
lamp*, for their inward or outward illumination,
nor of the light of the fun ; becaufe the Lord God
perpetually *enlightens them* ; ver. 1, 3 : *And they
shall perfectly reign* over their own thoughts and
affections ; and the holy commands of the now
glorified foul, fhall run with more facility through
every power of their natures, than royal orders
on earth had ever fwayed the different parts of
a kingdom : And this their reign fhall be *for
ever and ever*, as well over themfelves, as over
all their enemies ; in whofe doom, however dreadful, they fhall with pleafure fee every Divine perfection difplayed and honoured.

6. And he faid to me, Thefe words are
faithful and true ; and the Lord God of
the holy prophets, hath fent his angel, to

fhew

fhew to his fervants what muft quickly be done.

7. Behold I come quickly; bleffed is he who keeps the words of the prophecy of this book.

. 8. And I John *am he who* faw, and heard thefe things; and when I had heard and feen them, I fell down to worfhip before the feet of the angel, who fhewed me thefe things.

9. And he faid unto me, See, not; for I am a fellow fervant with thee, with thy brethren the prophets, and with thofe who keep the words of this book : Worfhip God.

Having finifhed that account of the celeftial city, which the Lord faw needful for us, the angel repeats a third time the affurance which had been given before, chap. xix. 9, and xxi. 5, that *thefe words are faithful and true*; and, adds he, *The Lord God of the holy prophets hath fent* me *his angel, to* open fome of his fecrets; and *fhew to his fervants*, for their direction, honour and comfort, *the things which muft foon be done* in fucceffion, till they are all accomplifhed.

And while the angel was fpeaking, his Lord ftept forth, and faid, *Behold I come quickly :* They are Chrift's words, *Rev.* iii. 11, and ver. 12, 20, of this chapter; as well as the fimilar phrafe, chap. xvi. 15 : And it is well known, that ' the ' fcripture, as well as every other animated ftyle, ' abounds with inftances of tranfition from one ' fpeaker to another, as well as of the perfon ' fpoken to, without any other warning of it ' than what the words themfelves give;' fee *Pfal.* xx. 5, 6, 7. *Acts* i. 4. *Rev.* xvi. 13—16. True indeed,

indeed, this angel will come with his Lord; and
the apoſtle John will probably diſtinguiſh him
from others, when he ſees him ſhining in his
great Maſter's train; but there ſeems nothing ſufficiently intereſting, either to our apoſtle or to
us, in his coming to make it the ſubject of ſuch
a declaration—Therefore our Lord proceeds, as
it was ſaid at the beginning of this book, chap.
i. 3, ſo I ſay again, *Bleſſed is he who* ſo hears and
reads, as really to *keep the words of the prophecy
of this book*, which affords to every humble eye
of faith, a brighter diſplay of the various glories
of JESUS, and particularly of his wiſdom, authority and power, than what appeared in his
ſtate of humiliation.

And I John am the perſon who *ſaw, and heard
theſe things; and when I had heard and ſeen them,*
notwithſtanding the rebuke I had had before for
the ſame, chap. xix. 10, *I fell down to worſhip
before the feet of the angel, who ſhewed me theſe
things;* and whom I had not ſufficiently diſtinguiſhed from the perſon who ſpake laſt to me—
Lord! what is man! Alas! with the pureſt in-
tentions in his heart he may, by one means or
other, fall into things which his ſoul abhors. To
ſuppoſe himſelf perfectly free from ſin, is not the
ſpot of God's children: Learn however from this
inſtance, to beware of giving undue honours
even to eminent ſervants of God, who have been
diſtinguiſhed inſtruments of good and comfort
to you. At the ſame time, obſerve from this
conduct of the angel; that the nearer men approach to angelic perfection, the more they ab-
hor and guard againſt being unduly honoured:
And he ſaid unto me, See! not! for however my nature, ſituation, and ſervices may be exalted above
thine at preſent, *I am* even now but *a fellow-ſer-
vant with thee, and with thy brethren the prophets;*

and in general *with* all *those who keep the words of this book: Worship God* with undivided, undiverted, and everlasting ardor; for he is all in all to us all; see *Acts* xiv. 11—18.

10. And he faith unto me, Seal not the words of the prophecy of this book; for the time is near.

11. He that is unjuft, let him be unjuft ftill; and he that is filthy, let him be filthy ftill: And he that is righteous, let him be righteous ftill; and he that is holy, let him be holy ftill.

12. And behold I come quickly; and my reward is with me, to recompence to every one as his work fhall be.

13. I am the Alpha and the Omega, Beginning and End, the Firft and the Laft.

14. Bleffed are they who do his commandments, that they may have a right to the tree of life; and may enter by the gates into the city.

15. But without *are* dogs, and forcerers, and fornicators, and murtherers, and idolaters; and every one who loves and makes a lye.

16. I J E S U S have fent my angel, to teftify thefe things to you in the churches. I am the root and the offspring of David; the bright and the morning ftar.

17. And the Spirit and the bride fay, Come; and let him that is athirft come: And whofoever will, let him receive of the water of life freely.

18. For

18. For I testify to every one that heareth the words of the prophecy of this book,
If any man add to these things, God shall
add unto him the plagues which are written
in this book:

19. And if any one shall take away from
the words of the book of this prophecy,
God will take away his part out of the
book of life, and out of the holy city, and
from the things which are written in this
book.

It was time for the angel to withdraw, and for
the Lord of angels to appear again, when his
servant was in danger of being mistaken for himself; and He it is who speaks in ver. 10, 11,
though he is introduced without the mention of
his name, till himself publishes it ver. 13, 16. But
with what rapture did the disciple *whom Jesus
loved* hear, if his Lord addressed him with a voice
akin to, or the same which he had used in the
days of his flesh, when he said to him, ver. 10,
Though I ordered Daniel to *shut up the words,
and seal the book to the time of the end*, chap. xii.
4; yet now *seal not the words of the prophecy of
this book*; nor let any of my servants seal it,
either by their silence about it, or by discourag-
ing men from studying it; but let them rather
tear off every guilty seal which either my enemies,
or mistaken servants have set upon it; *for the
time is near?* And if it was so almost seventeen
hundred years ago, it is still much nearer now.

And, as the last irreversible seal will soon be
set upon the characters of all men, so now, before
it is actually set, at the close of this book, with
awful justice I say it, ver. 11, *Let him that is
unjust, be unjust still, and he who is filthy*, after all
the means I have appointed for his purgation;

Z 4   as

as it is unreasonable that any further grace should be thrown away upon him, therefore this long-pitying heart now says, *Let him be filthy still:* But, as the contrary characters have been formed with infinite expence, by the Eternal Three; therefore with pleasure I add this immortal seal to my own gracious works; and say, *Let him that is righteous, be righteous still; and let him that is holy, be holy still:* For *as for God, his way is perfect.*

To the one and the other of these I say it, ver. 12, *Behold I come quickly*; and what my servants now see, may surely enable them to *behold* this grand event, both as certain and near: And as I shall come in that glory which is, and will be the just reward of my own humiliation, *John* v. 27. *Phil.* ii. 6—10; so *my reward, which I will give, is with me; to recompence to every one, as* the nature, the spring and principle, and the leading aims and ends of *his work shall,* in that day, appear to *be:* For however various the works of any man may now appear, when his chosen employments are traced up to their fountain head, they will appear to be but *one* continued work, *Matt.* xxv. 31—46. *John* vi. 29. *Rom.* ii. 10.

And that none may trifle with such a declaration, I seal again its immutability, by those solemn names of myself, which I have so repeatedly published; to be the *strong tower* of my people's defence, before I appear to the joy, or terror of every reasonable creature; viz, ver. 13. *I am the Alpha and the Omega; Beginning and End; the First and the Last*; see *Isa.* xli. 4. xliv. 6. and xlviii. 12. *Rev.* i. 8, 11. and xxi. 6. Therefore, whatever men may think or say, *Happy are they,* and they only, ver, 14, *who do his commandments, that they may have* ἐξουσια a new-covenant *right* or authority, founded in the purchase of Christ, and the promise and oath of God, *to the*

Tree

Tree of life; for though they can never attain any legal right, upon the terms of any covenant of works whatever; yet their keeping my command-ments, will be an evident token, that they have taken hold of my falvation, and confequently have a right, as the fons of God, to *enter through the gates into* that *city*, which has been fo fully defcribed, chap. xxi.

But, remark it, Reader, ver. 15. *Without are* thofe finners who refemble *dogs*; who here flew upon the affrighted fheep of Jefus, as long as they were within their reach, and whofe brutal natures render them incapable of enjoying the celeftial bleffednefs; *and forcerers*, who *poifoned* the fouls or bodies of men; *and whoremongers*, who funk their reafon under a load of brutality; *and murtherers, and idolaters*, who fet up fome-thing in their hearts and lives above God; *and every one who loveth and practifeth a lye*, to cover the fins he refolves not to part with.

Thus fpoke the Son of God; or if an angel uttered thofe words in ver. 14, 15, to give the greater folemnity to them, his Lord added, ver. 16, *I Jefus have fent my angel, to teftify thefe things to you in the churches:* And now I leave with you one more concluding name of myfelf; which will declare both my nature, and my federal re-lation to my covenant people, whom I muft guard during the night of their darknefs and conflicts here; for as God, *I am the Root* from which *David* fprung; and as man, *the Offspring* of that illuftrious *prophet* and *king*; who alfo, on a parti-cular occafion, wore a *prieftly* attire, that he might be the more lively a type of my three offices for the falvation of finners; fee 1 *Chron.*; xv. 27. *Matt.* xxii. 42—45. *Rev.* v. 5. I am alfo from and in heaven, as *the bright and morning Star*; and in a fovereign manner, I fhed my uncontrolled influence

fluence upon the earth, and particularly on Mount Sion, chap. ii. 28. Enough, will faith reply; for, when the Spirit applies these characters and glories to my heart, I want no more to ingage me to count all things but *loss and dung, for the excellency of the knowledge of Jesus Christ my Lord.* But what can a professor do, against the gigantic hosts who constantly oppose his entrance into heaven, without such a view of his Lord? or, *who is he that overcometh the world, but he that believeth that Jesus is the Son of God?* 1 *John* v. 5.

But lest the trembling soul should fear, that this glorious JESUS will not bestow himself upon him, he adds one more concluding invitation to every one who reads and hears this; which he also connects with his own preceding names, ver. 17. *And the Spirit and the bride* continue to *say, Come*; the former saith it by the word, ordinances, sacraments, ministers, providences, and by all the gifts and graces of his servants; as well as by his own immediate influences on the human heart: And the latter saith it, by her heavenly dress, by her holy conversation, by her serene and joyful countenance, by coming daily herself; as well as by word and deed inviting others. And I Jesus now command, *Let him that heareth,* not suffer this order to stop in himself; but as this is a word of life and death, to every man to whom it comes, let the favoured creature to whom I speak convey this call from me, to every one with whom he is connected, and in whom he has any interest; and *say* to them, in my name, *Come: And let him who is athirst* for the pardon of sin, for sanctification, for the Spirit of God, and for grace and glory, let him *come* immediately; for my heart is tender, and my arms expanded wide, as on the cross, to receive and
embrace

embrace him: And, that I may not ſeem to neglect the meaneſt worm who has any deſires after
my ſalvation, my every bleeding wound opens, as
it were, a new mouth to ſay, *Whoſoever will, let
him receive of the water of life,* as *freely* as this
all-bounteous heart can give it—Hark! ſinner;
this is the laſt call of ſcripture; and he that re-
fuſes it, dies *eternally.*

But as adding to, and taking from the ſenſe of
the word of God, was the ruin of our female
parent in Eden, *Gen.* iii. 3; the Lord will not
conclude the ſacred canon, without, as it were,
placing a wall of fire around theſe inſpired deeds
and writings, to ſecure them from daring eraſe-
ments, and ſurreptitious additions: And this
properly follows upon the preceding gracious
invitation; as ſuch alterations are moſt likely to
be attempted, with a view to make new terms
of our acceptance with God; therefore he adds,
ver. 18, 19, *For I teſtify to every one that heareth
the words of the prophecy of this book,* and gather
all my glories around to ſeal this awful truth to
him, *If any man add unto theſe things,* as if the
ſacred canon was not compleat, till he had debaſed it with his fancies and inventions; as he
has forged the broad ſeal of heaven, to the infinite detriment of all that follow him; therefore,
to all the weighty wrath which will fall upon
him for his other ſins, *God ſhall add to him the
plagues which are written in this book,* againſt the
beaſt and his followers; whoſe ſpirit he has ſo
ſhamefully imitated, though perhaps under the
lying pretence of great zeal againſt it; ſee *Deut.*
iv. 2. and xii. 32. *Prov.* xxx. 6. *And* on the other
hand, *If any one,* not through ignorance, or
miſtake, but in a daring arrogance, and to ſupport any hypotheſis of his own, *ſhall take away
from the words of the book of this prophecy,* and,
by

by a parity of reafon, from any other infpired
book; like another Judas he flies upon that
which is as dear to me as my life, therefore,
like him, he fhall be *blotted out of the book of the
living; and not be written with the righteous,* Pfal.
lxix. 28. *God will take away the part* which he
had *out of the book of life* of church privileges,
and treat him as a ftranger, and an alien; fee *Exod.*
xxxii. 32. *Rev.* iii. 5 : Yea, he will take away the
part which he would have had in *the holy city*
above, if he had fought it, as his external pro-
feflion feemed to intimate : But now the Lord
will feparate him for ever, from all *the* glorious
things which are written in this book—Hear and
tremble, ye papifts, who have taken away the
key of knowledge, and thereby introduced a ca-
tholic ignorance and impiety, to invelope and
deluge the world. And let thofe proteftants, more
immediately intended here, tremble too, whofe
high thoughts of themfelves, and *light thoughts of the*
perfon and offices of *Chrift,* have made it neceffary for them to quarrel with the obvious fenfe of
one infpired part and another of the facred canon;
which naturally and conftantly tends to a deiftical
difaffection to the whole of it ; whether it does
or not proceed fo far as to terminate in it.

But fee ! thefe holy ftreams of infpiration are
now going to be cut off from the infinite Fountain which poured them forth—That bleffed
Fountain will give us no more at prefent; *fo
Father, for fo it feemed good in thy fight* ; thy wifdom has confulted our weaknefs; and therefore
fealed up infinite eternal things in a compaffionate filence, after thou hadft furnifhed us with
the moft honourable and interefting employment
for devout meditation, even if our days fhould
be prolonged to the utmoft poffible date of frail
mortality—yet hear, for our apoftle, full of the
                                                    infpiring

inſpiring God, has yet a few words more to ſay in his name.

20. He that teſtifies theſe things ſaith, Surely I come quickly. Amen, even ſo come Lord Jesus.

21. The Grace of our Lord Jeſus Chriſt be with you all, Amen.

As though our apoſtle had ſaid, Whatever you forget, do not forget this one word, *Quickly*; and that you may not, as his miniſter, I thankfully take it up from the lips of my Maſter, and his angel; and oh! that God would ſound it out ſo loud, as to drown the noiſe of every intruding vanity; for *He who teſtifies theſe* ſolemn and glorious *things, ſaith, Surely I come quickly* by death to every individual, to ſeal up the ear which now hears theſe words; and at the final judgment I ſhall come quickly to all—Reader, are you ready? Can you welcome him? Where is the heart that ſays Amen to this declaration? Can the creatures whom he came to ſave, wiſh his continued abſence or delay?—At leaſt, ſays our apoſtle, my heart replies *Amen*; *even ſo come Lord* Jesus quickly as thou haſt ſaid; for what have I here, as from the earth, but what is mingled with ſin and ſorrow? I long, I pant for thy preſence too, my Dear All in All! My life is hid with thee in God! Oh! for compleat ſalvation! Come, my Lord, Come quickly. *My fleſh and my heart cry out for the living God.* And while thy chariot yet delays, I will imitate the mercy to which I owe all my hopes; and, with an eye lifted up to God, and a hand ſtretched out to men, with all the fervour of a chriſtian, I will ſay officially as a miniſter of ſalvation; May *the* illuminating, quickening, transforming, ſanctifying, comfort-
ing

ing and preferving *Grace*, which is in and *of our
Lord Jefus Chrift*, treafured up in him for the
ufe of dying finners, *be with you all*; to form
every power and faculty divine, fo that you may
perceive your heaven begun; and be able to fhed
the light and glory of the great falvation all
around you—And that the glorious *Amen*, Jesus,
to whom thefe laft words of fcripture are a folemn prayer, may grant in our favour this
apoftolic requeft, I intreat my Reader to join me
heartily in this concluding

PRAYER.

BLESSED be *God* for all his words and
works; and efpecially for this *Revelation of
Jefus Chrift, which He gave unto him, to fhew unto
his fervants things which muft fhortly come to pafs.*
And now let the power of our Lord be great, in
the accomplifhment of the glorious things which
he has here fpoken; and adapt thy people in
every future age to all thy will concerning them.

Forgive whatever, has been offenfive to thee;
in the fpirit of the writer or reader of this piece;
and, if it may be the will of God, fuffer no man
to read it wholly in vain; or without growing in
grace, and in the knowledge of our Lord and
Saviour Jefus.   If knowledge is, in ever fo fmall
a degree, increafed, let it not *puff up* any man;
but kindle upon the altar of every heart that
love which *edifieth :* And even now give us by
faith the fubftance of the things hoped for; and
fuch a prefent intercourfe with eternal fcenes, as
may difarm the temptations of life; that fo God
in all things may be glorified, through Jefus
Chrift; to whom be glory and dominion for
ever and ever.   Amen.

APPENDIX.

APPENDIX.

SOME complain that there are not sufficient *Data* (marks and characters) laid down, to enable us certainly to distinguish the events and times of this revelation. But that this charge, if it has any appearance of foundation, by no means lies against the far greatest part of this prophecy, is, I hope, evinced under the three last Trumpets, which clearly describe the grand events which the church and the world are to expect from A. D. 606 to 3125, and the times of each; as the last of those trumpets also clearly opens the things of eternity to our view; see chap. ix. to the end of this book. True, in the former part of this prophecy, grand events are pointed out, under the six last seals and the four first trumpets, without any account given us in the revelation itself, of the times of any of them; which was, no doubt, designed to intimate that, for wise reasons, the Lord would not give his church, at that time, so clear a view of this revelation, as he intended to give in the time of the sixth trumpet, and especially under the seventh; see chap. x. 2, 6, 7. But though it seemed needful, that some of these predictions should be vailed in obscurity, before their accomplishment, it by no means follows from hence, that we must always remain uncertain about the times of these undated prophecies: And as the three last trumpets describe an orderly series of events from A D. 606 to the end of the world, it is natural

to

to expect the same, with relation to the five
hundred and ten years which occur between the
opening of the first seal, A. D. 96, and the sounding of the fifth trumpet, A. D. 606. What
kind of events the intermediate seals and trumpets between those announce, and in what order
they will occur, the series of the prophecy sufficiently declares.   To arrive therefore at a certainty about these predictions, we have only further to enquire *where* we are to look for the
events described; and this must certainly be in
the neighbourhood of the church, which is the
guardian of these sacred oracles, that is, in the
Roman empire, (though not only there) which
arose to, and continued so long in its power for
the sake of the church. In that empire therefore
chiefly, we were necessarily led to look for the
calamities and judgments which open at the
breaking of the second, third and fourth seals.

Afterwards the sixth seal opens such a triumph of christianity in that empire, as obliges
us to think of Constantine the great, who reigned
from A. D. 306 to 337; and the date of this
triumph being thus fixed by history, both enables
us to fix the date of the second, third and fourth
seals, and throws considerable light upon the
times of the four first trumpets. By the time
of the sounding of those trumpets, it began to
be known that the Roman empire was but about
the *third part* of the then known world; and
this description of that empire under these four
trumpets, leaves no doubt on what place the
judgments predicted would fall: and the Western
part of that empire being ruined under the fourth
trumpet, A. D. 476, and yet more compleatly
by A. D. 566, this made it very easy to point
out the judgments intended under each preceding

ing trumpet; the firſt of which hiſtory aſſures us began A. D. 395.

Theſe things conſidered, I hope it appears, that there are in every part of this prophecy, ſufficient *data* to enable us, or at leaſt to enable the ſervants of God who ſhall live in the time of the ſeventh trumpet, to fix the date of every event deſcribed in this book ; though it does not appear that he deſigned that his ſervants in every age ſhould equally underſtand this revelation.

F I N I S.

AN
INDEX

SCRIPTURES more or lefs illuftrated in thefe Remarks.

A a 2

Ch.

Ch.

4

AN

AN
INDEX

OF THE

Greek Words and Phrases referred to in these *Remarks*.

AN

D

B b ing

147, 153. his war againſt the church, p. 152, 156, 157. when the dragon and his angels will be caſt down to the earth, p. 147, 152, 153. the dreadful ſtate of the world, when the dragon is caſt down among them, p. 154, 155.—The ſecond beaſt will *ſpeak like a dragon*, p. 171, 175. and give his power and authority to the Pope, p. 176.

Dukedom, the ſeventh form of government at Rome, p. 64, 140, 247.

E

EAGLES. See *Wings*.

Earth, ſea and trees, repreſent the political world, p. 40. hail, fire and blood caſt upon it under the firſt trumpet, p. 56, 57. a grievous ſore conſequent upon the pouring out the firſt vial, p. 221. its circumference, p. 327. will give up its dead, each in their proper time and order, p. 302. may perhaps be reduced to a chaos again, after the bodies of the ſaints are raiſed, p. 302, 303, 313. will not be annihilated, but purified by fire at the day of the Lord, p. 315, 316.

Earth the new, what it may probably be, p. 315, 320, 327.

Earthquakes, repreſent political revolutions, and religious alterations, p. 36. a great one expected at Rome, and when, p. 119, 128, 129. the *cities of the nations* fall by them under the ſeventh vial, p. 238, 239.

Eccleſiaſtical Hierarchy, ſecularized by Conſtantine the Great, p. 37—39.

Egypt, a ſouth kingdom from Judea, p. 76. a conjecture how long its plagues were apart from each other, p. 215, 216. the eaſtern world will be a ſpiritual Egypt, when the Greek church lies dead there, p. 124.

Eight

F

                                        Figures

Gospel

Gospel, compared to a *white horse*, and why, p. 20, 21, 274, 275. of John when written, p. 105.

Goths invade the Roman empire, p. 56, 57.

Grass and trees, represent men of low and high degree, p. 57, 79.

Grecian empire represented by a he-goat, p. 191.

Greek church, one of the two *witnesses*, p. 109, 110. sunk in superstition and blindness, p. 112.

Grosvenor Dr. his description of the *woman drunk with the blood of the saints*, p. 245.

Gun powder when it began to be used in war, p. 93.

H

HABITS, the popish, shamefully imposed in queen *Elizabeth*'s days, p. 43.

Hail, fire and blood cast on the earth, what they represent, p. 55—57. a dreadful *hail* under the seventh vial, p. 239.

Harps and vials the emblems of prayer and praise, p. 16.

Heads of the dragon signify both his hills, and his different forms of government, p. 139—141.

Heart, down through it the road to hell, p. 73.

Heaven opened, p. 2, 274. heaven and earth *fly away* before the judge of all, p. 301. the *new heaven and earth*, an account of them, p. 315—320. twelve properties of the saint's enjoyment there, p. 337.

Hell, not immediately opened by the Pope, only through its *well*, p. 70—73, 280, 281. a *lake of fire and brimstone*, p. 304, 322. adumbrated by *Sodom*, the valley of *Hinnom*, and *Rome*, p. 267, 268.

Henry VIII. assumes to himself an ecclesiastical supremacy, p. 252. destroys the monasteries in England, p. 86.

Hezekiah,

Miniſters,

N

C c

Thunder,

their fucceffes againft the Chriftians continued,
p. 95, 96. exact money for liberty to be of the
Greek church, p. 112. they, and others, fall
together in the land of Judea, under the fixth
vial, p. 227—237. deftroyed by fire from
heaven after the millennium, p. 295—297.

U. V

UZZAH dies for touching the ark, and why,
    p. 133.
Valentinian I. and II, and *Gratian*, when they
    reigned, p. 49.
Valentinian III. attacked by Attila and his Huns,
    p. 58.
Valley, *of Jehoſhaphat*, where it lay, p. 236. *of
    Shittim*, an eminent effufion of the Spirit
    there after the fixth vial is poured out,
    p. 237.
Vials, fall under the feventh trumpet, and are
    none of them yet poured out, p. 208, what the
    word fignifies, p. 218. muft be taken literally,
    p. 224. given to the angels by gofpel minifters,
    p. 218. by them God avenges his perfecuted
    minifters and fervants, p. 217. what time they
    will probably take up, p. 215—217. the time
    of the firft, fecond, third, fourth, fifth, fixth
    and feventh, p. 220—240. wherein the four
    firft vials differ from the three laft, p. 220.
    wherein the *vials* refemble, and wherein they
    differ from the *trumpets*, p. 220, 224, &c.
    they are the *laft plagues*, p. 239, 240.
Voices, thunders, lightnings and earthquakes,
    reprefent hoftile incurfions, p. 51, 54. *great
    voices*, what they fignify, p. 49, 131, 132.
    each of the three woe trumpets has two *voices*,
    p. 66.

W *WAR*

W

WAR reprefented by a *red horfe*, p. 22. by ftorms of *thunder, lightning, hail, and over-flowing rain*, p. 56. the war of Michael and his angels, againft the dragon and his angels, p. 152, 153, 156.

Warning, given of the three woe-trumpets, p. 65—67. the Latin church would not take warning by the deftruction of the eaftern empire, p. 97, 98. the world is warned of their danger, when the devil is caft down among them, p. 154, 155.

Waters, reprefent *people, multitudes, nations and tongues*, p. 227, 249. the waters of the fanctuary of different depths, at different times, p. 214, 215.

Well, of the abyfs what it fignifies, p. 70, 71. when and by whom opened, p. 70, 281. how the Pope defcended to open it, p. 72, 73.

Whitby, Dr. his treatife *on the millennium*, p. 286.

Wickliffe, when he lived and preached, p. 104, 153.

Wildernefs, what that word fignifies, p. 144. the nature, difference, and times of the woman's firft and fecond flight into it, p. 144—152. America probably the laft wildernefs into which fhe will flee, p. 144, 149. the world will be a wildernefs to the church, even in the millennium, p. 151, 152.

Winds, the emblem of commotions in the world, p. 40.

Wine prefs, trodden without the gates of Rome, when, p. 157, 204, 205.

Wings, of *the* Roman *Eagle*, when given to the woman, p. 158, 159.

Witneffes,

Z

A BRIEF

A BRIEF

CHRONOLOGY

OF THE

PRINCIPAL EVENTS, mentioned in
thefe REMARKS.

I. Before the Incarnation of Chrift.

EVENTS.	Years.	Page.
THE creation of the world,	4000	291, 307
Ifaiah began to prophecy,	760	299
The daily facrifice ceafed by Manaffeh, -	684	186
———— by Nebuchadnezzar,	584	ibid.
———— by Antiochus Epiphanes,	168	ibid.

II. Between Chrift's Incarnation, and A.D. 1778.

N.B. See the time of the ten heathen Roman
perfecutions, p. 28.

The Roman war againft the Jews, which continued feven years, began, A. D.	66,	22, 309
Jerufalem taken by the Romans,	70	22, 186
The *Revelation* given to St. John,	96	22
The gofpel, and epiftles, of St. John written, -	97	105
A temple erected to Jupiter Capitolinus, where the temple of God had ftood,	132,	187

A fa-

Events.	Years.	Page.
A famine in the Roman empire, began, -	138	24
A fifteen years peftilence in that empire, began,	251	27
Conftantine the great begins his reign, -	306	37
Above 12,000 Jews and Idolators baptized, -	312	42
The Pope falls as a ftar from heaven to the earth,	312	61
Arius fpreads his errors,	317	62
Conftantine removes the feat of the empire to Conftantinople	330	39
—————— he dies,	337	ibid.
Theodofius the great dies; the Roman empire is divided into the eaftern and weftern, and the Huns and Goths make incurfions upon it,	395	39, 56
Alaric and his Goths befiege Rome, and Pelagianifm, fpreads, -	410	56, 60
Attila and others fall upon the Roman empire, -	440, &c.	58
Britain calls in the Saxons to its aid, about, -	450	60
Genferic plunders Rome,	455	ibid.
The Roman empire crumbled into ten kingdoms, -	456	60, 247
Rome ruined under Momyllus,	476	64
Odoacer flain, -	493	ibid.
The Roman fenate, Confuls and Patricians, wholly deftroyed, -	566	ibid.
Purgatory firft feigned,	600	84

The

Events.	Years.	Page.
The monks raised to a level with, or set above the priests,	605	84
The emperor Phocas declares the bishop of Rome universal Bishop,		69
Mahomet retires to his cave near Mecca, -	606	77
And the holy city is trodden under feet, -		108
Patrimonies given to the church,	607	189, 190
Mahomet begins to call himself the apostle of God,	612	81
—————— he flees from Mecca,	622	ibid.
The light of the sun eminently darkened in the east, -	626	75, 81
The Latin service began to be used in the churches, -	666	178
The Saracens besiege Constantinople, -	672	80
—————— and again in, -	718	ibid.
The Exarchate of Ravenna gained for the Pope, -	755	248
The kingdom of the Lombard's gained for him,	774	ibid.
Tangrolypix the Turk puts a final end to the Saracen empire, -	1067	82
The first law against the abomination of Sodom made in England, -	1112	124
The synod of Thoulouse forbids the reading of the scriptures, -	1228	104
The Turks loosed, who had been bound near Euphrates,	1281	85, 95

Gun-

Events.	Years.	Page.
Gunpowder begins to be used in war, -	1342	93
Wickliffe preaches, -	1380	104
The art of printing discovered,	1450	ibid.
Constantinople taken by the Turks, -	1453	94
America discovered by Christopher Columbus, -	1492	55, 123
The reformation from Popery began, -	1517	100, 104
The order of the Jesuits established, -		153
And the *religious* houses put down in England by King Henry VIII, -	1540	86
The thirty nine articles of the church of England, first produced in a convocation of the clergy, -	1562	254
Arminianism spreads greatly,	1602	62
More than 2,000 ministers ejected from the church of England, -	1662	252, 254
The Turks gain the last of their victories over the Christians,		96
The *Revelation* begins to be more understood; and	1672	101, 104
King Charles II. gives a general indulgence to the English nonconformists, -		100
The act of toleration given to the Dissenters in England,	1689	252
The expulsion of the Jesuits,	1773	102

III. Events.

III. Events which the Author of thefe *Remarks*
expects after this A. D. 1778.

EVENTS.	Years.	Page.
The converfion of the Jews begins, -	1816	105, 193
The two witneffes flain, -	1862	120
Are raifed again, -	1866	ibid.
An earthquake at Rome deftroys 7,000 of their nobility and gentry, -	1866	129
The feventh trumpet founds,	1866	131
The Jews return to their own land, -		184, 193
The church puts off her fackcloth and is clothed with the fun, -		137, 146
The converfion of the Gentiles begins, -	1866	196
The Mahometans become papal Chriftians, -		176
And the Roman beaft becomes a dragon, -		179
The Grand Seignior calls himfelf the apoftle of Chrift,	1872	176
—— enters upon his full reign with the firft beaft, -	1882	ibid.
—— and goes to work miracles before him at Rome, -	1886	ibid.
The beafts wound in one of his heads, is completely healed ; but	1886	69
The church flees probably into the wildernefs of America,		150
The wine-prefs trodden without the city of Rome, -	1926	204

A Tem-

Events.	Years.	Page.
A temple built at Jerusalem,	1936	212--214
The seven vials darken and almost destroy the Pope's kingdom, from A. D. 1936, to	1942	206--240
The ten horns of the beast begin to hate the whore, and burn her with fire, -	1942	249, 250
The millennium begins, -	2016	278
Some unknown glorious event for the church, -	2091	230
The millennium ends, -	3016	295, 298
The world ends, and judgment begins, -	3125	304, 307
The judging of the righteous ends; and all the wicked are raised, -	3200	312
The judging of the wicked ends; and saints and sinners are removed to heaven and hell, -	3351	ibid.

F I N I S.